A Worm in the Head

Life is action and action is what you get in this novel—from the point of entry to the stage where the author puts a stopper on his creative outlet and you have to catch your breath; so fast is the pace, so absorbing the panorama!

The narrator himself is the actor and whether he is regaling you with his childhood experiences or dramatising his numerous encounters with comely and forthcoming females he generates a lot of thrills and excitement and deeply involves the reader in the action.

The story starts with the incident in the river where, still young and tender, the hero loses his even younger sister. He describes it so well and infuses it with such pathos that he virtually etches it into the reader's mind.

Then he describes his life in school, his growing up, his attempts at clinging to his job and his attempts all the time to escape from the larger responsibilities of life.

He treads a path studded with enchanting girls and he uses them with the resolve and reckless abandon of an incensed gladiator or a goat with a worm in its head, amply vindicating his youthfulness and virility. But he has a soul that keeps yearning for values other than these; for a fuller, more meaningful expression of its whatness and vitality and after a strenuous quest for this, he draws the curtains. It is at the point where the cycle assumes that puzzling appearance of being complete and yet not so complete! Give your verdict!

The author's action is as immediate, temporally, as it is dramatic. Most readers will agree that if we reduced our times to a hole, the author would appear as a rabbit winking mischievously at us out of that hole! And therein lies its value both as a means of entertainment and as an additive to the reader's experience.

SPEAR BOOKS

A Worm in the Head

Charles Kahihu Githae

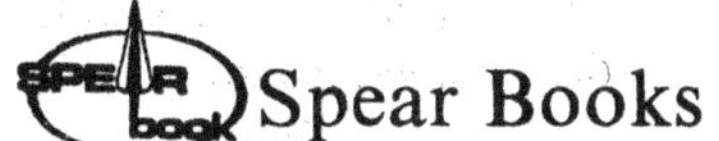
Spear Books

Published by
Spear Books, a subsidiary of
East African Educational Publishers Ltd
Brick Court
Mpaka Road/Woodvale Grove
Westlands
P.O. Box 45314
Nairobi, Kenya.

ISBN 9966 46 321 6

Printed by
Kenya Litho Limited
Changamwe Road, P.O. Box 40775
Nairobi

CHAPTER ONE

1

"Go to hell! You ain't gonna christen me! I grew a beard long before you!" That is Jackson Kabuthu addressing me. He is simply called Jack by his few friends. He has only a handful of friends; me included. Jack is always telling me to go to hell. I think one of these fine days I'll make a tour of the place. I'll ask Jack the way. Jack is again always reminding me the time he grew a beard. That is long before me, but he has never bothered to tell me exactly when. I think he has forgotten. He is very absent-minded . . . always forgetting this and that.

With his constant friend, 'Mr. Hangover', the bangs and clangs at the workshop, it is no wonder that Jack forgets a lot of things so easily.

I also forget things, easily. Take Rose, for example, my only girl-friend. I don't quite remember when she had her last flow and I am feeling in a tumbling mood now. I am afraid of asking her because she has told me repeatedly that that is one of the silly questions that men should avoid asking. So what? I'll ask her, all the same. If she tells me it's silly, but then removes her pants, I will easily forget the insult and consume the goods. Sweet, oh sweet; my Rose. But I am not suggesting that you do a bed-test with her. Oh no! That would earn you a black eye from my fist.

Jack is among my few friends—Rose aside. When I say a friend, I mean a faithful friend. Like him, I have very few friends. Guys don't like me because, as they say, I am a bit too rough, especially after a drink.

Right now, Jack is stroking his beard and giving me the most terrifying look he can manufacture with his eyes, nose, mouth and, of course, beard. I have just been preaching to him on the evils of drinking but Jack is not a person to be told what to do and what not to do. Not by me anyhow. I guess if he were told by a woman to stop drinking for two days at the end of which he would be allowed a lay, he would go through the two days a teetotaller just to show 'love'. He can really love a woman, so much so as to help her remove her pants when he wants a lay. He loves lays and drinks like nothing else.

I also love women. The two of us are real bird-chasers. Don't have any funny ideas about us, though. We don't remove one another's pants like I hear some guys do.

2

Last night, Jack came to my house and asked me to accompany him to Wananchi Bar. He had two pounds that he wanted to do away with. Two pounds of dough that could afford some few Tuskers and White Caps. We went to this bar and Jack ordered two beers. We swallowed those as soon as they were opened and Jack ordered some more which again soon disappeared. More and more and we were getting juiced. Then came the inevitable. Women. Two came in, had a look around and then perched their arses on the stools at the counter. They ordered Cokes and Jack told me that, by their looks, they could do with a beer each but maybe they did not have the money. Jack is always sympathising with these women. He beckoned the waiter and told her to go and serve the two 'ladies' with the drinks they preferred and foward the bill to our table. That was immediately done and the women took Guiness and soda. They were also 'kind' enough to join us at our table.

After some more drinks, Jack suggested that we move out of the bar and look for another as we had been in that one for too long. After some weak protestations, the women agreed and we moved to Malaika Bar.

A few more drinks and a new face entered. He just walked to our table and yanked the girl, the girl Jack had an eye on, on to her feet. We were all silent.

Then the intruder opened his mouth: "I can't go looking for you all over Nakuru like you are my wife or father while you are just here prostituting to mugs what I claim to be mine!" He would have done himself a favour if he had not made the mistake of calling Jack a mug. Mug! And Jack hates the word like you would hate a boil on your scrotum!

All eyes in the bar were focussed on us. I guess some trouble lovers were wondering what action we would take. I felt insulted alright but before 1 could plan my line of action, Jack acted.

He deliberately rose to his feet and politely asked the guy to withdraw the remark 'mug', or face it, but the guy was not in an apologising mood. He simply dragged the woman from right in front of our eyes and was heading for the door when Jack, in four hurried steps reached them, pulled the girl free and gave the guy a stunning blow right between the eyes. The guy fell, but not before Jack had landed a horse-kick right between his falling thighs.

There was no official announcement that war was on but within seconds of the guy falling, a bottle flew over my head missing me by inches and exploded against the wall. I was looking for the source of the missile when a punch landed on my right ear and threw me over the table to the floor. I got up, and the nearest boozer to me received my vengeance punch on his nose. Everybody seemed to be taking on everybody else and the situation was getting out of hand.

Then the bastard smashed the light bulb. Darkness—Jesus! I couldn't see a thing. I had to get out of the place. But where was the way? Someone was screaming while others overturned tables and chairs. Objects were wheezing past my head. I ran one way and hit the wall full-length. I groped in the darkness and found the window. I tried to escape but the bloody thing was wired. Noise, screams, bangs, clangs, howls and yells were competing. The bar-room was like hell. The only thing that was ringing in my ears was 'Get out—get out'.

Then there was the sound of a whistle. The cops! They had arrived. We were in for one hell of a night. In a cooler! Someone flashed a torch and I saw the door. Just a short glimpse and I made for it. No kidding. I did not care whether the cops shot at me or not but I beat them to it. I shot out through the door. Freedom! I ran like mad ignoring all the shouts at me to stop. I ran all the way home. Once in to my house, I bolted the door, jumped into bed, panting. I did not care where my friend Jack was.

For the whole of today, I have been expecting the cops to come for their interrogation but, fortunately, they have not come. I spent a very nervous day at the workshop. Here at home, I am jumpy and have got to peep through the key-hole every time there is a knock on my door. I even skipped lunch. I would not like to eat while going to the copper yard. I might puke in the 'bed' there. There is a smell there that you cannot compare to anything else. Not even the stench from the sewage cleansing works.

Jack, however, ate his lunch and swallowed a beer after that. He was not worried about anything. Last night he was not arrested and so, he does not care whether he was in the bar or not, when the fight was going on. He has just come and told me that, since those two women had drunk our beer, we should go out and look for them, so that they may 'pay' for the beer. He is convinced that the girl he had wanted had fully fallen for him and is sure that she also would be looking for him. When I ask him what place we should start looking for them, he suggests Malaika Bar. Malaika? The place we wrecked last night? Jack is not worried that we created a distrubance and so much property was destroyed in the place. He is again not scared that the cops will most likely be lurking around the place, looking for us and so it should be best that we lie low until the heat is off. Jack is a beast sometimes. He has this lousy mentality about self-defence that one day will lead him to the dock—on a charge of murder. He has told me that we were merely 'defending our honour'. No man has the right to call another a mug. Jack has gone further and told me that, if I don't go with him, he will go alone and will not speak to me any more. That's him alright. He is always sending me to Coventry; then he forgets! He is so forgetful.

One day, when he was drunk, he forgot to unbutton his trousers while pissing and after he had made a mess of himself, he unbuttoned the trousers for his prick to dry. But again he forgot to button up when the prick was dry.

Jack and I come from the same place. Maybe this accounts for our behaviour. I am a mechanic and so is Jack. We are both employed by an Asian. A pink-faced, onion-eating cheat. His name is Premji. He is the owner, manager, and all the other proprietory titles, of Premji Auto Garage. We repair all kinds of motor appliances and sell all kinds of spare parts. Some are new while others are old. Some of the used ones are, of course, stolen but that is not our bother.

I am a Grade II Mechanic while Jack is a Grade I. By all rights, Jack is supposed to get a higher pay than me but the blighter does not get a cent above me. This Premji does not care what Government Trade Test one has passed. He employs you as a mechanic and as a mechanic you are paid. Since I am single, I am supposed to be better off but then, I am not. Jack is cheated alright. When he budgets his wife's pants, I bugdet nothing and yet, when he complains that he is broke, I do the same.

When the finances are low and the demands at home rise, Jack ruefully laments why he ever got married. He then tells me that if women were like cars, he would be very happy because you can run a car when you have the money and when you do not, all you do is park it somewhere and wait for money. But women are not cars. Neither can they hibernate at given intervals—say between 5th and 25th of each month—as he would wish and then wake up only when the financial doldrums have been passed. I sure sympathise with him.

"Fred, I am telling you this for the last time. We either go together or I go alone and if I go alone, don't say hello to me any more," Jack again. He calls me 'Fred' when he wants me to do something in his favour. I like it when people call me Fred. You see Fred sounds like friend and I love friendship. I'd give anything to be your friend especially if you would buy me a drink if you are a man or allow me a lay, if you are a woman. I love beer and women. I don't know what I would do without them. I am a stinking addict of the two.

"Okay, big boy," I assent, "we shall go but meanwhile, why don't you spray that beard of yours with some kind of insecticide, the way you keep stroking it . . . you might be having mites for all I know. The *miguu sita,* you know . . ."

"*Miguu sita* or *miguu nane,* I don't care, let's go!" He insists. When he learns that you are softening to his request, he tries to make out that, all along, you really had no choice but to concede and toe his line. He at such times talks like a teacher in front of a standard one class. If he tells them that two plus two is three, the poor children have no alternative but to agree.

We start our walk to Malaika Bar. We are friendly again, but I am looking hither and thither in case a cop decides to jump on us. Jack is telling me how he escaped the coppers last night.

The cops had barred the door for everyone. They were now in charge of the exit, taking down people's names and addresses. Jack was simply left out when the names were read out outside the bar. Those whose names were taken were shephered into a waiting police van and driven off. Jack looked for the two women but they must have gone before the police arrived. So, Jack walked home, a free man.

We cautiously enter Malaika Bar and call for two beers. The waitress delivers them to us without taking any particular interest in us. The other few mugs who are here and at the counter don't even seem to see us. The atmosphere is very friendly today except that my heart is beating faster than normal. I am afraid that the cops might arrive any time and, well . . . We finish our beer and we go on and on with the next and the next. As the beers sink into me, I also discard the fear of the police. After all, I muse, cells are made for men.

Sure as hell, at around 22.30 hrs., the two women we lost last night just walk in. They head straight for our table and I am about to tell them to go and look for other company some place else when Jack beams and is already on his feet.

"Welcome dears," he says, "I hope all was well with you last night. Sit here. Hey, waiter! bring these ladies a drink!"

Sometimes Jack is too fast, even for me. I only have my mouth open as I shake the girls' hands. Jack has the situation like he had rehearsed it before.

"So what happened?" he is asking them. "I tried to look for you immediately after the commotion but you were nowhere to be seen."

The taller of the two answers, "You see, that was my boyfriend but

I left him several months ago on account of cheating me. Then the fool had the guts to come and announce our love—in a bar! And really, I have nothing to do with him!" she concludes.

"Well, I hope he learnt his lesson last night and will not interfere today, otherwise, he might land himself in a ditch too deep to climb out." That's Jack's reassurance. I wish I could believe him.

After a few drinks, we are wise and move out. Not towards another bar but towards home. My home, where I have two beds, one for Jack and one for me. I don't need to tell you what we do there.

When I have almost exhausted myself, I start thinking of the life that I am living. I live one hell of a life. I don't think of the future. I live for today only. When I look back at the past, I hate myself. Who am I, and what am I living for anyway?

I remember that both my parents are poor and needy and that I am the one who is supposed to fend for them. It is not written anywhere but then, I am their only living child. My parents were poor even when I was a small child. They had only two children: me and my small sister who got herself drowned at the age of eight. I was ten then. She drowned in Gura River when she was trying to retrieve her only nylon dress from the savage waters.

5

I recall that day very vividly. My father had just come home from a week's manual labour he had gone to do somewhere and he had brought us a bar of some hard blue soap. We did not ask him where he had gone to and he did not volunteer to tell us. We had been a whole week without soap. So, when this one was brought, we cut off a piece and ran towards the river.

On arrival, we jumped into the water, clothes and all and swam for about twenty minutes. We were swimming just next to the banks because there were some very unfriendly rapids at midstream. If you drifted towards the rapids, you would be a goner. For ever.

We cleaned our clothes, and put them on the granite rocks at the river bank to dry. Then we jumped into the river again, naked. We knew no nakedness anyway. My sister had only a nylon dress and poor quality pants and a nylon petticoat. I had a khaki shirt and shorts just to stop my small balls from falling to the ground. We had cleaned all these.

After swimming for about an hour, a cursed wind blew. I saw my sister's dress fly over our heads and being blown towards the middle of the river. I shouted to her that her dress was going and, at the same time, swam towards it hoping to catch it. My sister followed me. I had not noticed the rapids until I was right in their midst. I was tossed and rolled over. I dreadfully realised where I was and the only thought that came to me was how to get out of the waters.

I frantically tried to swim towards the bank but was making no progress at all. The waters had me and I was completely helpless in their midst. I was sucked under and twirled helplessly until I surfaced again, having swallowed about five mug-fuls of the evil water. Then, I banged against a stone and held there. I pulled myself onto the stone and panic gripped me. Where was my sister? Where? I turned this way and that way and what I saw was just the savage waters swirling and twirling around me. I also could not get out. I was right in the middle of the river and the waters looked wilder than I had ever seen them.

I started calling my sister in the loudest yell I could make but I guess she could not hear me above the roar of the waters. Then I started screaming and calling Mum and Dad to come and rescue me but, apparently, no one heard me. Maybe they thought we were having a swell time at the river. I shouted until I was hoarse and then decided that if I kept quiet and prayed silently to God, He would hear me. I did just that but my sister did not appear. I started crying.

I stayed perched on that stone until dark. That's when I heard a voice calling my name from very far. I shouted back and, the voice, which turned out to be my Mum's asked where I was.

"Here d-o-w-n!" I answered. Then I saw her silhoutte on the river bank. She also saw me. "Where is Wairimu?" she asked. "I -er- don't -er- know-mother please get me out of here!" I begged and started crying again. Crying because I knew I was going to be blamed for all that had happened simply because I was older than my sister; and now I was right in the middle of the river and Mum could not get me out. She did not know how to swim. "What happened and where is Wairimu?" she asked me. "Mother please, take me out of here, I am feeling very cold," I wailed. "We were swimming and she got drowned!", I said through tears.

"What?" Mum asked as she tried to put her right foot into the river. The particular place was deep and her leg sank up to the knee without touching the river bed and I shouted; "Mum—watch out! That place is too deep for you".

I could not see her face but could hear her voice muttering something like "... God ... why? ... what? ... why?" Then she raised her voice, "When did this happen?" and although I had no sense of time, I told her it happened 'a long time ago'.

"Okay, you stay right where you are while I go and fetch your Dad", and she left me. I looked around at the rolling waters and the darkness that was closing in fast. I could feel the cold getting right into my marrow but I could not do anything except shiver, sneeze and feel like the most miserably wretched creature on earth. I just wept and wept and wept.

Then she came back with Dad, and by then, I had exhausted my tears and was just whimpering away the seconds and minutes. Dad threw a rope end at me which I grabbed with both hands and I was towed back onto the bank, and safety. But when I stood next to Mum, she slapped me. That triggered off another stream of tears. I wanted to cry anyway. I wanted to speak through tears because I could not trust my mouth to tell all that had happened.

After I explained what I thought had happened, we went to where we had left our clothes and I struggled into mine. We picked sister's pants and petticoat and walked home. I was shivering and sneezing and I knew too well that I had caught a cold.

We arrived at home. Home, where maybe Dad would skin me alive. But, Dad left us and went to look for his two friendly neighbours and they went to the river again. They were going to try and comb the banks with a hope of finding my sister. They carried torches and Mum also went with them. I was left at home alone, to face myself. I reconstructed all that had gone on at the river and concluded that wherever my sister was, she was either dead or dying. There was some food on a plate by the hearth-stone but I did not touch it. I could not eat when my sister was not there. I just folded my legs and slept right there in the kitchen

Mum and Dad did not return that night. They spent the whole night combing the banks for either my sister or her body, but they did not trace her. They did not even trace the nylon dress that had caused the whole mishap. They came home at around 0900 hrs the following day and when I saw them, I started crying again. I expected Dad to beat me to death. If he believed, like Mum did, that I was the one responsible for sister's disappearance, then I knew I was in for some hiding with that bamboo cane that he kept under his bed.

When he came to me, I wanted to run away but on looking closely at his eyes, and noticing that they were wet, I stood my ground. He asked me in a very distant voice whether anything had happened in the night and I told him that all had been well. I asked him whether they had traced my sister and he answered in a single word: "No". Mum asked me whether I had eaten anything and when I told her, "No", she held my hand, led me to the kitchen and gave me food. It was a difficult process—eating, because I had a lump in my throat and try as I would, I could not swallow it. Mum was crying and cursing. I was almost surprised because none of them blamed me for what had happened. It was a feeling of relief, so intense that I thought it was not comfortable.

Mum was trembling all over. She must have been feeling hit so much. It was a wound that could not be fully healed. Death is forever. Death is never amended or simplified. When you die, you are dead. Maybe you will be lucky to go to the place they call heaven but that is neither here nor there. You are dead and that is all there is, to me.

The search for my sister lasted two weeks. Two long and painful weeks that left Mum looking ten years older; Dad—a wreck, and me, as thin and shaky as a reed. They were two weeks that taught me that we human beings are very fond of the dead and hate the living.

Each morning, Dad and Mum accompanied by scores of others would set out for the river, stay there the whole day, combing every inch of the cursed bank and coming back each evening, more sorrowful than they were when they left in the morning. People I had not even seen before would come and help in the search. Our home which was usually dead asleep by nine at night would be awake until past midnight and on some nights, when the searchers had come from very far, we would sit until morning, with only the talk of the rivers and drownings. People who usually chased me from their shambas when we went to steal oranges would come and hold my hand in the most sympathetic and loving way. All this sympathy added to my tears and I formed a habit of going to hide behind the house every time some new faces came. This world is funny. I experienced some ups and downs during the two weeks. But still there was nothing. Neither my sister nor her body was found. Not even the nylon dress.

One evening, when the search had been abandoned, we were sitting around the fire. There was me, Dad and Mum and one neighbour. We had just had supper and I was dozing but not feeling in a mood to go to bed. Dad was tense and pulling his moustache this way and that. Then he started talking. He was addressing God:

"God, you gave me these two children and I have been trying to look after them in my very poor state. Why did you take one away? Why didn't you allow me to stay with them, poor as I am? What have I done to you to deserve such a severe punishment? Oh God, God, God". He was beating his chest and his eyes were closed. Then he started weeping and gnashing his teeth. Mum and the neighbour followed suit, and I was the last one to cry with a loud wail. I was very unhappy.

Each night, in dreams, I was seeing her. With her innocent face and timid eyes. In one particular dream, we were chasing butterflies and she was faster than me. I tried to get her but she ran ahead of me. Then we came to a river. She was running on the water and was not sinking. She kept running on it and she was calling me to follow her, but I was refusing I started walking back home, but she called me back and said that she knew of a place across the river where there were some very beautiful flowers; and urged me to accompany her and see for myself. I refused to get into the river but then she held me and started dragging me towards the waters. I was scared stiff but too weak for her. When we got in the waters, I started sinking and she was laughing at me. I screamed . . . and woke myself up. I was panting and sweating, like a pig. Mum asked me what it was and I pretended to be dead asleep. I shelved that dream in my memory and prayed that it should continue some day, but it never recurred.

CHAPTER TWO

1

At the age of twelve, Dad decided that I should start going to school. The school fee was not very high those days and, if he continually got the manual labour that he was doing, he could afford the money.

I joined the village primary school and the change from my daily routine of looking after our one cow to going to school each weekday was both exciting and taxing. I was bought new khaki shorts, a shirt and a vest. The first Monday morning when I put the clothes on, I eyed myself in the mirror and I felt so excited that I had to wink at the shaven head that gaped at me in the mirror.

I was escorted to the school by Dad and, on arrival, we went to the Headmaster's office where several parents were standing, waiting to go in and pay fees for their children.

There were so many children of different sizes and colours and I felt very small and scared in their midst. Some were laughing and chasing one another around the flower beds and when one big boy came to me and said hello, I lost my voice and just gaped at him. He looked at me contemptuously, spat at my feet and pinched my nose before running away towards other children who were playing foot ball with an orange.

I touched my nose, where the brute had squeezed and felt some wetness. At first, I thought it was blood but felt both relieved and ashamed when I noticed that it was only mucus and tears. I decided that I would tell Dad of the episode but abandoned the idea when I realized that I would not be able to pinpoint the bully brute from among the hundreds of khaki-clad brats in the school compound.

Dad came out of the Headmaster's office smilling and holding a pink printed piece of paper—the fees receipt—which neither he nor I could read. He told me that he had paid my fees and that he hoped that I would benefit from the sacrifice. Then, he left me and went home. I felt desperately lost without him or Mum around me. It was only through sheer strain that I did not run after him and return home to the cow-herd routine.

The Headmaster, a brown tall man with a bald patch on his pate, wearing a gaunt face with a whiskery moustache, his height well-slid in a dark brown suit, a white shirt and a string tie, emerged from his office flanked by liutenants, a horde of some seven men and three women in different colourful drapes. They stood outside the office. A hush fell among us even without anyone telling us to keep quiet. The Headmaster cleared his throat and placed a large file in front of his eyes.

"Except the children who have arrived today", he said "I want the rest of you to go to your classes and wait for your teachers there. If any of you makes noise, the prefects will note the names down and, you don't need to be reminded of what will happen to such people."

There were a few giggles from among the girls as the children tripped to their classes.

The Headmaster and the teachers then gazed at the miserable crowd that was left. We looked like drowned rats. Long, thin arms and legs and hobnobbed heads with funny ears and vacant but hopeful faces. The lot that had taken up arms against illiteracy.

The Headmaster smiled at us. A very welcome and re-assuring smile, especially for me.

"Good morning, children," he said in a loud baritone. A voice completely different from the one he had used while sending the other children to their classes. He was answered by a few giggles and titters from a few of us. I held my breath.

Undaunted, he waved his right hand to cover the whole bunch of us, saying: "You have now started school. I am glad that you have come and I wish even your brothers and sisters who are of school age but were left at home were here. My first word to you is, 'Welcome'. I hope that you will gain something from the teachers here and that none of you will be braving the cold to come here each morning and go home each evening without gaining a thing.

"These, here," he continued, facing the teachers, "will be your teachers. I will tell you their names so that when you want to speak to them, you will not refer to them as 'Hey, you'." There was more giggling and even the teachers smiled. "Immediately on my left, here, is Mister Elijah Muthama. He is my deputy and also the school Geography Master, but you will not need him until you reach Standard Three.

"Next to him is Miss Rosemary Wanjiru. She is the English teacher for Standards One to Four and is also the Standard One mistress." On and on he went but after introducing Miss Rosemary Wanjiru I did not follow on to the others. I allowed my eyes to pore over Wanjiru.

She looked very small and young. She had long braided hair and a round innocent face. She looked like she would be sorry to hurt anyone. I immediately developed very intense liking for her. The Headmaster was still running his monologue: "You will be told about the basic rules about attendance at school, cleanliness and lessons, etc by your class mistress.

"Meanwhile, you will be shown your class by Miss Wanjiru and I hope that you will obey her. Once again, welcome." Somewhere behind me, a child started clapping hands and we all clapped our cold hands loudly.

Miss Wanjiru took us to a class and seated us two at each desk. She did this calmly and with a perpetual smile on her lips. Then she left us in the class and went away.

<h1 style="text-align:center">2</h1>

We had a chance to look at one another. Most of my classmates were complete strangers to me but there were a few faces which I could swear to have seen before. My deskmate was a total stranger, a tiny girl who shuffled her feet and bit her fingernails when I stared at her.

"What is your name?" I whispered. She looked at me warily and then hid her face in her hands, tittering. Just then Miss Wanjiru came back to the class, holding a bundle of exercise books, both red and green covered. Then, she issued us with two books each—a red one and a green one, a pencil and a rubber.

"Open the red books," she said in a soft sweet voice, and we all obeyed. I looked at mine and it had feint-ruled squares. "That is your Arithmetic book. Now, if you close it and open the green one, you will notice that it is ruled and not squared; and that is your hand-writing lessons book. The pencil will be your sole writing implement until Standard Three, when you can use ink-pens. The rubber is to erase mistakes." My deskmate had started gnawing at her pencil.

"These books should be kept clean and tidy and, if anyone tears his or hers, they will be punished severely. You will also take the greatest care that you do not lose them, or the pencil or the rubber that I have issued to you. Is that clearly understood?" she paused and we all said, "Yeees!" as she walked out.

The day dragged on and by eleven I was so hungry I would have given away my exercise books for a meal. We had done no lessons and the atmosphere in the classroom had been so tense that I was still unaware of my deskmate's name. I had not asked her again.

At about 12.30 hrs, Miss Wanjiru came back to the class and told us that we could go home and report the following morning. I was already on my feet, ready to run home and even before she had left the class she noticed me. She smiled at me and asked me: "What's your name?" and I started trembling. I could not even speak. My deskmate was giggling again and that kind of gave me some courage. How can such a tiny girl laugh at me? So I told Miss Wanjiru my name and even my Dad's name. She walked over to me, patted me on the head and that very touch re-assured me so much that I felt that, given Miss Wanjiru, I would do without Mum or Dad. "Don't be afraid of me, okay?" she soothed me and I nodded my assent.

When I got home from school, I showed both Mum and Dad the books, pencil and rubber. I also told them about the wonderful teacher I had met. Mum told me that I should exploit her kindness by extracting every bit of book knowledge that Miss Wanjiru could spare for me. Then, Mum presented me with a khaki bag for my books.

The weekdays were monotonously routine. I would be roused at about 0600 hrs, wash my face and have a hurried cup of tea, strap my school bag over my shoulder and half-run-half-walk all the way to school; do my lessons and enjoy the P.E. lessons more than Arithmetic and go home at 12.30 hrs. I was hopefully looking forward to weekends when I would not need to rise at 0600 hrs and would spend the day looking after our cow.

At home, I would boast about my lesson and put extra emphasis on the P.E. lessons which Dad sagely described as laxatives when the brain was tired of other lessons. I should not give P.E. lessons priority. I acceded. I tried as much as I could to put more effort into book lessons and less in P.E. lessons. My young brain was porous and I could absorb the lessons without much difficulty.

It was always my pleasure to stand in front of the class while other pupils clapped their hands for me, after the teacher declared me number one in a test. I was the smallest in the class and when the big boys threatened that they would beat me, I always told them to try and beat me on the pen and paper game, but I would not dirty my hands fighting fists. Anyway, it was not dirtying my hands that I did not want but some of the boys could knock off my teeth with one blow. I had to keep away from them when we were going home especially after a hand-clapping session.

Each evening, Mum would hold me in her arms and beg me to take all my intellect, plus that of my sister and put it together. She would beg me to put all efforts into education so that our poor unknown home could one day grow big and known. Then she would lead me to bed. I would sleep. I would sleep and dream that our home was multi-floored and Mum and Dad were in beautiful clothes and that we ate meat every day. Such dreams made me very happy.

Life in primary school was hardly anything to talk about. You went to school in the morning, did your lessons and came back home in the evening. The girls were there and yet not there. They were for the big boys. The big boys were the ones who followed the girls to the toilets. I don't know what they did inside there, but each time a boy and a girl did that, they came out about five minutes later, running in different directions. Later in the class, the girl would not raise her eyes to the teacher and the boy could not answer any questions put to him. What they did must have a very bad effect and so I did not want it. I came there to learn and would do just that. I would learn and fulfil the promise I had given Mum and Dad.

I sat for and passed Kenya Preliminary Examination very well. I was among the first lot to receive invitation letters to a government-aided secondary school. I was invited to Kiangoma Day Secondary School. There were some hostels, but they were for the children of the rich. There was a separate payment for the hostels. My first term school fees were obtained through donations from friends and relatives and, needless to say, if there was any remainder, it was being reserved for my next term. I had to take a twelve-mile journey each day. Six miles going in the morning and six miles in the evening. The journey was long and I was wearing my heels flat, fast. I don't know how many kilometres I was making since the metric system was still unheard of then; but I don't even know why I did not become a national walking champion. Maybe it's because nobody was timing me. I was wearing my heels because I had no shoes. They were a costly luxury which a poor farmer's son could not afford.

3

Life for first formers at Kiangoma was not very pleasant. The Form Two boys, calling themselves 'Seniors' called us 'Monos'. And they believed that we had no feelings whatsoever and that, unlike them, we were created like mules. Monos were there for the sole pleasure and amusement of their masters, the seniors, anytime, anywhere. They believed this like a piece of Gospel. They would force us to clean their uniforms; hard khaki uniforms. They would wait until lunch break and then gather us into one hostel and do all the abominable things that one could think of. They would insult, beat, spit on, pinch, kick and torture us in any way they wished to. You name it, and they were doing it. After cleaning about ten khakis of shorts one would be left to nurse one's aching biceps, if not bleeding knuckles.

I remember this one very obese mono, who was forced to run round the hostel naked. On account of his obesity, the seniors had doubted his sex and wanted to see the organs, just to ascertain. Then he was forced to run, with his shrunk prick hitting both thighs alternatively. The seniors were laughing. Laughing like monkeys, or was it like hyenas? But we, the other monos were quiet. In fact we were sweating. We did not know who would be the next one to run round the hostel, naked. Me, I was thin. Very thin indeed, but you never could tell. If the seniors were deriving pleasure out of a fat mono running round the building, there was no reason why they should not want to see how a thin one would run. After that, the seniors would promise us a drink in the evening. But as I was a day-scholar, I did not have to wait for their drink.

Every evening, at home, I would take out a book and bury myself in it, revising all that I had learnt during the day. I did not go out to where some other boys went; but they were telling me some funny things that they did to girls.

At the end of the first term, I got a shock. I was not at the top of my class as I used to be in primary school. I was number six. Six! Gosh! Even without going with the other boys to do the funny things to the girls! I had to put more time in study. I could not believe that I had slackened my pace so fast.

When Dad asked me what number I was, I at first thought of telling him a lie, but then my integrity prevailed and I honestly told him the truth. Number six! He gasped, looked a the clouds above, and asked why I had "deteriorated so much"? I told him that most of the lessons had assignments which required references to books that were only available at the school library. I explained that we were allowed access to the library only after normal lessons in the afternoon and as I was a day-scholar, I could not afford the time for evening references and as such I had to be content with teachers' lectures. He shook his head in sympathy and promised that he was going to do all that was in his ability to see to it that I got what the other children were getting. Meanwhile, he advised me to dig deeper into the available text books. And, that's exactly what I did. I dug deeper into study.

At the beginning of the second term, Dad was able to afford my hostel fees. I did not know where he had got the money from until I saw some people fencing the lower part of our small piece of land. Dad have sold it to them. I could not believe it and so I asked him. He sadly told me that he had sold it so that I might not get too tired each day going to and coming back from school. He told me that he had sacrificed it so that I could learn comfortably, pass my examinations, get a good job and re-buy the same land from those people. It was no joke. The rich bought the lower part. The part that bordered the river. The river that had swallowed my sister. Really, I wished they would all drown.

The proceeds from the sale of the land furnished me with the requirements for the hostelers. Besides the cash payments, I was required to buy myself a bed, a mattress, two blankets, a pillow and a pair of sheets. I accompanied Dad on this shopping tour and we selected all the items from among the cheaper ones on display in the dukas. I was bought a $2^1/_2$-foot banco bed and a $2^1/_2$-inch foam mattress. The blankets and sheets were of the same low quality but they did the job that was envisaged.

4

On the opening day of the second term, I was escorted to school like royalty. There was Mum carrying the bundle that comprised my bed and mattress while Dad carried my wooden box, full of clothes and books as I carried the lighter piece of luggage—a carton in which were my blanket and sheets. A neighbour had also consented to accompany us to the school so that he could see for himself, the institute which taught children of the village how to speak English like Englishmen. We trekked the six miles and, on arrival, Mum could not but declare that the journey was the main cause of my retardation in the class.

As we entered the school compound, there was the usual hullabaloo created by students on such occasions—just like monkeys trooping back into the forest after a successful raid on an unprotected shamba.

A few seniors were glaring at me enviously and hostilely as we entered the hostel; and one of them forbade me to make my bed before I was properly allocated a place by the school captain. So I kept my belongings at the extreme corner of the hostel and then escorted Mum and Dad and the neighbour to the gate; but no sooner had they waved me good-bye than I felt my heart sink. The few remarks I had heard from the seniors around the hostel had already scared me. At least I realized I was still a mono.

I wasted a good number of minutes with the gate-keeper before gaining enough courage to brave the short, yet long walk back to the hostel.

For monos, the hostels meant much more than just buildings with several beds inside. It was like living in a cobra's hole, expecting venom any time. The seniors had more amusement in the night than during the day. They would give us the drink that they had promised during the day. Brine. A very sweet drink for a cow or a heathen goat. Bitter, salty brine. Brine that was served in big mugs. They told us that since most of us were young and capable of wetting our beds, they were giving us brine so that such 'accidents' may not occur. We would be made to sit on our beds each evening and the brine administrator would come to each of us individually. He would force us to swallow a full mug and this normally left us vomitting or crying for water. Water that we wouldn't get.

After the brine ceremony, they would pour water in our beds and then force us to go to sleep, in the wet beds—and cover our heads with our blankets. Then, they would pass by the beds and we would receive strokes of the cane, ranging from one to ten. Then they would pull the lower part of our folding beds and the beds would collapse and they would laugh, and tell us that they were taking us to 'Kampala'. We got so much of this that I felt like leaving the hostels and becoming a day scholar once again. But then there was this twelve mile journey. God! What a nasty life!

One evening, a senior ordered me to accompany him to the shops. The shops were outside the school compound and there was this rule that we should not leave the compound after dusk, but when I pointed this to Waciira, he told me that I was too green to lecture him on what to do and what not to do. He even promised me a double ration of brine if I did not go with him. "The choice is yours," he told me. "You either come with me and miss the brine or stay behind and . . ." and he walked away. I stood there, hesitantly, considering the implications of the choices in that statement; and then, reluctantly walked after him. I felt awful, but walked on, a step or so behind him.

When we reached the gate, we found the watch-man and he stopped us. Waciira gave him some excuse that I was not too keen to hear and we were allowed out. And just a few yards from the gate, Waciira told me that I was going to buy him some cigarettes at the shops. I stopped abruptly on hearing that. He also stopped. Cigarettes! I wondered. Spend my money on cigarettes? Those damned sticks! The money I had, yes; because Dad used to spare me some five to ten shillings for my pocket money. But I never spent it on luxuries. I spent it sparingly and usually by the end of the term I used to have spent just about a half of it. But now. Well—I had two shillings in my pocket, and I was not ready to part with them. Two shillings; convertible to twenty ten-cent coins. No. Oh no! I would not part with them. Not even with a double or a treble ration of brine. They were my shillings and I was going to keep them; come what may!

Despite the protestations in my mind though, I didn't have the courage to tell Waciira so. "I haven't got the money," I told him, as I fumbled the coins in my pocket. I wanted to hold them tight in my hand lest they make any noise and betray me to this brute. But the damned silver pieces did it; and Waciira heard it. He heard the sound—and went berserk. He jumped on me, swearing that a mono should never tell a lie to his senior in all his life and, before I could say 'Kiangoma', he slapped me so hard on the mouth that I thought I had lost some teeth. There was a salty taste in my mouth. He gave me a

22

kick on my balls and I felt my prick shrink. But I thought quickly. Why did I deserve any kick—more so on my balls? I had not committed any crime. Was it an offence to defend myself from a robber, a person who, being my senior ought to have been coaching me on how to conduct myself in a secondary school rather than treating me like a slave?

I decided to take no more of this; and the pain in my mouth gave me the courage I needed to answer back to this intimidation. As if what he had done to me was not enough, Waciira came for a follow-up with his fists, but this time he met with some resistance. I whacked him with my-strength punch on the mouth and he thudded on his back on the road. He tried to get up fast, but I landed a kick on his balls and he crouched. Then he started to scream—screaming loudly, hoping that at least the watch-man would hear him, and come to his rescue. The watch-man did not come; maybe he didn't hear the scream or heard it and thought it must be a mono facing the routine music. Besides, even the watch-man could not expect a mono to have reversed the trend. And I also did not expect Waciira to scream in the first place; the way he had always led other seniors in torturing us had put him at nearly the top of the loathed gang. Was he this weak? I asked myself, as I tried to pull him up so that we could have a fair fight, but the bastard could not get up. I left him there, walked back to the gate, told the watch-man a lie and was allowed in.

<h1 style="text-align:center">5</h1>

But I couldn't go to the hostels. No. That would be tantamount to sliding the noose around my neck and only patiently waiting for Waciira or his fellow-torturers to come at will and pull the rope. I went straight to the Headmaster's house. I knocked on the door and, even before there was an answer, I was already inside. The Headmaster looked at me from his table and either was too slow in asking me what I wanted or was familiar with such surprise visits by monos, or I didn't give him the time to decide which words to use in finding out my problem. I looked him straight in the eyes and, without mincing words, told him that I had been kicked on my balls and for all I knew, I was impotent. I also outlined the kind of life we were being forced through down at the hostels, exaggerating it so much I thought the Headmaster was just going to pick the phone and call the police immediately to come and carry out some investigations if not to arrest our oppressors. But I was wrong. He was only slightly moved by the story and told me that he would warn the seniors against such acts of indiscipline the following day and that, meanwhile, I "should go back to the hostel and sleep."

Sleep? Had I heard it clearly? What a teacher! A headmaster! Or was he half asleep while I told my story? How could I go to the hostel, where, at the time, Waciira might have mobilised all the seniors, and now lay in waiting or maybe looking for this mono who had dared to do the incredible? Sweat was oozing out from my forehead, my armpits, my back and beneath my pants. I wanted to ask the Headmaster whether he was sober and knew what he was asking me to do, but the question could not get through my vocal cords. A lump had blocked the way. He waved me out of his house, and I did step out of the house and shut the door behind me, cursing as I stealthily tried to lift each of my feet, putting one in front of the other, in well-calculated steps that took me to the hedge that surrounded the Headmaster's house.

I stopped, stooped, detected no silhouttes of human beings, then straightened, pulled out my prick, pissed on the hedge and tried to remove the lump in my throat. I might need a clear throat for a big scream, I told myself, as I resumed the short, yet long walk to the . . . well, to the hostel? Yes and—and no!

One thing made me go back to the hostel, though. I remembered that I never had a big brother and I had to fight my way through thick and thin and, if going back there meant death I would have to face it—die fighting for my rights.

Back in the hostel, I found my beddings soaked, either with water or brine, and a note placed on the bed. It read: "You have struck a Senior with your cursed hand. Make sure you do not come here because when we get you, only the Lord may have mercy on you."

Well, how stupid! How would I have known they were hunting me down, without coming over and reading the note? Anyway, I tiptoed out of the place since I did not know when the intended threat would be implemented—whether in the night when I was already going through a dream or the following day before or after the Headmaster—himself a part of the torture system—had given his warning. Time was not in my favour either. I would have preferred to face the ordeal then, when I had the courage. But I couldn't. It was already 22.30 hrs and noise was strictly prohibited after 2200 hrs. And, as expected, every one else was in their beds—the seniors possibly wishing that if only the clock could be turned back were it for one hour, now that I was in; and fellow monos heaving sighs of relief, thanking the Lord for having had mercy on them and brought the hour to 2200, ending the day's brine session, and hoping that the following day would be a hastier one, the week—faster, and the term and year lifted off by a space vehicle, just to ensure they woke up in the not too distant future to find themselves in Form Two—the liberator of all Form Ones from the savage seniors.

Standing out there, at the entrace to the hostel, I realised that I was breaching hostel regulations and going back to the hostel was still 'another breach'—of a threat, but after pondering over the two, the regulations prevailed over the threat. So I tiptoed back, watching out for any possible pounce from the seniors, although some kept clearing their throats as I passed by their beds and even as I undressed while sitting on my wet bed. I removed my shoes, but my slippers were not there, under the bed and, as I scanned around for them, there was more throat clearing which was getting into my nerves. My heart was actually racing.

I decided to do without the damned slippers and continued to undress, but something stopped me. Something thudded heavily on my back. I turned with such quickness as might have scared the would-be attacker, but it turned out to be an old shoe, hurled at me from behind by one of the mugs. The source of the missile could not be located as the shapes of all the students while in their beds were all similar and as still as dummies.

The missile launcher must have been a coward, I told myself, as I picked the shoe and put it on the floor. But before I could resume my now-nearly-ceremonial undressing . . . another bang! This time a stone, landing right on my head! And the blow bruised my temple and started a tom-tom in my head. I couldn't wait for more. I rushed barefoot and reached outside before other two bangs-on the door behind me.

Out there, under the security light, I stood shaking with fright and rage, clenching my fists, wondering why most of the bad things on earth never happened at the right time. The duty-teacher ought to have been there then, to see it for himself, to confirm my story to the Headmaster, to facilitate the revelation of torture in the hostels. I stood there, hoping that some telepathy would work on him, but it didn't. Instead, a stray dog, on its usual nocturnal missions, came sniffing around the dustbins, turning them over in a bid to secure a bone, a bite, an item on its menu; but finding not much, it looked up, saw me, growled, but curled its tail between its hind legs and scampered into the shrubbery below the hostels. I watched it disappear into the shrubbery, wished it luck, and imagined I could fare as well if I walked behind it, into the bush. At least it was luckier than I. It didn't have to go to school to be eventually independent in life!

I wasted a good half an hour before finally making up my mind on what to do; and I, at last decided to go and wake up the cook. Maybe he could be of some help, I thought, as I walked through the lawns to his house. If the cook refused to accept me, I would join the watch-man at the gate. What I was not going to do was to spend the night in the hostel receiving missiles from unkown sources.

I knocked at the cook's door and he opened without hesitation. I entered, sat down and told him briefly what had happened. He understood my position and sympathised. At least he was better than the Headmaster. And he went on to tell me how he, and some other farm-hands, had tried to talk to the school captain about stopping the torturing initiation, but the captain had maintained that there was 'monoism' in every school; that he had been a mono himself and received the same kind of treatment, etc., that appeals to the school administration had been fruitless and that any other approach to the subject had been met with stubbornness and so the cook and the other would-have-been liberators had despaired and hoped that things would sort themselves out and settle in time. A very hopeless hope by any standards, but considering who the anti-monoism advocates were, I felt they had probably done their best.

After our warm discussion the cook gave me some food and then allowed me to share his bed with him. I slept very soundly except for the few occasions in my sleep that a bug or a flea would startle me awake. And I dreamt most of the time. A wonderful dream I had; that the cook was our Headmaster and that the Headmaster was . . . not the cook, but rose flower, planted at the flower garden beside the hedge that surrounded the Headmaster's house; and that everytime I went around to see the now friendly Headmaster, I pissed on the rose flower on my way out of the house. But everytime I had pulled out my prick and aimed the jet on the highest petals, the Headmaster would call me back to the house. Oh! only to find that the call was being made by the bug or a flea.

Things did change and, I felt the hero of the day. My report to the Headmaster did not go unheeded; and we had peace for the rest of the year.

CHAPTER THREE

1

It is during the Christmas holidays and I am feeling fine. I will be away from hell for at least a month and a week. There is nothing like a transfer from hell to heaven. You ask anyone who has undergone such a transfer and they will confirm my words to the dot! I am at home with Mum and Dad and other young men and women who are also on their holidays. The atmosphere is so friendly around here. No one wants to hurt another and apologies for trifling wrongs are exaggerated. I was at number three in the terminals and Dad actually smiled at that, and then told me that he would like me to be number one always. I promised him that I would do my best and be just that.

I am feeling very highly educated. The other day, I told Mum in English to make tea for me and some friends who had come to see me; "Tea for three, Mother, I've visitors,"—those were my very words. She looked at me and then told me to repeat what I had said. She told me through laughter that she did not go to school and as such she did not understand the English language. I pitied her and said that there was still a chance for her. Mum smiled and told me that, if she by a miracle would be young like me again, she would study so hard that she would obtain all the academic degrees that there were in the world. Dad had the same view. I didn't argue with them.

It was during those holidays that I met Gladys. Gladys Muthoni. She was then a Form One student at Tumu Tumu Girl's School. She was a first former and as such I did not fear her so much.

I was scared of girls who were in higher classes than me. There was this one who was in Form Six and I dreaded her like death. I did not want to even go near her. I feared that I would contaminate her with my 'small' education. One day, she asked me to dance with her and I pretended that I was having a headache. When she asked me why I had gone to the dance hall knowing that I had a headache, I smiled stupidly at her and she caught my hand and dragged me onto the dance floor. It was a cold night but after only two minutes of waltzing

I was sweating all over. I stepped on her toes as she tried this and that movement and at last she gave up. She patted me on the head, the way you pat a small dog and I felt absolutely a cad. From that day onwards, I kept out of her way, despite her seeking me diligently, especially during those dances.

2

Yeah, I was telling you about Gladys. I met her at one of those dances. They were being organised by a secondary school students' association, for the sole entertainment of and attendance by secondary school students. It was my third dance to attend but it was Gladys' first. I was getting used to hopping all over the dance floor, not caring whether I was taking the steps of rumba when the song was intended for waltzing or vice versa. On the contrary, Gladys was very nervous. I was dancing and generally feeling groovy and what have you. Then, I spotted her. She was all alone at a corner, just sitting and sipping a coke. She did not seem to be really drinking. It was like kissing the bottle because she did not seem to be swallowing anything after each kiss. I walked over to her.

"Good evening, miss," I said.

She looked at me, turned her head away and then continued kissing her bottle. She did not as much as answer my salutation. I wondered where I had gone wrong but then, I could not figure it out. I had to try once more. I don't usually give up the first time.

"I say, miss, care to dance with me, just one dance and then you can sit down again?" That was even more crude, but then, she respondend. Not positively anyway; but I just wanted her to open her mouth. I wanted to see what was inside those lips. I guessed she had gold in her mouth.

"I don't want to dance!" she said so fast and readily that I was not even able to see what I wanted to see.

"Why?" I asked. I was standing in front of her and I was feeling the first rays of embarrassment.

"Should there be a reason why?" She asked, her voice having an edge. I started regretting my intrusion into other people's affairs but then, because I had started it all, I had to carry on, possibly to the end, sweet or bitter.

"Well, maybe, may I please sit next to you?" I begged. She looked at me, sipped her coke again, and moved sideways to make sitting room for me at her side on the bench. I sat down but made sure that we were not touching at all. She had finished her coke and placed the empty on the floor. The way she swallowed the last gulp made me feel thirsty.

"Tell you what, I will go and get two cokes, one for me and one for you and I think, as we drink, I might as well get to know you." I said. That was meant to save my face. I pactically knew zero of the proper procedure to approach a woman. The truth is, that was the very first girl I had asked for a dance. The previous two dances had been a success for me just because I had been asked to dance by the girls themselves.

I walked to the counter where, for the convenience of the dancers the students had organized a mini kiosk and had aptly named it "DARWIN'S CORNER" and then below that, in red letters, "SURVIVAL FOR THE RICHEST". They were selling soft drinks and cheap cakes and chocolates. As I was walking to the kiosk, my brain started calculating how much money I had and how much would remain after doing the purchases that I was intending to do. Dad, on this day, had given me five shillings and I had already used one for the gate fees. The sodas were at ninety cents each. Thus, two would cost me a shilling and eighty cents! The chocolates were fifty cents each and I was planning to buy two. So, after the purchases, I would remain with only one shilling and twenty cents! Poor pocket! Dad would not give me another five shillings if he would know how I was spending it.

When I went back to where the girl was sitting, another boy I knew was sitting just where I had been seated before but the silence surrounding the boy and the girl told me that the boy was also not making any progress at all. I felt relieved. It's good to fail on one thing but the whole situation turns sour if another person succeeds where you have failed. The boy, on seeing me with the two cokes walked away. I offered one of the cokes to her but she declined saying: "I've had enough of cokes!"

"But . . . but . . . " I could not go on. What a peculiar woman! After all the sacrifice! I could not believe it. She was not looking at me. She was looking at a small note-book she held, completely oblivious of my presence. I was standing, flabbergasted, still with my peace offering in my hands. I looked like a sinner who had gone to confess but had found the confession priest out! Two or three minutes passed before she raised her eyes and seemed almost surprised to see me standing there. I also found my voice again.

"Just take it, please. It's not meant for any ill motive—it's just . . ." I did not finish. I looked closely at her eyes and noticed that they were misty. Her lips started trembling and before I could querry the reason for the sadness, a tear rolled down her cheek from her right eye, followed by another from her left. Then she sobbed once.

"Please, go away, leave me alone!" she was waving her right hand at me. I at once changed from an offended suitor to a nursery school matron.

"What's wrong?" I asked frantically. The tears were then rolling freely down her cheeks.

Just then, Florence came to my rescue. Florence Murugi. She was another Form one girl that I knew. She was going to primary school with me and she was kind of friendly to me in a remote way.

"What is it, Fred? You two look unfriendly. Have you met Gladys before?" she asked looking friendly towards me but really being more concerned about the plight of her friend than about the previous coming-together. I started to lose my temper. I like to handle mustangs like Gladys alone. That way, when she finally removes her pants, I congratulate myself without having any thoughts that so and so helped me up the ladder. My successes on that line were few. Very few indeed in practice.

"Nothing is amiss, Florence. We are just getting acquainted with . . . what did you say her name was?"

"Gladys," the girl herself said and then hastily added: "we are alright." She had wiped the tears from her face and had undergone a complete change from a snivelling baby to a mature school-girl. I wanted to kiss her just for her words. She could have been another me who wants to work things out alone !

Florence hurriedly left us and was immediately swallowed by the dancing mob. I perched myself awkwardly on the bench next to this 'queen' because I still had the cokes and the chocolates in my hands. But one thing was certain: I was sure I would advance rather than retard.

<h1 style="text-align:center">3</h1>

"Well, Gladys, why are you so unhappy?" I asked not knowing whether that was the best form of opening a dialogue with a total stranger. She stretched her hand and I proffered the coke and chocolate to her. That settled one score. She looked at me, placed the coke on the floor but remained with the chocolate in her hand. Then she spoke.

"I would not say that I am really unhappy, but I am not in my happiest mood." She was smiling. "This is the first public dance that I have attended. I do not know how to dance. Now, you men have been pestering me all along to dance with you so that you may see how awkwardly I will dance and then tomorrow, you may have a joke to share with your friends. Isn't that so?" She asked matter-of-factly.

"Not really, let me tell you something," I said after a long pull of my coke. I started unwrapping the chocolate eyeing her from the corner of my eye and saw that she was doing exactly the same. She was eyeing me furtively and unwrapping her chocolate! I felt a surge of triumph in my chest.

"When I attended my very first dance here, I was also very nervous and, to tell you the truth, it was a girl who saved me. She took me to the floor and slowly told me how to follow the beats which I successfully did. You see, this is not a dancing competition and so there is hardly anybody who is really interested in the way you dance. Do you see all these jovial guys jumping up and down here . . . ?" I asked, waving a dismissing hand at the helter-skelter dancing mob, "None of them is really bothering to follow the beats. Their main idea is to relax their muscles and sweat. If you say you will step into the floor after 'you know how to dance', you never will!" I sounded philosophical even to myself.

"But . . . but—if you yourself do not know how to dance, then we are going to form a very clumsy couple." She giggled. "Besides, I am not in a dancing mood I have other problems. She sighed and once again, her face started to cloud. It was fascinating to watch the rapid changes on her face as mood after mood took effect.

"What other problems? Surely at your age, which I note is still under sixteen, you don't have such problems as can stop you from dancing when you are already in the hall?" I could not understand her. She was an enigma!

"I came here to get away from it all! To feel at least some freedom—I mean—just to free myself from the claustrophobia—you will not understand even if I try to tell you. I. . .

"No! No! Maybe I would understand. Besides, sharing a problem with a friend has been known to be a sure way towards solving it." I advised. I particularly used the word 'friend' to see how she would react. I was keenly observing her but she did not seem to have taken any particular note of the word.

Her eyes misted again. She opened her mouth to say something but then closed it again. Then she started weeping. Not yelling or howling all over the place, but a tear rolled down her young cheek. It was followed by another and then another. She was weeping alright. Shedding them goddamned tears. Something she had in her mind must have upset her so terribly. Or was it me? But, what I had said and done did not warrant any tears. She had accepted my coke and chocolate in what looked like good faith and I had just suggested that she open her heart for me. Surely weeping is not the best way to express one's problem. Or, maybe she wanted me to see the tears and guess the weight of the problem in her heart!

The tears were then joined by spasmodic heaving of her chest and choking sobs. I was moved. I was so moved that I felt a lump stuck fast in my throat. I was dumb.

Through her sobs, she slowly opened her cheap handbag, produced the small note-book again and threw a passing glance at some pages. Then she slowly closed it and replaced it in her handbag. She then raised her eyes at me and I immediately understood what she wanted. She wanted me to comfort her but then, where was I to start? I did not know what she was weeping for. She might have been weeping because she had missed her boy-friend at the dance and that would not be my funeral at all. She might have been weeping because she did not have a boy-friend but then . . . there I was! All she needed to say was, 'love me' and then I would have shown her how much I can love instead of weeping and whining and whimpering and snivelling and wetting her cheeks like a boy at his father's funeral.

She looked at me again and this time, she was a real pitiable sight. All around us, the other people were still dancing and generally forgetting that we—that is me and the girl—were in the hall. I wished I had not in the first place joined this mourner. I would have been among the dancers—utilizing my shilling! She looked at me and must have noticed that I was at sea and she gave me a cue:

"If you want love and you have none, you cry. If you have love and then you lose it, you cry too. Life is miserable but I wish—oh how I wish I knew! Look at me." She inclined her head towards me. "At my age, this is the first dance I have attended. My father is so . . . I mean—he does not think that I am even old enough to use hair oil." I automatically looked at her hair and noticed that her father's refusal to buy her hair oil had not been very effective. Her hair looked good enough to me She continued; "And here I am, not knowing where I am heading to or when to start heading where . . . !" She told me between sobs. She was at breaking point.

"Please stop crying. You are going to break your heart as well as mine." I told her. It was meant as a warning. If she continued shedding them goddamned tears, I was simply going to walk out on her. I was going to leave her at the mercy of Providence. At that age, I did not know how to go about solving problems or disputes between fathers and daughters.

"My heart is already broken and if you know what love is, then you would share my sorrow—that is—if you love me." She whispered. Were my ears failing me or had I heard right? Did she say 'if you love me?' This is the evening of all evenings !!

"I love you but, please, look here. If you do not tell me what's making you cry, I simply cannot know by just looking at you. If I don't know the problem, then I would not possibly look for a solution. Please do tell me what's so adversely affecting your heart," I begged. My heart was beating twice as fast as normal. I had got myself a girl so easily. Trouble was, the girl I thought I had won over was just weeping. That's not love, by my standards.

"Please take me home, I can't bear it any more." She told me.

"Finish up your drink and then let us get going!" I urged her. I was not ready to waste another shilling just like that.

"Let's share it," she said. Then as abruptly as she had started, she stopped weeping and her face again brightened.

There was an interval in the dancing and everyone started looking for a place to rest their weary bones. Florence came galloping towards us but found us too busy. She shied away and we finished our drink.

4

We walked outside the hall and only a few paces from the door, she sat on her haunches and pissed. Just a foot from where I was standing. Gosh!! I started getting very uncomfortable. Then she pulled her pants up and released the waist band and the tap it make almost drove me crazy! Then we started our walk with my mind completely blank.

That is when she related her story to me. She told me how she had been repeatedly insulted by her girl-friends because she did not have a boy-friend and how it was not her wish to stay as she called it 'unloved' but no boy dared approach her for love or anything else. Her Dad was so cruel and had threatened to slit the throat of any boy who would be found lolling around their home or whistling past the home. She was promised a severe beating if seen even walking with any boy except her brother. She had actually received several strokes of the cane when she had been seen handing a text book to a boy and the father had gone through the book, looking for 'love letters' as he had said.

Going out of her home compound was strictly forbidden after six in the evening. It was lucky on that day because, as she informed me, her father had gone to see his brother in Nairobi. That was why she had been able to attend the dance. Her mother had promised her that her Dad would not know. Poor woman, she surmised, she also received a slap from the 'lion of man' when she had tried to intervene during one of Gladys' beatings. I understood her plight.

When we got near her home, which was about two miles from the dance-hall, I asked her for a lay but she told me that she was in her 'red days'. I informed her that I would not mind the redness but she insisted that it was unhygienic to do it then. She was mine and I could have her as many times as I wanted when the storm abated. I swallowed hard but did not argue any more.

When we reached her home, I told her that I would leave her there because I did not want anything to happen to her: but I meant happen to me. But she assured me that my throat would not be slit because the old man was not in and further that her brother had on that day gone to see their aunt who lived in another village about ten miles from Gladys' home.

I would have liked to hang around the place but then, there was still the journey home, my home to be undertaken by me—alone.

I did not even return to the dance-hall. I went home and slept. That night, I dreamt that I was laying Gladys and wetted myself terribly. I was always dreaming doing the act andwetting myself every other night. I hardly laid any women and so it was satisfying to dream. Served my purpose. Shitty me!

I met Gladys on two other occasions during that holiday, but I did not lay her. We were always meeting in awkward situations. Once, I met her at the shops. She was with her mother. I just winked at her and she winked in response. The next time I met her, I was with my old man. We were coming from Gakindu, a bigger market town than my home trading centre. We had gone there to sell a goat so that the proceeds could be added to the little money Dad had, for my school and hostel fees. I did not as much as look at her. She was loving alright. She even sent me a Christimas gift; a coloured hanky, through Florence. I kissed the hanky and kept it in a very special place; my wooden box. I would go to the box while looking for anything and kiss it. It was to me a very special gift from a very special person.

She did not attend any other dance. I went to the dance-hall each time with a hope that she would be there but, I was constantly disappointed. I guess her father did not go to Nairobi again. I was so mad at him that I wished him dead!

CHAPTER FOUR

1

Back to school—back to books—to lessons! to timed wakings and sleepings! That is what I am saying as I am walking down this road with my wooden box on my shoulder and a small carton in my hand. The holidays are over and though I felt them short—that is—they kind of ended before they began—I still have got to toe the line!

Back to brine? Ay; but not as a receiver because I am going to Form two now. But instead I will be a brine administrator. I wll make sure that those poor monos have it real rough and sour down their throats. It will be done in secret, of course, because all those initiation rites were banned after I had reported to the Headmaster. I had thought that he would not take any action but then I was wrong. That night, when I was talking to him, he must have been having a very cute girl that he was thinking about.

The following day, we were all assembled in the foot-ball field. The Headmaster warned the self-styled seniors that if any reports of 'monolisation' reached his ears, there would be no alternative but to send that 'senior' who had done it home, ". . . for an endless holiday." He went on to tell us that the institution was only a secondary school and not an Army training college. "Anyone who feels that he must fight is free to leave school and join the army or G.S.U." He closed his address with a glare that left us all quailing.

The senior were scowling but we, the monos were smiling. I wanted to go and shake the Headmaster's hand but then abandoned the idea because I did not know whether the seniors would heed his warning.

Three days later, a senior was caught being carried 'pick-a-back' by a mono and was so unceremoniusly expelled that monolisation died a sudden death.

No one ever touched us after that. Even my punishment was not meted out. Of course there were verbal threats that they would do it, but the time never came. I only experienced open hostilities in minor incidents. One time my wet clothes were thrown from the drying line onto the dusty ground and I had to wash them again. On another, I found my Mathematics book crudely painted—a whole bottle of ink had been splashed through all the pages. On yet another occasion, I found my slippers cut to pieces. Very cowardly acts, I thought.

On arrival at school, there were the usual holiday stories that students tell. One tries to quieten the others by telling them how many new girl-friends he had acquired, and how many he had left high and dry. How many screws he managed etc, etc. Not to be left out, I told them the story of how I acquired Gladys and even showed them the hanky that she had given me. It convinced them.

Others declared that they were men—no longer boys—because they had been circumcised over the holidays while others doubted it, yet others went to the toilets to show the Thomases that they were really men.

As I was not yet circumcised, I changed the subject quickly, by asking them what they thought we should do to the monos when they arrived. There were many suggestions but they all led to one thing: pain to the monos.

We were still chatting and exchanging pleasantries when the first batch of monos arrived. They were unlucky. Very unlucky indeed.

2

"Monos!! Monos!! Come here!! You will be our horses tonight!! We shall circumcise all those who are not circumcised! We shall . . .!! We were running and shouting at them like vultures running towards a carcass. They wanted to run away but it was too late. We were on them! No more formalities—we pinched their ears and kicked their asses. We made them have one hell of a rough time. We were enjoying ourselves at the monos' expense when, wao! The headmaster's volkswagen appeared at the corner—coming at full speed. There were very slim chances of running away but then, we all knew that he did not carry a gun. We all beat it. If he had recognised any particular face, then, that person would have been in trouble. I ran all the way and hid in the shrubs below the hostel. No one could see me there. Most of the other boys were hiding there with me. No one was talking but you could hear the hearts of some pounding. Nasty situation to be caught in—that one! I crouched very low and listened. There was not a single sound except the songs of birds in the bushes, which had been temporarily halted by our hurried entry into the shrubbery.

Then, the sound of a car starting came to my ears and some of us sighed in relief while others still held their breaths. We waited until the sound had faded away and then, one by one, we raised our heads from our covers and cautiously walked towards the hostels.

As we learnt from some of the seniors, the monos did not complain of being terrorised. One of them had explained that we had just been welcoming them. Very wise of him. Anyway, the Headmaster had told them to report anything that they found irregular in the 'welcoming'.

That night, the monos who had arrived had it hot. We gave them all the torture that we ourselves had received from our seniors and even invented some new methods of 'initiation' which were more painful.

We invented a new game in which two monos of almost similar gait and strength woud take part in a fist fight in a fake arena. The one who would be beaten would receive a mug of brine while the victor would be slapped by a senior—whom he himself chose.

We also warned them that, if they reported these incidents to the Headmaster, they would be expelled. We convinced them that they were no longer primary school children and that, in every school, there were rules of initiation which were laid down by the school committee! We further told them that, in some other schools, the initiation was far much worse than what we were doing! Did they believe it or didn't they!! None dared report to the headmaster for fear of being expelled and so we had a nice time. Nice but short-lived. Everything that has a beginning must come to an end some time, and that includes school days.

3

On the second day of my second term in the second year, I was expelled from school. I beat up an epileptic mono and I was sent away. The Headmaster had stuck to his warning. Strictly no mercy for mono teasers. I went home. Not alone, of course. We were eight. We were real tough mono disciplinarians and we made sure that they suffered in our hands. We were eight mugs forming an extremist group calling itself 'Mugg's Group'. The leader of the gang was a big bully named Mugugu and we had derived the name of the gang from his name.

The epileptic mono whom we beat without knowing he was epileptic had refused to clean the uniform of one of us and so justice had had to be meted out without delay! I had given him a slap that you could have heard from Nyeri, and he had fallen, tightened and started foaming at the mouth and farting foul gases. Me, I thought he was dying and the heroism I had felt while administering the 'justice' had rapidly turned from fear to dread.

You should have seen us. We scattered in all directions like locusts in the wind. We left the mono still lying there on the ground at the mercy of the other monos who had no idea what was happening to their friend. The matter reached the headmaster's ears and he summoned us all to his office.

The mono was able to identify us all, not without the help of the other monos and of course some unscrupulous seniors who would rather have cleaned their hands than be condemned with us.

We went to the Headmaster's office. He was very bitter about the incident. He told us that we were not even fit to live in this world, leave alone in that particular school. He called us human mistakes without putting it in so many words. Then, he expelled us. We had thought that there would be the usual sending us home to return with our parents, like he did when we went wrong before. We even thought that we would be given a chance to defend ourselves but this was not to be. There was only the refund of the caution money and then we waved bye-bye to Kiangoma secondary school.

I went home. I had to carry all my baggage, bed and mattress included because, as the Headmaster put it, he did not want anything that would remind him of us in the school. The load was too heavy for me and I had to leave the beddings at a house which was just outside the school compound, to be collected later.

The headmaster had killed me. Really, what kind of job woud I get with the amount of education I had?

4

On arrival at home, I told Dad a lie. I told him only some truth about the epileptic mono but when it came to the role I had played, I said that it was some other boys who had done it but that the victim had picked on me just because of the colour of my skin. I went further and told him that the Headmaster did not like me very much. When he asked me why the Headmaster should hate me, I told him that he had a small brother who was attending the same class with me and that I used to beat the brother in every subject that we were taught. The headmaster was envious of this and so he had a remote hatred for me. The case of the epileptic mono served very well as the chance the headmaster must have been looking for all along to put me in trouble, which he had done.

Dad did not argue. Neither did Mum. Mum believed almost everything I told her but I could sense some doubts in Dad. He was only half-convinced. When he suggested that he should go to the school and at least try to plead with the Headmaster about my re-admission, I protested and told him that such an act would only earn him foul words from him. I told him that re-admission on such basis would cloud my future school days and darken them completely. He agreed with me. Gosh! What a mess!!

That evening, as I slipped between my blankets, I wept. I wept bitterly and wondered what I was going to do. I could not hope for any job other than maybe that of a farm-hand. My age was not good enough for that. There was no chance of going back to school. Where would I go? I wept and cursed these hands of mine for taking part in the beating of the epileptic mono. I cursed all my friends in the Mugg's Group for having involved me in the fight. I cursed everybody and everything but excluded Mum and Dad. They were the only people I felt were innocent in the whole world.

Dad suggested that the only thing I could do was to take a jembe, go to the shamba and dig. And that is exactly what I did. I took a jembe, went to the shamba and dug. I blistered my palms and still got on digging. I wanted to prove to myself, Mum and Dad and the world at large that I was not a born failure in all aspects.

I was such a hard working boy that Dad did not hesitate to make preparation for my circumcision. I became a man; or did I?

Digging is a pleasant job if you are a born-peasant. I bet I was not, because I was getting bored and exhausted. Stiff bored by the daily routine of getting up in the morning, taking a jembe, spending the whole day throwing dust all over myself, taking a swim before going back home to eat maize and beans, day in day out. I could not go on much longer. I was straining my tether every single day.

After eight months of digging, I gave up. I ran away from home and swore never to go back there. I would go to the towns and see what the other men see there. The trouble was, although I felt a man—that is because I was circumcised, I otherwise did not feel a man at all. What had I accomplished successfully in this world? Nothing at all. I had even failed to complete my school days. What a failure! But all the same, I would not dig any more.

I decided that towns like Nairobi and other Provincial Headquarters were for real men. I picked on Nyeri. Nyeri was till very small and the fare back home was only a shilling and fifty cents; so that, any time I felt like playing the prodigal son, I would afford the fare back. Worst point was, I did not have any money of my own. I had to wait until Dad kept his money within reach so that I could steal. This chance came one day when he hung his over-coat behind the door and went to look for a friend of his. Ten minutes later, I was heading for Nyeri with ten shillings, which I had picked from the over-coat. There was a total of a hundred and thirty and it's only that I felt 'honest' otherwise I would have picked more.

5

On arrival at Nyeri town, I got hooked to a butcher. This butcher came from near our home and he had no objection to my helping him roast meat at the rear of the butchery. He also showed me his hides and skins store where I would be sleeping. The place had a stench like rotting carrion but I just pinched my nose and slept comfortably nevertheless. The butcher also promised me that he would be giving me all the assistance that I would need as long as I served him. He would be giving me twenty shillings—depending on the market—and would raise it after observing my performance. Not bad for a beginner anyway. He would also provide me with meals.

Besides tea and half a loaf of bread in the morning, Mathuku, my employer had made arrangements with the owner of an adjacent hotel that I should be taking my meals at his hotel. The arrangement was that I should have fried maize and beans (githeri) for lunches and ugali and sukuma-wiki for suppers—strickly no meat. I felt that, as a roaster of meat, at least I had a right to have meat. I also felt that the exlusion of meat from my meals by Mathuku was because he was expecting me to steal it.

So I roasted meat and ate it. If a guy brought a pound of meat for roasting, I made sure that I ate a piece out of that pound. I was not going to starve when guys, sons of men like me, were eating their full and giving the left-overs to dogs. I was also starting to put on weight. Nice job, that one. You never go hungry.

I was beginning to know my way around town and had even moved from the hides and skins store and was living with a friend I had met. We were sharing his single room at Blue Valley and he had started to show me what he called 'routes'.

These were whore-hunting expeditions which occasionally rewarded us with some inexperienced young girls who did not demand too much from us for 'services'. Maximum charge was two to three shillings a tumble. The problem was, no matter how much I scrubbed my skin and clothes, I still retained a faint smell of meat.

The butcher also moved me from the rear of the butchery to the counter. He employed another mug who had not gone to school at all at the kitchen. Because I could do some addition and subtraction, I was to stay at the counter, helping him in the selling.

I could miss the meat eating mischief alright but then, I was fully employed. My meals at the hotel were also improved, to include meat for supper but the lunches remained the same. My pay was raised from twenty shillings a month to sixty and Mathuku helped me open a Post Office Savings Bank account. He told me to at least be saving twenty shillings a month for a rainy day, because, as he put it, there is an end to business sometimes.

He also warned me against stealing his money. He told me that if he discovered that I had stolen anything from the till, he would take me to the police station where, he threatened, I would be put in a dog kennel overnight, with a police dog as a companion! He did not need to exaggerate so much. I was not going to steal from him. I swore that to him and to God.

It was pleasant to handle hundreds and hundreds of shillings at the counter but, unfortunately for me, out of all the thousands that passed through my hands each month, only sixty shillings belonged to me. I was getting bored with the whole muck. I guess I was born a rover.

CHAPTER FIVE

1

"By the left, quick maaarrch!! Left, right, lef, rai, lef, rai, ay, ay, . . ." That is Sergeant Wilfred Kago. He is our Segeant. Our drill instructor. Kago is a brown lean man. Shorter than the average cop with a very handsome face. Especially with his trimmed moustache. His uniform is always impeccable and it fits him so nicely that I always envy him. He looks likeable. He is also very lenient and does not punish us so much when we go wrong.

"Haaalt!!!" there is a lot of dust raised by our abrupt stop and we are all silent now. We are all at attention and our unloaded guns are pointing menacingly at the sky.

"Left tuurn! Order Arms!! Stand at ease!" We do a different thing at each order. Everything here is so systematic. I wish you would see us. We are sweating but no one dare wipe the sweat. Even if it comes right into our eyes, all we do is blink and blink.

"Stand easy!" Now we can wipe our sweat, adjust our caps and scratch where one itches. We cannot, however, move even an inch from where we are standing. That is against the rules of this place, rules which are enshrined in one major and dreaded phrase—'Force Discipline'.

I am at Kiganjo, Kenya Police College. I am training to be a cop. I want to be a cop and besides other things, arrest all my enemies. I think I will first arrest the headmaster who expelled me from school and then Gladys, that girl who was once mine but just faded into thin air even before I laid her. I will arrest her and fine her one lay.

Gladys' arrest will not be as legal as the Grey Book. What I will do is, go to whatever place she lives and invoke the powers of entry into almost any premises that cops have, and see her. Then I will talk to her and I think my five common senses plus the sixth police sense will be able to convince her that she still owes me allegience and that her affirmation of loyalty can be realized or expressed in the form of a lay. I hope I will remember a few legal terminologies to impress her with like 'cognizable and non-cognizable offences', 'equivocal and unequivocal pleas' and maybe even a few sections of the law like 40 of the Penal Code for Treason and 275 of the Penal Code for Theft. But the way I will spell them out will be different; I might as well say, 'Section 275 of the Penal Code, cap. 63 of the Laws of Kenya' and might even tell her that cap 63 is in Volume 2!!

I am no longer a blinking butcher. I got tired of that. I guess I am a drifter. I will gather no moss, maybe no riches either!!

Just when I was about to act the prodigal son, at the butchery, I heard through meat eaters, that the Police recruitment team was coming to Nyeri to recruit constables. I did not know what constables were and so I asked: "Do they wear the crown?" Stupid question, though.

"Yes—of course, a constable is like the one you just saw here sometime ago buying meat, that one who had a white cap on. That one is in traffic duties. Lots of dough, man," a wise-acre told me. I pressed on: "What do they need, I mean like education standard and such?"

"C.P.E. and above—they don't need much," was the reply.

If constables were like the cop who had just bought meat at the butchery then there must be a lot of money in being a cop. That guy had a fat roll of bank notes. I made up my mind.

2

I asked where the recruitment was taking place and as soon as I was told, I informed my employer that I was going to try my luck and he told me to feel free. I went to the rear of the butchery and discarded my white overall and then ran to Blue Valley where I discarded my working clothes. Then I put on some smart clothes, eyed myself in the mirror and decided that I was passable. Before I left I told my employer that should I fail I would go back to the butchery and continue serving him. He promised me that my vacancy would be there until I went back to tell him the outcome of the interview.

At the Ruring'u Stadium I was astonished to find hundreds of young men. It must be a very good job, being a cop. All this time I had not really come face to face with a cop. I had not been arrested and I really knew zero about them; but how I wished I was one. Luck would fall on me, I told myself. God bless me.

Hundreds of us were lined up, without our shirts and shoes on, and a uniformed cop came measuring our height with a yard-stick disqualifying most of the job-seekers. I passed the height interview.

Then we were grouped into two, those with academic certificates and those that had never seen the inside of a classroom. Those of us with certificates were then taken for an aptitude test that included sixty one-minute questions that I found easy but tricky; before the whole lot of us were subjected to a medical examination. I had not expected and neither could I have shunned it but I really don't like the idea of having someone make my prick a toy. I mean milking it just to find out if I had had a rotten woman of late. They should just have asked me about it and believed my honest answer—that I had had nothing to do with rotten women. I was clean.

Anyway, I went through all the tests without a hitch and got my blue card, admitting me into the college for training. Then we were told the few things to carry with us when reporting to the college.

On the following day, I returned home for the first time in over a year. I had stuck to my word of not going back there until I could afford a pound of sugar. I carried some presents for Mum and Dad, but on seeing me, Mum shed real tears and accused me of being a bad boy for having left them without a word not long after my sister's departure. I felt I had wronged her and the way Dad was eyeing me and trying to assess my perception of Mum's remarks, told me something awful was going to come out of Dad's mouth, if not from his walking stick.

This is what I wanted to avoid. I had to stop it, and in time. But Mum didn't seem to want to allow me to say anything, in defence of my absence. She continued, even reminding me how I had stayed wriggling inside her tummy for nine months and that whatever the case was, I was, by blood, supposed to go and see them more often. I decided to cut her short, and break the news that I had been recruited into the Police Force, that I had gone home to inform them that I would be employed, be on regular pay, on which we could all count for the improvement of our home, and would be in a better position of seeing them more often.

This worked. Mum kept quiet for a moment, then sighed with relief, and held her chin in her hand, before half-gazing, half-shying at Dad. Dad kept nodding at my explanation, stealing a wink every now and then to express a wish to Mum that maybe she should not have rushed to condemn me, but I apologised instead, on my own behalf and on behalf of Mum. Then he started to explain pro-verbially how people sometimes leave home thinking it would not take them long before they went back, but how certain unforeseen problems kept them away from the very home for periods beyond imagination. "But," he conclusively told Mum, "as the saying goes, .. *'na ni ma gutikiri i kahii itagaakiriguo mutwe'.*

Mum later escorted me to the road where I kept promising I would go back to see her soon. And when the bus eventually came and I boarded it she kept waving good-bye until I could not see her any more, behind the cloud of dust that covered her as the bus sped off.

Kiganjo. This is where I have been for the past four months. Four months of toil. Four months of hard labour. Four months of soul hunger. While training you, the guys at Kiganjo make sure that you become a real cop. They ensure that you completely forget the easy time you might have been having outside those guarded gates. They want you to walk, talk, look, hear, see, smell, think and even dream like a cop. I wonder whether they do not want to make a robot out of you? They would probably also want you to lay women like a cop. I wonder what dreams cops dream—must be something to do with the Law or Discipline. Two words that form the very essence of a cop.

Training to be a cop is not an easy task. It means more than just six months of no woman and six months of no smile. Oh, they would like you to feel at home there; but, how can you feel at home when all the things you are supposed to do are new to you and the teacher who is trying to teach you supposes that you knew them all along?

After three months however, we were given some seven days freedom; mid-course holiday. They allowed us to get out of the gates then, to go and empty our over-full balls anywhere we wanted.

During that mid-course leave, I went home. I arrived at about 1000 hours in the morning and spent the whole day with Mum and Dad, telling them the wonders of the Kenya Police Colege. Mum even commented that I was walking like a cop. I felt great. There are some remarks which are very pleasing especially when they come out of one's mother's mouth.

Then, in the evening, I went to the shops to see whether there would be any faces that I would recall. But, there were no friends of mine. The few mugs who were lolling around the bars were too old for me. We could not amiably mix. Besides, I was not a boozer then, so, I got fed up with the trading centre very fast. I started for home.

3

Only a few yards from the shops, I overtook a girl. I was not in a talking mood but she greeted me. I answered her and to show her that I was not interested in her, I accelerated my pace but she called after me and told me not to leave her behind. As it was getting dark, she asked me whether I was going to Mutwe-wa-thi so that I could accompany her. Although my home was in a different village, I told her that that was where I was going and so we started walking side by side towards the destination. We were talking about this and that and she convinced me that she knew me well.

When we came to Nyaguathi river, I asked her for a lay. She told me to go to hell. I said that I was capable of laying her even without making the damned request and she threatened that she would scream. To counter that, I told her that I would strangle her. I had then stood infront of her and she was glancing right and left, looking

50

for an escape avenue. I placed on the ground the small parcel I was carrying comprising the few items I had bought at the shops, which I had thought would be required at home; soap, sugar and tea, and held her hands firmly, with both my hands. She did not scream and I quickly wrestled her to the ground. Her parcel flew into the bushes.

She lay on her back and after a bit of struggle, I had my way.

I was so excited that only a second after I entered into her, I had my eclipse. Gosh! That was wonderful! Nothing better than a woman's softness after three months of celibacy. She was muttering some word to me, telling me to do it again, which I did. She told me that even if I had not used any threats, she would have thanked me anyway, when we reached near her home. That touched me somehow, and I half-heartedly apologised. I dismounted and helped her to get onto her feet and dress.

I walked her all the way near her home and when we reached there, she allowed me to do it again. She even removed her pants and we used my coat as a carpet to lie on. I wished I had not in the first place used force on her. It was her own offer and it was beyond all description. She knew how to give it to me and I accepted her. I really did enjoy her. She even booked me for a later date but my time was running out. I was due back at Kiganjo in only a week's time.

That week was spent mainly in helping Mum and Dad in the farm chores. I promised Dad that I would save enough money to re-buy that lower part of our land which I had forced him to sell to get my school fees. I felt so ashamed of myself.

CHAPTER SIX

1

After recruitment, we were all gathered in 'C' Mess and our posting orders read out. I really do not know what method they use to choose places for trained recruits but I found that I had been thrown to Western Province. Western!! Such a hell of a distance from home!

My dream of ever arresting the Headmaster faded into the distant blue; but, after all, the police were going to cover my expenses for the journey. Besides I had sworn, with the Bible held high in my hand, that I would serve the Republic as a Police Officer, anywhere where I would be posted within the Kenyan soil or outside. I had to accept Western.

Mum and Dad were there to see me off and I had given them a hundred shillings each out of the four that I had been given. That is the time when I learnt that the authorities had been keeping something for me each month. It was explained that since we were going out into the world, where we would be required to cater for ourselves, it was only appropriate that they should keep something for us, to give us a comfortable start. I thanked them.

I arrived at Kakamega twenty hours after leaving Kiganjo. We had to take a train ride all the way to Malaba, and then board a bus to Kakamega.

We boarded the train at Nairobi Railway Station at about 1400hrs. and the policemen we found on board told us the train would arrive at Malaba the following day at 0800hrs. A whole 18 hours later.

I was accompanied by three other graduates, two Luhyas and a Mkamba. The Luhyas had travelled in a train before but the Mkamba and I had not.

We had to travel third class—according to our Rail Travel Warrants, but the cops who were on board, and who we came to learn belonged to the Railways and Harbours Police Department, told us that cops should not mix with the sundry who travelled third class. There was a second class coach reserved for them and, because they'd be on duty throughout the night, we could sleep in the coach if we wanted.

My Luhya companions happily agreed to sleep in the coach but I requested the cops if I could accompany them on their 'duty rounds' so that I would familiarize myself—so to speak. They exchanged glances and nodded their assent. My heart was overjoyed.

The train came to life and started crawling slowly out of the station, with the two cops hanging at the doors, checking whether there would be any 'jumpers'. These, they told me, were people who jumped into the luggage compartment when the train started, so that they would not pay the fare and, because the goods coaches were not checked after the train left the station, they would arrive at their destinations safely, unmolested. I asked them what action was taken if one was found stowing that way and they told me that those with money were charged double, while those without money were forced to do dirty chores on the train—like cleaning the bogies and loading and unloading the train.

Trees, buildings and the land-scape rolled by as the 'iron-caterpillar' wound its way, meandering in and out of what the cops told me were the rolling hills of Limuru, through farmlands and then into . . . I thought it would plunge right down into a ravine, but the cops said we were now entering into the escarpment—the land of beauty. It was scaring to me!

I threw my pair of eye-balls across, to see nature's mighty power of creation and destruction, imagining what it would be like, were this iron caterpillar to roll on its side, towards the beautifully-shaped pieces of agricultural land down the valley. And what, I asked myself, may have prompted the white man to cut through the side of this escarpment, spending all the money, the labour and not minding the risk, in a foreign land?

The proverbial snake rattled on, down into the base of the escarpment, beside Longonot, the mountain of fire, crawled on past indifferent gazelles and zebras and the wild, stopping at few stations, past tors, and eventually made a full halt at Nakuru; reputedly the cleanest town in East Africa.

A few passengers disembarked and an almost equal number boarded the train which whistled shrilly as we left the station.

After Nakuru, my cop friends told me that it was high time that we accompanied the Ticket Examiner in his rounds, to check whether all the passengers had paid their fares. The ticket-man turned out to be a lean, oldish railway employee. He walked with an easy gait and carried out his duties nonchalantly. He declined to check the tickets in the First Class coaches because, as he put it, First Class coaches were numbered right from the originating station. Besides, no first class passenger would allow swindlers on board.

The second class coaches were checked meticulously and one old couple asked why there were so many cops on the train on that day. He was not answered by anyone and we proceeded to the third class where on entry into the first coach, I was met by smothering heat and a blend of stenches from that of fish to ripe bananas. The passengers were in such a haphazard state, each trying to get room where they could stretch their legs and, at the same time, keep guard over their belongings. There was an incessant buzzing like in a bee hive, interrupted frequently by a squeal or a shout by one of the passengers. Our entry reduced the volume of the noise and some of the passengers eyed us hostilely while others went even to the extent of clicking their tongues. The ticket examiner was over-meticulous in his job here and seemed to doubt even the very tickets that were shown to him.

From the third class coaches, we picked four youths who had no tickets, despite their protests and pleas that their tickets had been picked from their pockets at Nairobi. We shepherded them into the guard-room where they were to be detained until we reached Bungoma Station where stowaway cases were dealt with.

At 0300 hours, the following day, I was feeling so sleepy that I begged leave from my friends to take a nap, at least for the remaining hours of the night. They allowed me to retire and I went and joined my Luhya friends and stretched myself on the bunk. It was very comfortable, especially with the rocking of the train and I must have slept so heavily because I did not stir until we arrived at Malaba and I was roused by the duty cops.

Me and my friends alighted from the train after intermittently waving the other cops and found a Police van waiting for us just next to that station platform. We rode on that and it took us to Kakamega.

2

I arrived at Kakamega and my six hours assessment of the place branded it lousy. I did not know what was coming but I felt that somehow, I was not going to enjoy the stay very much.

Only thirty minutes after booking my arrival in the occurrence book at Kakamega Police Station, the lines sergeant marched me to the office of the officer-in-charge where I was given a copy of the station standing orders.

A list of seventeen 'don'ts' which included one underlined 'don't' prohibiting me from bringing to the lines, any visitors, male or female, without prior consent from the officer-in-charge.

"Even at night?" I querried. The officer-in-charge looked at me and told me that, to avoid having to take visitors to him for scrutiny, either during the day or night, I should avoid bringing any visitors to the lines.

My first deployment in duty was a night beat in which I had to patrol the town from 22.00 hours each evening to 0600 hours the following day, stopping, questioning, searching and arresting suspicious characters. This I found to be very difficult because there were no special differentiating marks betwen an honest and a dishonest night-walker.

The cop who was supposed to acquaint me with this job was an old timber, his force number having only three digits, and apparently, he had some extra role to play every time we stopped a reeling drunkard.

He would tell me to stand aside and then take the drunkard to a distance, always out of my earshot, and whisper some things to him. Most of the times when he did this, money would change hands; from the drunkard to the cop and then he would rejoin me complaining about the cold night; but then I would notice that his eyes were twinkling with new light.

Each morning, before we reported off-duty, the cop would hand to me anything from twenty to thirty shillings, telling me to go and have a warm cup of tea, to thaw the cold from my bones. I would thank him profusely and think what a magnificient god-father he was, until much later when I came to know the real source of the money.

On the eighth day of my stay, I went for the fist operation, which opened my life into the police world and gave me what must have developed into a police heart.

I had spent the night on beat and was dozing in bed, resting. I did not want to fall into heavy sleep and yet I wanted to rest my weary self before preparing for another night on beat. A half-doze which was creeping into me was blasted into nothingness and full alertness by the station alarm, screaming full blast.

In a Police Station, the alarm is the last resort to a dangerous situation and its sounding is only done or ordered by the most senior officer in the station. Even the booking in the O.B. is done in red, to show that it is not an every day event.

That realization made me jump out of bed, and into my trousers. I donned the police over-coat and cap in less than three minutes. I slipped on the boots, without socks or even lacing them and joined the other cops who were all running towards the Police Station.

3

At the report office, I found a corporal who was waving his hands frantically, showing us all the way to the armoury, without saying a thing. I arrived at the armoury door and the lines' sergeant was issuing every new arrival with a self-loading rifle and three clips of ammunition. There must have been a dire urgency in whatever was happening because even the sergeat did not seem to worry very much about our force numbers, ranks or names as is usual in handing out arms and ammunition.

We then paraded in front of the station and the deputy station commander came running. The lines' sergeat welcomed him to the parade and then the second-in-charge took over. He cleared his throat and stated:

"A bank robbery with violence has been committed at Kisumu. The vehicle used is believed to have been stolen from Kericho this dawn. It's a Peugeot 504 saloon, white in colour, registration number KLH 776. I repeat the number; KLH 776. The vehicle is believed to be headed for south Nyanza but you never know with criminals, they might decide to come this way. If they do, they are our game.

"The occupants are believed to be five, including the driver. They are armed with what is believed to be a revolver or pistol. These people are killers and they gunned down a security guard at the bank during the robbery. We will mount road-blocks at Shirere and Kaberengo but, as I said earlier, this is just as a precaution because the bandits were last seen heading for South Nyanza.

"The following will man the Shirere road-block, Number ...." he called out five names, headed by a corporal and then five other names for the Kaberengo road-block. My name was called in the second detail.

My heart was already beating wildly. I had a feeling that I was going to confront the gangsters for the first time and was very anxious to 'meet' them and at the same time, I was scared stiff at the prospect of the gangsters gunning me down.

I had had time then to lace my boots and load the rifle and felt almost ready for anything. The other four officers who were to accompany me were familiar faces but due to my newness to the place, I had not had any chance to work with them and as such, I hoped and prayed that they would be crack-shots with the rifles and brave enough not to start looking for cover when the bandits fired at us—if they ever came our way. I was not very sure that I could fire at anyone, bandit or no bandit.

The only firing of guns I had done was at the Kenya Police College range and then, I had been firing at standing card-board targets which I was sure would not fire back at me. The very prospect of meeting an armed robber, who would definitely aim and fire at me was very scaring and I said a silent prayer that the gang would go to South Nyanza or anywhere else, but not the Eldoret/Tororo road.

The corporal in charge of our group ordered me and another constable to load the spikes on the back of the land-rover, a difficult job due to the weight of the spike-boards and the noon-day sun which was beating mercilessly down on us. Wearing the Police caps was intensifying the heat instead of lessening it.

We also carried reflecting signs written 'POLICE CHECK' on one side and 'ACCIDENT AHEAD' on the other plus hurricane lamps with red chimneys. That made my heart sink even further. It was only 1230 hours and carrying the lamps meant that the operation might continue even after dark. It's one thing confronting an armed robber in daylight and quite another doing so in darkness.

The preparations, that is from the time the alarm sounded to the time we were ready to move to Kaberengo, took almost thirty minutes and I wondered whether that is what is usually referred to by the Press as 'quick police action'. However, I did not ask anyone because what I would have actually preferred was a longer delay so that by the time we arrived at the road-block place, the bandits would have passed and gone their way.

<h1 style="text-align:center">4</h1>

The Land-rover at last took off with me and two other constables sitting in the rear while the corporal and another constable sat at the front with the driver. The corporal was armed with a revolver and an ultra-high frequency set; the only means of communication with the station as the very high frequency set in the Land-rover was out of order.

"Scared?" a fellow cop asked me, smilling slyly. I guessed he had attended several road-blocks before.

"Why?" I asked him, scowling and trying to put on a bold front although I knew that my hands were actually trembling and I had to grip onto the rifle tightly to steady them!

"Nothing . . . you just look like you have swallowed a bee . . . alive," he chuckled and was joined by the other cop in laughing at me. I bit my lower lip and cursed my anatomy and physiology for showing my adrenal feelings so openly.

"Have you ever swallowed one?" I asked the cop, looking at him with hostile eyes. My glare put him down to size and he muttered a hasty apology and added; "Let's reserve all the fight we have in us for the robbers. Be of courage . . . the bandits might not even turn up and we shall have no need to be scared." Coming from someone else, the words were very reassuring to me and I even sighed in relief—inaudibly though.

Amid the bumps and clatters of the road-block paraphernalia, we reached Kaberengo and chose a spot, about seventy yards from the Kakamega/Eldoret/Tororo junction road and parked the Land-rover on the left hand side of the road. We jumped out and the cop who had almost riled me earlier helped me in removing the spikes.

We placed one spike-board on the left-hand side of the road and the other some fifteen yards from the first on the right hand side of the road.

The reflecting signs were placed each fifty yards from the spikes on either side.

When the road-block was thus mounted, the corporal called Kakamega Police Station on the U.H.F. set and informed the control that all was set and ready. He also told two cops to go each to the reflecting signs while I, the corporal and the other constable were to remain at the spikes, checking on cars. The driver was to stay in the vehicle, which he had then turned to face the way we had come, ready to chase any vehicle whose driver refused to stop at the road-block.

The first vehicle to come was a matatu from Turbo, as over-loaded as it could carry. When the corporal saw it, he orderd me to get into the Land-rover while he signalled the matatu driver to stop and park on the side of the road.

I hastily did as told and waited, not knowing what for.

Three minutes later, the driver of the matatu came to the Land-rover, grinning and holding some crumpled notes in his hand.

"I've been told to come and see you by the corporal," he told me even before I had had time to open the door of the vehicle. He had stood against the door, apparently barring me from getting outside and he dumped the crumpled notes on my lap before muttering thanks and running back to his matatu.

I opened my mouth to call him back but, before I uttered a word, our driver, who had been watching me intently, put his right hand palm on my mouth with his left hand.

"How green are you?" he asked me. "Have you never worked as a Traffic Police Officer?" He looked so surprised.

I physically removed his hand from over my mouth and wiped his 'touch' from my lips.

"What d'you mean by that?" I asked him harshly. He just looked at me, straightened the notes and then counted them. There was a total of seventy-five shillings, all in five shilling notes and, as I watched him counting the money, something slowly opened in my brain. This, I realized, was what was termed in loose terms as 'chai' and in harder terms as 'bribery and corruption'!! Seventy-five shillings for the six of us. I did a quick mental calculation and found that, shared equally, each of us would get slightly more than twelve shillings. I also leafed through my law memory book and was so appalled to realize that those same twelve shillings could land me in jail for a period of as long as three years!

"Keep it," the driver said, handing the money to me, but I quickly withdrew my hand.

"No! You keep it—and I don't want any share of it!" I said quickly as I got out of the Land-rover. I walked to where the corporal was inspecting yet another matatu, while the first matatu driver was driving off, waving at me and smiling.

"Go back to the Land-rover!" the corporal barked at me, looking at me with admonishing eyes.

"No, sir, send someone else. I'd rather stay here at the spikes . . . please," I pleaded with him although I had made up my mind that I was not going back to the Land-rover. I had left the station to come and wait for armed robbers and not for my first lesson in corruption.

"Why?" he asked me smiling.

"Well . . . nothing. I just . . .," but I did not finish. There came, through the U.H.F. set, the call sign of the set we had:

·"Kakamega mobile two from control." At first, the corporal did not seem to know what was going on.

"Kakamega mobile two—Kakamega mobile two—from control— how do you read me over?" The voice seemed agigated and urgent.

"We are being called," I told the corporal, who quickly unhooked the mouth-piece.

"Control from Kakamega mobile two—you are coming fine—go ahead." His hand was trembling as he held the mouth-piece.

"Kakamega mobile two—flash SITREP—vehicle registration number Kilo Lima Hotel figures seven seven six—I repeat Kilo Lima Hotel figures seven seven six—earlier reported stolen and used in a robbery is heading your way after jumping a road-block at Maili Tisa—are you with me over?" The corporal had to swallow twice before he could answer. I was so shocked that I was trembling from head to foot!

"Roger—roger—control—go ahead."

"I go ahead—Charlie India Delta personnel from Eldoret are on chase stop—detain the vehicle and occupants stop shoot if necessary stop—are you with me over?"

'Roger."

"Reinforcement has been dispatched from Kakamega stop— confirm arrival of car and action taken stop over."

"Wilco—wilco, over."

"Good luck, over." Good luck? Yes. Even the fellow at the control knew that I needed the luck.

Then followed the most frantic efforts by all of us to completely block the road. We hurriedly placed the spikes together, end to end, thus completely blocking the road on either side. The corporal shouted to the matatu driver to 'get the hell going!' and to the police driver to '*Kaa chonjo*' and then turned to the rest of us.

"You heard control? These bastards are armed and may try their target practice on us. Don't fire in the air. Shoot straight at them and . . . " and before he could finish, there sped towards us, from Turbo direction, a yellow car. The driver must have noticed the spikes just in time because he applied emergency brakes, making his tyres screech, just a few yards from us.

I had leapt some five feet from the spikes towards the grass verge, cocked my rifle and my finger was itching to press the trigger of the rifle which I had levelled on the car with surprisingly steady hands. The other constables were all aiming at the car but the corporal was pressing the mouth-piece of the U.H.F. set without saying a thing.

The driver of the yellow car, a Datsun 1600, came out of the car with his hands reaching for the skies muttering "Please, don't shoot . . . pleas don't shoot . . ." If only the corporal had as much as started to say any word which started in 'sho . . .' I would have blasted the daylights out of the driver's universe.

"Where the hell do you think you are? . . ." Corporal started asking him but, before he could finish his question, from the same Turbo direction, there appeared a fast moving white car, which had its head-lamps on as was its klaxon, full blast.

All my attention was diverted to the new arrival and my heart performed a double somersault when I noticed that the car was a Peugeot 504. I immediately decided that it was the gang's car and I held my breath, as I sentenced the occupants to death!

5

The car came on, without checking its speed and was on us even before I could pull the trigger or read the registration number. It was heading straight for the spikes as the other officers dived out of its way. I heard myself shout a warning to them as the front wheels of the Peugeot smashed into the spikes, bursting in a cloud of dust as the vehicle swerved out of control, staggered on the road from left to right with its fractured fore legs and in its crazy swaying, headed straight for the police Land-rover which it smashed into, so heavily from the side that the Land-rover was physically lifted off the road, hung for three undecided seconds in the air and then landed on its side on the road-side gutter. The Peugeot followed the Land-rover and landed on top of it.

I was watching the horror scene, which had taken less than ten seconds, with my mouth very open, my ears full of buzzing bees and my brain completely muddled.

A movement at the pile of both vehicles snapped me back into consciousness and I found myself blundering, heavy booted towards the cars. The first thought I had was of our driver, whom I had left in the Land-rover, holding seventy-five shillings, and I was determined to go and see what had happened to him.

When I was about twenty yards from the pile-up, a full blast of a self-loading rifle from my right stopped me short. I watched for the movement which I had seen at the pile-up, just in time to see a man, who was trying to get from the Peugeot's driver's door, hold his chest momentarily before another blast of the S.L.R. crumpled him to the ground.

The left-hand side door of the Peugeot was flung open and a man, with a black object in his hand, came out. He looked right and left and started blundering towards me. I braced myself, shouted at him to stop but, instead, he raised his right hand and the black object was instantly 'transformed' into a hand gun. I closed my eyes and pressed the trigger of my S.L.R., and its vomit of lethal death sent my whole body shaking like a man with palsy. I released the trigger and opened my eyes. The noise around me was like a replay of a sound-track from 'The Berets'.

About five yards from me was what was left of the man who had held the black gun. My blast had caught him around his middle and, although he was still on his feet, his whole front looked like it had been soaked in red paint.

I saw him take a hesitant step forward, both hands holding his belly, with blood oozing through the fingers and flowing down his thighs and legs. I looked at his face and noticed that his mouth was tightly shut but his eyes were open. It was such a horrible sight! His hair seemed to be standing on end and his breathing, through his nose only, was wheezy and laboured.

Then, he opened his mouth and released a sound, half-human and half-animal and then spat out a mouthful of blood, before his knees sagged and he fell head-long onto the tarmac. A die-hard. He had been on his feet for more than five seconds!

On the ground, his hands and legs twitched for only three to four seconds and then all was quiet. Even the other officers had stopped shooting. The war was over, the victors still standing on their feet while the losers lay on the ground.

'You have killed a man!' I heard my conscience accuse me but, immediately, the same conscience defended me, "He could have killed you if you handn't killed him!" And for the first time I felt a burning sensation on my thigh. I looked down on my thigh, parted the police over-coat and noticed a small hole on my trousers. It was quickly filling with blood which was spreading onto the cloth and making a very conspicuous carmine on my grey trousers.

I touched the hole and my finger felt the hollow in my body and pain started in the wound. I was just about to scream when the corporal came to my side.

"Are you hurt?" he asked urgently. I looked at him and noticed that he was levelling his pistol at me. I didn't know whether he wanted to give me the mercy shot or what but the last thing I remembered was me telling him, "I think he nicked me . . . ." Then I felt my legs give way. I dimly saw the corporal, dropping his gun and stretching his hands to hold me.

I was jerked back into conciousness by a jolt from my head banging against something. I felt like I was swimming in the air and before I opened my eyes, I heard voices and the persistent scream of a siren. I realized that I was in a car which was moving fast, and that the bang I had flet was my head hitting against the thigh of someone who was cradling my head on his lap.

"It's not serious, it's just a scratch but I think what scared him was the blood," one voice said.

"Or the fear of death. I bet that was the very first time he has shot at someone . . ." There was soft laughter from both of them.

Then the scream of the siren slowly petered off and I warmly welcomed the silence that followed.

"But you should have seen him," the first voice said. "I've never, in my twelve years of Police work, seen a man confront an armed gangster the way he did. He just stood there, emptying the whole magazine on the thug even though the thug had shot him first!" There was pride in the voice. Then, they laughed softly again. "That's one for the record . . ." More laughter.

6

I opened my eyes slowly and discerned the inside of what must have been a small car. I was on my back on someone's lap and my legs were slightly touching the floor boards of the car. I racked my brain and tried to connect the past events and remembered that I had been at a road-block and had been shot. I activated my brain and tried to feel the pain in my thigh but apparently there was none. I tried to move the leg and that is when I felt a leaden weight on the whole of the leg and a very remote ache on the thigh, which was more of an itch than pain. I closed my eyes again as the vehicle started on a series of twists and turns with the siren coming on and going off in short blasts. I decided that I would feign unconsciousness and hear what my companions would say.

"Does this place have a casualty entrance?" I heard a voice ask.

"No. Just drive to the main entrance and clear the path with the siren . . ." and he trailed off in laughter. I had all along been trying to place that voice and attributed it to the corporal who had com-manded the operation at Kakamega. I automatically knew the voice which had questioned about the casualty entrance. It was that of constable Otoigo, the C.I.D. driver at Kakamega. There was only one voice which I could not place but the knowledge that I was in the hands of my own station personnel made me feel really at home.

The car came to a halt and I heard the doors open before I was physically lifted by one person. I must have been very light or the person must have been very strong. Another hand was holding my leg, keeping it straight. I dared not open my eyes but I could feel the late sunshine burning onto my face. A short distance and then we started climbing stairs. Then, the unmistakable smell of hospital precincts; ether, iodine, methylated spirit and disease!!

"This way," I heard a female voice.

"Good afternoon, sister," I heard my carrier say.

"Good afternoon, officer—this is the victim of the gang?" the same female voice. Kakamega Police must have called the hospital.

"Yes, sister, but, he isn't very seriously wounded," the corporal replied.

"Then, why doesn't he walk?" The sister asked as I felt myself placed on a trolley which someone started to push.

Another short distance and I was transferred from the comfort of the trolley and put on a hard surface. Here, the smell of disinfectant was smothering. Someone was removing my trousers and, except that I was 'unconscious', I would have stopped them.

"Go and wait next door. We shall tell you of the findings," the nurse addressed someone and I heard a faint 'O.K.' followed by the thud of boots, slowly fading away. A door closed and opened somewhere.

The person who was removing my trousers had got them to my knees and then, I heard her gasp and murmur, 'Oh!'

"What is it?" Another voice—female too, asked.

"Nothing. It looks like a burn—he must have been shot from very **close quarters—what the police call point-blank range . . ." The voice** giggled.

Then, I felt a maddening pain on my thigh as someone was **dabbing it with something and I could not hold my 'unconsciousness'** any longer. I opened my eyes and tried to sit up but a gentle hand pushed me back onto the couch. I looked at my tender and noticed that she was a young pretty nurse. She was also looking at me, smiling. Another nurse was at the corner of the room where there emanated steam—like something was being boiled.

"How'd you feel?" The nurse asked. The question made the other nurse turn sharply. She was older than the one at the couch.

"Oh! He's come round?" She asked, at the same time hurrying to the couch.

"How are you?" She inquired, smiling reassuringly.

"Fine," I replied although the throbbing pain in my thigh was almost unbearable. "Where am I?" I asked her.

"Kisumu—New Nyanza General Hospital and your colleagues are just next door," she told me still smiling.

"Thank you. How is the wound?" I asked her.

"Not very deep. The bullet bruised you as it passed. There is only a slight burn. I don't think we need to admit you," she finished.

"That's fine with me. Can I go home, now?" I asked trying to get out of bed. I had my legs over the edge of the couch when the nurse rushed to me and held me.

"Not so fast! We haven't even dressed your wound!" And I looked down at my thigh, having raised myself on one elbow. My shirt was open from top to bottom and my trousers were down at my knees. The only piece I had of apparel, to cover my nakedness was my pants and that sort of made me embarrassed. My eyes had been deliberately avoiding to look at the wound all this time, but I had to, at last.

I saw what looked like a burn, with unbursted blisterettes all around. There was a gaping wound in the form of a furrow, about two inches long and half an inch wide and about a quarter of an inch deep; but the main cause of my uneasiness was the angry red flesh that fringed the furrow and the blisters.

The nurses had given me all that time to examine myself and then one threw a glance at my face before dipping some lint into an open bowl, containing a yellow mixture and then dabbing the wound again. The pain was so excruciating that I shot out my right hand, grabbed the wrist of the nurse and shouted at her, 'Wait a minute!"

I guess I was holding her too tight because she winced and begged me to release her hand. The pain in me was so severe that I felt sweat breaking all over my body and my mouth turning dry.

"What is that yellow stuff?" I asked the nurse, holding onto my thigh with both hands and trying not to scream.

"Iodine; is it painful?" She was still smiling. I guessed she must have seen so many people gnashing their teeth on application of iodine.

"Painful? If you put that lint on that wound again, I am going to walk through that door!" The other nurse was looking at me with eyes that conveyed mercy, pity, concern and a tint of love, all in one. "I am not touching it again," she assured me. The pain made my memory even sharper.

"What happened to our driver?" I asked the nurse, momentarily forgetting the pain in me.

"Which driver?" the nurse asked.

"Our Police driver who was crashed in the Land-rover?" I was trying to blot out the picture of the man I had shot as he stood in front of me.

"What do you mean, crashed in the Land-rover?" She was shaking her head. She did not understand.

"You told me that my fellow Police Officers are next door?" I asked her, hope making me smile.

"Yes, they are next door."

"Could you please call one for me?" I begged.

The nurse gave the other a knowing glance and the one who had been standing far from the bed shuffled her feet as she walked towards a closed door on the far end. The one who remained made herself look very busy arranging and rearranging the wound dressing. I guess to avoid having to look at me. My wound was still agape and I felt like someone was tapping softly on it. I pulled my trousers and covered my nakedness. The blood on the trousers had dried but had a faint smell, like burning sugar.

The door was flung open and Cpl. Matolo came in. He was grinning from ear to ear.

"Hi! Hero of the year! Congrats, man!" He came and shook my hand vigorously and patted my back several times. "Well done, Fred!"

He at once became serious, cast an eye at the nurses who stood at the corner and almost whispered to me, "What you did today is beyond all imagination. The truth is, I, myself, would not have done it. That's why I am calling you hero of the year. It's not sarcasm or flattery. You did what even the commissoner himself would call a perfect job. Even the Division commander had ordered that you report to his office immediately you are on your feet. Not for the usual disciplining but for a pat on the back," he looked serious alright. Then I remembered the driver.

"What happened to driver Kinyua?" I asked him.

"Why?"

"Where was he when the Peugeot rammed into the Land-rover?"

"He was with me at the spikes. The Land-rover had nobody inside."

I felt almost ashamed of the relief that came with that piece of news.

"What about the other officers?" I asked.

"Everyone of us is as fit as a fiddle . . ." and he laughed.

"The robbers . . .?" The picture of the dying man was again looming menacingly.

"We only got one alive—he is in Kakamega General Hospital with a broken collar-bone, out of the car-accident. He was not shot by anybody. The rest are more dead than this wall. I guess it was our round, that one. Except you, and your injury is of course not very serious, we suffered no other casualties," he finished and then beckoned the nurses over. He told them to dress my wound so that we would check whether I could stand.

Again, my trousers were pulled down to my knees and I noticed that the younger nurse could not help looking at my crotch.

Ten minutes later, I stood from the couch and felt my whole right leg very heavy and half-numbed. However, with the corporal on my right hand and one nurse on my left, I made five toddler's steps before I told them to let go of me and I tested my game leg. It was okay but when I tried to balance my whole weight on it alone, pain shot through the thigh and I had to hold onto the nurse to stop myself staggering. I wished I would stay holding her just like that!

We were fully engrosed in the testing of my leg when the door burst open and five men and three women, all in white dust-coats came in. Four of the men had stethoscopes dangling from their necks while one woman had what looked like a surgical compact.

They all stopped short, in the middle of the room when they saw us. One of them spoke:

"Is that the Police casualty . . ." pointing at me.

"Yes, Doctor Adala . . . he just wanted to test the stability of his leg. I . . . " she didn't finish.

"You mean 'he wanted'? But you are the nurse here and you should know what the patient needs and what he doesn't need. Get him back onto the couch!"

To prove that the nurse had done nothing wrong, I walked back to the couch, trying as much as possible not to limp and I sat myself on the couch. The doctor, accompanied by the whole entourage came over.

<h1 style="text-align:center">7</h1>

My trousers were again rolled to my knees and the doctor, without saying a word, ripped the bandage from the wound and the movement was so hasty and uncared for that blood welled up in the wound once again. I also felt pain start throbbing all over again.

"Iodine swab . . ." he said without raising his eyes, and the nurse who had treated me earlier ran to the corner and brought the required swab.

When I saw that it was the same yellow stuff, I opened my mouth to protest but the doctor assured me, even without me uttering a word, that he would not touch the wound with the lint. He did not. Instead he cleaned the surrounding area and then bandaged the wound again. His actions were quick, deft and expert and within five minutes, he had finished. He looked at his watch, took the head-chart and noted something on it.

"You may go home and go to Kakamega Hospital for a check-up after three days, Fred." He was smiling, for the first time, as he discharged me.

"Thank you doctor," I told him and, even Cpl. Matolo thanked him.

We started walking out of the small room and at the door, I turned and smiled goodbye at the nurses. I read the inscription on the door: 'Observation Ward'. I was holding onto the corporal who was muttering to himself about "The long journey from Kakamega to Kisumu . . . lousy doctors . . ." and I interrupted him by asking:

"What was the reason for my being brought here instead of being treated at Kakamega General Hospital?"

"The idea was that, because we did not know how seriously wounded you were, Kisumu was more appropriate in case we needed the Flying Doctor's Service as the airstrip at Kakamega is not in a safe condition for an aircraft to land," he told me. Stupidly enough, I felt that I should have been more seriously wounded so that I would have had the first ride in an aircraft!!

Outside the hospital entrance, I found the Police Ambulance still parked where we had left it.

I checked on my wrist-watch and noticed that it was already 1810 hours. I had been in the hospital for slightly over an hour.

The driver of the ambulance and a C.I.D. sergeant, whom I had known for a long time and I guessed was my companion-on the journey from Kakamega to Kisumu, came out of the car, at a run, when they saw us.

"How are you, Fred?" The sergeant asked.

"Fine, thanks. I just got a slight laceration which does not need a doctor's constant watch and so there is no need for admission." I answered him.

"Okay, let's get back home, and Fred . . ." he pulled me to one side, away from the others and held my right hand "Congratulations Fred." He was smiling contentedly.

The journey back to Kakamega was fast and eventless. At Kakamega Police Station, I noticed that half the Police personnel from the Provincial Headquarters, Divisional Headquarters and the station were all gathered there. I at first thought that there was going to be mounted another road-block and wondered when the robbers will give the Police a rest.

However, the whole crowd surged forward when I stepped out of the ambulance and every one of them was shaking my hand, muttering something meant to tell me about ". . .a wonderful performance . . . jolly good show . . . congratulations . . .crack-shot . . . keep it up . . .lesson to the thugs everywhere in the world . . . should be in C.I.D. . . ." and at the end of it all, my biceps was aching and my thigh had once again started throbbing in pain.

My night-beat companion at last held my hand and led me to my house. He told me that the O.C.S. had declared two days off-duty for me and him because of what I had gone through. The way he analysed it, I noticed that he would have liked to go to the night-beat alone and thus pocket the proceeds from the job—alone.

I got to my house and when I had put on the light, my beat companion told me that I should not worry over supper, as he was going to fix something for me. Then he left me.

I unzipped my trousers and pulled them down to observe the wound again and a loud knock on the door made me pull them up hastily, banging the wound in the process before I welcomed the knocker.

"Come in." I said, hating the caller even before I knew who it was.

The door opened and Cpl. Matolo came in. He carefully closed the door, glanced at the window and proceeded to remove something from the inside pocket of his coat.

His hand came out with the same crumpled notes that I had seen at Kaberengo and I wanted to tell him to get them the hell out of my house but I checked my tongue.

"Fred," he said in a voice just slightly above a whisper, "me and my companions have decided that you take this as a reminder of the dangers of this work. Just have a beer, or buy yourself something else." He handed the money to me and I accepted it and put it into my trouser pocket.

Then it started burning a hole in the cloth and through to my skin and I had to remove it and hold it in my hand.

"Thank you," I told the corporal and he left my house.

I thought of the best place to keep the money and had difficulty in coming to a decision. At last, I put it in an envelope, folded it until it became a very small parcel and buried it inside an opened packet of flour! I had successfully finished my first course in corruption!

The following day, I was marched to the Divisional Commander's Office, in civilian clothes, where I shook his hand, was offered a chair and left his office fifteen minutes later, after a warm cup of tea, smiling like the cat that swallowed the bird.

"Keep it up, my boy," he had told me. "I can see a very bright future in you as a Police Officer. One day, I hope that you will sit on such a chair as I am sitting on. Once again—well done!"

Overnight, my small unknown name had spread like bush-fire in Kakamega Town.

'Wonder-cop' was the nick-name got from Government officials, while bar-maids, matatu operators, businessmen, would-be thieves etc all kept quiet when I passed wherever they were and wore embarrassed grins and smiles in my presence.

I really did not know why they reacted that way to the death of a gangster. After all even the other Police Officers had played their part and I could not understand why I had been the hero. I had nearly lost my life! If the gangster had as much as raised his gun, just a foot above what he did, I would have been as dead as a wall—to use the corporal's phrase.

Anyway, the reaction was very embarrassing to me. Despite the hero-worshipping I received from the *wananchi,* the first two weeks were awful to me.

Even after spending the whole night awake, harassing drunkards and late movers, sometimes I would be required to 'help', as the sergeant put it, in taking prisoners to court and sometimes I was so weary and exhausted that I was repeatedly dozing, right there, inside the court-room, while on the duty of guarding prisoners.

It was also during those two weeks that I had a vicious attack of malaria and ended up being admitted for four days at the Kakamega Provincial General Hospital where I was reportedly half-crazy.

I was told that I slapped a nurse and that I was asking for Mum and Dad to come and take me back home. Even the doctors had a very hard time keeppig me under control and medication.

I was having illusions of all kinds and feeling very depressed.

Malaria was sapping my strength, but so was the police force and I wished I had not joined it, that in fact I had stayed at home, with Mum and Dad—digging our small shamba. Maybe we could have dug more, maybe deeper, and . . .

However, despite all these misgivings, I found solace. I spotted the women. Big women. Amazons, if you want. Women with fannies that don't need a pillow under them during the ritual of Venus. Women that make you feel that you are in bed with a woman—not a hole of muck!

After two weeks on night beat, I changed duties and was deployed in day patrol. I was supposed to be acquainted with this job by a young cop—just about my age—who was a far better teacher than my first collegue. Njagi did not have extra roles to play with suspects out of my earshot and he was the one who told me where the few shillings that the former colleague used to give me came from.

He said that, to survive, one had to have an extra cent here and there and that even when one took prisoners to the Police station where they were subsequently charged and taken to court, the fines which emanated from such procedures benefited only the higher authorities without a single cent being given to the original arrester.

After reporting off-duty each evening, Njagi would request me to accompany him to town where he would have a beer or two and I would have a soda or a glass of milk. I had refused Njagi's offer of a beer despite his reassurance that a bottle or two would not make me drunk. I had not tasted beer before and was not very much inclined to start drinking.

Most of the evenings, after the drinks, we would go home, me alone but Njagi would be accompanied by a woman whom he would pick from anywhere within the bars. Sometimes I would also feel that I could do with a woman but always shied away from the idea.

8

Then one day, it happened. We went to town as usual but on this day, instead of the way Njagi used to pick his women at the last hour, he took his pick immediately we got to town and the woman accompanied us into the first bar that we entered.

Njagi called for two beers, one for himself and one for his woman and a soda for me. As we were drinking, the woman excused herself and went out, only to come back some few minutes later, accompanied by another woman. The new woman was introduced as Judy Nekesa—Miss and there was even extra stress on the word 'Miss'. Njagi called for her drink and she said she'd take a soda. He friend urged her that one beer would not change the orbit of the earth and she smilingly agreed to take beer. Thus, I was the only one having a soda at the table and Judy was quick to comment on it.

"Why is my friend only taking sodas?" She asked smiling. I did not know what to answer and so I grinned. Njagi answered for me: "He is a clergyman." And we all laughed loud. I was feeling embarrassed though.

"Where is his church?" The woman went on. This time, I had to answer myself: "In my house; that is where I preach to women only and they have to receive the 'word' while naked!" More laughter.

"Then, I would like to hear one sermon," she giggled and sweat started to make my face shine.

It's not that I was impotent or that I was not capable of the game but somehow, my newness to the place, the distance from home and other displeasing aspects of life which had welcomed me to the place, had made a real celibate of me. Njagi was eyeing me from the corner of his eye. I bet he thought that I was going to blast the woman for her open offer but I was having other ideas about her. I looked at her and noticed that she was pretty in a rough way. She had a small round face on her small round head with her hair cropped short. Her bosom was, however, full and her waist small, giving way to what appeared an over-sized derriere and comfortably mascular legs. Her teeth were small, even and white and her lips were slightly upturned at the corners and frequently parted in lop-sided smiles. She was seated opposite me and I ogled her shamelessly. Right there and then, I decided that I was going to take her home, if she consented to at least . . . christen my house.

"That's a splendid idea," I said. The good thing about my church is that one does not have to carry a bible." We all laughed. Then Njagi suggested that, because Judy was going to receive a sermon from me, it was appropriate that we should sit together so that she might be used to the smell of the clergyman. We altered the seating arrangement and Judy came and sat next to me while Njagi and Deborah, his woman, sat together. We formed bar-couples and my stupid heart started beating faster. We took three other drinks each before deciding that we should go home.

I had a terrific night with Judy. Immediately we got into bed, she stripped to the skin and literally undressed me. I was still shy about removing my pants. When I was naked, we fell to. She was sighing and cooing and gasping and when I came to the climax, she screamed and held me so tight around the middle and bit my shoulder while at the same time she was scratching my buttocks and the whole of my back! Then it was all over. I lay panting on top of her and she eased the grasp that she had on me. She then thanked me and I was so surprised that I had to ask her what she was thanking me for. She told me that she had had sensations that she had not felt before and thus the need to thank me.

We hardly slept that night. Most of the time was spent in exploring one another.

The following morning, she told me that she would be going to her birth home, in Chavakali and I gave her some two pounds. By the way she thanked me, I suspected that I had given her far more than she had expected from me. She also gave me her address and told me that I could write to her and invite her to come to my house anytime I wanted. I was sad to see her go.

Njagi wanted to know how it had all fared and I told him that if life were like that throughout, then men would not have cause to cry.

I wrote to Judy three days later but the fool did not reply. I was very bitter about it and decided that even if she came on her own I would not welcome her to my house. There were other women. Bigger and better women and the field was open to me—to choose.

76

9

Then I met Charity. Charity Wangui. She was a cop. A very charitable cop. She taught me lousy screwing manners and styles all for free. When I look at it from both sides, I feel that Charity was the cause of the beginning of my downfall. Not that she stole anything from me but she changed me. I was a nice, innocent, meek, humble and promising youth before I met Charity. She made me the opposite of all those things. She changed my being.

My meeting with Charity was very funny. When I arrived at Kakamega, she was on leave. She came after I had stayed for over a month.

On that day, I had gone to the canteen to look for some cigarettes and just as I was leaving the canteen, I met with her. She was entering the canteen, but . . . my God! She was the most beautiful thing I had ever set my eyes upon. 'Thing' because I could not believe that such beauty and shapeliness could be in a human being. She was more beautiful than any other woman I had ever seen.

Other than giving her way to enter the canteen, I just stood there, gaping at her. I was bewildered. She sized me up, smiled, and said hello—in a soft, musical voice that astounded me. I could not believe my eyes or ears, even as she stretched her hand towards me. I took it and just held it lightly, my hand trembling. Then I released her hand, quickly, muttered an apology, and let her pass. I walked to my house and tried to figure out whether I was dreaming or not. Still day-dreaming, I walked back to the canteen, to look for her, but she was not anywhere around.

I had not tasted beer since I was employed but I surprised even myself, my collegues aside, when I called for a Tusker Export. I swallowed that. Not bad at all, I told myself. I called for another, and swallowed that one too. My friends who knew me as a teetotaller noticed that I was drinking and they started competing in buying me drinks.

I didn't know exactly how many of those small bottles I emptied, but I got so drunk that that night I puked in my bed and had a splitting headache the following day. My advisors told me that what I had was just a hang-over and they 'prescribed' that I drink two beers to make the head 'straight'. So I went to the canteen and drank two beers and, surprisingly, the headache was gone within a few minutes. But it was replaced by a want of more beers. I did not even report on duty, but the boss must have known all about it because when I told him that I had failed to go to the office because of a headache, he said he was sorry about it.

That evening, as I was arranging to go to town, I saw Charity once more. She was putting out some clothes on the line, outside a house which was just a short distance from mine. I walked back into my house, and prepared myself to accost her; preparation which included eyeing myself on the mirror to see whether I had anything offensive on my face. I straightened my jacket, cleared my throat and left my house, locking the door behind me. I walked towards her but instead of looking at her, I had my eyes focussed beyond her—in the distance. When I reached her, I pretended to be surprised to see her once again, I cleared my throat. She turned and faced me.

"Hello," I said and hastily added, "how are you?"

"Fine, thanks," she answered and smiled broadly revealing some even white teeth.

"Do you think the clothes will dry in the night?" I said to keep the conversation going. I could not think of anything else that I could say.

"I hope they do. I would have cleaned them during the early hours of the day but then I was sent out on duty. These people here are merciless. I just arrived yesterday from my leave and instead of them giving me at least one day off to 'get back to station', they just told me to report on duty." She said and laughed. The laughter to me was like music. Not loud and yet audible. . . .

"Oh, I am sorry, how was your leave?"

"Just fine, no rain and yet not so hot," she told me.

"Where is your home?" I asked, just to keep her talking.

"Nyeri, and what of yours?" She had stopped her work and was now just standing there, looking at me with deeply appraising eyes. I felt shy—under her stare.

"Nyeri, as well. Where particularly is yours?"

"Mathira, at a place called Kiawarigi. Do you know it?"

"Yes, I've heard of the place but I have never been there!"

"Where is your home, in Nyeri?"

"Kaheti, Kaheti Village, where we have one of the oldest Roman Catholic churches in Kenya," I boasted. "Have you ever heard of the place?" She had started on her work again. As she was bending to pick the clothes and put them on the line, I noticed them . . . I mean her thighs. A smooth pair of promising softness, stretching further above the knees and disappearing into her dress. I was getting transfixed. Her breasts were straining against her dress as she reached for the line and then relaxing as she bent. I was having wild calculations and imaginations. That dress should be removed to at least allow me to see what was beneath it!

"I've in fact been to the place once," she told me. "I had gone to watch the Nativity play that was being acted there every Christmas. Do they still act it?" She had finished putting the clothes on the line and I was afraid that she would go but she reassured me by just standing there, once again poring over me with her eyes.

I did not know what answer to give because I used to attend those plays a hell of a long time ago. Come to think of it, the last time I had attended any church service was long long ago. *

"I should think they still act them, it's hard to break such an old tradition," I said.

"I see, by the way, when did you come here? You were not here when I went on leave," she had picked her clothes basin. Gosh! She wanted to go. I wished I could keep her longer. A few fellow cops had passed us as we chatted and I had noticed that not one single cop passed us without addressing a salutation to Charity. They were also very careful to particularise the addressee of the salaams—Charity. I had also noticed some dire longing in the eyes of most of them, which was turned to open hostility when the eyes were turned on me by the by-passers. Most of them were clearly envious.

"I've been here for about one and a half months now." I answered desperately.

"So, you have not been polluted by the women of this place?" What was that she said?

"What was that again?" At that, she laughed loudly. She twisted her body this way and that way and I was just about to go and grab her.

"I am telling you that we have some women here who, if you do not watch your steps, will make you completely forget your home. You .know you are very far from home and if you get over-involved in them, you will forget your home and you might even be spending your leave days here chasing them like there are no girls at your home. I know of quite a few people who have been thus victimised." She was serious and her face darkened, I guess at the memory.

"Well, I have not yet met them and anyway, I am quite sure that no woman can make me forget Mum and Dad even if she tries to bewitch me." I answered firmly, although I had met one already and was not very sure about forgetting home and all that.

"And where were you going just now when you stopped here?" She asked and laughed again. The way she was looking at me was not explicable.

"Not to look for them, of course," I defended myself.

"Okay, if you were not going to look for them today, what of tomorrow?"

"Even tomorrow and the day after that and . . ." she did not let me finish.

"And what will you be doing when you want . . .?" She did not finish. She ran off into her house and I was left standing there with my roused desires, my mouth very dry and my knees full of jelly. I just stood there. Over a minute passed and that is when I realised that I was standing in someone's door-way. So I moved. Not towards the town but towards my house. I went on to my bed and lay on my tummy. I pictured Charity and felt that I had to have her or no woman at all. I got out of bed, put on the light and went to the kitchen. Then I felt that I was not hungry at all and so I went to the table-room. My mind was completely blank when a knock on the door froze me. I thought it was Charity knocking and had wild hallucinations.

10

"Come in," I said in a voice, scarcely above a whisper. The door knob twisted and the door opened slowly and Nekesa came in. She was smilling, but I was scowling.

"Hey—how are you, man—you've been lost!" She was coming towards me and smiling all over but I did not even want to see her.

"I've been just around," I answered her tersely. I didn't even offer her a seat. What if Charity came in just then and found the woman in my house? What would I say the bag of flesh was doing here?

"What's wrong, Fred. You look sick?" She came towards me and wanted to hold me but I backed two paces from her.

"Don't touch me!" I found myself saying. She was startled. She also moved a pace or two backwards and then stopped. Then there was another knock on the door. This time, I went deaf and blind for at least two seconds.

"Come in," I croaked.

The door was flung open and Charity came in. She stopped abruptly on seeing us, whirled around and went out again. I just heard her voice as she said something like . . . "Sorry, I did not know you had company . . !" and she was gone. I heard her retreating steps and cursed the woman standing there with her big derriere and her everything! Then I flopped on the chair and sighed.

The woman must have realised that she was not welcome and she hastily bade me good night. I could not find a voice to reciprocate. I just placed my head in both hands and wished that Charity had not come into my house when that woman was still there. Maybe she would not want me any more. What a mess!

Then, I went to the kitchen, so angry with myself that I was unable to cook. So, I went to the canteen.

At the door, I met with the lines' sergeant who demanded a beer from me telling me that he was the one who had saved me from possible disciplinary charges for failing to attend duty. He told me that he had talked to the O.C.S. and explained everything. I did not ask him what everything meant. I bought him two beers, bought myself a loaf of bread and a pint of milk and went back to my house. I felt that if I stayed in the canteen, I would drink myself silly or unconscious.

Back in my house, I ate half of the loaf of bread and drunk the milk and then flopped on the bed. I slept very fitfully. The whole night was full of torments. I did not wholly blame myself on what had happened but I really had nothing tangible to commend to myself. I noticed that, despite having met another woman in my house, she had developed some kind of sisterly friendliness towards me.

'She would invite me for supper for which, at first, I gave lame excuses. But, eventually, I found that I could go to her house, have supper, chat a bit and then leave. I was afraid of mentioning the real thing; for I did not want to try and fail, because that would force me to avoid her, yet I could not. Besides, she also never tried to encourage me. We would talk about beds, but never about sleeping in the beds. We would mention love—at a distance— but never about making love. We would discuss anything, save those which would lead us to bed, together.

When I tried to steer the subject to the you-know-what, she tactfully but quickly diverted it to safer grounds. She could look at me straight in the face, especially when trying to explain a point. She would flatter and wring her hands when she missed a straight word and I, the animal thing in me having been roused, would look at her hypnotically and wish a thousand things.

She did not sit carelessly for once and her skirt was strictly and always below knee-level and even when she thought that a skirt was too short, she rallied the assistance of a lesso and thus her knees were always out of sight.

I was getting so much used to her. My friends said behind our backs that we were lovers. They even mentioned that I spent most of the evenings at her place instead of at my house. I had literally brushed aside Njagi's invitations to got to town and I was going to town only when expressly necessary. Njagi once told me that I was behaving like a novice when I confessed to him that all those evenings spent at Charity's place had not yielded a lay. I let him have his opinion, anyway. I had nothing to lose.

Sometimes, when we were chatting the hours away, she would steer lie on the bed and when sleep crept in, I would dream the cursed dream. Then I would wake up in the morning and swear that the next time I went to Charity's place, I would ask her for a lay—come what may! But I would go there and the same thing would happen. I would find no words for it.

Sometimes, when we were chatting the hours away, she would steer from safe grounds and then when she realized it, she would feel embarrassed drop her eyes and avoid looking at me. At such times, I would feel a leaden weight above my stomach and a lump in my throat.

She told me all about her life history and I told her about mine but you can bet I did not mention my butcher-man days. I had realized that she was very sympathetically sensitive to poverty, she herself having come from a poor family. I lied to her that I had been chased from school for lack of school fees and that I had resorted to the only job that I qualified for: being a cop. She shook her head and I could read something in her eyes—something of motherly protection towards me. Yes, it was there. Something beyond pity and yet, above friendliness. Something I could not explain.

My birthday was approaching and I had even mentioned it to her. She had told me to warn her beforehand so that she could know what to cook for the 'big occasion'. We had even discussed what would be the best meal for that day and we had concluded that *Chapati* and *Mutton* which were our current favourite dish, would do. I had also put it in my diary that on that day, the birthday, I would break the ice and bluntly ask her to kiss me. I was sure she would not refuse. But, what if she refused? Then— hell!!

Three days before my birthday, I went to Charity's house, just like

I had done so many times before. She seemed happier and ready to laugh at the flimsiest excuse. While eating, she did not sit opposite me like she used to do but came and sat on my left side and we were actually touching. After the meal, she took the dishes to the kitchen and when she came back to the table, she sat just where she had been; next to me and this time, I even thought that she was closer. I could feel her woman warmth seeping through her clothes and radiating into me and I started getting uncomfortable. She was sighing repeatedly and then she started singing. Her song went thus

> Oh, I wish I had someone to love me,
> Someone to call me his own,
> Oh, I wish I had someone to love me,
> 'Cause 'am tired of living alone.

She laughed after that. I looked at her and then, like a shipwrecked survivor who sees land after several days of floating on water, it dawned on me. So she had been waiting for me to make a move! And I had been the goat that I am!!

"Charity, do you know exactly what you are saying now?"

"Yes, I do; I wish I had someone to love me." and she looked quite serious about it.

"Okay, then, I love you," I just said it. I don't even know where the words came from.

"Are you serious?" she asked. If there had been a Bible around, I would have sworn by it!

"Honest, I am very serious. I have been afraid of saying it for all this time but you have been in my heart from the day that I met you at the canteen door." I stammered on.

"What have you been afraid of?".

"Well, I really cannot say but I feared that you would not accept my love. I mean—I felt that maybe I was not suitable enough for you and that you would let me awfully down if I made a move". That was the absolute truth. She looked at me silently for a full minute and then her eyes filled with tears.

84

11

And so, it happened. That night, I laid Charity—even before the scheduled birthday. I laid her and found her to be the warmest—I mean the hottest woman I had ever laid. That woman had it—I mean what it takes to make a woman. I almost ate her with my teeth. I would have liked to swallow her and keep her in me so that no other person would be accesssible to her. She was above all and she filled my heart to the brim.

From that day, I laid Charity on every single day of the month except of course the three to four days per month when her dam broke up. But even on those days, we shared the same bed. She grew very possessive and did not want me to say hello to, let alone touch, another woman.

She taught me some very quaint styles of the bed-game. We could do it sitting, lying, standing, sleeping, rolling, crawling and kneeling. We could do it anywhere: in her house or mine, in the bathroom, in the bush in the evenings, at the golf-course after dark and we even did it once in the office. She taught me how to kiss—in the mouth and emphasised that kissing is even more loving than making actual sexual love. She was telling me that kissing is what feeds the love affair and that we were doing it like Whites. It's aping of course but it seems that we Blacks have got to ape the Whites from time to time—just to feel civilized. Very good thing—this civilization. Anyway, White civilization is not bad at all. They brought it here to us, togehter with all the atrocious civilized crimes that accompanied their entry and thus the dire need for a Police Force. That way I got a job; not forgetting that they also brought education, and trained the teachers who taught me and even the headmaster who expelled me from school. They were very good teachers—these Whites. Blinking colonialists!!

Me and Charity were actually living as man and wife. I was even thinking of marriage. When I come to think of the part I played, the part that bred the bacteria which started the decay on our cord of love, I sometimes wish there would be a mule around, to give me a real heavy kick right on my balls! I did not play my part right. I let her do all the loving. She even referred to me as her husband. Even when chatting with her friends, she would look at her wrist-watch, gasp and hurry away, leaving her friends laughing at her last word: "Let me hurry home and cook for my husband!"

I had literally moved from my house to hers where I took all meals. Charity just fed me without even asking for subsistence and I felt so much of a sucker. I had repeatedly tried to offer her money to buy the foods but she had bluntly refused my offers and even one day, she almost lost her temper when I went to her house with a pound of meat and told her to fry it so that we could have a meal. She just looked at me, looked at the still wrapped piece of meat and told me: "Fred, I can afford all the meat that I need in this house".

"But, I . . . I just want to sort of help you in . . ." I tired to explain. She would not let me finish.

"Did I tell you that I need help? Did I . . .?" She was getting worked up and I solemnly apologised.

Even when the meat was finally cooked and we were eating, she still retained that hurt feeling in her tone of speech and her eyes and I decided that I would not be buying any foods unless and until she asked me.

That year's Christmas found us at the height of our love and I thought that it would be the most appropriate time to give Charity at least something for all her love.

I went secretly to Kisumu and bought her a dress, a pair of shoes and four silk pants. To crown it all, I bought a bottle of Cinzano which I had noticed she cherished. I came back to Kakamega and 'hid' them in my house until the eve of Christmas day and I told her that we should have a meal at my house.

She prepared a stuffed chicken and the rice was cooked in coconut gratings. A very delicious meal. We sat as usual at the table and she was spoon-feeding me and I was enjoying every minute of the evening.

After the meal, I went to the bedroom and came out with the gift parcel, still wrapped and presented it to her.

"What is it?" She asked quizzically.

"Open and see!" I was smiling shyly. She undid the wrapping and the dress was exposed. She looked at it, dismayed and then fingered it reverently. Then, she removed the shoes from their box and placed them beside the dress, on the table. She tore the paper wrapping on the pants and they cascaded on the table. She shrieked in delight.

"Are they for me?"

"Yes . . . yes . . ." I had to clear my throat.

"You bought them for me?"

"Yes, it's your Christmans present."

"The dress . . .?"

"So that you may remember me everytime you put it on . . . "

"The shoes . . . ?" She was examining each item as one in a day-dream. I could not believe that Charity could be so fascinated by such small presents. She had several dresses and pairs of shoes, not forgetting the tens of pairs of pants that littered her every box.

"For dancing . . . I don't know whether I chose the right size of heels . . ."

"And these . . ." pointing at the pants. They were in four colours. White for Sunday service; blue for the day following a heavy loving night, green for a sign of readines for a love making bout and red for 'hell days' as she called them. I had chosen each with a purpose. "These are . . .?"

"To protect you from cold." I chuckled.

"Why did you buy all these . . .?" I could see that she was trembling. Her eyes were getting that far-away look that preceded our love-making. Her 'in-the-mood' look. She looked at me and a smile flashed across her lips. She shrieked again and was on me before I could duck. She threw her arms around my neck and smothered me in kisses muttering, "I love you, my wonder cop. I love you . . ." not giving me time to tell her the same and our embrace tripped us onto the sofa set.

Then, we got up and I ceremoniously produced the bottle of Cinzano from the cup-board and she was so thrilled by the very sight of it that she spilled some of it as she was trying to break the seal, in a hurry.

"I believe it now," she said matter-of-fact. "I believe it now when you tell me that you love me," she stopped. She looked at me for over a minute and then asked: "Fred, will you take me, as your wife?" My mouth popped open but I quickly hid my surprise in a smile. I cleared my throat but, before I could answer, she went on, "I know that's the most important decision to make in one's life and so, I'll not demand an answer just now. Please think about it but don't forget that that was an offer . . . " she laughed and kissed me again. I did not know what to say. Our love had really reached a deeper dimension.

<h1 style="text-align:center">12</h1>

Then, one day, things changed. Changed for the worse for me. I did one thing that Charity, with all her love and devotion, could not stand. She was so possessive.

That day, I went to town. Charity did not accompany me as she used to do every day. I was just going to pick my suit from a laundry and rush back home and I left Charity so that she could do her cooking meanwhile. I had told her that it would take me a maximum of fiteen minutes to walk to and from town.

As I was walking down Kenyatta Avenue, I saw Mary Wambui. She was my village-mate at home—in Nyeri, and the very sight of her made me remember home. Home which was out of sight and out of mind. Fate just arranged that meeting and I can swear that I had not known that she'd be there when I walked down Kenyatta Avenue. What a woman she had grown into!

When I was in school, Mary was a tiny girl. Not yet fit for human consumption. Now, there she was. As big and as mature and as fit as I like them. She was almost as good looking as Charity but then, I did not know whether her downstairs was cold or hot. At first, I thought it was a case of mistaken identity but then she turned her face towards me and although she was at a distance, I confirmed that she was the same Mary I knew. She was gazing at some clothes at a shop window. A thousand querries swirled for priority in my head. What had she come to do at Kakamega? Of course not shopping. Then she moved.

She moved and entered into Flamingo Hotel. A middle class hotel, where you do not go except at the end of the month. The way she swayed her derriere as she entered the hotel, was a promise of a warm comfy night. She had not seen me and I felt like a hunter when he closes in on his game, unseen.

I wanted to know exactly what she had come to do at Kakamega. I hesitated some minutes outside the hotel and then I entered. The hotel had its share of sparse diners and I quickly spotted her at a table—eating and drinking. She was having some milk and some slices of unbuttered bread. A lousy meal especially for supper. This time I moved quite close to her and made sure that she saw me. And see me—she did. She stopped eating and gazed at me. I was also gazing at her. Then she smiled. Recognition dawned on her. She smiled broadly and opened her eyes wider. Gosh! What a beauty! Before I even said hello, I had made a mental note that, come what may, I would lay this woman.

"Hello, Mary, or am I wrong?" I asked knowing too well that I was as right as rain.

"You are not wrong, Fredrick—is it really you? It's a happy surprise—God! How lucky I am—there will be no problems for me tonight . . . so you live here, Fredrick? I had almost even forgotten your face . . . you must have noticed that I looked at you too long." She said all those words so fast and happily that I believed that she was happy. But there was something that she had said. About night problem or was it a problem for the night? I had not fully grasped that one.

"Night problems, Mary—what did you say? Do you have any problems here ?" I asked her. I was smiling like the cat that swallowed the bird.

"Well, let me tell you, I came here looking for my brother. He is supposed to be teaching at Kakamega High School but when I arrived, I was told that he had left this morning for Nyeri. As it was, he was to give me my fare back home plus of course a place to sleep. I carried only a one-way ticket fare. Now I was wondering what to do with myself but thank God, here you are." She finished.

I was still standing over her. Laundry forgotten. I sat myself opposite her and inquired about home. Mary told me only about the persistent drought and the way animals were dying, et cetera. I asked her whether Mum and Dad were still existing and she told me that they were very much alive despite the inflation pressures that were making them age faster than normal. I did some quick thinking and realized that I had neither written to them, nor sent any financial help for a period of over six months. Six months! What a prodigal son! Then I quickly changed that flow of thoughts by inquiring about the meal on the table.

"Is that your supper?" I asked bluntly.

"Yes, I could not afford . . ." she was wringing her hands.

"Sorry, I know how it is," I surmised, pretending to know what I really did not know. I called a waiter who had been all along hovering around us and ordered chicken and rice for me and for her. As it was being brought to our table, I remembered that, just then, Charity must have been busy 'cooking for her husband—me!" But I quickly covered the line of thoughts with more questions.

"So, your brother has been teaching here all this time—and I did not even know?" She explained that her brother had been in Kakamega for over three months but since he was not a boozer or a 'chaser', having been converted into the religion of Christendom, he hardly left his house after classes. That explained why I had not met him.

We were eating then. She had left the bread and milk like she was not the one who had ordered for them. It was not her wish that she should have such a lousy meal for supper but then, she could not afford anything else. Reminded me of my school days. Damned days they were.

We finished our meals and I paid for everything—milk and bread included. This, I felt, was just the beginning of a long evening. I wanted to show Mary around town.

Just as we were leaving Flamingo Hotel, I met Gachanja, a fellow cop. Gachanja started talking trash and eyeing Mary greedily, trying to tell me a few unimportant things, just to make sure that he took all the details of Mary.

Gachanja was a reputed gossip and I knew that that unfortunate meeting with him might be the subject of discussion the following day. I only prayed that word would not reach Charity. Anyway, Charity had an open dislike for Gachanja and so, or so I thought, I was safe.

I was feeling kind of thirsty for a beer and so we went to Blue Mountain Hotel. It's a posh place where only big shots, either in Government employment or business haunt. There was no rule that we, small timers, should not go there but then we just felt out of place. What with your own bosses occupying fifty per cent of the seats! All the same, I led Mary there and we occupied the table farthest from the door and nearest to the toilets. That way, I could have clear covering of all the tables and would not need to pass among the bosses when going to piss.

I called for a Tusker Export from the waiter who gave me a none-too-welcoming stare but whose eyes softened when he looked at Mary. I asked her what she would have and she said Fanta. I made the order as well.

On the third Export and her fourth Fanta, I ordered Sherry for her. High Life Sherry. A very arousing drink. She at first protested saying that she was still in school and as such, she should not touch anything alcoholic but I managed to convince her that Sherry was a very gentle drink, a particularly mild type of wine that would do her no harm and that kind of won her over. She agreed to take it but insisted that she would only take one small bottle. I argued that she should take one for herself and one for me and we settled on two none-too-small bottles of Sherry.

We were drinking and chatting and she was getting very excited. One of my bosses was seated on a high stool at the counter and was throwing venomous glances at me and Mary but I was trying to show no fear. My courage, being fed with the spirit of alcohol was at that time something to reckon with. If we had gone on for long, I would even have confronted the boss by asking him for a cigarette light. I was feeling as bold as that. Besides, I was not going to show Mary

that there were some people who coughed and I answered 'Yesir!!!'
Oh no!

She was laughing very loud and getting over-excited and even
careless with her dress and drink which she repeatedly spilled on the
table. The waiter, every time he came to wipe the table, gave me a
knowing look which seemed to say; "Get this bloody bitch from
here!" She had taken four Sherries—two too many—and I then had
eight Exports but when I have my eyes on a dame, I don't get drunk.
You might as well give me a hose-pipe direct from the breweries and I
will still be fit for the night service! That's me.

She was telling me some childish stories about school life and I was
telling her some bits about my life as a cop. I did not tell her that I was
a constable though. No! No! I could not let her know that I was in the
lowest rank in the Police Force. I told her that I was a sergeant. I
wanted to tell her that I was an inspector—like most cops pretend to
be—but then I did not see the reason why I should decorate myself so
much. She believed me like I was telling her that she was a girl.

It was high time that we went home. I called the waiter and paid the
bills. I took her small hand-bag and we started walking out. As we
neared the door, she reeled and would have fallen but she held on to
the nearest table, shaking it so violently and almost spilling all the
beer on the table. The occupants at the table gave her a cold eye. My
boss had left but that did not mean that the fellows would not go and
tell him of the mishap. The girl was letting me down. I had to get her
out of the place, and quickly too. I took her hand to steady her.

13

I was also wondering where I was going to peform the 'ante-
mortem'. I was counting the number of friends in the Police Lines
who would allow me to use their visitors' beds for a few tumbles and
then leave the woman there and I found that if that was to happen,
the house had to be very far from Charity's. I thought of Njagi, my
friend but then I realised that, although Njagi's was last in the row of

houses, I had to pass at Charity's before getting to his. I did not want to think of what would happen were Charity to see me with Mary.

She almost fell over the stair-case as we were climbing down and when we reached the foot of the stairs, she started puking. I pulled her to a corner, away from the glaring lights and she puked. She puked everything, including the chicken and rice. Blast!

She got more drunk than she was before. I realized that that must have been the first time she had tasted Sherry. I dragged her out of the corner and we started our walk home once again. She was staggering and reeling and rocking and just as we entered the Police lines— Wao! . . . Tuikong! Mr. Robert Tuikong arap Songok—the Provincial Police boss was there. Just in front of us. He was coming towards us. No mistake. I had to stand at attention. What a situation! He was looking at me the way you would look at a nameless creature you encounter in your deep-sea travels.

"Good evening. Sir," I stammered. I was not standing at attention because Mary was pulling me. She did not know why I was standing there. She had no idea what 'Force Discipline' was. She was muttering things that only the devil could interpret. I was getting one hell of an embarrassment. My boss was just standing there, clenching and unclenching his huge fists. I bet he wanted only the least excuse to land one punch on me before throwing both of us in cells.

"Who is she?" He asked. He did not bother even to answer my respectful greeting. All he wanted to know was who Mary was. I had to tell a lie. I simply could not tell him the truth.

"She . . . er . . . ah . . . is my . . . relative from home, Sir." I said. He did not seem convinced. He was looking at Mary with Naja Naja eyes. Mary had incidentally started hiccupping. Gosh! I didn't want her to start puking again. At least not in the cop's yard! The boss looked long at both of us and then he spat. He spat right there in front of us and then he started walking away. When he was about ten yards from us, he turned:

"I want you in my office tomorrow morning at eight, do you hear me?" I noticed that he had a lot of difficulty restraining himself from actually shouting.

"Yes, Sir, I will be there, Sir," I said. Geese and Ducks!! All the beer I had drunk evaporated immediately. I felt sober. As sober as a saint. You would need to be a cop to know the difference between a Police Constable and a Police Officer, holding the powers over a full Province. An Assistant Commissioner of Police!! At least I knew that the following day I was in for some marching. Some unusual marching whereby you do not put your belt and cap on. Some marching which leaves you in bad terms with the sergeant. Some marching that reduces your pay at the end of the month. That is what I was in for the following day. All because of a school girl. You should have seen her. She had started hiccupping again. She was making some noises only heard in a pig-sty. I hated her. I did not want to lose my job only because of a lay. I was getting steadily and quickly annoyed.

"Let's go home and please try to pull yourself together. You are making a mess of yourself," I said bitterly. She muttered some things that I did not understand. I had to half-carry, half-drag her for the rest of the journey. One thing was certain; I was going to lay her and then, the following day, I would go to the boss's office and explain. Very stupid explanation I would have. Ninety-nine per cent lies and one per cent fabrication.

At last we came to my house. I sat her on the ground against the wall as I fumbled for the keys in my pocket. I opened the door and led her in. As we entered and I snapped on the light, I remembered one thing—rather one person—Charity! All this time, as I boozed and caroused, I had completely forgotten about her. What explanation would I give her if by a fluke of a chance, she came and found Mary at my house? Would she listen to anyone telling her anything? Well, that was the question.

I left Mary sitting or rather lying on the sofa-set and went to Charity's house. The time was past eleven but I knew that she would not go to bed before seeing me.

I found her seated at the table, embroidering one of her table cloths. I tried to smile but the light seemed too bright for me. I did not want her to suspect anything. I went to her and planted a kiss albeit lightly, on her cheek. A very short kiss and then I sat myself opposite her. I did not want to sit too close to her otherwise she might have sensed that my heart was beating a trifle too fast. All the same, she eyed me suspiciously, conspicuously looked at her wrist-watch and then asked;

"Where have you been? I have been to your house twice this evening but found the door locked." It was a plain demand. Not a request.

"In the town, of course . . . babe?" 'Babe'—the term I used towards her only on occasions. She liked it very much and I was using it this time to please her.

"But, where particularly? Surely not just sitting in a bar drinking. Look at what time it is now . . . you have not had supper . . . you have not even loved a bit and . . ." She did not finish. There drifted a voice from the direction of my house. Someone was calling my name. I knew too well who it was. I started sweating. This school girl was going to ruin my everything.

"Who's that . . . listen . . . who's that calling you?" Charity asked, cocking her ear towards the source of the sound. She was listening very attentively. She was at the same time looking at me with dangerous eyes. Since the day we had declared our love for each other, I had not told her any serious lie. I was going to start the lies and the task seemed quite difficult. I frowned pretending to be unknowing.

"I don't know—who can be calling me at this hour?" and I looked at my wrist-watch to avoid Charity's eyes. I pretended to be more puzzled than I really was. She looked at me steadily and then asked me whether I was sure I did not know who was calling. Thanks to the small amount of beer that had not evaporated when I had encountered my boss, I was able to look at her straight in the face and re-affirm that I, Fred, did not know who was calling. The caller had kept quiet.

"Let's go and check," she suggested.

"No, it's not necessary. Whoever is calling will go on calling and when he gets tired, he can go and sleep," I opposed. I used 'he' and not 'she' so that she might not suspect that I knew who was calling.

"That's not a 'he', Fred, it's a 'she'," she corrected me.

"Whoever is calling will go away after they get tired!" I was talking too loud. I wanted to pretend to be very angry. I knew she dreaded my anger because it would lead to a few days of no kisses. She was scared alright.

"Are you angry with me, Fred?" She asked timidly.

"No, am not, but if you start getting worried about trivial things like that, I will surely have the right to be angry. What do you care? If someone wants me when I am with you, she is in for a blank draw. Suppose it was you . . . you are at my house and then someone starts calling you from outside . . . would you go? . . . And at the same time, would you suggest that we go and check who that person is . . . ?"

"Of course not, darling . . . please don't be angry with me," she pleaded and came to me, held me around the neck and kissed me long and sweet.

There was something about Charity; every time she held me and kissed me, I did not think of anything else except how I would make love to her. Honest. She had made me a one-woman-man. Right then, I wished we were in bed. She nibbled my ear and begged me to forgive her. I told her that I had forgiven her, from deep inside my. heart—that was.

I ate another supper at Charity's house. I could not bring myself to tell her that I had had another supper elsewhere. As I was eating, she was sitting on my lap. She was spoon-feeding me. That was her favourite hobby. That way, I could use both my hands to explore her anatomy. I never seemed to get tired of that. Each time, there seemed to be a new contour here and there. I loved her.

I was eating mechanically—that is chewing and swallowing, but my mind was somewhere else. I did not have the whole of my mind on Charity. I did not know what Mary did after calling my name four times. She might have gone outside the house and missed it on coming back. She could have been moving around the houses looking for me. She might even have knocked on Charity's door in her search. At that thought, I threw a glance at the door and noticed that it was not latched. I was so deeply involved in that thought that I kept chewing a particular mouth-ful too long. She started me back to the old track:

"What are you thinking of, darling. Please do tell me and don't be angry with me." She pleaded.

"I am thinking of what position I will sleep in tonight—whether on your right or on your left. I have been sleeping on your right for too long. Would you like to sleep on my right tonight, babe?" I asked her.

"Of course, dear—any side you choose—and tonight . . . we are going to try that new position we read about in that book—I think it will be exciting." She laughed happily.

That was another of her special treats. If we read a book, and we came across a new bed-style, we would, as a must, try it and most of the times, it was very exciting. I looked at Charity and wondered why I was not contented with her alone. I had by then known all her likes and dislikes and if only I had brought Mary early enough, and introduced her to Charity, she (Mary) would have been treated so kindly—like a child being nursed by her mother. I knew that she would have suggested that we leave Mary at Charity's house and spend the night at my house. That way, we would have avoided any kind of scandal and everything would have been alright, but no! I have got to complicate things—even at the apex of our love—and with Charity, someone who was ready to sacrifice almost anything for me. She would not allow me to give her money for food or any other household needs. A person who was so generous that I was feeling ashamed of her kindness!!

I finished the supper that Charity had prepared for me. She gave me some orange juice and as I drank it, I felt my tummy distended to its limit. I also felt tired and sleepy. I started yawning.

I had thought of what I would do about Mary and found that I could do nothing. I had to leave her to herself. Maybe I could sneak after Charity had fallen deeply asleep, go and check what she was doing but then I was not even sure of that. Charity used to sleep with one arm around my neck and even the slightest stirring on my part would rouse her. So, I was going to leave things to work themselves out just like the universe unfolds.

"Let's go to bed, darling . . . you know it might take us some time before we can master that new game . . ." She trailed off in laughter. I stood up and just as I was going towards the bed-room door, there came a knock on the outer door. I froze and the cigarette I held in my hand dropped. Charity was mid-stride as she was going to lock the outer door and when she saw the shock on my face, she too froze. The knock was repeated, this time louder.

15

"Who's there?" Charity asked. I was hardly breathing. I picked the cigarette with an unsteady hand.

"Is Fred there?" A man's voice from outside. I recognized it immediately. That was the voice of Njagi—my friend.

"Yes, what is it?" I asked and you could feel the relief coming over me from a mile off.

"Let me see you for only one minute, please. It's something to do with the office," Njagi begged.

I walked outside Charity's house and left her standing at the door as Njagi hurriedly pulled me towards the Canteen. He was so excited about something and the grip he had on my arm was actually turning into a pinching grip. We were hardly out of Charity's earshot when he whispered almost hysterically:

"Brother, there is a very cute dame in your house. I was just passing when I saw that the door to your house was ajar. I thought you were in and so I entered even without knocking—you know I have no manners to portray to you. Then, there she was! She's so good, *bwana*. I startled her awake and she asked me whether I had seen you anywhere. She did not know where you keep the key to your bed-room and she was dozing on the sofa-set. *Bwana,* that dame is real good. Leave Charity for tonight and go and taste her. I bet you will find that she is hotter than Charity. Don't let her sleep alone. *'Matunda ya uhuru', bwana*." He was so worked up and talking so fast I had no time to say anything. Then, he took a break. He was panting. Right then, a solution came to me. If I told her a lie, touching official matters, I was sure Charity would believe me. I hurriedly whispered to Njagi:

"Let's go back to outside Charity's house and you tell me that there is a road-block operation at Shirere. Try to make it that you are trying to convince me to go while I am adamant. Also mention that, the Police Woman at the Provincial Ops. Room had earlier come to call me and that she had returned to the office and said that I was not at my house. I will of course vehemently object and protest against going on duty but you will go ahead and point out to me that, the Duty Officer is waiting for me outside the Police Station, okay?" I was also worked up. I was planning to kill two birds with one stone. If the plan worked, I was not going to need any other explanation as to who was calling me and at the same time, I would go and lay Mary.

So, we walked slowly and stood just outside Charity's house. I knew that she could hear all that we were saying and so I put up the strongest protest against going for that 'road-block'. Njagi played his part so well. I told him, rather reluctantly, that I would be meeting him at the Police Station and stormed into Charity's house, wearing a frown. As I pulled the door to, I clicked my tongue and swore that I would not go for that duty.

"No darling, you must go. You know the O.C.S. does not like you very much on account of our love and so he will be looking for the slightest excuse to put you in trouble. Please, you must go. Kiss me and then go before he gets impatient." That was Charity herself. It was almost as if she wanted me to go and lay Mary. Anyway, the acting part was not over yet. I said:

"Just when I want to have the best night, with the best person in the world—the fools come and pick on me. Are there no other Police Officers who can man a road-block in this damned station?" I pretended to be very bitter.

"Please, darling, just go—I am all yours all the time. There is tomorrow—please."

"You are telling me to go as if you also do not want me, are you expecting someone tonight?" I asked. She looked at me like she had been stabbed through the heart. She opened her mouth but no words came out of it. I pitied her. Then, she started weeping and I gathered her in my arms. I took her to bed, kissed her and apologised. I told her that I was sorry and that I would not leave her house until she had also told me that she had forgiven me.

Seriously speaking, I had over-acted. If you hurt Charity, you would know that there are some people who are more affected by one thing than others. I had done the same some time earlier and had to spend hours soothing and coaxing her before she smiled.

When I went out of her house, I did not go straight to mine. I went to the Police Station and lolled there for about ten minutes before walking on tip-toe back to my house.

Lucky me! Although my name was not in the list of those supposed to man the road-block, surely there was a road-block at Shirere.

When I got into my house, I found that Mary had at last spotted the key to my bedroom, and gone to bed and was snoring her head off in deep drunken sleep. I undressed, got into bed and although she was already asleep, I hoped for a good night.

CHAPTER SEVEN

1

"Next time I see or even hear of anything like that, I assure you that you will go home. This is the last warning that I am giving you. Now, get out of my office and think twice!!" That is my boss—Tuikong! He has warned me against something. He did not tell what was the specific wrong I had done but he just warned me. He told me that I was behaving like a Bushman who did not have any idea what Force Discipline was. He even told me that I had completely forgotten the small amount of discipline that I had had when I passed out of Kiganjo —Kenya Police College. He even called Mary a drunken prostitute and warned me against bringing *'walevi wa chang'aa'* to the Police Lines,

'Walevi wa chang'aa'? And then he told me to think twice! I think he is the one who is supposed to think twice. He called a school girl a drunken prostitute! Blast him and his balding head! I am tired of him and his half-cooked philosophies.

I walked out of his office and spat. The sergeant was there with me and was trying to get from me what had happened last night but he could bet his last grey hair that I would not tell him.

I told him that if the boss had not seen the need to tell him the problem, it is possible that the boss did not want him to know. I went further and explained that being called to the boss's office was not automatically a sign of error on my part. I could as well have been called to receive special instructions on how to handle a particularly difficult case!!!

That is the other problem with us cops. The sergeant is just told to march me to the lion's den but the bastard himself does not know what for. As many of these sergeants are only literate in Kiswahili, when you argue with the boss in English, the sergeant nods his head like an iguana, not knowing the head or tail of the whole issue. He just follows you outside the office pestering you with monotonous questions. *'Ilikuwa nini bwana, mimi naambie nikupeleke kwa mkubwa?''* And if you don't want to tell him, simply advise him to go and ask the boss and that really puts a full stop to his questioning.

This morning, as early as 0600 hours, I made sure that I had taken Mary to the bus stage, where she would board the bus to take her home. Before she left my house, we had a good laugh because she did not know exactly where she was. She just woke up, and because she could not see me in the half-light, she asked me who I was. A very strange question to ask of somebody who had spent almost the whole night making love to you. So I had to tell her who I was and where she was and we had a good laugh at that. She had to wash down four aspirins to cool her head which she complained was having a tom-tom drama right inside. I gave her five pounds for her journey and she thanked me profusely. I was indirectly paying for her screw but I did not tell her so. She had been good—real good and she could even have been much better, had she not been drowsy all along. I had to slap her rump twice to stop her from going to sleep while I was still 'on'. At last I allowed her to sleep and I explored her curves unassisted.

On leaving the boss's office, I went to Charity's house. I found that she was still in bed. I knocked and she opened for me. She had that see-through night-dress of hers. I could see that she had on, green pants but no bra. I could even see her nipple, dark and prominent and I felt some excitement run through me. She looked very lovable and sleepy.

"Well . . . morning, dear . . . are you not going on duty today?" I asked her checking on my wrist-watch and noticing that it was already 0830 hours. On entering her house, I held her and kissed her lips. The lips I should have kissed the previous night. She still retained a faint smell of tooth-paste. She melted in my arms. She started cooing.

"Not in the morning. I will be reporting at 1400 hours," she told me. Anyway, the day was my 'off' day but I had to act some more. To cement last night's lies—so to speak.

"How lucky! And you know what—I am off-duty because I went for that lousy road-block last night!" I managed.

"So, what do we do with the day?" She asked with a lop-sided grin. I grinned back.

"Spend it, of course."

"How?"

"Well . . . we could . . . let me see . . . we could go to the golf-course and see whether the grass has grown . . . " she started laughing. We had earlier gone to the golf-course and had wanted to make love there on the green but the grass had been short and dry and we had abandoned the idea but promised to go there and do it when the grass grew greener.

"Yes, we could do that, but meanwhile, have some breakfast."

She gave me tea and buttered bread. After the tea, she went into the bedroom and called me in. I did and found her already between the sheets.

I undressed and joined her in bed and, you know why I praise Charity so much? Do you know? Last night, I completely exhausted myself with Mary but Charity is able to keep me balanced throughout the game. There is something that she does with her hips that makes me stay 'on' all the time. I love her—my Charity. As I make love to her, I silently beg her heart to forgive me for running away from her.

We did not go to the golf-course. We spent the day making love and eating.

Four days later, it was house cleaning day. Charity used to clean mine and her house. She also cleaned all the sheets, that is at my house and her house. That was one occasion when I was able to pay back at least some of her kindness. She allowed me to buy all the detergents she would need for cleaning.

On this day, I went to town and left her cleaning the sheets and singing as she did so. She was quite happy.

2

On my return, I found that she had cleaned all, sheets and houses and was sitting on a stool outside her house, listlessly glancing at a weekly newspaper. Her countenance showed that she was far from happy and I immediately demanded to be told the cause. She looked at me with those searching eyes of hers and asked me:

"Fred, have you bought any hanky, recently?" I could not remember the last time I had bought a hanky. All the ones I had been using had been bought by Charity herself.

"No. Why?" I asked. I was sure I had not bought myself a hanky anyway. What a tricky question she had asked.

"I see," she sighed and kept mum. Now, what was it? What else had I done involving handkerchiefs? She looked at me and then turned and stared unseeingly at the far horizon.

"Well, I found a hanky under your bed but I don't remember having bought you that colour of hanky of late. It was old and pretty gummed up. I was wondering whether it was yours!" She concluded.

I saw at once where I had gone wrong in answering the question in the negative. Within half a second, the whole thing dawned on me. The hanky she was referring to must be the one which we used to wipe our wet parts when I had that game with Mary. That's it. There is nothing else to it. What a mess!!

"Can I see it? Maybe I would recognise it." I said not because I really wanted to see it but just because I could not simply keep quiet. I was almost trembling.

"I threw it away—it looked awful. I mean like it had been used to wipe—you know—after a game," she blushed and dropped her eyes and I felt ashamed of myself. "It was awful and I thought a lot of bad things—I mean—I could not guess how such a thing came to be under your bed. It's a long time since we made love at your house and you know that and there is no place that I do not clean every time but ... anyway, let's forget it. What have you brought for me from town?" She resigned. Mishaps never come singly. Just today, when the smallest present would have been needed to please my dear Charity, I completely forgot to buy her anything.

"Let's go back there—I mean the town, I forgot to bring you candy, my sweet." I was feeling so guilty that I wished she would slap me.

We went to town and I bought her all kinds of sweets that she wanted. Then, we went home, and made love. During one break, she told me a funny recount of a dream she had had. She told me that she had a dream in which, she was the best-maid in my wedding and I was getting married to a White woman. We laughed it off but not before I told her that dreams are not things to worry about. I had to quickly change the subject so that she could not ask me for my answer about the connubial proposal she had made to me earlier. We made more love and I secretly swore that I would not lay another woman as long as Charity was my woman. I even decided to hasten the day when I would declare her my wife.

CHAPTER EIGHT

1

"You are idle, negligent, lazy, disobedient and utterly uncouth. Indisciplined and God knows what else! You are not fit to be in the Police Force! I will give you only this last chance and if you don't change your attitude, you will go home. Home I mean! I have nothing to lose. I am your superior and by gum, I am tired of you! Do you hear that? Tired! That's what I am!!"

He is my new boss, the Bungoma Divisional Police Headquarters commander and you should see him. He is heaving and sighing and gnashing his teeth. He is livid. Real hot! That's what he is. He is boiling. Gosh! I am always getting into trouble with my bosses. This one had called me to his office because last night I got myself drunk and walloped a woman. A bar-woman. A damned prostitute. I gave my hard knuckles and she accepted them. Not in a hand-shake but in a showdown.

Last night, I went to this bar they call Cool-In. I was feeling above normal temperature and so I was going to cool my throat with an ice-cold beer. On entering, I found this woman who was seated all alone at a table having a Guiness and soda. Prostitutes are always having Guiness and soda. I guess it's because both drinks combined cost a little more than the other beers and the only thing that the greedy and merciless prostitutes want to see is the empty wallet of a buyer. After that, they can go and prostitute their stinking holes elsewhere. So, I joined this woman at the table where she was, greeted her and ordered my Tusker Export. Before the waiter had left our table, she asked me whether I was so selfish as to have ordered my beer only, seeing that she was at the same table with me and that she was drinking. So, I, as a Good Samaritan, called for her drink. We now sat and discussed the only subject that prostitutes are proficient in; money and drinks.

A prostitute will never mention the weather to you. She knows that

106

her hole is well covered and that no rain can wet it or sun dry it. So I
sat with this one and we discussed money and drinks. She was
swallowing faster than me and was surreptitiously looking at her
watch from time to time and I guessed that maybe she had another
man's pending arrival and as such she was checking on the time to see
whether he had been late. I did not mind that. I was not really after a
woman. All I was doing was being a Good Samaritan. I had some
surplus money from a job and I could drown her in drink if she so
wished. A smuggler had bribed me handsomely that day.

After four beers each, I asked her about her plans for the night.

"What do you suggest?" She was smiling. I don't know why but I
felt that that smile was not sincere.

"A night at my place with you . . . I bought a new bed and it has not
been tested yet." I declared. We both laughed and then she added;
"That's a good idea—you mean I will be the lucky one to formally
'open' the bed?" She raised her eye-brows.

"Yes, I think we might as well borrow some cello-tape which we
will stick onto the bedcover and then you will cut it to declare the bed
'open'." We laughed again and then I called for more drinks. I.told
myself that I had a woman for the night, or had I?

At about 22.30 hours, she told me to excuse her. She was going to
remove her over-coat so that we could go home. She was a bar-maid at
another bar and, as she put it, there were no customers and so she
could afford to slip out of the place without other bar-maids making
too much noise.

She left a half-full bottle of Guiness at my table—a sure sign that
she would be coming back. I waited for her for over an hour and then
I decided to go and look for her. I had decided that if I did not see her,
I would just go home. If on the other hand I saw her, I would tell her
to forget our small talk as a stale joke and then I would leave her.

I checked on her in four different bars without fruit and found her
in the fifth. She was with another man and just as I was entering, she
was kissing the man—in the mouth. I went blind with rage and even
ignored the few *salaams* that were thrown at me by the few friends I
met in the bar.

However, I went to her and politely told her that I wanted to talk to her in private, for a minute or two. I did not want to grab her from her new-found love and, besides, I was not really in a mood for a woman. I just wanted to ask her why she had kept me waiting for her all that long when she very well knew that she would not return to the place she had left me. I had learnt that to fight in a bar, and over a prostitute at that, could be very scandalous. It can damage your name permanently.

The woman just looked at me and went on sipping her Guiness and soda. This must have been bought by the man she was kissing. Jeez!! These women can never go hungry as long as there is a man who has an active prick around. I told her to excuse me again. The man she was drinking with pretended not to be seeing me. The woman spoke for the first time:

"Are you talking to me? Do you know me? Go your way and don't bring your drunkenness to me." I have never heard of such language being addressed to me by a woman. I don't really know what I felt but, within a second or two, the woman was on the floor, with her drinks and her friend's drinks. I just yanked her up and she carried the table with her. I lifted her and gave her several slaps on the face. She started to scream but a slap right on her mouth stemmed the screams. Then I gave her a kick at I guess the wrong place—her crotch—and she collapsed and rolled her eyes.

The guys in the bar did not say anything. Even the guy who had been drinking with the woman just looked at me, agape. They all knew me for a cop. There is no better privilege than when mugs recognise you as a cop. You smack a woman—bang!! and the guys there pretend not to have heard or seen anything. They just sit on their goddamned asses sipping their foaming beers. Very respectful— these guys are. They know that you wear the head-dress inscribed '*Utimishi kwa Wote*' and I guess they think that the slaps you give to a woman are part of the '*Utumishi*'. Fuck the blighters!!

I left the woman lying just there on the floor and got the hell out of the place. I went to my house and put off all lights and hopped into bed, hoping for a good night. The fight had released my pent-up feelings and I did not even need a woman then.

However, I did not sleep for long before there was an impatient knock on my door. I went and opened the door only to find the night-duty cop standing there wearing a worried look. I told him that he should take his funereal countenance from my door-way but instead of him going away, he got into the house, told me not to put on the light and whispered agitatedly that there was a woman who had gone to the Report Office and reported that I had beaten her. She had a swollen face, bleeding lips and several other injuries. He further told me that the Divisional Commander was right there at the Station when the woman arrived and that he, the Divisional Commander, was the one who had sent the cop to come and fetch me.

There and then, I laid an egg. If that matter had reached the boss's ears—and eyes too, I knew too well that I was in for some stew. Some perfumed stew served on a rat-poison tin-lid.

I told the cop to go and tell the Divisional Commander that I was not in my house. The cop was a friend of mine and besides, not all cops have read that story of Ananias and the lie he told to Peter before he collapsed and died and as such, a lie, even if being told to the Divisional Commander would have little if any effect on the cop. The cop saluted me mockingly and left.

I went back to bed and closed my eyes. I also plugged my ears. I did not want to see or hear anything.

2

This morning, the boss called me to his office. That is where I have just been and that is where he has just warned me. If he knew my character fully, he would not have warned me. He would have sent me home. Dismissal would have been the word. Trouble is, he does not know me fully as I have been in this Division for only two months. Two short months and I have been called to his office twice and received two warnings. Today was the third day and, as he termed it—the final warning.

I was transferred from Kakamega Division because the bosses could not allegedly stand my behaviour. They accused me of gross misconduct. A very grave accusation especially coming from one's bosses. They again did not specify the particular misdeed that prompted their decision to transfer me but I had an idea—albeit remote. I had snatched a girl from one of them.

I left Kakamega in real disgrace. Charity had long said good bye to me. She too, could not stand my behaviour. I had laid another woman and she had found me out. She had met me right on top of the woman. She did not need any other proof that I was unfaithful and she did not even give me a chance to defend myself or even state my case. She acted as the Judge, Jury, Assessor, Advocate, State Counsel and all other members of the Bar that you can think of.

What happened is, I had gone to town to look for a beer. I had said good bye to Charity that afternoon. She was going home for a long week-end which would start on Thursday and end on the following Monday. I had seen her off ceremoniously and had even kissed her—at the bus stage—in front of all the other commuters—and she had wept a little as the bus took off. Then I had gone towards the town, with the aim of looking for a beer or two before retiring to bed.

As I was passing at the Muncipal Hall, I saw a woman standing by the road-side. She was waving every car and bus and lorry that passed on the road and I thought that she must be either crazy or stranded to do that.

As part of the *'Utumishi kwa Wote'*, I went all the way to her and asked her if she had any problem. She told me that the last bus that was going to Turbon, her destination, had left her and she had nowhere to go and that was why she was trying to stop every vehicle that was moving on the road with the hope of a lift. I wished her luck in the thumbing and added, as a by-the-way, that if she completely missed the lift, she could find me at Teacher's Bar. Just as a by-the-way anyway. She asked me where Teacher's Bar was and, from the position where we were, the Bar was actually visible and I pointed it out to her. I then left her.

I went to the bar and when I was having my second beer, in came the woman. She came straight to the table where I was, with another cop friend and told me that she was tired of waving at vehicles that were not stopping. I welcomed her to sit down and I had an idea that the cop friend I was boozing with had got himself a woman just out of the blue. I called for a beer for her but she told me that she was a teetotaller and so she preferred a Fanta instead. As she was sipping it, I asked her what her plans were, now that she had missed a vehicle. She told me that she was going to try her luck and trace another bar-maid, who had come from her home place and was working somewhere in Kakamega, failing which she would be forced to hire a room to sleep in. She added that the hire would be a handicap to her as she did not have so much money to spare. I was doing all the talking with her and my friend was just sipping his beer and ogling the woman without making any conversational contribution. I decided to test the chastity of the woman.

"Why waste all that money on lodgings and such when there are beds that would 'feel' privileged to be slept in by a person like you?" I was smiling amiably. She blushed, frowned a bit and then smiled.

"Where are those beds?" she asked.

"Just around here. For example, there is one at my house that has not had the smell of a woman for ages," I lied.

"Are you sure?" she asked.

"Yes, of course," I emphasised. All this time, I was waiting for my friend to make a contribution so that I could hand over the responsibility of the woman to him but he just sat there completely oblivious, or so he pretended to be, to the on-going conversation. Then to my utter dismay and surprise, he told us good bye. He just got up from the seat, paid for his five-beers and left. I was so surprised that I did not even ask him what he wanted me to do with the girl; but the girl was thinking different:

"Now that we are going to be together for the night, what is your name?" She just asked out of the blue.

"Fred," I answered. And despite the fact that I really did not want her, nor really intended to take her to my house or anyone else's for the night, I thought that she was too good a girl to let sleep in a lodging—and alone at that.

"Fred, that's a nice name and I am glad to meet you, Fred," she laughed and I scrutinised her then. She was of average beauty and size and to be frank, I thought she was good enough for anyone. I thought of Charity and at that, I could have sent the woman packing and going without hesitation. The woman was far below the class of Charity in all aspects—as I saw it. Then I remembered that Charity was miles and miles from Kakamega and so there was no chance of her knowing of my night exploit over this woman.

After another two drinks, we left the bar and went to my house. Just like that: and when we got into the house, without further preliminaries, we just went to bed.

3

I was working it out and she was encouraging me with fake screams when the door burst open. I must have forgotten to bolt it. Some one was having a torch ablaze and was coming direct to the bedroom. I at first thought it was my friend, Njagi and so I told him to get the hell out of the house and sharpen his manners. He came all the way to the bedroom door, which was ajar, and directed the torch-light towards the bed where I was. Then, he snapped the light on and he was transformed into the last person I expected in my house at that time: Charity!!

My prick just shrunk. I felt hot, then cold. My mouth went dry. I was still there, on top of the woman. I was paralysed. The woman under me was also rigid. She did not know who was who and so she kept quiet. Charity spoke: "I am sorry, Fred, for interrupting your enjoyment. I just came to check whether you would have supper at my house but then, I am sorry." She was looking at us with cobra eyes. She went on: "My bus got broken down at Eldoret and I thought it better to come back and be with you instead of hiring a room there. I am very sorry." She did not go on. She just stood there, squarely at the door.

"What am I living for?" She asked, taking deliberate steps towards us, tears dropping from her eyes and when I saw the tears, I came back to my senses and called her name: "Charity . . ." and I think my voice must have roused her anger even more becaue, without warning, she picked my shoe which was on the floor and banged me so hard on the head.

"Will I be cheated all my life?" She asked as I was trying to get out of bed, a process which I found quite difficult with the sheets having entangled my legs and my sight affected by the bang on the head. I managed to get out of bed and wanted to run out of the house and go to a place where she would not see me. But, I just stood there, naked as a new-born baby, facing my prospective wife.

Charity took a walking stick which I usually kept in my bedroom and started pummelling the woman. The woman screamed for mercy. I had to do something, but what? Charity then threw the stick away and went on the woman with bare hands. She got hold of her hair and dragged her from the bed. The woman thudded on the floor and that's when I thought of the easiest thing to do: I switched off the light. That made Charity leave the woman and she came looking for me. She found me at the door and hammered several blows on my face with her weak fist. The blows had no effect. Then she held me so tight and screamed loudly. There was someone already at the door trying to ask what was going on but I told him to go to hell.

When she released me, she put on the light again and the woman was crouching near the wardrobe. Charity jumped on her and this time, she held both her breasts, naked as they were and started pulling them. When I saw the naked woman, I also became aware of my own nakedness and instead of trying to separate them, I went looking for my pants but they must have been misplaced during the struggle between Charity and the woman. I could not find them anywhere and so I slipped on a pair of trousers. Then, I faced the two women.

"Cut it out, Charity!" I commanded. I had to hold the situation otherwise the woman might even have been killed in my house. My shout startled Charity back into her senses and she obediently released the woman. She came to me and gave me a slab that could have been heard from Kisumu. Then she turned to the woman and roared: "Get out, you dirty bitch!"

The woman forgot all her pains and very easily picked her clothes from the tangle that had been created by the fight. She even threw my pants at me. We were all silent now as the woman picked her pants here, hurriedly slipped them on and walked out. As she was going out, she had to pass near me and I gave her a wide berth. Then Charity bolted the door.

"Well . . .?" She said. "Who was she?" The atmosphere was calm now. I was even breathing like nothing had happened. Then something struck my head. I realised that I had not even known who the woman was. I had even forgotten that name that she had told me. What she was was another matter altogether.

"I do not know," I said, as clouds of distant rain covered me. This was surely the end of me and Charity. Charity and her sweet everything. What was to be done, anyway?

"I am sorry, Fred," she said. "So sorry to have caused your sweet heart to leave you. Please forgive me." And she walked out of the house. I went to the tableroom, and just stood there. Five minutes later, Charity came back.

"I want you to make love to me, now," she told me, sort of an order. I hesitated, not knowing what to say, how to say it, or even what to do. I just gazed at her. Then she held my hand and led me to the bedroom. She undressed, removing all her clothes, making me feel that that was the last scene in the whole act. She was beautiful. She had a body, a really beautiful body. Maybe she was removing her clothes to give me a chance of comparing her beauty with that of the other woman, I thought as she took a step towards me, taking it on herself to remove my clothes. I did not question her course of action. I obeyed her, like an automaton. My naked manhood was just droopy. She held it and at once it became alert. Self-protection. She may even have thought of pulling it off. Something that I did not want to think about.

"Now, come on, Fred," she said, "do it. Do it for the last time. This is the last time, you know. You will not enter my body after this.

114

Please make love to me!"

She was getting crazy, twisting my prick this way and that way. I felt like screaming. I wanted to cry. How could she force me to make love to her? Still, I wanted to apologise. I wanted to do all the things that would show her how repetant I was. I would have done anything—but making love . . . it didn't strike me as a way of apologising. How was I going to start? I would have liked to do it—if only to prove to her that I was real sorry. But my weapon just dropped. It had also agreed with my school of thought. Neither my mind, nor my prick could be forced to apologise the way Charity wanted. I opened my mouth to say something but Charity was at it again: "Please, Fred . . . do me the favour. I will not finish your manhood. I will reserve some for you pick-ups. Just this once dear, and I will be satisfied. I know that I have been very unkind to you all through but, please, accept me this once." There was no doubt about it. She was insane. Stark raving mad!

"Please, Charity, you know very well that you have not been unkind to me. It's all my fault. You have nothing to blame yourself for. I know this accident might leau to my losing you but I can not even have enough words to tell you how sorry I am. I am sorry from right deep inside my heart. I wish there is anything that you would want me to do to prove how sorry I am. Just say it . . .' I found myself saying all this. The words just came out. I was in a real tangle.

"Yes, dear," she said in a low voice, "sure there is. I have told you the only thing I wish for in this world—making love to me. A mere tumble is all I need." And she climbed onto the bed, passing her fingers over this and that part of her body as if to feel whether or not she still had them intact, her lips about to display a smile, but her eyes very hard on me.

I looked down at her as she lay there stretched on the bed. Yes. I was feeling my manhood livening and it seemed then that the only solution would be to make love to her. I was wishing I could make it. Damn! Why had I involved myself with that woman?

She continued studying me, even as my manhood started hardening. She seemed to like it that way. I braced myself for the onslaught, to meet her request. I cleared my throat, wishing there was something I could say but nothing came to my mind. I pulled myself together and started for her, my manhood, the only weapon left, at the ready. But suddenly, she jumped out of the bed. Then, she quickly put on her clothes and by the time I reached the bed and sat on it, she was fully dressed. I shuddered in agony. Life! Then she walked out of my house and slammed the door shut behind her, without saying a single word either to me or herself.

4

As I sat on the bed, I felt relieved and at ease. I ponderd over the whole episode, the effects of the several Exports I had taken earlier in the evening already gone. I felt like laughing. And I did actually laugh until my sides were aching and my eyes were wet. I really do not know why I was laughing but the whole thing seemed so funny.

That night, I slept even without covering myself and in the morning, the laughter lines were still around my eyes.

The following day after I reported off-duty, I went to my house and started working on a plan of how to recover Charity. I knew that I would need hours of coaxing before I would be re-accepted. I planned my peace-plan and was satisfied that it would work.

Then, I shyly went to her and found the door locked from outside. I went back to my house and Njagi, my colleague came. We started talking of the previous day's episode and that's when I learnt that Charity had, in the morning, applied for ten days leave, on compassionate grounds. Ten days! That would be too long but then, Njagi assured me that by the time Charity returned to Kakamega, her anger would have abated and she would probably listen to me.

So, I waited until the ten days elapsed. Those were some of the most trying days in my life.

I had not gone to the kitchen to cook for over eight months and I was not going to start then. I became a *'nyama ya kuchoma'* man. After eating the meat, to avoid going to my house and staring at

Charity's portrait on the wall, I became such a hard boozer that I was most of the time one of the 'gentlemen' who left the bars only when the barmaids started sweeping the places.

Every night, I went to bed—a very cold bed—and would wish Charity were back. At least I could know whether it would be love or hate. She would tell me whether she would accept me or not and I would know how to go about my sex life then. If she completely refused my apology, I would start looking for another woman. If on the other hand she accepted me, I would apologise and 'pinch my ear'.

At last she came. Her arrival raised my spirits a mile high, only to be hurled down with such force that I have never fully recovered since then.

When she arrived, I gave her about twenty minutes and then cautiously went to her house. I knocked on the door and she invited me in. I pushed the door open and when she saw me, she opened her eyes wider and then fixed them on me.

"What do you want?" She demanded.

"To talk to you." I cleared my throat.

"About what . . . what is there to talk about?" She was breathing heavily and her lips, those beautiful lips, were trembling. I suddenly did not know how to start.

"Aren't you inviting me to sit down?" I asked and looked at the wall behind her. I could not bring myself to look at Charity's face.

"What for? I don't think what you have to say will take such a long time that you would need a seat," she said and I noticed that there was pain in that voice. She was all this time looking at me with eyes that expressed something between regret and accusation.

"Anyway, well . . . I wanted to tell you that whatever happened was an accident and because I do not think that I can explain it to you, I will beg you only to be . . . I mean . . . I want you to be the judge of this. I am sorry for what happened and would like you to take it from me that—I still have the same feelings towards you as before." I finished. She had then sat herself on a chair and was looking at her hands which were on her lap. I did not think I had made even the slightest impression on her.

"Fred . . . Fred," she swallowed hard. "I don't want to cry. These last ten days have been too painful for me but now I am alright. I have noticed that love and devotion to a man like you is all rewarded with bitter shame." She was on the verge of tears, but she continued; "You know that was not the first time that you have cheated in our love. There was the other occasion but I pretended that it was nothing, even after a friend of yours who knew all what happened had told me all the details of the woman you had on that day. I refused to believe him. I wish I had believed him then and would have loosened myself from your net before it closed too tight . . ."

Then she broke down. She sobbed once but before I could go to her, she hid her face in her hands and spoke through sobs; "Please go away, Fred, please go . . . I can't stand seeing you here in my house I don't want to say that I am fed up with you; but you know it . . . just go," and she rushed into her bedroom and slammed the door shut.

I stood for about half a minute. I was in two minds. One was to follow her into the bedroom and maybe in the process of comforting her, I would win her back. The other was to leave her house and go because following her into the bedroom was taking a risk. What if she did not want my kind of comforting? What if I went to the room and she chased me out? But, before I decided what to do, she came out of the bedroom. She had wiped off her tears and was having one of the most terrifyingly hostile looks in her eyes.

"I told you to get out of my house. If there is anything which belongs to you here, I give you five minutes to pick it and get out!" She snapped at me.

Something in my head snapped as well. I looked at her and all her beauty was completely lost to me then. I saw her just like any of the hundreds of women that pass on the streets. I did not have any words to tell her but went out of her house and walked towards the canteen.

I was in such an irritable mood that, after six beers, a fellow cop came to me and made a joke about something stupid and before I knew what was happening, I had landed a full-weight punch on his corrupt nose.

The cop, too surprised and stunned to react, just asked me: "What is it, Fred? Why did you just punch me? What is it?" and he was wiping blood from his nose with his handkerchief. Instead of answering him, I pointed my long finger at him and told him to behave.

I stormed out of the canteen and my legs seemed to know just where I was supposed to go. I found myself inside Wananchi Bar. Even during my high-love days with Charity, I had spotted a bar-maid at Wananchi Bar, who was either a top-class hypocrite or a holy prostitute. She did not even once show the money 'mania' that most barmaids have. She had even refused to 'keep-change' once. I was determined to know which category she fell into. A man must always keep a substitute in case of desertion.

I perched on a chair at an unoccupied table, amid hellos from the few friends I found in the bar.

5

The barmaid I was going to 'try-out' was seated all alone at another table and I beckoned her to come over. She walked towards my table with that air of nonchalance that I had noticed in her and said a very soft hello. I grinned and told her to sell me an Export. Before she left, I added that it was my birth-day and that I could buy her a drink if she had the time to sip one. She smiled and I thought that she lifted one eye-lid higher than the other one in a wink. To me, the game was set.

She came back with two drinks; my Export and an opened bottle of Coke. I felt disappointed. Me, when I want a woman, I like her to drink something that will weaken her defenses and make the wooing game easier for me. When a woman takes a soda, you can be sure that the negotiations will not be as easy as A.B.C. and I protested at this immediately.

"Surely, you can have a beer. I can afford even two . . . after all I told you that today is my birth-day?" I was smiling invitingly and waving my hands actor-like to stress the dire necessity of a beer for her. She looked at me, looked at the door of the bar and sat on the chair next to mine.

"Where is your wife, today?" she just blurted out. I felt my face swell in anger but I quickly composed myself. I even managed a very insincere smile. The changes that had occurred on my face were not lost on her and I noticed that the mischievous smile that was starting to form on her lips had died off.

"She died or rather, our marriage died . . . ten days ago," I replied casually.

"Oh, I see," she swallowed a sip of the Coke. She was loooking at me intently.

"What about that beer I offered you?" I asked as a peace offering.

"I don't start drinking beer before eight in the night and now," she consulted her wrist-watch, "it's only 6:30," she giggled. Then she sighed, and looked at the door again before adding; "Anyway, I can drink it now. After all, it's your birth-day," she giggled again, picked my empty bottle and headed for the counter. By just closing my eyes, I could almost see her removing her pants for me.

When she came back to the table, I licked my lips and asked for her name. She was so taken aback that she spilled some of the Guiness which she was pouring into her glass.

"What?" she demanded, "you want to tell me that you . . . of all people . . . do not know my name?"

"I would not have asked you if I knew, would I?" I tried to sound so much unknowing. Did she think that she was the Mayor of the town that we all should know her name?

"And how did I come to know yours, you are Fredrick, aren't you?" She was smiling so triumphantly.

"Your knowing my name does not necessarily mean that I must know yours, does it?" My voice had an edge. "Mine starts with a 'C', can you guess it?" I was very soon going to lose my temper.

"Carol!" I almost shouted at her. I did not want to imagine that Charity also started with a 'C' and I would not have liked her name to turn out to be Charity. If Carol was wrong, then I was going to guess 'Cow'. The way she slowly shook her head told me that I had failed.

120

"Wrong, anyway, it's Christine, Christine Nafula from Ndivisi in Bungoma," she sounded very proud of her place of origin. Pride which reminded me that I also came from a place which I had almost forgotten and adopted Kakamega as my birth place. Just like someone had told me during my very first days at Kakamega. Unfortunately, that same person was the main cause of my forgetfulness. I did not want my thoughts to follow that line.

"That must be very far from here," I suggested.

"No, it's only . . . anyway, I don't know how many miles but, we pay six shillings to Bungoma and another three shillings to Ndivisi by matatu—it isn't very far."

We chatted more and more and as more and more beer cascaded down my angry throat, so did my feeling of utter loss disappear.

She mentioned Charity and I was surprised to find that, I could discuss her without flinching. Christine at one time told me that she felt like a thief to have me all to herself but I reassured her that, even in the law of 'Offences against property', a boy-friend, and a jilted one at that, was not capable of being stolen.

At 10.30 p.m., half an hour before closing time, she winked at me as she moved through the rear door. I hurriedly swallowed the dregs in my glass, stood up and checked my equilibrium, which I found to be grossly impaired, and casually sauntered through the front door. I found her standing against an electric pole—as if hiding from a casual glance from anyone entering or leaving the bar. I held her hand to steady myself and together, we started for home.

The distance from the bar to my house was not very long but it was burdensome due to the excess drink which I had taken. She had to half-support me as we jumped over the road-gutters.

When we entered the Police compound, I wished Charity were able to see us together!

Then, on close scrutiny, I noticed that Nafula had protruding upper teeth. Something that reminded me of a laughing horse—if the beast ever laughs. She also had a walking gait that resembled the canter of a horse. For no apparent reason, I thought she also smelt like a horse and started having misgivings about her suitability as Charity's substitute.

However, I had made the decision of taking her home, and I had to take her there, horsy or not.

6

We reached my house without encountering Charity and I opened the door, welcoming my new 'find' home. There was nothing that we were going to do at the table-room and our main job was in the bed-room. We went into the bed-room, stripped and united.

She was bottomlessly hollow and after only one round, I decided that we rest our weary bodies despite her appeals for ". . . . some more . . . I have not had enough . . . you can't bring me all this way for only one . . ." I dozed off leaving her very wide awake.

The following morning. I offered her a pound for her services but she refused. She just looked at me, pretending to be insulted then pointed out to me that she was employed. She added that she was not the type that sold love. Love? All I could tell her was, "Thank you, Madam."

I met Charity regularly but, because she had refused to answer my greetings the first day we met, we passed one another just like total strangers. Njagi mourned the death of our love for almost a month before he realised that, me, the bereaved, was not mourning with him.

One evening when I arrived at my house, with an Amazon at my side, I found a small carton outside my door. I did not call for the bomb-disposal unit but took the risk and conveyed the carton inside the house. On opening it, I found that Charity had returned all my photographs, letters and all other small gifts that I had given her; including a cheap ring that I had placed on her finger, as a sign of 'ownership'. Without stopping to think, I took the carton outside my house, poured kerosene on the contents and set them afire, just like they burn bhangi outside the law courts.

It was only after I had a hand-ful of ashes left that I realized that, all that I had burnt was actually my own and that there was no loss to Charity.

All the relationships that I had with women were temporary to me and I had no intention of getting married to any of them. There was plenty of time to romp about before I got myself tied to the nagging life of a husband—I told myself.

I was also not planning to breed kids all over the town and although the bouts cost me a fortune, they also provided healthy exercises. I think the real reason why I was romping all over town was to shut out the picture of Charity. I was looking for idemnification for the loss of Charity.

Marriage was still a far note to me until I met Judy Nekesa again, in different circumstances though.

It was this hell of a weekend when everyone feels a milionaire. I was having a beer in town, not thinking of anything in particular and generally feeling in love with the world. I had had a satisfying meal of *chapati* and mutton and still had plenty of money on me.

I was in a new shirt, a new pair of shoes and, that afternoon, my doctor had certified that I had been completely cured of a 'clap' that I had contracted earlier.

The clap, besides giving me a hell of a pain around my 'protected area', had cost me five pounds and had given me a very uneasy week!

As wise as anyone who does not over-indulge in alcohol at the end of the month, I bought myself a packet of cigarettes and started for home, unaccompanied.

I had to pass through the Police Station to report my return to quarters and even before I entered the report office, I was aware of excessive noise coming from the cells, which were adjacent to the report office.

My mind clicked and I remembered that earlier, some officers in a 'Black Maria' had been dispatched from the station for the usual end-of-the-month swoop. A swoop which netted all kinds and sorts of petty offenders from drunks, vagrants, loiterers, idlers, solicitors for immoral purposes etc. Even the town residents had dubbed the swoop 'jaza' because, as they said, the main intention of the Police was to fill the Black Maria with people, whether offenders or non-offenders

Almost everybody who was found in the streets after 1800 hours was stopped and questioned and as most of them would be smelling of alcohol, the end of the interrogation would be arrest and detention at the Police Station, pending charges. Several people would be released depending on who the Duty Officer was for the day, but several others would ultimately be taken to court.

I entered the report office where the din was deafening despite the report officer's shouts at the prisoners, threatening that he would pour water in the cells, if the prisoners did not keep quiet.

Most of the noise was coming from the female part of the cells while from the male side, came a combination of unmelodious songs which were all out of tune and over-pitched.

"Full house, tonight?" I asked the report officer.

"Over-full! Damned it! I am wishing this clock would run and 2300 hours come so that I report off. Spending a night here would render one crazy". He complained.

"*Pole, bwana*, I just want to book my return," I told him as I took the Occurrence Book and borrowed his pen to do so.

"Lucky you! You fellows working in crime branch are luckier than some of us here. We are imprisoned here the whole day and even when we walk in town, people don't recognise us as officers! I am totally fed up with this," he threw his hands up in despair and then he turned his mouth to the cells, "*Nyamazeni! Ghasia . . . . malaya!*" He shouted at the top of his voice to the women and a comparable silence followed his bawling. He turned to me then,

"By the way, there is a woman who was asking for you. She is here in the cells, but I told her that you were not around." At that, I stopped writing. My lewd brain told me that a woman who would have been asking for me was a potential date and I quickly inquired,

"What's she like?"

"She looks new to this place—I mean I have not seen her in the streets but again, owing to my daily confinement here, I cannot claim to know many women. You are lucky . . ." I knew that he was going to start complaining to me about this 'confinement' and I had to cut him short. I waved him to silence.

"You mean you don't know her?" I asked him.

"No . . . I don't . . . you could check in the cells register . . ." I did not let him finish but quickly took the cell register and hurriedly leafed through the pages until I came to the days' entries.

I ran my eyes down the name column, reading the numerous Nanjalas, Nafulas, Wanjalas, Queens (wondering why anybody chose Queen for a name!), Odakes, Khaembas, Wangilas, Ongetis and at last I came to a name that somehow seemed to ring a memory bell in me.

"Judy Nekesa," Offence: "Loitering with intent".

I remembered that somewhere, sometime in my earlier days in Kakamega, there had come a certain Judy Nekesa in my life but her existence had been quickly brought to an end by the arrival of yet another woman.

I operated my memory buttons and tried to picture her but several indistinct negatives passed through my mind's screen and I would have taken longer except the report officer roused me back to the present.

"Got her?" He asked me, joining me at the counter.

"I think so—I think she should be this Judy Nekesa . . ." He stopped me by banging the counter top, "Yes! Now that you mention the name, I remember—she should be that Judy Nekesa!!"

I went to the cell door and was unable to see anything in the cell through the three inch square hole on the door. I told the cell sentry to open the door for me. Nasivili, the cell sentry, was an old friend of mine and he obligingly opened the door.

I almost told him to shut it immediately he had opened it! There emanated from the cells some liquid stench of unwashed bodies and a din that, as the report officer had earlier said, would render one crazy!

When they saw me, several women started calling . . . 'Fred . . . Fred . . .' and I had to shout them down, "Shut up! All of you or I . . ."

Silence fell. No wonder the report officer had complained of not being recognised as an officer by the public. I looked at them and I realized that I could have sworn to have seen twenty-six out of the thirty in the cell.

"Judy Nekesa!" I called out and the women once again got a chance to open their mouths. They repeated the name "Judy Nekesa' severally, until Judy, the same old Judy, came shyly from behind the others. I at once noticed that she had been weeping and took pity on her.

I thought she would smile and start pleading with me to activate her release but, instead, she just stood there, looking at my feet, not saying anything and about ten seconds must have elapsed in the embarrassing silence. I had to break the ice.

"What are you doing here?" I asked her, sizing her up and wondering what I had found wrong in her the previous time.

She just looked at me, seemed to swallow something and blinked her eyes.

"Why do you just keep quiet—say something!" I told her.

"Like what?" she could hardly pronounce the words.

"Well . . . for example, wouldn't you like to go home?" I found myself asking. This time, she looked at me straight in the face, swallowed hard and then focussed her eyes on my feet again. I guessed she was admiring my new shoes and almost felt proud to have them on!

"Yes. I would like to go home, but, how can I . . .? I am a prisoner . . . here . . . I am . . ." she sobbed once. My pity was quickly transformed into annoyance. I found that I had difficulty in restraining my temper and voice. I hate tears. To me tears are a fraudulent way of hiding something. I have a chauvinist's belief—and a very strong one—that women hide their misdemeanours in tears!

"I am asking you whether you would like to go home. Answer me that only!" She looked at my face again and I thought there was a flicker of hope in the eyes. She tried to smile but I guess that needed a lot of effort, and she gave up.

"Yes, I'd like to," she told me.

"Yes, that's all I wanted to know. Now, wait while I see what I can do." I was going to push the door to, but she held it with her hand, "and please," she told me, "I've got my cousin here with me . . . I don't know whether . . ."

"Name?" I cut in.

"Queen—Queen Abungwa. We were waiting for a bus . . ." I waved her to silence.

"Okay—okay—just wait there," I noted the name in my mind and told the sentry to re-lock the door. He was pushing the door to but the women all started calling my name at once . . . "Fred . . . Fred . . . even me . . . even me . . . Salome Nanjala please . . ." Some were holding the door and the sentry had to use his upper masculine strength to push it closed. He latched it, cursing and then we went back to the reports counter. Musenjeli, the report officer, was laughing his head off. Nasivili scowled at him, "What's so funny?"

"Nothing . . . I was just watching Fredrick Wamatu and all his women . . ." He laughed off and then pretended seriousness. "Tell me, have you had an affair with all those . . .?" he waved his hand towards the cell.

"Of course not! Most of those have at one time met me when they had problems or as witnesses in cases. I'd need artificial insemination equipment to serve such a herd!"

"We all laughed as I leafed through the cell register again. Queen Abungwa was also charged with 'Loitering with intent.' So were most of the other women in custody.

I checked on my wrist-watch. A relic from my hey-days with Charity. She was the one who had chosen it, had paid half the price for it and had actually strapped it on my wrist. I remembered her every time I looked at the watch!

The time was 2110 hours. I threw a glance at the wall-board where the names of the Duty Officer, Provincial Orderly Officer, Stand-by personnel, Orderly sergeant, Crime stand-by officers and even the night-duty driver, were listed. My name was in the crime stand-by list.

Inspector Fanuel Nzuki was the Division Duty Officer. The only person who would release a prisoner. He was familiar and friendly to me and I had run some unofficial errands for him sometimes earlier. I was going to ask him a favour. I knew it was a long shot but I had to try.

My reason for wanting Nekesa released was not based on love. what made anxious to see her free was her indifference. I had thought that she would see me and literally fall on her knees, begging me to release her. Instead, the look she had given me was almost unfriendly if not downright hostile and, actually, it was me who had suggested the idea of release. I thought that maybe she doubted my powers at the station and that thought made me decide that I would even kneel in front of Nzuki, to see that she was released.

I checked myself and found that I was sober alright. My breath had the faintest traces of alcohol but that would have to be put up with. After all, Nzuki was a hard boozer himself—I told myself as I nervously rapped on the Divisional Operations Room Door, avoiding looking at the inscription on the door: STRICTLY NO ADMISSION.

"Come in," I heard a voice invite me in, and as I twisted the door-knob, I braced myself.

The first thing that attacked me was the heat and the unmistakable fragrance of perfume. The lights seemed very bright and the Stonner Set at the corner was craking incoherently.

Nzuki sat at the Very High Frequency Console, reading something but my attention was diverted to the far end of the room where the Telex Machine was. The Operator, who had stopped manipulating the machine on my entry now tried to go on with her job and I caught my breath sharply when I realized who it was. I could hardly guess what words I was going to tell Nzuki—with Charity in the room.

"Good evening, sir," I stood at attention.

"Evening. Wamatu. What can I do for you?" Nzuki querried and added, "do sit down." And I perched myself at the chair opposite his. However, I could not bring myself to start talking.

"You are on Crime Stand-by?" Nzuki prompted me.

"Yes, sir," I answered.

"Has anything happened?" He raised his eye-brows and I was almost glad to note that his eyes had that extra-redness, which meant that he too had had his share of alcohol.

"Not really, sir, I mean nothing on the 'hard' crime line but we have more than enough 'intent' cases in cells," I said casually.

"Yes, it seems that the swoop lot had something against the women-folk today . . ." he chuckled and threw a fleeting glance at the direction of Charity. I also glanced at her and noticed that despite her placing her hands on the Telex key-board, she was not typing and was listening intently to our conversation.

"That's why I am here, sir. The truth is there are two girls in the cells who were arrested while they were waiting for a bus to take them . . ."

"Waiting for a bus!!"

"Yes, that's what they told me and it was confirmed by one of the swoop officers," I lied firmly. I did not want to look at Charity. I knew that she would be having that half-smile and spiteful knowing look on her beautiful face.

Nzuki pondered over my statement for half a minute and then seemed to come to a definite decision.

"What are their names?" He asked me as he took a pen from his pocket and tore off a page from the signal pad on the desk. I told him both names. Then, he told me to wait in the Ops Room, while he went out.

When he was gone, Charity spoke, "You mean your latest pick-up is in cells?" There was a very bitter note about the pronouncement. I did not know what to tell her and so I let her question hang. I just looked at her with cobra eyes and she muttered a soft 'sorry' and then started hammering on the Telex machine in such a speed that I knew she was making seventy five spelling mistakes out of every one hundred words. I had a mind to follow Nzuki in the Report Office but the V.H.F. set came to life:

"Control from Butere." I looked at Charity who was still very 'busy' at the Telex and thought that she had not heard.

"Five Yankee India Two Control from Five Yankee India Seven— how do you read me over".

I grabbed the handset. "India Seven from India Two—five go ahead."

"Roger, Sir, I want to submit my Delta Charlie India Romeo over."

"Wait one, over." I looked at my watch again. 2130 hours!! Quite late for any station not to have submitted its Daily Crime and Incident Report for the day to the Divisional Headquarters. I also realized that Charity, as the Telex operator for the day, was supposed to have received the reports from all the stations before relaying them on Telex to Force Headquarters after they had been checked by the Provincial Orderly Officer. I looked at her and noticed that she was still bent over the Telex. I wanted to tell her what Butere had wanted but then I did not want to talk to her.

Over a minute passed in silence and then the telephone on the V.H.F. Console came to life with a shrill ring. I almost jumped out of my skin. I let it ring a second time before I picked it up.

"Ops Room." I answered.

"Hello—can I speak to Charity Wangui?" The voice of a man.

"Who's calling?" I asked looking at Charity and noticing that she was not typing.

"I want to speak to Charity—what has my name got to do with you?" The voice asked and I felt mad at that.

"One moment," I said. I don't know what came over me but I felt that I should not allow that man—rude as he was—to speak to Charity. I slowly replaced the receiver and looked at Charity and she had resumed her pounding of the Telex.

"*Ukuigua uguo.*" I told her silently.

8

Then, the door opened and Nzuki came in, followed by two girls. Charity stopped typing and half-turned her chair to face us.

"I will release these two—but, they are the only two I will release tonight. The rest can be sorted out tomorrow." He told me. I thanked him profoundly, using words which implied that he would hear more about that gesture of kindness and consideration. I was gesticulating with my hands as words were hard to come by in the situation and environment.

Nzuki, an old timer, understood and nodded sagely as I, accompanied by the two ladies, left the Ops Room.

"Have you left anything in the Police Station?" I asked them as a way of opening conversation.

"No. Nothing!" Answered the other girl. Queen. I was already having misgivings about releasing them. I did not quite know what would happen after that and so I had to ask.

"And now, what do you propose to do?" We had stopped mid-way between the Report and Inquiry Office and the Ops Room.

Judy cleared her throat to say something but then kept quiet. Queen laughed softly and then said, "I think we shall bother you some more by asking you to 'lodge' us for the night. We can sleep on the floor in your house . . . it's better that way than sleeping on the floor in the cells and . . . and . . . as Judy had mentioned," she turned to Judy, "you two are old pals and . . ." She laughed off again.

The security was partially obstructed by a guava tree which grew between the station block and the armoury and so I could not see their faces clearly. I'd have liked to see their faces, especially Judy's and note her facial reaction.

"I guess that can be arranged," I said softly.

"What's the time?" Judy spoke for the first time. I turned towards the light and checked my watch.

"It's a quarter to ten," I answered. Judy turned to Queen

"Do you think we could still get a bus home? I think the Kisumu O.T.C. passes here at ten-thirty. I think . . ." but Queen cut her words.

"Go to the stage again? With the possible chance of rape if not arrest! I am not going . . . I'd rather take myself back to the cells instead of risking a second arrest." She said firmly.

I was listening to the dialogue, bemused. I was also wondering what Judy was thinking. I was wondering whether it had been very wise of me to have put all that effort—including lying to the Duty Officer—to see that they were released. I was wondering why I had done it.

"Fred," Queen spoke to me, stretching her right hand and holding my upper arm, "I think Judy has been upset by the events of the day. Please bear with her. Let's go home and maybe while there, she will regain her confidence and with it, her mood." And she started pulling me towards the Police lines.

I did not need any arguing. I had decided that if they had continued to argue about the time and O.T.C. buses, I was going to leave them just where they were and get back to my house. Judy followed us meekly.

Queen was telling me how neurotic Judy could be sometimes and how ungrateful she must be not to realize that I was her saviour and how they would have spent the night on a cold floor amid stinking drunks . . . I found her very garrulous and could not keep pace with her rhetorical questions and comments and so I let her do all the talking.

We came to my door and I noticed that Judy was some five feet behind us. Queen was still overly excited and was muttering some things about her first arrest, first day in cells. police unfairness and apologising to me for that! How good it is to be a friend of a friend of a cop etc and when I had opened the door, snapped on the light and welcomed them in, Judy rushed to the toilet and Queen, without warning, threw her arms around my neck, standing on tip-toe to balance our heights and said several 'thank yous' before she released me and flopped on the sofa.

On her return from the toilet, Judy's mood must have also changed because she smiled, came to me, held my hand lightly and I thought she was going to lift her face for a kiss but, instead, she told me,

"Forgive me, Fred, if I misbehaved, but, you can't imagine the pain that I have felt today. Thank you very much for what you have done for us." I looked at her and noticed that she appeared very small and helpless.

"Don't mention it," I told her and released her hand.

"I think I had better rush to the canteen and see whether there is any milk or bread left. I am sure you must be feeling hungry and as I don't cook in this house, there is hardly anything that can be fed on here. You poor girls will have to do with tea and may be bread only," I laughed off.

"That's a splendid idea . . . the truth is, I was going to suggest just that but was feeling . . . you know . . . shy . . ." That was Queen. She was ready with a word in any situation.

"So, why don't you go to the kitchen and put the kettle on? I am sure Judy knows where the kitchen is." I told them as I left.

I hurried to the canteen and noted that not only was there plenty of milk but that there were also several crates of bread. I should have known that the canteen manager would stock to the ceiling, at the end of the month!

I bought two packets of milk and two loaves of bread. I also noticed that there were eggs and I bought six. When these items were being wrapped, I felt a hand touch the back of my neck and I turned to see who it was but found no one. I looked at the counter again, dismissing the touch as that of a flying insect but it was repeated. This time I turned fast enough and caught Njagi before he squatted on his hunches as he had done the first time. We both burst out laughing as we shook hands vigorously.

"Where have you been hiding, you son of a gun!" He asked.

"Hiding?" I asked in mock shock. "I've been so much in the open today—re-connecting old wires and practising polygamy!" I told him laughing.

"Polygamy? How is that?"

"Polygamy to the very last letter of the word," I told him. Then, a bit more seriously, "Let's go to the hall and I will try and explain to you what is going on," I suggested. The 'hall' was a euphemism we used for the bar part of the canteen. I picked the two loaves of bread, the two packets of milk and the eggs and Njagi asked me, "What are all milks and breads and eggs about?"

"Part of the polygamy . . ." more laughter as Njagi orderd mine and his beer. When they had been opened and the waiter had gone from our table, Njagi asked again.

"So—what about the polygamy?" He pronounced the word 'polingame' I cleared my throat, pretended to be very serious and said:

"This evening, at about 2110 hours, I triggered the release of two Luhya female adults from the cells. Their names are Judy Nekesa and Queen Abungwa. Then, I took them to my house where they complained that they were hungry and I went to the canteen and bought two loaves of bread, two packets of milk and six eggs all valued at seven shillings and eighty cents. That is all I have stated," I finished.

"Read over correct by Njagi?" Njagi finished the statement format.

"No! Self recorded," I told him and we both laughed. Then, I dropped into a more serious whisper, "Guess what! I think we had better finish these drinks, take these foods to the girls and you will have a chance of looking at the specimens then. And then, after that we can come here for another beer and probably planning the night." I told him and then, something that had been bothering me all evening at last surfaced. I had all the evening been trying to connect Judy to Njagi but somehow, the link was missing. This time, when everything became clear, I banged the table, so loud that the waiter came almost running and Njagi pretended to cower away from me.

"What has gone wrong?" He asked in mock surprise.

"Wrong? There is nothin' wrong. In fact everything is right. I have just remembered something that will make you laugh." I was looking at him.

"And what do you think would make me laugh . . ." he was already laughing.

"Does the name Judy Nekesa ring any bell in you?" I asked him.

"Should it? . . let me see Judy . . . Nekesa no!"

"Then, let me tell you, Judy Nekesa is a girl who was introduced to Fred Wamatu by a friend of Njagi, some months—in fact several months ago."

"You don't say . . .!"

"I am saying it!"

"Then, let's go . . . but, first . . .," he dropped his voice again. "I have got a specimen in my house, bearing new registration numbers but I am yet to test the engine and driver comfortability . . . so I think you will have to practise polygamy to the end."

134

"That's bad . . .eh," I told him.

"Not really. Queen can sleep on the sofa set while you take Judy to bed or vice versa . . ." he suggested.

"Do you think it would be wise . . . I mean the vice-versa hint?"

"It depends on who is who to you . . ." We laughed as we finished our drinks and left the canteen. Njagi was telling me about the new 'car'—as we dubbed women. The body-work was perfect, not many dents and did not appear to have been refilled after any accident. No visible blemishes but he had not opened the bonnet yet to check on the engine. But he hoped the engine would be clean if not perfect.

We got to my house and found that Judy had prepared black coffee and they were drinking it while dancing to the music coming from my radio-gram, which they had put on, at a volume too high for the hour. The dance died upon our entry and I walked purposefully to the radio-gram and lowered the volume.

9

I introduced Njagi to them and noticed that Judy could not remember him. He had to remind her point by point of the previous meeting at the bar and at the end of it all, the way Judy nodded her head told me that she was only half-convinced. She seemed to remember that there was a previous meeting but the venue was not in a bar! We let it remain that way. Then, she cocked her head comically to one side and told Njagi:

"I think it's my turn to introduce you to a girl . . . meet Queen . . . Royal both in name and office . . ." We all laughed.

"And where is her palace?" Njagi asked still holding Queen's hand. I had been observing what was going on on Queen's face as she was introduced to Njagi. At first the face had clouded but after a second scrutiny, she had accepted him and had actually smiled. The question by Njagi made her laugh more loudly than necessary. Women!

"Still under construction . . . the kingdom was established about three hours ago . . . " more laughter.

"Why don't you call it 'queendom?" I asked and we all laughed as
we mixed the coffee with the milk, cut the bread into slices while Judy
smeared excessive margarine over them and then we sat at the table. I
told Judy that I already had had my meal and would only have a cup
of coffee to keep them company but Njagi said that despite his
having had supper he would eat and drink the 'queen's toast'!! And
we had a merry time over the coffee and bread. Then, I thought the
right time to ask a question which had been bothering me all along
was come. I had wanted to ask what these two girls had come to do at
Kakamega but I had not had the right moment.

When Njagi expressed his sympathy at the two girls having been
arrested while waiting for a bus, I took the opportunity and asked,

"So you had finished whatever mission you had here in town and
were ready to go home . . .?"

"Yes," Judy answered and then kept quiet.

"Was the mission just around the bus-stage?" I asked desperately. I
wanted to ask her point blank—'What had you come to do here?' but
I thought it would have been impolite. My impatience was again
telling on me.

"No, we had come from the hospital, where we had gone to see our
uncle, who is admitted there. The poor man was mauled by a leopard
yesterday. When we had seen him, we went to the bus stage to wait
for any matatu or bus and that is when the police truck arrived and
when almost everybody else ran away. We were left standing there
and we were picked . . . it's like a curse . . . our uncle is in the hospital .
. . we are in cells . . . and my uncle was only lucky to have escaped
from the beast's claws alive . . ." Then I remembered that we had
received a report of a marauding leopard and we had sent word to the
wananchi that they should report a second sighting of the leopard so
that the Police could try and capture it if not to kill it. The previous
report had talked of slight injuries on the victim of the leopard.

"Sorry to hear that . . . and how is your uncle now?" I was clucking
my tongue—the only way I know of expressing sorrow.

"Not very bad . . . but . . . his hands and face will bear witness to the
encounter for the rest of his life," Judy said sadly.

"It's better to be ugly and alive than beautiful and dead!" That was Njagi and we all laughed, despite the prevailing circumstances.

After the coffee, Njagi announced that he had to go away and Queen could not help showing disappointment on her face. I escorted him outside the house alone and bade him good night; none-too-friendly.

I went back to the house where Queen was slumped on the sofa set and Judy was clearing the utensils we had made dirty.

"Feeling sleepy?" I asked Queen as I sat myself on the set opposite her. She looked more fair-skinned than Judy and I had to admit that she almost had a right to her name. She was extremely beautiful and except Judy was there . . .

"Not really . . . I just want to get used to this bed of mine," she was pressing the settee with her hand.

"Why don't you try stretching on it—for size?" I suggested and she quickly pulled off her shoes. Even before she stretched on the settee, I knew she would be too tall for it. She wriggled into position, having folded her legs at the knees and the knees protruded at the edge.

"Five marks out of the test of royalty . . . queens are supposed to be neither too tall nor too short." I told her as she re-sat on the settee. She looked sad and I guessed she had put some hope on Njagi and was feeling the loss of his going away.

Judy had finished cleaning the utensils and she came from the kitchen rubbing her hands together.

"Queen is too tall for the settee," I told her and she laughed.

"I knew she'd be. I guess we are all going to share the bed. After all, it's only for a night and then tomorrow . . . " Judy said with a finality.

"How?" I asked. I admit I had had several affairs with several women, but, an affair with two women at the same time was just not in my line. Judy must have had a very queer mentality.

"How?" She mimicked me. "I mean going to bed and sleeping—the three of us," she put extra emphasis on the word sleeping.

"I see," I said although there was nothing to be seen. I simply could not imagine how I would spend the night with two women!

Queen was already on her feet and Judy was propelling her

towards the bedroom. I had made myself busy; locking and bolting the outer door, checking on all the windows and even straightening the curtains and keeping the books on the shelf in line—and all these chores took about ten minutes. Then I went to the kitchen and put off the light, which Judy must have forgotten to do, switched off the tableroom light and joined my ladies in the bedroom. Their clothes were hanging on a chair and the girls were actually between the sheets.

<h1 style="text-align:center">10</h1>

I started undressing, so much conscious of their double gaze that I had problems unbuttoning even my shirt. I don't know how I would have reacted if by a bad stroke I had found that my feet were stinking.

I removed my coat, which I carefully put on a hanger and took to the wardrobe, taking my time. Then, the shirt, being careful about looking for a hanger and a nail on the wall where I could hang it. Then I removed my shoes. The only smell that came from them is that of newly tanned leather and I felt at ease.

I peeled off my trousers and, if I had had to put it in the wardrobe, I would have had to walk five feet from the bed, with only pants on and with the double barrelled gaze still on me. I decided to throw the trousers on the chair at the far end of the room—to see whether my previous darts sessions had paid their dividends.

I carefully folded the trousers and aimed low at the chair and threw the trousers. They landed squarely on top! I realized that I was so strained that I was humming a nameless tune!

"Push a bit," I told Judy who I noticed was the extreme outer edge of the bed and had left a small gap betwen her and Queen who was at the far end.

"No—you will sleep in the centre of the bed," she said and made more room there. Queen also moved an inch or so towards the wall edge of the bed. I was standing naked and despite the warmth in the room, my upper arms and thigh had developed goose-pimples all over.

"What d'you mean at the centre?" I asked holding tightly to the leash of my temper.

"This . . ." and she threw off the sheets which had covered her so that I could slip between her and Queen. My eyes caught the blue of Queen's pants and the white of Judy's. I also had a passing glance at both their voluminous bosoms—which were naked to the skin revealing warmth and comfort! And their buxom flanks. I had no choice but to slip between them, wriggling gently into position, more conscious about the warmth around me than the sweat on my nose. Judy pulled the covers over us and turned to lie on her back. Queen had faced the wall but she also turned to lie on her back. I was surprised that my bed could comfortably 'lodge' three people.

"Anyone needing a light?" I asked them and noticed that my throat was extemely dry. I would have to wake up and go for a cup of water!

Judy asked, "What for?" as she snapped off the light through the bed-side switch. That was better! In the darkness, without their probing eyes, I felt more confident.

I was lying on my back with both my hands at my sides and I felt Queen move her hand stealthily to my crutch. I held my breath for a second. I wanted to remove her hand which was surreptitiously caressing my 'man' and which in turn was making its life and existence known, but I knew that a sudden movement would have made Judy know that there was something going on.

Judy suddenly turned to face me and shot her hand at my belly. She touched my navel and then her hand started moving downwards; slowly but purposefully it traversed downwards.

My body tensed involuntarily and Queen must have felt it because she quickly jerked her hand away just as Judy's hand reached its apparent destination, where it started doing things which almost made me scream in ecstasy; but I quickly turned and lay on my belly.

I had a lousy night with the girls and as the Agikuyu say, *Mbogo nyingi itiri nyama.*

At 0715 hours the following day, I was up and bathing. the cold shower only helped ease half of the tension in me. I didn't know what I was feeling but then, there was a small voice saying 'You are inadequate . . . you are a fool . . . you should have . . .' I finished the shower with only the thought to get the girls out of my house as soon as possible.

When I went back to the bedroom, I found that the girls had snuggled closer and Judy had one arm over Queen's bosom. I clicked my tongue as I picked my clothes to go and dress in the table room. I could not possibly dress up when the two girls were lying so lovably in front of me! I would have been tempted to go back to bed and . . .

When I was lacing my shoes, a knock sounded on my door. I checked on my wrist-watch and noticed that it was 0800 hours, Sunday 30th. June, before I called the knocker in.

The door-handle twisted but the door would not budge. I then remembered that it was still locked and I went with one shoe still unlaced and unlocked the door. Outside, the report officer was smiling at me,

"Good morning, Fred," he greeted, stretching his hand.

"Morning, Matheka," I answered, and went about lacing my shoe. I did not invite him in. He was one of the known gossips and was ready to magnify trifle scandals into bone-chilling outrages.

"Well . . . ?" I asked him as I finished lacing the shoe.

"You are required at the station. There is a follow-up of the marauding leopard's report from Chavakali Chief's camp. The leopard has been spotted again and this time it has snatched someone's goat . . ." He laughed after that.

"I'll be coming soonest," I told him.

"Yes, the duty officer is waiting. Meanwhile, I'll go and call the sergeant for the keys to the armoury and also driver Kinyua . . ." He went on although I had no need to know all the details of what he was going to do! When I didn't say a thing, he left and I went back into the house. I thought of waking the girls up but then decided against it. I went to the wardrobe and retrieved my coat, threw a sweeping glance at the sleeping forms, clicked my tongue again and went out of the house, closing the doors gently so as not to awake my sleeping beauties.

11

At the station, I found four men who looked like they had just finished a twenty-one mile cross-country. They were still panting and they looked exhausted, that is from their heads, through their clothes to their dusty feet. Even the walking sticks they carried looked weary.

I grunted a greeting at them and instead of replying, they all stretched their hands and I had to go through the ritual which the Abaluhyas seem to so deliciously relish: shaking each person's hand vigorously, muttering, '*Swa-swa-swa*'.

The duty officer, I.P. Muriuki who had relieved I.P. Nzuki was smiling slyly at me.

"You behave more of a Luhya than a Kikuyu these days," he told me.

"Indoctrination, sir—two years is not two hours with the same community!" And we both laughed. To crown it all, I stretched my hand towards Muriuki who took it in his and I shook it even more vigorously than the Luhyas. He winced in mock pain, withdrew his hand and blew on to the fingers.

"Well, now that that is done," he turned I.P.—in front of P.C. all over, "these Wasakhulus have brought a follow-up report of the leopard which attacked a man the other day. It was reportedly seen hauling a goat into a thicket and the bush has been surrounded, so that it can not escape. I am sending you there, knowing that you are a crack-shot from early days to go and bring that culprit—dead or alive, but I'd prefer him dead as we do not have any cells for animals here. You will go with driver Kinyua and P.C. Onyango.

"Go and take a rifle or would you prefer a revolver?" He asked me. Arms have a feeling that they create in each individual. A revolver makes me feel more of a detective and I like it when I am patrolling the town or visiting a scene of crime within the town.

On the other hand, a rifle makes me feel more military and its weight alone gives me more confidence than the bullets inside. I even change my walking gait when I am carrying a rifle.

"No, sir, I'd rather have a rifle as I am not planning to get so close to the cat as a revolver would demand," I told him.

"Okay, rifle then, and as many bullets as you think you will need for a hunt in the bush. Carry as many as you can. There is no limit in that." He dismissed me and I went to the back of the station where the armoury was and found P.C. Onyango, already armed and practising silent drill—alone—with the S.L.R. which is supposed to be carried at shoulder arms.

"Hi," I shouted at him and he in turn moved the gun to 'present arms' position and saluted me. Onyango! He had an exhaustless store of fun and amusement.

I entered the armoury and the sergeant handed me a rifle. I took it in my right hand and balanced it and then took three clips of ammunition, slipped one into the magazine slot and put the others into my coat pockets. All in all, I had thirty rounds of ammo. Enough to kill thirty leopards dead!

"Where is Onyango?" The sergeant asked me.

"Outside, practising Denham Drill," I answered.

"That's all he is good at—and when it comes to the actual drill, he cannot differentiate 'mark-time' and 'slow-march', the sergeant remarked as he noted down my name, number and rank, type of gun removed from the armoury, type and number of rounds of ammo. And at last I signed in the register and went back to the station.

"All set?" I.P. Muriuki asked.

"Just one thing, sir, I had not locked my house and would like to go and do just that," I begged.

"Five minutes only!" Muriuki said as I ran towards the Police lines with my rifle and ammunition.

I knocked on the door hurriedly, entering even before I was invited and found that Queen was in the bathroom while Judy was in the kitchen, brewing coffee.

"Good morning, dear," I greeted.

"Don't endear me! You refused to even kiss me last night," she accused and then her eyes fell on the rifle, "and what's the gun about? You are not going to shoot someone . . ." I decided to ignore the first part of her statement and answered the second question, "I am going to kill that leopard which mauled your uncle." I informed her. "You don't say! That's the best news I've heard in a long time!" She clapped her hands.

"Yes, it should be and I've only five minutes—no—two minutes in which to drink my coffee and get back to the station. The driver is waiting for me in the vehicle and the engine is running. I also think that if you be ready in the same two minutes, we would all take the same vehicle and go to your area. After all I might even visit your home after killing the leopard—how would you like that?" I asked her knowing that she would only answer in the positive.

"Yes, I'd like that very much!" she was bubbling with joy.

"Then, get Queen out of that bathroom and let's get going," I told her as she put some coffee in a *sufuria* and started swirling it round to cool the coffee while she blew into it. She then transferred the coffee to a cup which she handed to me together with a slice of bread reset in egg and I gobbled them down quickly. The coffee was still hot and I had to blow into it before every sip.

The girls in turn must have realized our time limitations because by the time I finished the coffee, they were already fully dressed.

Queen muttered something about men's houses having not even a trace of lotion or hair oil and Judy suggested to her to settle in the house and stock it with all the cosmetics that she needed.

"How can I settle in 'your' house?" Queen asked. "I am not a home-breaker," she added and we all smiled. They were hurriedly drinking their coffee and I was pacing, with a cigarette dangling on my lips, impatiently. The five minutes which Muriuki had given me had quadrupled and I was expecting an impatient knock on my door any second.

We were all ready at last but just as we reached the door, ready to move out, Judy broke off and ran back to the bedroom. She came back a minute later holding her head-square in her hand and we started again for the door but Queen broke off and ran towards the W.C.

Judy looked at me and without warning, threw her arms around my neck and raised her face, closing her eyes and I kissed her long and sweet. However, I could hold her with only one hand because I still had the rifle on the other.

Queen flushed the toilet and we broke our embrace but I could see that Judy's face had become all soft and mellow.

"That, my dear girl," I told Queen, "is what we call the eleventh hour rush. Now, is there anything else to be done in this house?"

They both looked at one another, shook their heads and we all trooped out of the house. I locked up and we started our walk to the Police Station.

Lucky it was Sunday and most of the Police Officers were still in bed, nursing self-inflicted hang-overs and only a few eyes pored over us as we walked to the Police Station.

We passed in front of Charity's house. The door was tightly closed and I could not help imagining that the fellow who was calling on telephone the previous night was in there, savouring his 'morning call-up'.

That though made me quicken my pace involutarily and I shouted to the girls to 'get a move on' and Queen noticed my sudden change of mood because she asked meekly, "What wrong have we done, now?"

"Nothing, sorry—but please let's hurry," I apologised as we came to the Police Station.

"Hey!" That was I.P. Muriuki, "Your five minutes have turned to twenty-five and you come here with a whole platoon of women!" He expostulated as I opened the rear door of the van and indicated to Judy and Queen to get in. The van was a Ford Transit which was usually used to transport prisoners to the law courts.

They both hesitated, Judy wringing her hands and it was ony after Kinyua had started the engine of the van that they got nervously in. The men had sat themselves next to the driver's cabin and Judy and Queen sat just next to the door, as if deliberately keeping away from the men in the van.

As I closed the rear door and rushed to the front, Muriuki signalled me to stop and told me; "You are the operation commander and I don't want to hear that anything has gone wrong!" It sounded more of a threat than a warning.

Operation Commander? Of a leopard hunt! Suddently, I started thinking of what we were required to do. We were going to seek a wild animal from its natural habitat and possibly kill him. The animal was a leopard—one of the fiercest cats in the world. This cat had already attacked a man—which meant that it was not going to give in without a fight!

12

I had read and re-read parts of the Wild Animals Act and knew that a wounded leopard is the most dangerous animal one can encounter. When hunting a leopard, one had to shoot to kill. I of course knew where the heart of the leopard was—the first target, or the head—so as to destroy the brain immediately, but, what if one was not in a position for a brain shot? And I was the dammed commander of the hunt.

"Have you ever hunted wild animals?" I asked Onyango.

"Yes. Of course," he readily answered. We were driving down towards Shirere River.

"Using what? Bows, arrows, spears . . ."

"Nets," he said firmly.

"How do you go about netting a leopard?" I asked puzzled. The way Onyango tapped his foot on the floor boards of the van told me that I was going to hear one of his silly, yet funny jokes.

"I didn't mention leopards. I mean I have been hunting fish for a long long time. Are they not wild animals?"

"Yes. They are."

"Does that answer your questions?"

"Yes. Thank you vey much." Kinyua, who had been listening to our dialogue without a word hooted at a cyclist as he overtook him and slowly shook his head.

If the only wild animals that Onyango had met were Kamongos, then I was really going to work for the title of 'Operation Commander'.

"Onyango," I called to him softly.

"Yes, sir!" Mockingly.

"Have you ever seen a leopard?"

"Yes. Several times."

"Dead or alive?"

"I think dead, because they were not moving."

"Where did you see them?" I had to know that.

"In Bata Tourist's Guide to Kenya, June edition." He told me very confidently.

"I see!" I had to swallow that—bitter as it was.

"Anyway, when we come to the thicket or rather when we see the leopard, just blast the S.L.R. on him, okay?" I instructed him.

"Of course, I will make sure that he does not steal any other goat."

"I hope so—just don't panic," I added when I noticed that he was gripping his gun so tight that the knuckles had turned white.

"And what will you be doing?" He asked me.

"I will be there, to help you kill him" I told him as we branched off the main road and joined a dirt road that would lead us to the Chief's camp where we would know the latest location of the leopard.

About a mile from the main road, the window between the rear and the driver's cabin of the van, was rapped impatiently. I told Kinyua to stop so that I could check on what was going on.

I jumped from the front and ran to the back.

"What is it?" I asked through a side window.

"We would like to alight." Judy told me. I opened the rear door and Queen and Judy alighted.

"So where is your home?" I asked her and she pointed to the right, towards a cluster of thatch houses which were all dwarfed by one large house with corrugated iron sheets and a chimney.

"There," she told me.

"Okay, we shall pass there on our way back to the station," I told her although I was not very sure of that.

I climbed back into the van and Kinyua started again. Only about three hundred yards from where we had stopped, the window was again tapped. Kinyua stopped and I again went back to the rear of the van. The men at the rear were already climbing out and one of them, their leader by age and size spoke;

"We shall have to leave the vehicle here. The animal is about half a mile towards this foot-path," he indicated an overgrown foot-path on the left. Already, curious residents were coming one by one and standing at a safe distance to watch us. I went to the front of the van and communicated the information to Kinyua and Onyango.

"Onyango—get off there and let's go and kill a real wild animal not wild fish. You, Kinyua will remain here and look after the van. I can't trust our hosts," pointing to the curious on-lookers, "with the car . . ." and Kinyua nodded his assent as Onyango climbed out of the van. I added, "I hope we shall not be long . . ." and Kinyua nodded again and wished me luck. I needed it.

Onyango was looking like one who had been having dyspepsia for a whole week as he clutched his rifle and walked with me and the four men down the bush-track.

"You are sure it's half a mile?" I asked the leader of the men just to open conversation. Sometimes, half a mile could turn out to be two whole miles.

"Just that or thereabouts—it isn't far from here," he answered me and I turned my head to see a long queue following us. I knew that such a bunch would be hard to control and I noticed that they had an assortment of weapons from mallets, spears, pangas, clubs and stones. I told the leader to warn them against noise when we reached the thicket where the leopard was hiding.

"Don't worry," he told me, "most of these will not dare venture to two hundred yards from where the leopard is . . ." and he laughed. "Most of these are 'men' only where food is concerned but not where bravery and men's courage are needed!" And he dismissed them with a wave of his hand.

Further down the path, we came to a group of men who, by the startled looks they had on seeing us, must have been doing something illegal or highly suspicious. One had to be physically held by his colleagues to stop him from bolting into the bush.

They exchanged greetings with our group and then fell into a fast conversation—in their local dialect, which I could easily understand.

Our leader was telling them that we had gone to kill the marauding leopard and that we needed all assistance from the wananchi and that it was unwise of them to smoke *'ijaka'* in our presence and . . . . So that was it. The blighters had been smoking bhangi! One of the raw narcotics which I thoroughly detested, but I did not mention it to them. I had a more difficult task ahead.

Our leader signalled us to go ahead and we crossed a stream which was lined with wild bush and lianas. Suddenly, the air was filled with shrilling and chirping noises from insects and birds and I knew that we had entered the forest proper.

The bush suddenly cleared on our left, to expose a grassy glade and further on was a thicket which looked like an island in the sea of grass.

Around the thicket, standing ten feet apart, were men with spears, clubs and sticks. One of them put his finger on his lips, as a signal for silence as we approached them.

"He is here," one of them told us pointing to the thicket of thorn bush around a tall eucalyptus tree which stood, drooping its branches to caress the tops of the shorter trees, like a Maasai father blessing his children.

"Where particularly is he?" I asked him. I was using a loud voice because I could not bring myself to whisper. Whispers have a scaring effect on me and I don't like them!

"He should be at the base of the tall tree," he whispered.

"Are you sure? Speak up! The leopard knows you are here already and whispering won't change his mind!" I was playing for time. I did not know what would have prompted me to go into that bush and seek the cat out!

"Yes. Yes—of course. We have been here since he entered the bush and we would have noticed if he left. We have some dogs which we had leashed and we can use them to get him out of the bush," he told me and I felt more confident. At least there was something to seek the cat out.

"Send for the dogs, then . . . and don't bring the whole village here.

We are going to use guns and needless to say, bullets do not know the difference between human beings and leopards . . ." I warned him as he told one of the guides to go and call the boys with the dogs. I looked at Onyango and noticed that he was holding his rifle, muzzle pointing down and he was chewing a blade of grass.

"Stop eating grass! The leopard might mistake you for a goat and . . ." before I finished, Onyango had thrown the blade of grass far away, had spat twice and held his gun at the ready with his eyes bulging. I lit a cigarette to hide a smile and when I had puffed only twice, one of the guides told me to stop smoking, as the leopard could be riled by cigarette smoke and attack us before we were ready! I threw the cigarette on the grass and crushed it under foot.

From our left came the cacophonous chorus of yaps, yelps and barks and whines and I looked to see a parade of mongrels of different colours and sizes, all straining against their leashes in the haste to enter the thicket.

The dog show in Nairobi would have scored zero against the paraded specimens. I hoped that they would at least keep the leopard busy while I aimed and shot. The handlers of the dogs were admonishing them to be orderly without much success and when the noise grew unbearable, I told the boys to release them.

13

I held my breath as the mad pack entered the bush at different points and waited for the first sign of the leopard.

"Onyango, go to that side . . ." I pointed to the far end of the forest "and wait for him there." I waited for Onyango to go but he did not.

"Onyango—you heard me?" I tried to sound commanding.

"Yes, sir, I heard you but . . ."

"But what?" He was looking down at the grass.

"I'd like to be near you," he said with finality.

"But, we . . ." I stopped. A pained shriek came from within the thicket and about a dozen dogs appeared from various points in the bush, all with their mouths very open and their tails between their hind legs. I looked at the scattering dogs and then raised my eyes just in time to see a blur of movement on my right. Onyango was standing on my right and I could not fire at the fleeing leopard without blasting him dead.

The rest of the men all started running towards where the leopard had entered the bush and any shot from my gun would have killed a man. They were all shouting to the dogs to follow and I also found myself shouting at the top of my voice and running towards the same spot. A few men had been able to release their weapons but I guess none had even touched the leopard. The leopard had then reached the fringe of the forest and disappeared into the undergrowth.

I shouted to the men to stop and they all obeyed. All in all, without counting Onyango, there were about twenty men and I had to use my loudest voice to make them understand.

"Don't run in front of me!" I shouted at them against the noise of the barking dogs. "Keep behind me and wait for me to shoot the damned beast! We are here to kill only the leopard—not a man for God's sake!" I was wondering why the bastards had not tried to kill the leopard before our arrival.

"Now, let the dogs seek him out again and I will try to shoot him—do you hear?" And some nodded with shiny faces full of sweat. I also had to wipe sweat from my face although the hour was still before 0900.

The dogs entered the bush again all howling and barking and a second later, most of them came out of the bush with their tails folded and I peered at the point where they had exited the bush. Inside there, a dog let out two whining yelps and then all fell silent.

The sun was coming up and making patterns of light on the undergrowth and these patterns all looked like leopards to me. Sweat had got into my eye and was making focussing very difficult as I had to blink and blink.

I looked carefully again and thought that I saw one light pattern which was not swaying with the movement of the wind like the others. I carefully lifted my rifle, aimed, held my breath and emptied the whole clip of ten onto that pattern.

Beyond the roar of the bullets, I thought I heard a screaming noise as the leopard, now wounded, left the bush and headed back for the island thicket, being trailed by three dogs which still had some fight in them while the rest of the pack followed at a far distance. I only had time to re-load and follow his entry into the thicket with a hail of bullets, noting with dismay that four or five dogs went down with the bullets while the rest wavered in their pursuit, hesitated and then about-turned and headed for various directions, all away from the thicket. The leopard once again shot into the undergrowth.

Deafening silence followed the volley of bullets and I had to wriggle my fingers in my ears before I could hear what was going on around me. The men were whispering again—this time saying that the beast was definitely shot and that he would need only one bullet to 'finish him off'. I also thought I heard some groaning from the thicket. On looking around, I could not see Onyango anywhere and I asked the nearest man where he had gone. Instead of the man answering me, he pointed towards the bush-track that we had entered the glade by and by the way he shook his head with a half smile, I knew that Onyango must have made a hurried exit. I dismissed him and concentrated all my attention on the bush.

I had to smoke or I would have blown my top off. I did not care whether the leopard would be riled or pleased but I found that if I did not smoke—I was not going to fire that rifle again. I also had a chance to wipe the sweat from my face and blow my nose. The cordite fumes had already started an itch in my throat but I held it back. The men in turn had collected their weapons and had re-assembled some three dogs which did not look very enthusiastic about the hunt any more.

"I think I have wounded the demon. If you could muster enough courage and seek him out again, I will finish him," I told them as I crushed the cigarette filter under my heel. The men exchanged glances but none of them looked at me.

"You could seek him out with bullets," one of them suggested. I shook my head, "But, I do not know where particularly he is—one would need a cannon to blow up the whole bush here if . . ." and I stopped as pounding feet approached the glade. I turned and saw Kinyua, wielding a self loading rifle running towards us with four administration Policemen—all in uniform following him. I guessed they must have dressed to escort the Chief to a function. They were all armed with batons! Behind them came a rowdy crowd of gesticulating shouting men. These were the men who had waited at a safe distance for the kill to be made so that they could come and celebrate, I thought ruefully.

Kinyua came and stopped in front of me. "Have you got him?" He asked breathlessly.

"I think I have wounded him—seriously—but maybe he is still alive. Onyango returned to the car—eh?" I asked him.

"Yes. I am sorry, Fred but do you know something . . . he will have to walk back to the station. I am not going to have him in the car after what he has done to you!" Kinyua vowed and clicked his tongue and then added, "But first things first—where is the animal?" He asked recovering his breath. I pointed to the bus with the muzzle of the gun. Kinyua had the rifle ready and was trembling with ecstasy. I turned to the A.P.'s.

"As you are not properly armed, just keep off the firing line and be ready with your eyes only. The beast is moving with lightning speed from one bush to the other and spotting his point of entry into the bush is very important."

The guides still had the four dogs, which were not as eager to attack as previoulsy. I told them to release them into the bush but, try as they could, the dogs would not enter the bush. They stood their ground firmly and growled bare-fanged with their spinal hairs bristling. The men started whipping the dogs and I told them to stop. I was averting my eyes from the four carcasses which had died of my bullets but Kinyua forced me to look at them: "Did the leopard kill those dogs?" He asked and I answered him in a single word, "Yes."

"What do we do now?" He turned to me for guidance.

"I think what we shall do is throw missiles into the bush and the leopard will come out again." I turned to the men and told them what I thought we should do but one A.P. opposed the idea.

"I think if the animal is wounded, he will not have much fight left in him. I could try and go inside and rouse him again." He added. I looked at him and noticed that he was merely a youth. One of the people employed, not because of loyalty and devotion to the State, but just to earn their daily bread. Like Onyango, I thought the closest he had got to a leopard was on a magazine page.

"Do you know how dangerous a wounded leopard is," I asked him, dismayed.

He looked at me as if by doing so he would read how much knowledge I had of leopards and he answered, "Yes," confidently.

"And yet you suggest that you will confront him?"

"Well, he might not even be wounded. I . . . ."

"Why don't you go into the bush!" I shouted at him. "Why don't you go in there bare-handed? You think you are going to accost a goat—don't you?" I was fuming furiously.

Instead of answering me, he held his baton firmly and started walking towards the thicket. All of us were watching him as he passed where the four carcases of the dogs lay and headed straight for the opening where the cat had entered the thicket. He hesitated for a second before he bent his head and parted the bushes with his hands.

14

Then, the scene exploded in a blur of movement and I saw the big cat pounce on him with such speed that the A.P. did not even have time to cover his face.

It hit him fully on the chest with the front legs and man and beast landed in a heap—the leopard on top. It had held him on the neck with both front paws and the hind legs started raking him with quick printer's strokes, like it was painting a crude picture with its claws on his belly and thighs, using red paint. The man screamed once, a gurgling form of a groan and then the whole crowd of men surged forward towards them.

Kinyua was a bit faster than most of them and reached the heap before all. He had his gun at the ready but I guessed he would not use it on the leopard without shooting the A.P. He turned, dropped the rifle which exploded as a bullet fired itself automatically, grabbed a club from the nearest man and swung the clup overhead and brought it down with full force on the head of the leopard. The blow made the leopard scream as it tried to turn to face the new attacker but Kinyua had already raised the club again and brought it down between the eyes of the leopard. He lifted the club again and again brought it down and I noticed that Kinyua was also screaming.

The head of the leopard burst like an over-ripe pumpkin but Kinyua still swung the club—up and down—up and down—battering the animal. The rest of us were watching—horrified by the insanity of Kinyua's strokes. His face was shining with tears and sweat and his clothes from belly downwards were splashed with blood and brains from the leopard. He went on even after the leopard was apparently dead.

I went to him and called him softly but he did not seem to hear. I had to hold him and drag him away and even as he left the mess he had created, he was still muttering incoherently and tears were still streaming from his eyes. He was shaking like a naked man on a snowy mountain top and then he suddenly steadied himself, retched once and sicked copiuosly on the grass. He looked down at his trousers and again sicked and I had to hold him to stop him from falling. He was staggering drunkenly.

The rest of the crowd had all gathered at the place where the A.P. lay, with the leopard still holding his neck in an obscene hug and were trying to release the neck of the A.P. from the leopard's grip. The leopard's claws had embedded themselves into the man's neck and I guess they had even curved further at death.

I sat Kinyua down, left him holding his head in both hands and joined the others. The leopard was the biggest I had ever seen and even minus its head, it still looked fierce. It had stretched itself beside the A.P., whose belly, groin and thighs were all fleshy mangled wounds and blood. I noticed with dismay that the A.P.'s belt of thick leather had been clawed into two. One look at his face, though covered with blood and brains and skin pelts from the leopard told me that we did not need a First Aid team for him. I felt bile rush to my mouth and swallowed it bitterly.

Most of the men who were with us were howling mournfully and the din they were creating was beyond description. Some were rolling on the ground while others were pulling their hairs and beating their chests.

The only calm persons were the A.P.s. They were bending over their dead colleague's body trying to prise the leopard's claws from his neck. They stood and gave me room when I bent over the bodies.

"Jesus Christ!" I mouthed and suddenly crossed myself, not to bless the dead but to sanctify myself from the blasphemy and the A.P.s looked at one another. From the corner of my eye, I thought I saw one A.P. cross himself.

The long claws had gone so deep that when I tried to pull the right paw clear of the neck, the whole head of the dead A.P. was lifted from the ground and fresh blood started flowing from the wounds. Some flies had already started buzzing around us, some settling on the dead A.P's belly-pit and thighs and some even trying to settle on my eyes. I brushed them away and again tried to prise off the leopard's claws.

"Hold his head firmly down," I told one of the A.P.s and he held the dead A.P's head down with his own head turned to one side, and his eyes tightly closed.

I heaved, holding both leopard's paws and the claws ripped off some flesh as they disengaged from the neck. The force I had exerted sent me sprawling on the grass on my back and I quickly stood up.

I bent over the A.P., touched over his heart and certified him dead.

The crowd, which had by then doubled its size was chanting war songs and slashing at the bushes with their weapons while others were pounding the ground with their clubs and sticks in a frenzied orgy which, to watch, was both fascinating and saddening.

They were then chanting a rhythmic song—with one group calling the tune while the rest answered in time with the beating of feet on the ground and the thud of the clubs. The word '*ingwe*' was prominently featured in their song.

Then, all of a sudden, they all converged at the body of the leopard and hacked and clubbed and slashed and after only about five minutes, what was left of the leopard was only a muddy mess of bones, blood, flesh and pulpy nothingness. Then, they resumed their war dance.

I was watching them all this time, not knowing what to say or do but feeling a hollow in my belly—a sign of utter loss. The leopard was dead—yes—but, with it, a man. I remembered that it was me who had provoked him into that silly act of going into the thicket. I was biting my lower lip ruefully, trying to think of an appropriate way of apologising to the crowd but finding no suitable words. Then, someone touched me on the shoulder and startled me back to the present. I thought it was the crowd coming for their revenge and I turned sharply and saw an Assistant Chief, in full uniform, from boot to beret, standing beside me. There were also other people and I noticed that even women had joined the crowd.

15

"What are we going to do?" he asked in a soft feminine voice. I cleared my throat.

"We shall have to remove the body to the mortuary for post mortem and . . . of course the remains of the leopard" I answered him.

"Will the body of the officer be removed from here without having been photographed?" he asked me, twitching his whiskers and looking like Solomon.

I did not know how to answer that one. Yes, bodies were supposed to be photographed at the scenes of death where possible. I had no right to remove the A.P.'s body before the photographs were taken.

I again understood what his question meant to him. The photographs were not only to show the lie of the body but there was a widely held belief that the photograph would even show the killer of a person.

Even when a person was killed at one place and the body dumped at a different place, there was a belief that the photograph would show the killer and in some instances, even the weapon used.

"I guess you are right," I told the Assistant Chief, "we shall leave these other officers guarding the body while we rush to Kakamega and call the Scenes of Crime Team from Kisumu. We would have called Kakamega Police Station from the van but the 'over-over' is out of order. I used 'over-over' because it was the popular name for the V.H.F. set, by the public.

"Yes, we should do that but I don't think there is any need for you people to drive all the way to Kakamega. I will send one of my men on a bicycle and he can take your message to Kakamega. Meanwhile, I would like you to join me in my house which is near here for a cup of tea or a beer if you would prefer . . ." and I felt that I would do with a beer.

"Give the instructions to the officers," I told the Assistant Chief. I could not bring myself to tell them myself because I still felt that I had been responsible for the officer's death. "Tell them to make sure that the body is not touched by anyone before the photographs are taken or before our return."

Out of the crowd, someone had brought a blanket and it had been spread over the body. Due to their closeness, part of the leopard's remains, now having more flies than a Maasai manyatta, was also covered by the blanket in what looked like mutual comradeship in death.

I checked on my clips of ammunition and noticed that I had expended twenty rounds. Twenty rounds of the 303 ball which had resulted in the death of a leopard, four dogs and an Administration Policeman!

There was no way of bringing order among the enchanted mob of mourners and we left them to their grief. As we left, I thought I could smell bhangi being smoked somewhere in the crowd and I saw, from the corner of my eye, a gourd, which must have contained an alcoholic drink, being passed around.

Kinyua led the way, holding the rifle indolently and I hoped and prayed that his hysterics were over and he would not do anything stupid to Onyango—with the gun. I followed him, puffing furiously at a cigarette—now that the leopard was dead—and the Assistant Chief, followed by a few mourners closed the rear. We met more and more people on the way going to the scene. Most of them had to press themselves against the wall of thorny bush to let us pass while others hailed us and even others picked short conversations with those who followed us.

The walking distance from the scene to the road seemed longer this time and I was panting as we reached the van. Onyango was sitting at the front, clasping his hands under his chin. Kinyua handed me the rifle and went straight for the driver's door.

"Go to the back of the van—we have an Assistant Chief who will sit at the front," he told Onyango in a falsetto which was more commanding than the actual words.

Onyango obeyed and by the way the Assistant Chief said hello to him, I thought the two had met earlier.

The Assistant Chief got into the front of the van and I joined him while Onyango went to the rear and Kinyua got in and started the van. He engaged the gear and drove off as a dozen or so people tried to wave at him to stop while others were shouting at him. Kinyua turned a deaf ear to all of them and I immediately knew what had happened.

Kinyua had locked the rear door of the van, and his telling Onyango to go to rear was just a way of making him step out of the car. He had carried out his threat of not allowing Onyango to ride in the van! I had to stop him.

"Kinyua please . . . we cannot leave him here . . . just stop . . ." I commanded although I was not feeling in a very commanding mood especially when the command to be delivered was to wait for Onyango, who had, incidentally, let me down!

"We are only going to the Assistant Chief's place and the place is not very far. He can walk the distance . . ." and he accelerated even more as we bumped along the road and I could not bring myself to argue with him. I peered through the window connecting the driver's cabin to the rear of the van and I noticed that the rear door was all metal plates and as such I could not see what was going on behind the van. The Assistant Chief was looking at his hands as if he had not seen them before. I sighed as we reached the path leading to the Assistant Chief's home and Kinyua slowed, pressed the indicator lever and turned left into the path.

It was overgrown with grass and only two clear ruts were on either side of the road and Kinyua had to concentrate on his driving fully, while I looked at the land around us.

Lining the road were flowers of differnt kinds, while beyond the flowers, I noticed that the residents grew the same crops as are cultivated in my native district—Nyeri.

Maize, beans, bananas, coffee, though in very small scale, numerous varieties of citrus fruits including guavas, oranges, grape-fruit and many, many more. There were rows upon rows of potatoes, green and healthy looking and even the sweet potato runners were so much alive.

16

I was enjoying the vista so much and the arrival at a barred gate interrupted it. We had reached the Assistant Chief's home. I had to get out first so that the Assistant Chief could alight and he went to the metal gate and shook it, making it rattle loudly. On either side of the gate ran a barbed wire fence which was implanted with cedars. There was evidence that the cedars were watered every day but their growing progress looked mangled and stunted. I guessed that the climatic zone was not suitable for them. As we were waiting for the gate to be opened, I turned to the Assistant Chief.

"We have very good farmers here," I told him, waving my hand to cover a wide area.

"Yes, thank you. But there are some who still worship 'kwete' forgetting their land. I have to almost force my neighbours to tend their farms and that is why you find very promising crops. Further inside the location are some tracts of land which have been left idle or uncared for and I sometimes wish the Government would enact a law, penalising those who leave their land idle." I was shaking my head sagely as a youth came running down the path to the gate.

The Assistant Chief gave him an admonishing scowl and told him a few bitter words all aimed at reminding him how precious time was—how the gate should be answered promptly—especially when the 'honourable chief' had 'honourable visitors' in an 'honourable government vehicle.'. He crowned it all by telling the youth to at least affect good manners while there were visitors around. The youth was nodding his head as he heaved with all his strength to open the ten-stone gate.

At last the gate opened and glided smoothly on its hinges and the Assistant Chief signalled to Kinyua to drive in while he trotted up the path, telling the youth to re-latch the gate.

Inside, I saw three hirstute Angora goats cropping at the short grass on what looked like an evenly mown lawn. Kinyua had driven further ahead and parked beside an old junk of a car which I thought had long ceased to be used on the road, but he was still sitting at the wheel of the van.

"You have some very fine goats here!" I exclaimed to the Assistant Chief who smiled contentedly and dismissed them with a wave of the hand.

"They would have been even better looking, except they had worms which cost me a fortune to eradicate," he told me. The goats would not have been any better to me. With their distended bellies and shiny coats of fur, they looked fine although I could not know what had distended their bellies—worms or fat.

They gazed at us briefly, with the characterstic bovine non-chalance and went on crunching harshly at the grass. There were three thatch roofed mud walled houses and we walked on until we came to an imposing stone house which was flanked on either side by smaller mud walled houses with iron sheet roofs and as we neared the door of the big house, out came a girl.

I had completely forgotten Judy and seeing her again made me catch my breath, miss a step and what the Assistant Chief was telling me about the homestead. I had not even connected the home to the dwelling she had indicated as she alighted from the van earlier. She had changed clothes and she looked so radiant and warm and I could not help regretting I had not done what the previous night . . . .

When she saw us, she stopped mid-stride and opened her mouth but nothing came out of it. The Assistant Chief spoke, pointing at her. "This is my daughter—the third—she finished school about two years ago and has been lying here idle—she can't get a job—or a husband . . ." and he chuckled. Judy had retreated into the house.

"What class?" I asked and turned towards the van and noticed that Kinyua was still at the wheel.

"Form Four—she had fifty four points! I don't know what other passing these employers want. Every letter of application is answered 'regret . . . regret," and he clucked his tongue in either annoyance or disgust.

"Sorry to hear that," I tried to console him, 'let me go and see what the driver wants in the car," I broke off and walked to the van.

"Aren't you coming out for the 'Mukasa's cup of tea—I bet there will be some beer" I asked Kinyua.

"You tell him to bring mine here—I will be guarding the car and you can also leave your gun here—there is no point in going with the guns there like home-guards on a raid," he told me.

"But, they are used to guns now. I . . . ."

"No! Please remember the state my clothes are in."

"Oh! Sorry . . . I understand. I understand . . . I had forgotten. I will tell him to deliver whatever he has to the car and d'you know what, the girl you gave a lift in the morning is his daughter," I told him turning slightly to see whether the Assistant Chief was within ear-shot. I noticed that he was still standing at the door.

"You mean the girl we brought from Kakamega this morning?" he asked.

"Yes—she is the one who was standing at the door just now."

"You and women! I wish I had the same stamina as you," he looked envious. "How they all fall for you—and you are not their tribe."

"Diplomacy, man! Tactical diplomacy and of course a little bit of luck and also a bit of sacrifice . . . a hell of a combination—eh? I laughed out loud as I walked back to the Assistant Chief after handing over the guns to Kinyua.

I told the Assistant Chief why Kinyua would not leave the vehicle and he understood at once. He then looked behind me and I saw his lips curl in a smile and I also turned and saw Onyango—with the youth who had opend the door for us at his feet, marching purposefully up the path. He had a way of concealing his feelings and one look at him would not have told me what he felt about the whole episode. He passed the Police van without as much as throwing a glance at it and came directly to where we were. I expected him to start complaining about what we had done to him but instead he just removed his handkerchief, wiped his brow and said, "Phew—that was a real healthy exercise—walking all that way!"

We exchanged embarrassed glances and then we all entered the big house. The room we immediately found ourselves in must have been the table-room—sofa sets lined the wall—all bedecked with embroidered cloths and occasional tables littered the middle of the room which was warm and inviting.

"Welcome . . . please sit down," to us and then he raised his voice, "Mai . . . !" and I heard Judy answer from somewhere within the house. I was looking at the walls which were embellished with framed portraits of the Assistant Chief and what must have been his family. Dwarfing all these was a wreathed portrait of the Head of State.

The table-room looked highly cared for and classy.

17

Judy came into the room from a door at the far end of it and the Assistant Chief had some words for her about undue shyness and then ordered her to shake our hands.

"You tell her your names and she will tell you hers. You are the ones who practice English mannerism" and he smiled as he sat himself on a straight-back chair at the corner, near the window while we shook Judy's hand. Onyango was nearer her and he said, "Timan Onyango—child of God." And he crinkled his face, pretending to be hurt by Judy's shake. I was not amused.

"Judy Nekesa Wepukhulu," she said and then came to me. I was praying that she would not do anything stupid—that would arouse suspicion—as she shook my hand.

"Fred Wamatu," I said in a voice scarcely above a whiper. She had twisted her fore-finger in a way and was tickling the inside of my palm.

"Judy . . ." she stopped, looked at me, looked at the unceilinged roof and pulled her hand away even before I had time to practise the English mannerism of 'glad to meet you'!

"Your mother has not yet come from church?" the Assistant Chief asked. I looked at him and noticed that he had doffed his beret and his head was all grey with very little streaks of black.

"No. I think they have left the church and are at the place where the leopard is . . . was being killed." I noticed the change of tense.

"And we did not meet her on the way . . : anyway, you will take her place.—After all you should be practising running your own home. I am almost eager to start drinking your bride-price before you spill it or drink it alone in bars." He was saying all those words with a half-smile and Judy was so embarrassed she was shuffling her feet and wringing her fingers and twitching her lips. She looked so beautiful! "Well, go to the cupboard and see whether there is any beer left and bring it all here . . . and call Masinde for me." He instructed.

"That leopard is a curse to my family," he addressed us, "it almost killed my brother the other day and killed two of my sister's dogs yesterday. This morning it snatched the goat of my brother-in-law and the most severe blow has come in the death of that officer. If I would relate properly—that is my son. His father and I attended the same initiation ceremony! Such a promising hard-working youth! Now gone beyond reach! There must be someone in the family who has done something which has turned our ancestors' spirits against us and they are punishing us. After the burial, I am going to assemble my clan for absolution rites. Except I am a Christian at heart, I would have summoned Wetangula, the location witch-doctor for prognosis but, I want to do away with all those traditional beliefs now."

I noticed that he had developed a far away look and even his face appeared a bit older. I was slowly shaking my head in sympathy and wondering how much longer Judy was going to take to fetch those beers.

The youth—Masinde—came in and started. "You sent for me?" but the old man cut him short, repeated the same counselling he had done at the gate, putting on extra emphasis on the kind of manners which the youth should portray to strangers and then ordered him to shake our hands.

He shook our hands with a dirty hand and I had to surreptitiously remove what looked like a speck of cow-dung from my thumb.

"That's better," Wepukhulu said. "Now go and fetch water and a towel for the visitors to clean their hands." Masinde left and Judy came in, balancing several beers on a tray. She hesitated, I guessed not knowing where to put the tray until her father told her to put it on the table next to me. That done, she left and I counted eight bottles of White Cup and three Tuskers, on the tray, before Judy came back with three glasses and placed a glass each at our tables.

"I can't locate the opener," she told her father while gazing at the door. She was standing only three feet away from me.

"Take this" Onyango had one at the ready, "and keep it," he added. He was seated next to me and I felt a surge of annoyance pass through me.

Judy took the opener from Onyango and started saying, "Sorry, there are no Exports," as she opened a White Cap for me and then she must have realised what she was saying because she checked herself, looked side-long at her father and opened the White Cap for me.

"Does Wamatu drink Export only?" Onyango opened his dirty mouth and Wepukhulu turned to us. Judy hesitated before opening Onyango's Tusker and when she did, the effort she applied was so furious that a lot of foam and beer spilled from Onyango's bottle. I had to change the subject.

"There's the driver in the van outside," I pointed out.

"Oh! Yes. See how easily we forget things! And what happened to Masinde? These young boys!" Wepukhulu's exclamation sent us all laughing as the door opened and Masinde came in with a basin half-full of water, a towel slung over his shoulder and a piece of soap floating in the water. He placed the basin on the floor at my feet and I washed my hands, taking care to remove any blood from the nails and wondering whether Onyango would need to clean his hands.

"You don't need to clean your hands, or do you?" I asked him as Masinde pushed the basin towards him and I was towelling my hands.

"Why not? For hygiene, one has to wash his hands before and after every meal," he said as he soaped his clean hands thoroughly.

Judy had already taken a bottle of White Cap to Kinyua at the car and she presently came back with the bottle and said that Kinyua, had said that he would not drink any beer at that hour and would prefer a soda or a cup of tea.

"Then get him a bottle of soda, I am sure there are still some," Wepukhulu told her as he took a swig from his bottle. He had a glass but was not using it. Judy went to the inner room again and came out with two bottles of Fanta which she took to Kinyua outside.

Wepukhulu had once again started his lamentations over the 'curse' in the family but I was only listening half-heartedly. He had sent Masinde to the hen-coop to select three one-colour hens, tie their legs and keep them ready.

I was in the middle of my second beer when the unmistakable sound of a land-rover engine came to our ears. I looked through the window and saw the white Police land-rover outside. The driver was talking to Kinyua.

"Those will be the photographers," I told Wepukhulu and we all left our beers and went outside.

I greeted the driver and he told me that he had left the Scene of Crime Personnel a the scene and had just come to fetch me. I knew that the photographs would have been taken even without me, but, I remembered that there were professional divisions in the Police Work.

18

While the Scenes of Crime took photographs, the General Duties personnel from the Station had to get the list of the witnesses who saw the incident while the Criminal Investigation Department recorded the statements of those witnesses and the Prosecution Branch would conduct the Inquest in court. Every department had its role, except the Special Branch who acted like unconcerned spectators, making me wonder why the Government needed such a department.

And one day, I was brave enough to ask the District Special Branch Officer Kakamega what they did behind the doors marked 'KNOCK AND WAIT"

He smiled at me, the way you would smile at a mad man you knew, and answered me in one single word; "Plenty," and then quickly changed the subject by remarking about a woman who was passing by.

"Do you know her?" he asked me.

"No. I don't," I answered him.

"You should . . . she is the K.A.N.U. Vice-Chairman in Butsotso Location . . . excuse me," and he left me to go and greet the woman. I looked right and left and marched off, vowing that I would one day endeavour to know what they did—I mean what role they played in the complicated gears and wheels of Government machinery.

As at that day, when I was climbing into the S.O.C. land-rover to go to a scene of death, it being three months since I had questioned the D.S.B.O., I still did not know what the department did.

Judy came running from inside the house just as I was slamming the door of the land-rover shut. She stopped some six feet from the car, threw an eye at the van where her father had got in and asked softly.

"Are you coming back?"

"Yes," I answered in a whisper.

"Please . . . ." she was saying and then her father called her.

"We are going to the scene again and I hope that we shall be back soon—prepare lunch . . . okay?" Wepukhulu told her.

"Yes," she answered and walked back to the house. The Land-rover started and we followed Kinyua's van which was already ahead of us.

We left both vehicles at the same spot where we had left them earlier. The S.O.C. team had brought a stretcher from Kakamega Police Station and Onyango, even without being told by anyone, removed the stretcher from the land-rover and wanted to carry it all the way to the scene but Wepukhulu ordered a by-stander to carry it. The fellow silently obeyed. I noticed that the residents had a lot of respect for their Assistant Chief.

The beer I had taken had cleared the melancholia and cob-webs in me and I was hearing and seeing things in very sharp perspective. The insects which had been dominant in making noise in the morning had **quietened down but had been replaced by various birds. I thought I** could even hear the shrill screeching of a spider-monkey—an animal I had heard was a delicacy for the residents.

The animal and bird sounds escorted us until we crossed the river and then gave way to the mourning song from the scene of death. Even a drum had been brought and I could hear its 'tom-tom' from far off.

The mourners were less hysterical this time but their number had trebled. Women had easily outnumbered the men and as we entered the glade, I could see that the dancers had moved to one side and had left the S.O.C. officers at the bodies.

The photographs had already been taken and after I exchanged greetings with the officers, the body was placed on a stretcher.

Wepukhulu then handed me something wrapped in an old newspaper. I unwrapped it, not having the vaguest idea what it would be and found twenty-one empty cartridges. Someone had been very careful in collecting the shells from my gun and the one from Onyango's which had automatically fired on being dropped by Kinyua. I thanked Wepukhulu. Then I told him to get some wananchi to help carry the corpse to the vehicles and when he told them that we needed bearers for the stretcher, the whole crowd surged forward and the stretcher, normally carried by only two persons, was carried by more than a dozen men and women. Some, who could not get a place to hold it were holding onto those who were actually carrying it and we started on our journey back to the road, leaving the remains of the leopard at the scene, and escorted by the mourning song of the pall-bearers.

The crowd led us, singing, while I fell back and we started a light conversation with the officers from Kisumu.

They complained about the number of fatal accidents on the roads, which were keeping them busy every hour of the day and night; about the new Provincial Police Officer at Nyanza who had **come from North Eastern Province with a war-operational mind;** about the hippo which mauled a tourist at Hippo Point.

I was still very much aware that I had left a half-full bottle of beer at Wepukhulu's. I wanted to go and finish it plus of course seeing Judy and at least arranging a date as well as collecting the three hens that I was sure were intended for us.

I was planning that the S.O.C. team would take the body to Kakamega General Hospital mortuary, escorted by Onyango, while I could possibly urge Kinyua to rush me to Wepukhulu's house.

"I don't think we shall need to go to Kakamega. I will send the photographs as soon as they are ready. We had better rush back to Kisumu," the head of the S.O.C. team told me, interrupting my thoughts and making me stop abruptly. What of the beers? I almost asked him! I had to try and convince him.

"I thought you would take the body to the morgue, seeing that you have a land-rover. We have only the van and it is not designed to carry a stretcher," I pointed out to him, waving my hands at each item as I mentioned it and pleading with my eyes which I was trying to open wider than normal and gazing at the fellow!

"We'd like to—in fact very much," he could not look at me. "But you see our mobile V.H.F. set is out of order and we would not know when we are required unless we were at the base. This is the end-of-month week-end and we unfortunately expect more calls than usual." He told me and I forced myself to understand.

Kinyua opened the rear door of the van and the stretcher was slid in. It could not fit in and had one end protruding outside the van. **Two A.P.s joined it in the rear while one was to go back to the Chief's** office and make a formal report. Onyango said that he would sit at the rear of the van—to stop the stretcher from sliding out. I guessed he did not want to walk back to Kakamega.

Wepukhulu insisted that he would accompany us to Kakamega and I bye-byed the S.O.C. team as they waved heartily and left.

The crowd had then formed a ring around the van and were singing and dancing—calmly. Kinyua started the car and had to drive slowly—to avoid raising the death toll for the day, and when we were clear of the people, he stepped on the gas and the vehicle bumped on the rough road until we reached the tarmac. The change from the rough road to the smooth tarmac made me feel as if the vehicle was not moving at all.

At Kakamega General Hospital mortuary, we filled the necesary forms, which I signed and one A.P. counter-signed and then **deposited the body, after I had searched it. There wasn't much! A few** shillings, a bunch of keys, his certificate of appointment and a dirty handkerchief.

Except for the certificate of appointment, which I handed to Wepukhulu for forwarding to the Chief, I handed all the items to the **A.P.s. Then we all drove to Kakamega Police Station.**

I was ready to answer any questions but, contrary to my fears, that I would be blamed for the death of the A.P., no one seemed to know what part I had played.

The sergeant was there to take the rifles back to the armoury and he congratulated me when I handed the expended shells to him.

Kinyua was supposed to drive Wepukhulu and company, back to Chavakali but the way the sergeant ordered him to do it had riled him since he told the sergeant point blank in front of all around that he would not drive that van any more on that day. He told the sergeant further that it was a Sunday, that he had been working since morning to that hour—1600 precisely—and that it was high time the Station administrators, the sergeant included, got another driver for the station so that they could work in shifts—Amen!

He hung the van key on the rack, filled the work-ticket which he put on the shelf and walked from the station block towards the lines without another word or turning back.

I finished booking the situation report and also walked to my house, after telling Wepukhulu to remind the witnesses that their statements would be recorded the following day at Kakamega Police Station and not at Chavakali—and that therefore, they should make themselves available at Kakamega Police Station as early as 0800 hours.

CHAPTER NINE

1

The following day, I recorded my statement and handed it to the C.I.D. personnel. I then had a very busy time in the Crime Branch office until about 1500 hours when Judy was ushered into the office by the report officer.

She had a small suit-case with her and before I shook her hand, I looked at her head and noticed that the hair looked unkempt and that her eyes were red, showing that she had been crying.

"Your visitor," the report officer announced and left.

"Welcome . . . ." I told Judy and indicated a chair to her. I was in the middle of taking the finger-prints of a confessed burglar. Judy shook her head.

"I'd rather wait for you at your house . . . "she said in a tearful voice.

"What's wrong! What has happened?" I was alarmed.

"Nothing . . . I will tell you when you come home," she said and I noticed that she was on the verge of tears. I gave her the key to my house and she left with her head bent in sorrow.

I took the finger-prints extra fast and had to bang the fingers of the burglar twice—to soften them when they stiffened. Finger-print taking was one job that I claimed to be an expert in but the finger-prints which I took on that day were worse than a novice's!!

I rushed the burglar back to the cells, went back to the office and hurriedly compiled his file and then ran to my house. I entered without knocking and Judy was not in the table-room and so I went straight to the bedroom. She was there, lying on her tummy on the bed with her suit-case on the floor near the wardrobe.

"Judy, dear, what has happened?" I asked her as I sat on the bed and placed my hand on her back.

She broke off in a fit of sobs and I started feeling the heralds of annoyance. I gave her a minute to get herself under control and then asked the same question again. I was caressing her back.

"He beat me!" she said through sobs. "He beat me and instead of father defending me, he also beat me! I am not going back there! I'd rather die! She raved uncontrollably.

"Who beat you?" I asked her.

"The stupid drunkard—he had the guts to even use his belt on me!" She was pressing her fingers on the eyes. I think to stop the tears from flowing, but she was not succeeding.

"Who?" I shouted shaking her. She got startled by my sudden change to violence and she sat bolt upright on the bed and looked at me with very wide but very wet eyes. Her lips were trembling lovably.

"My brother . . . " she answered and controlled her tears.

"Which brother? surely not Masinde!"

"Another one . . . Khaemba . . . the older one . . . the idiot does nothing except steal from father, drink himself silly and impregnate people's daughters, making father pay compensations every year. He is hitting the thirty mark now and he is still a bachelor and he had the guts to call me a prostitute! Me? A prostitute! Oh God! . . . " and she again went into her hysterics and I slowly pushed her onto the bed.

I had read in some books that emotions like those could easily be removed with a pinch of brandy but I had not brandy in the house. The closest I had to brandy were the numerous jerry-cans of chang'aa which were at the Station exhibit room, but I was not sure whether they were still palatable. I was mumbling soothing words to Judy and trying to reassure her that she was out of the reach of her brother's hands, as long as she was in my house. When she developed some relative calm, I asked her exactly what had happened.

She then told me how her brother had come home as soon as we had left on Sunday and how, instead of even asking her where she had spent the previous night or even the circumstances which led to her sleeping out just started accusing her of practising prostitution from her father's house, of being a failure in life and even threatening her with eviction if by a stroke of a chance she got pregnant.

When Judy asked him on what authority he was issuing the threats the elder brother had turned wild,

"I am the eldest son in this home! Just because Dad is too old and does not whip you any more does not mean that I cannot!" And Judy had to challenge him to try, whereat he had ungirdled his belt, doubled it and said, "Like this . . . " whipping her all over her body.

Their father had come in while this was going on, but instead of stopping it or inquiring what was wrong, he had commented, "I know she must have done something quite awful for you to do this to her . . ." and had proceeded to use his swaga-cane on her.

"I am not going back there!" she declared again, "I'd rather starve to death than go back there!"

"And what do you propose to do? How do you hope to cater for yourself all of a sudden? You have no job for instance. You have . . ."

"Job? I'll get a job . . . all these bar-maids around town did not have to go to school to get . . ."

"Stop that!" I said raising my voice. "You want to start practising what your brother was accusing you of?"

"No! Not all bar-maids are prostitutes," she said.

"Of course—not all . . . but most of them are. How will you escape the net? You think you will . . . or tell me . . . what do you propose to do to your physical attractiveness so that we drunks will not see it and fall for you?

"I don't have to do anything. After all I am not very beautiful. All I need to tell them is that I am not for sale!"

"And you hope they will murmur 'sorry lady' and leave you alone, eh? That's what you think!" I could visualise her with five men, all holding money in their hands and queing for a go!

"What would you do in my place?" she asked calmly. She had swung her legs over the edge of the bed and we were sitting side by side. I had put my arm over her shoulder.

"Marry," I told her.

"Marry? Marry who?" she sounded astounded.

"Fred Wamatu . . ." I named the suitor.

For the first time since she had got into my house, she smiled.

"The problem with you men, is that you take things and twist them this way and that way until at last you make them jokes. Do you now know that you are making a joke of my whole life and future?" she was holding my left hand fingers and she released them when she finished talking. She half-turned to face me.

"A joke—I am proposing to you. Honest. Judy, will you marry me?" l asked her. I sounded serious even to myself. She turned rigid and her whole body tensed. She was looking straight ahead and even my holding her close passed unnoticed. I guessed she was weighing the question before giving me an answer.

My heart was raising its tempo as a distant memory loomed distinctly. Someone had asked me that same question, but I had taken so long to give the answer that events had occurred rendering the question useless.

I was starting to reminisce over the past and I had to shake my head to cut the line of thought. Judy was speaking:

"Yes . . . yes . . . Oh Fred . . . you can't understand. I don't know how or what to . . . " and she held me and we kissed, broke off and we looked at one another and both burst out laughing together!

"And, like a good wife, you should not be sitting on the bed at four-thirty. You should be in the kitchen preparing your husband's supper!" More laughter as we left the bedroom and together we went to the kitchen.

We checked the items of the food which we needed to buy, noting them one by one and then we went to the table-room where we budgetted. It was still within the month-end and I could afford to be a little extravagant. Even when we went to do the actual shopping, I did not strictly follow the budget and the end result was over fifty per cent more expenditure than anticipated. Then, we went back home and prepared supper together. Judy insisted that I should be in the kitchen all the while she was cooking so that I could show her how much of this and that I needed in this and that meal. I was bored stiff and I told her, "Prepare a meal that you yourself would like to eat and enjoy eating. Let me look after the pocket while you look after the cooking."

2

The following day, I reported on duty feeling like a million dollars. The first married night had been such a success to both of us. After a delicious supper, we had sat down and properly laid down our 'dos' and 'don't's and what 'likes' and 'dislikes' we would practise and avoid respectively. Then we had gone to bed—a warm bed and even made warmer for me by the very presence of 'my wife'!

When I said hello to Njagi, who was unaware of the previous night's developments, he looked long at me and told me,

"Be open. Tell me, what's going on?"

"Why?" I asked him smiling.

"You are so happy that your bliss is radiating all the way from your heart and literally shining on your clothes!"

"Should I not be happy?" I asked him, mocking offense.

"Why not! I'd like you to be happy, Fred."

"Thank you. To tell you the nude truth, I am now a married man and you bachelors have got to exercise a little bit of manners when you knock on my door," I announced solemnly.

"Ma-rr-ied?" he was genuinely surprised. I nodded my head.

"To . . .?"

"Mrs Judy Nekesa Frederick Wamatu nee Wepukhulu."

"Hell's teeth! That's news—eh? You are not serious."

"But I am!"

"Since when? I thought you transported her back to her father's kraal on Sunday?"

"Yesterday—yesterday at 1530 hours."

"So she is in your house now?"

"Yes. And for keeps. I have decided . . ."

"I guess you know what you are doing, Fred."

"I hope to God, I am doing right."

Then I told him all that had happened and what had led Judy to my house and how we had decided to settle. At the end, he told me,

"I am not a very good counsellor on matrimonial matteres, seeing that I am still a loner, but you are my friend and I've just told you that I'd like you to be happy. You are my best friend, honest and your happiness is very important to me. I'd like to think that Judy is also serious about this issue and also hope that her family will not spoil any or everything. That's my wish. I hope you will be happy." And he stretched his hand and we shook hands lightly. He looked sad and I questioned him immediately.

"You'd like me to be happy and you don't look very happy yourself."

"I am alright," he told me without looking at me and he excused himself to go and check on what 'route' he would be on that day. He was in traffic duties then. I looked at him as he walked away and noticed that his head was bent and his shoulders looked slightly humped. It was as if he had an unseen heavy load which was making him drag his feet as he walked.

I entered the crime branch office and started to doubt whether the decision I had made had been really wise. Again I told myself that Njagi had his own life to live the way he wanted it and I had my own. He should not make me doubt or worse still, change my mind.

I started working, putting all concentration on my work. I did not have to worry about where to have lunch or any other meal for that matter. I even planned how I would sit for the Inspectorate Examination, the first step towards promotion. I felt that I needed to be promoted so that I could earn enough to keep Judy and me clothed and fed.

What did I need to be promoted? Quite a lot!

There were examinations to be passed. I had already done the Police Literacy Examination succesfully. I had once booked the Inspectorate Examination but had failed to turn up at the hall and had been disqualified from sitting for two sessions besides being deducted five shillings per paper. The two sessions were then over and I could book and sit for it.

I had also to improve my work, to attain what the police bosses refer to as 'merit'. I had only one commendation, following my gunning down of the robber but that had been long covered by other folios, three of them adverse to my chance of advancement.

There were two disciplinary charges, one for breaking out of Police Lines and the other for using insubordinate language towards a senior officer. I clicked my tongue when I remembered how that one had come about.

3

I had taken Charity for a film in Kisumu. At about 2130 hours, when the film was over, we had joined Kabue, an old friend of mine from college days, for a drink.

Then, it had started raining cats and dogs and we noticed that we could not possibly go to the bus-stage and wait for a bus in that rain. We did not have enough money to hire a taxi from Kisumu to Kakamega—which would have been hard to find anyway—and so we decided to put up at Kabue's until the following day.

In the pouring rain a bus had plunged into the river and although there were no casualties as the bus had been moving slowly, the Police had been called to the rescue.

The alarm had been sounded and Fred Wamatu had not appeared. A check in his house and even Charity's—as the sergeant told me— had been fruitless.

I tried to explain but he would not listen. I was charged and fined twenty shillings for the offence and another ten shillings for an offence emanating from the first charge.

When I was marched to the station commander's office for the formal charge, I shouted at him trying to tell him how I had no control over the rain or sunshine and how it was only by luck that I was not in that bus, which incidentally was being driven from Kisumu to Kakamega and when he told me that the decision to charge me had been made by the duty officer, I asked him who held more powers in the station—the O.C.S. or a mere Duty Officer and the O.C.S. added a charge against me for using insurbodinate language.

Charity was not charged with me and although I loved her so much
and would not have liked anything bad to happen to her, I felt that
there was partiality in the way the whole affair had been handled. The
Discipline Book procedure would have been that we get the same
charge—i.e. me and Charity. I felt cheated.

After those charges, I grew so unfriendly towards the sergeant and
the officer in charge that he used to call me on duty only when
absolutely necessary.

The third adverse folio was the letter from the Officer Commanding Police Division, informing me that my pay would be less by
fifteen shillings at the end of the month following my non-
appearance in an examination hall where I was required. The
O.C.P.D's letter had actually asked me to show cause why I should
not forfeit the fifteen shillings but before I could reply, the payslips
were handed out and mine indicated a miscellaneous deduction of
fifteen shillings.

I had really to do something to make the bosses forget about those
three folios.

The leopard incident would be of little help. Kinyua had proved
the hero of the sad day and I had played second fiddle.

As I sat there, completely absorbed in compiling case files, I
wished that a real big case would come somehow. A case which I
would successfully investigate and have a better name in the station;
revive the 'wonder-cop' image so to speak.

I was determined to be good and even made a habit of going to the
office as early as 0700 hours, a whole hour before official time so that I
could clear anything which might have been left the previous day
before the prisoners were taken to court. I sometimes left the office
long after the official 1630 hours and on occasions, I would even
return to the office at night to compile any urgent case file.

I was feeling confident that I was making headway and even the
various comments from my bosses indicated that they too had
noticed my 'work', when everything was shattered to nothingness.

CHAPTER 10

1

It was three months after Judy's arrival and I hade gone to Lurambi for a case of stock-theft. We had successfully arrested the rustlers and recovered the stolen heads of cattle; five prime beef bulls and had taken them to the Police Station where they woud be held until indentification in court, before being handed back to their rightful owner.

I was handing back the S.L.R. I had used for that duty when the report officer casually informed me that I had a visitor at home.

"What kind of visitor?" I asked him. I wasn't very much interested. I had so many visitors coming to my house. Some were plain nuisances. I would find a visitor waiting for me in my house just to tell me thank you for releasing his brother on bond! I had got used to them and hated them!

"Your brother," he answered me equally casually.

"Brother?" I asked surprised, "What brother?" The report officer was smiling slyly and I was just about to lose my strained temper. I had spent the day running up and down the forest in pursuit of stolen cattle and I was not in a very amiable mood.

"That's what the fellow said—he was drunk anyway . . .

I finished booking my return and walked purposefully towards my house. Something was telling me to hurry and yet I could not know what it was. I was tired and thought that the feeling of alarm was coming from the tiredness. Brother? Who would that brother be? I decided that if I found that he was a drunk coming to ask for his brother's bond, I was going to charge him for trespass!!

When I was about fifty yards from my house, I saw some four or five officers all standing outside my door and I quickened my pace. When I came to them, one of them muttered something like, "Thank God, you've come."

"What is happening here?" I asked waving at the door of my house which was closed.

"We don't know," answered one cop, "but whatever it is, it is not very constructive. There have been some thudding noises and when we came here, the door was closed and bolted and even our calls have not been answered. I think you'd better . . ." I did not let him finish. I went to the door and rapped it impatiently calling out; "Judy!!" There was no answer and I put my ear against the door. At first I could not hear anything; but after a second or two, I heard what I thought was rustling of clothes and a heavy sigh. The sounds seemed to come either from the bedroom or bathroom.

"Judy!" I shouted again and when no response came, I moved three steps backwards and then rushed at the door with my shoulder. The door was made of very hard wood and I bounced back, clutching my shoulder which felt broken.

I went to the door with my foot, aiming at the lock and my kick burst it open and I almost fell inside.

The scene that met my eyes shocked me. Littered every where were broken pieces of furniture. The radiogram speaker was also on the floor. But, what held my eyes was the scene on the sofa-set.

A man was astride Judy who was lying on her back. The man had a long gash on his face from which thick blood was still dripping and falling on Judy's upturned face. The man had both hands on Judy's throat and I guessed he was squeezing the life out of her. Judy had her mouth open and even as I looked, a drop of blood from the man's face dripped inside the mouth.

My violent entry did not seem to have been noticed by the man, who was still holding Judy's neck. I jumped over an upturned stool and reached them, gave the man a horse-kick bang on his face and sent him sprawling over his back to the corner of the room. I followed him there and administered another kick, this time aiming at his face, which he held in both his gory hands. He collapsed in a heap and I turned my attention to Judy who was already surrounded by the officers I had found outside my door. One had her blouse and bras open, spilling her ripe breasts, and massaging her chest. I thought that the officer was relishing his job.

180

I cleared them away and knelt beside her possessively, "Judy . . .
"Judy . . . my darling . . .' I called to her but her eyes were closed and
her arms were limp and lifeless. I frantically felt for her pulse and was
thankful to God that it was there, albeit faint.

I looked at her face and noticed that it was swollen. Her neck was
also swollen and I realised that what she needed was not massaging
but the attention of a qualified doctor. I braced myself, told the cops
in the house to check on the man at the corner who had all this time
been neglected and I lifted Judy in my arms. I checked her weight and
noticed that, despite her buxom appearance, she was light enough for
me to carry.

I started walking out of the house with two cops trailing me,
muttering apologies and at the same time trying to keep Judy's hands
and feet from swinging or getting in uncomfortable positions. I
looked straight ahead to avoid catching a glimpse of her increasingly
swelling neck and face and at last we got to the Police Station.

All cops rushed to me to see what was happening and I shouted at
them to stop gaping and get driver Kinyua as fast as possible. Two of
them ran in different directions while the rest wanted to know how it
had come that Judy's neck and face were swollen. I did not want to
tell them that I did not know and so I did not answer them.

Kinyua came running from behind the station and even without
the unnecessary questions of what happened, he hopped into the van
and told me to get in. I climbed with difficulty into the van, still
holding Judy in my hands. I placed her beside me on the seat so that I
could hold her and was relieved to note that she could sit by herself
and lean against me. I called her again but she did not answer.

Neither did she open her eyes.

When the van started, she briefly opened her eyes and tears
streamed from them. She closed them again. As we joined the
tarmac, Kinyua put the siren on and it screamed all the way to the
entrance of **Kakamega General Hospital.**

The hour was past 1700 hours and we found nurses engaged in
their idle banters, but a sharp word from Kinyua sent them
scampering here and there.

"This way please . . ." one was showing us the entrance into the

observation ward. We placed Judy on the provided bed and the
nurses started fussing over her and asking their questions:

"What happened to her?"

"Attempted murder by strangulation . . . ." I told her as I stretched
my arms. They were aching all over.

"How . . .?" One asked. She had here bespectacled eyes upon. I
almost put my hands on her neck to show her practically but, instead,
I raised my arms to my own throat, "Like this . . . ." I told her. Then
the senior nurse sent us out of the room: "Would you two wait
outside there," she pointed to the door, "we shall tell you of our
findings."

"Yes, of course," I answered promptly and we left the room. When
we were finally outside, Kinyua turned to me.

"Fred, what happened?" He looked concerned.

"I don't know. I guess that fellow is her brother. I found him
chocking the life out of her. Gosh! You should have seen the bizarre
spectacle! At first I thought he was raping her . . . he was on top of her
and there was blood everywhere . . .."

"Why would he want to kill her?" he asked looking far away.

"I can but guess. The way she came to live with me was not
approved by the family. You see she was running away from what she
called maltreatment by the father and brother . . . it's a long story . . . ."

2

Then, the sound of a siren came to our ears and we both turned
sharply towards the entrance of the hospital.

The police land-rover was coming full-speed, with its head-lamps
ablaze and the siren cutting into the still evening air. The storks on the
trees above our heads which were making their evening calls flew
away in a flurry of wings and when the siren was put off, the silence
that followed would have swallowed the boom of a cannon. The
driver stopped the car, jumped out, rushed to the back and half a

minute later, he re-appeared holding onto one end of a stretcher while another officer held the other side. They had to pass where we were standing and my heart jumped into my mouth when I saw the face of the casualty who was on the stretcher.

"Accident . . .?" Kinyua asked the driver of the land-rover.

"Yes. And near-fatal!" The driver of the land-rover answered, smiling wryly at me as they passed.

"That's the brother, Kinyua—damned it! I didn't know I had done so much damage to him!"

"You did that to him?" Kinyua asked astounded. He involuntarily moved a pace backwards to widen the gap between us!

"I had to!" I tried to sound apologetic. "He was killing her. He needed only another five minutes and we would have taken the woman to the morgue rather than the observation ward. But the cut on the face was still there when I got into the house. I only kicked him."

"But it looks like his head has been crushed between two rocks?" he said.

"That will be blood only . . . don't you remember how much blood you had on you after killing the leopard and yet you were not even bruised?" I reminded him, I cast my eyes at my shoe and noted that it was shining with clotted blood. I looked up at once. We had been standing there for over twenty minues and it was getting cold.

"Fred . . .!" someone called me from behind and I turned and saw nurse beckoning me. I almost ran to her. She ushered me into the observation ward and on looking at her I noticed that she was very sad. I avoided the couch on the right hand side of the room, where the nurses were hovering over someone and clucking their tongues with their eyes wide open and faces showing consternation. I strode to the bed on the left of the room.

Judy lay there. She was covered up to the neck and she appeared sound asleep. One nurse touched me on the upper arm and asked me,

"Your wife?" I nodded.

"She was pregnant . . ." The statement almost made me scream.

"I . . . I . . . don't . . . maybe . . ." I stammered.

"Yes. She was but unfortunately, she has miscarried. I guess she must have received a blow, and a heavy one, on her lower abdomen." She was no longer looking at me. I closed my eyes, bit my lower lip until I felt pain as a milllion thoughts whirled around my brain. I opened my eyes and for the first time directed them at the corner of the room. There was a china basin full of bloody clothes.

"You'd better go home and come to check on her tomorrow morning," she suggested and I started walking out. I was in a trance and my legs automatically lifted and fell and we came to the police van. That is when I noticed that Kinyua had been holding me all the time.

When I sat in the van, Kinyua started it and I heard myself utter: "That's it! May the bastard die!" but Kinyua did not say anything.

The drive back to the Station was occupied by thoughts of what the nurse had said. So Judy had conceived. Yes! I should have known. She had had mild maladies in the mornings, usually preventing her from joining me at breakfast table! I should have known. She also had started growing all soft and warm and slow in a lot of things. But then it was all over; too soon! The pregnancy had been pre-maturely terminated by her own brother! Did he do it deliberately— I wondered. Was he against her carrying my baby? My first progeny!

I felt pain as I imagined how wonderful it would have been to have had my first-born and by Judy!! I also vowed that her brother would pay for his act, through the nose.

The decision made, I felt relieved, sighed and turned to Kinyua.

"Thank you for all you have done for me, brother," I told him and except he was driving, I would have shaken his hand.

"Don't mention it . . . you could have done the same for me," he told me and smiled.

"Yes. I guess so," I told him as we parked the vehicle outside the Police Station.

I had expected a mammoth turn-out of officers and I left the van with a scowl and clenched fists, ready to tell any nosy inquisitors to go and jump in the lake! But my preparations were unnecessary as I found only the report officer and sentry at the station. Even the cells were unusually quiet.

I picked the O.B. to book the occurrence and then stopped short. What was I going to book? The assault on Judy? . . . the miscarriage? . . . the trespass by her brother? I could not make up my mind and so, after only reading a few of the day's entries, noting with relief that nothing of the episode had been booked, I closed the book and walked out towards the Ops. Room for Duty Officer's advice.

"You could land yourself in a mess in this one," he said sadly after I had told him the whole sorry story. He had listened without interrupting until I had come to the very last word. I had to tell him the whole truth and I trusted that he would understand why I did what I did and would not immediately order me to take myself to the cells!

"What do I do now, sir?" I asked him.

"Nothing! Don't do a thing. Don't book anything in the O.B. **Just let the matters follow their course. If even their father comes here,** don't talk to him about the episode. Just refer him to me if he has any questions to ask. I will also talk to the O.C.S. about it but be careful. **Don't even go to see that woman in the hospital. Keep off and call it** quits—for good. Okay?" he had turned all cop and his words almost had a scaring effect on me.

End up my love for Judy? Call it all up? Judy ! Judy! Judy! The first woman to carry my baby? Then I got my doubts. How old was the pregnancy? Had it been really mine? I decided to ask the nurse that question first thing in the morning.

"It's okay, sir. I will do that," I told him but I knew that at least I would go and check on her condition the following day. I would wake up early and be there at 0630 hours, just have a look at her and then rush back to the station. It would be secret of course, because I would have to obey the Duty Officer's word.

3

I walked out of the Ops. Room, feeling thoroughly but unfairly chastised.

I hurried to my house and found Njagi there. He had tidied the table-room and cleaned all the blood from the floor and the sofa-set. Faithful Njagi! He told me in a rush of words, " . . . they will have to look for another scene . . . not this house . . ." and I had no words with which I would have felt good enough to thank him. I checked on the door and noticed that he had repaired the earlier burst lock.

I went to the bedroom and the first thing to meet my eyes was Judy's dress on the bed. I'd have to pack her things and . . . I didn't know what to do with them. I went to the wardrobe and checked in the niche where we used to keep money.

Judy was a very thrifty girl and had managed my financial matters exceedingly well for the previous three months and I had felt so happy about it. Inside the niche, despite the awkwardness of the date, I found over five hundred shillings—enough to keep me going until the end of the month and I felt that I had many reasons for missing Judy—if I was going to call it quits. I picked one hundred shillings and joined Njagi in the table-room.

"Let's go to town and have a beer. I need one," I told him.

We went but Njagi would not allow me to buy the beer. He told me that he could afford to drown me in drinks and I let him proceed.

He had to hire a taxi for me at 2300 hours. I was so drunk I could not walk the short distance from town to the Police Station. That night, I pissed on the sheets which Judy had so carefully washed and ironed.

The following day I was roused from a drunken stupor by someone banging on my door, impatiently. I opened my eyes and had to close them immediately. They were aching and exposing them to light made them water. I rubbed and opened them once again. I checked on the wrist-watch, with the knocker still banging on the door and I could not believe my eyes. The watch indicated 1000 hours! I put the watch against my ear and heard it ticking. I could not believe it. I opened my mouth to tell whoever was knocking to stop it but I felt like I could not shout loud enough.

"Fred, Fred! Is he dead?" I heard the knocker ask.

"No! I am not dead!" I answered him as I swung my legs over the edge of the bed. I had removed only my shoes and coat and was otherwise fully dressed in socks, shirt and trousers I tried to stand up and staggered back onto the bed. The fellow at the door was telling me, "You come to the Station. The O.C.S. is waiting for you. You'd better have something pleasing to tell him. He is not in a very friendly mood!" I staggered out of the bedroom and went to the table-room. My head started a tom-tom as I walked to the kitchen, gurgled water and spat it out. I checked on the small kitchen cupboard and took four Aspirins from the bottle and washed them down with water. Why had I drunk so much? I asked myself as I went to the door and opened it, again blinking at the sunshine. The knocker, who turned out to be Nasivili, the day's sentry, was tapping his fore-finger on his wrist-watch.

"10:00 hours! What is wrong, Fred?" he asked me and I felt annoyed by the way he was looking at me.

"I think you have made your point clear. You have been sent to call me and that is all. Isn't it? Now go back to the Station." I told him as I slammed the door shut in his face. I went back to the bedroom and hurriedly changed my shirt and socks. I put on my coat and walked out of the house. My hair was cropped short and I just passed my hand over it. I did not need a comb.

I went straight to the O.C.S.'s office, feeling lousy from my self-inflicted malady and knocked on the door. He called me in and I entered and closed the door. He eyed me from head to toe, shook his head and looked at his wrist-watch. Not to be out-matched, I also looked at mine. 10:15 hours.

"I guess I don't have to tell you what time it is, seeing that you also have a wrist-watch but I would like to know whether you have formulated your own hours of reporting on duty?" He said and I was relieved to note that his voice was not harsh.

"No, sir. I overslept and . . . "

"I can see that. You want to tell me that you drunk too much last night?"

"No sir. I think that would be tantamount to . . ."

"To pleading guilty to a charge of failing to report on duty, which you have done anyway," he remarked. I was feeling that if I did not sit down, I would collapse and he must have noticed that.

"Sit down!" He offered me a seat and I thankfully sat down and folded my hands on my lap.

"I don't know what to tell you. I don't know how to start. You are **becoming unmanageable! Tell me; why can't you keep out of** trouble?" He was looking at me just the same way I used to look at an ex-convict while taking his finger-prints a second or third time.

"Sir, I think I can explain what happened." I told him.

"That I know. You abducted a girl and when the brother of the girl came to fetch her home, you knocked five of his teeth out!" Gosh! The way he said it, one would have thought he was there from the beginning to the end.

"That's not true, sir, I didn't abduct her. She is the one . . ."

"Forget it. The mess has been done. I am not asking you to tell me **how it all started. I would have liked to know how it came that you** almost killed the poor fellow."

"I guess I used too much strength . . . I mean I was annoyed. He was killing her. I would have done the same if I had found him with any other woman. Part of my duties as a Police Officer is to stop the **commission of atrocious offences . . ." I was raising my voice and he** waved me to silence.

"But it happened that this was a woman you loved?" He was smiling. I could not believe it. He was actually smiling. I felt something move inside my chest.

"Yes. I loved her." I declared.

"So much so that you were ready to kill for her."

"I guess so, sir." I told him. His smile was infectious and I found myself smiling.

"You can smile if you want," he said, still smiling. "Why I have called you here is to tell you to go to your house and bring all the clothes which the woman left there. Her father went to the hospital this morning and picked her when she was discharged. He came here and was threatening to sue you; but I warned him against it. I told him to first look for an excuse for his son's entry into police lines and the action he did there, before he raised his complaint and I can assure you that closed the chapter. What he does not want is you having anything to do with his daughter. Just go and bring all the clothes here and forget about the woman."

"There isn't much, sir. When she came to my house, she had only three dresses. I have bought all the others . . ."

"Just go and bring her clothes. Her own clothes, okay?"

"Yes, sir," I said and stood up to go.

"And next time you want to over-drink, choose a week-end, okay?"

"Yes, sir. Thank you, sir."

"What are you thanking me for?" he asked, the smile still playing over his lips.

"Well, sir, I must admit that I was worried about what would happen but now I feel . . ."

"Relieved—eh? Go and bring those clothes!" He shouted at me and I literally ran out of his office to the lines. I passed many cops who wanted to know what had transpired between me and the O.C.S. but I told them to go and ask the O.C.S. himself. I went to my house and packed Judy's clothes. Even what I had bought for her. They were too many and could not fit in the small suit-case in which she had carried her three dresses. I put them in my own bigger suit-case. I told myself that for all the love and happiness which she had given me the past three months, I could at least thank her by giving her the suit-case and the clothes. I wanted to write a note to her, to tell her that I still loved her and that as time went by, we would be together again, but I didn't. I thought her father or brother would receive the suit-case and would probably search it before handing it to her. I took the suit-case to the O.C's office and handed it to him.

"Everything is in there?" he asked me.

"Yes, sir. I thought there is no point of leaving old clothes in my house," I told him.

"Okay, get to the crime-branch office and start working. I will make sure you leave the office at 22.00 hours tonight—to compensate!" He said.

I went to the office. I could not work. I was cursing myself for having drunk the previous day. I had over-slept and had missed to see Judy in the morning. Then, I felt that it was all over. I guess our move was not blessed. I had to let her go and forget her.

4

The first step towards that would be getting myself another girl-friend. That would be easy, or so I thought. There were so many girls who at one time or another had told me they liked the length of my nose. Yes. There were plenty.

The mood at the Station changed against me again. I don't know what people want. Some commented that I had got away with the case too easily. Some even suggested that the O.C.S. who was my tribe anyway, had used tribal bias to snub the Assistant Chief and that that episode had strained the relations between the Police and other Government administration departments. What had seemed to be a relief for me had turned into a burden once again. I resorted to the only solution I thought I knew: drinking. Drinking and picking whores all over town.

One evening, about three weeks from 'Judy's day' as I called it, the O.C.P.D. caught me necking with his nurse-girlfriend. The bugger was old enough to be the girl's father but he would not see that. The following day, I was transferred from Kakamega Division in Western Province to the Northern Division of Nairobi Area. I guess the bosses in Western Province wanted to transfer me so far from their sight that we would hardly meet—either socially or officially.

However, the transfer livened my hopes. At last I would be nearer home and I would be able to more easily contact my poor parents.

Nairobi, however, is where the fast pace of development both in good and evil at first overwhelmed me and I had to stay for a long time **without coming to grips with the pace. It was there where calamity** followed calamity.

I then made up my mind that I would cease to be a cop. The things I had done in the service would surely bar my promotion. Four disciplinary convictions and two warning letters were lodged in my file. I did not want to age a constable. I would have liked to be promoted to a sergeant; so that I could live up to the lie I had told Mary. All the other boys I was with in college had been promoted some were even Chief Inspectors.

One day, on Tom Mboya Street, I bumped into Wafula, who was such a dirty thick-head in college. I was whiling my off-duty away and looking for a bribe here and there..Wafula was in uniform and you know what rank he held? I.P! An Inspector. He told me that he was the deputy O.C.S. at Bondeni Police Station. Wafula? I did not want to think of him as deputy O.C.S.

He asked me what my rank was and instead of telling him, I wrote the word Constable on a piece of paper and handed it to him to read. He muttered an apology and bought me some drinks.

I felt cheated alright, but what was there to be done? I was afraid that some day Wafula might be transferred to Parklands Police Station as the officer-in-charge and God knows I would not call him 'sir' even if he wore the medals of a General!!

The others had been made Non-Commissioned Officers. People like Njoroge, who could not even make his boot shine in college! I did not want to think of his likes. I remembered that, when we were sitting for the Police Literacy Examination, Njoroge had made everybody, including the invigilator laugh. There was an essay question which required the candidates to write a short composition on 'Little things that annoy me'. Njoroge finished the paper in three minutes. We did not know whether he had refused to do that question or whether he had written the composition earlier, thus needing only to hand it in, but on looking at his paper, when we were handing them to the invigilator, I noticed that, Njoroge, besides his index number and heading of the essay, had put only one word: 'MOSQUITOES'

Another day, I asked him what he thought a sexton was and he told me without hesitation that a sexton must be a woman with a one-ton posterior!

But, maybe I was wrong. Maybe the Wafulas and the Njoroges were wiser than me. That is why they had been promoted and left me at the base of the ladder, marking time!

I had to resign! Damn it! I had to. I could not stand the humiliation any more.

People like Kiarie whose uniforms never lacked a dirty spot were also inspectors! Others like . . . there was really no point in counting them. Those who had not been promoted had resigned and were employed elsewhere. Why not me? Why not resign and go through what the others had gone through when they were seeking jobs?

My decision to resign was also influenced by the transfers. Never settled in one place and on being transferred, my marching orders invariably included a confidential note to the receiving officer since, on arrival at any new station, I would be called to the boss's office and get a warning, 'not to take the indiscipline' I had at the previous Station to his Station.

Then came the crunch and I felt like I could kill all the Police Officers in the Republic before killing myself. Something happened that I, with all my patience, could not stand. I could not even believe it. I could not believe that the Police, being my employers, could take me to court and charge me with a fabricated charge and then, I remain in the same Police Force, calling some of those same bosses 'sir'. There was no point. There would be no 'policemanship' in me when I met on the street with someone with whom I had shared a cell in remand. I was too proud for that.

2

The dull yellow cold beams of the early morning sun were just peeping through the holes in my window-curtain as I opened my eyes and blinked. I had repeatedly reminded myself that I should buy new curtains. I consulted my watch. A cheap Kienzle; a gift from a friend. It indicated 16:45 hours, 18th March, the day that I would, for the first time in my life, stand in the dock as an accused person, to answer a charge of wrongful confinement and assault. Wrongful Confinement? By me? A Police Officer? If an arrest by a Police Officer, having all powers, privileges and immunities as conferred to him by the law, can be termed wrongful, who then should arrest criminals!! Wrongful! I wish they had used the term 'unlawful'. With the word 'Law' in the charge, maybe I would have felt that what they were charging me with was legal.

I yawned. My eyes were burning. My head was still heavy with sleep. I had hardly slept. I had spent the whole night dodging in and out of short naps which were interrupted by one monstrous dream. Every time my eyes closed in a doze, a picture would form in front of my eyes. It would start remotely, with a running rider-less horse, **which had no mane. The horse would be running towards a pool of** water at the far end of a paddock. But before reaching it, it would turn into a dog and the dog would be chasing me. I would try to run away from the bare-toothed monster but would make no progress. The dog would start slashing at my calves with its long fangs and then I would fall down. Then, the dog would stand on my chest and start licking my face with its blood-red tongue. I would scream and wake myself up to find the echo of the scream still within the confines of my room. I would fumble for my box of matches, strike one for a light. I don't see the horse now, but sweat is oozing out of my face. I discard the match and wipe the sweat from my face with the corner of my bed-cover. Time would go as I stare into the darkness. Then, I would doze again hopefully, but unsuccessfully. The horse would reappear and the last scene would be incomplete when I managed to fully wake up.

I rolled out of bed and slipped on my slippers and wrapped a towel round my middle. Another yawn and I walked towards the door of my room. I was surprised to note that it was not bolted. I must have forgotten to bolt it last night in my mental torments.

I went out to the first common bath-room and found that there was an earlier bird than me. Someone was having his shower and whistling through the water-spray.

I went to the next bath-room and closed the door as soon as I had **opened it. Shit! Someone had mistakenly relieved himself there.** Can't blame him though. Without lights, all cats would look black at night . . . or was it deliberate? I wanted to go to the third bath-room but the 'whistler' in the first bath-room had had enough of the cold waters and was leaving the bath-room. He grunted a greeting and I grunted back. I went into the bath-room and peeled off my towel and pants; bracing myself for the first splash of the cold waters. The water was not very cold though. I soaped myself and tried to whistle through the spray as I showered but I could not form a tune. So, I concentrated on making a clean body of myself. You never know. I may make myself a good impression on the magistrate's mind, by looking clean. I have heard that a person's appearance may work wonders in the mind of the magistrate. I sauntered back to my house and put the kettle on. I had to have coffee because I was not sure whether or when I would have another cup. In prison, they do not serve you with coffee. It would be too costly owing to the inflated number of prisoners we are having in jails these days.

I carefully combed my hair and proceeded to dress in my Sunday-best; new socks—bought when our pay had been increased—about three months ago, brown safari boots, old but cleaned for the occasion, a wrangler jean—navy blue and smart—real smart, a terry young shirt, only five months old and, although the collar is starting to lose its deep blue dye, still looking good. A heavy tweed jacket, **normally reserved for dates with new girls but has to be used now** because of the dire importance of the occasion. A wide Klook tie— very immaculate and finally, my most fashionable Y-front pants.

I strapped my Kienzle back on my wrist and drunk two mugs of coffee. Then, I brushed my teeth feeling them shrink from the cold water after the steaming coffee. This was to remove the bitter after-taste of black coffee. Ready to move, I picked my wallet and counted the small change I had. Twenty-five shillings in currency notes and seventy-five cents in coins. Gosh! It was only the eighteenth and I was that broke!

I picked my cigarette packet and found that there were only seven sticks. Enough to keep me going until . . . when? I suddenly realised that I did not know what tomorrow would have in store for me. Of course I had been assured by the police—fellow colleagues—that I would be released on bond after my plea but this assurance was slowly turning into mist as I locked my quarters and pocketed the key. I walked towards the place where we would take an official car to town—a vehicle that I would not be able to use again from them until the criminal proceedings preferred against me were over. I had already been interdicted and was on half-pay.

As I walked, slowly, puffing on my cigarette, I weighed the chances of being released on bond or being remanded in custody. It all depended on the way the magistrate saw it. But his word would determine whether I would see the inside of my quarters tonight or the four grey walls and a wired air-aperture. That is what I call power. Just a word from a fellow human being like me and the graph of life changes.

3

The ride to town was rather quiet except for the usual remarks that cops can't spare: a lady dressed too heavily in the warm weather; a motorist who leaves his lane and tries to overtake but is forced back into his original lane; about how much longer the meagre monthly emoluments were going to be awaited etc.

Nevertheless, they avoided one thing: commenting on my summons to appear in court. They were only too aware that their comments would have multiplied my steadily growing hopelessness rather than easing my conscience. Only the driver wished me luck as I dropped outside the court-house.

I lit a fresh cigarette and puffed furiously. It was only 0820 hours then, a clear fourty minutes before the magistrate arrived in court. My summons had instructed me to report to the court at 0900 hours and remain in attendance until otherwise directed by the magistrate or a Police Officer.

As I walked towards the court room, a cop came along in an apparent eleventh hour rush; but I stopped him, to kindly show me where the toilets were. He must have mistaken me for one of those senior young men to whom he dutifully owes respect because he both directed and saluted me! I felt pleased. At least it seemed my Sunday-best was working. It would probably make the magistrate smile, I thought.

"John Kimtai, Peter Mwasya, James Fredrick Wamatu, you are all charged with wrongful confinement contrary to section 263 of the Penal Code and Assault contrary to section 251 of the Penal Code in that, on the 26th day of October . . ." We were standing, me and my two co-accused. My heart was beating in an usual rythm and I was feeling dry-crawed. I could also feel some slight tremor around my knees. The magistrate rumbled on until he finished reading the particulars of the charge as the Police had framed it. I was quite surprised and very angry to hear some of the fabrications. Damn them! Did they have to tell open lies? Was it to impress anyone and if so whom? I should think that if the idea was to impress, then the impression went beyond Criminal Records Office finger impression!

"Do you plead guilty or not guilty?" the magistrate asked us.

"Not guilty, Your Honour . . ." the voice of Kimatai, followed by the croak of Mwasya as he said: "not guilty, Sir." Then, I braced myself to give my word. My word had been predetermined by the previous night's conversation between me and the investigating officer. He had told me, and this in a conspirator's whisper, to plead 'not guilty' after which I would be released on bond, pending hearing, on a date which the magistrate—preserve his almost almight power!—would fix. I have heard that the hearing date is again determined by the diary. A mere pen and paper job. If 1st. April is engaged, so to speak, 2nd. and 3rd. April have got to be looked into.

If both those are also filled up, then, 4th. April will do.

Anyway, I did not need to scramble my mind for so long.

"Your case will be heard on 19th. and 20th. of May and you will be remanded in custody." The magistrate finished.

"Your honour, could we please be released on bond?" My voice. I could not even recognise it myself. It sounded like a dreamy croak. When the hunter gets the hunted, the blood spills. When alternatively, the hunter turns into the hunted, blood also spills but this time, thick blood. Treacle, thick blood. I could feel it choking me. I could feel it with every desperate thump-thump of my heart.

"They are asking to be released on bond, Your Honour," the interpreter told the magistrate.

About half a minute passed before the magistrate looked up from his scribbling and set his eyes on us, eyes which were scaring my guts cold. For no apparent reason, the eyes reminded me of my twenty year dead grand-mother. She had the same eyes. Slightly curved inwards and slightly blood-shot around the irises.

"Prosecutor, do you have any objection to their release on bond?" he finally asked. The prosecutor stood up, pulled the lapels of his well-starched jacket and said; "No, Your Honour." They can be released on bond." My heart started dancing inside its cage. I felt relief flowing from my forehead all the way to my belly. Even my **balls kind of nudged one another. So the police had been right! We** would be released on bond!

"With or without sureties?" the magistrate did not even take his eye from the table.

"With sureties, Sir," replied the Police prosecutor.

"The accused persons are remanded in custody until 2nd. of April when they will be brought for mention but they may be released on bond of five thousand shillings each with a surety of like amount for each." The magistrate put his pen on his desk, rapped the table once and was out of the court even before the scanty crowd of spectators of justice had enough time to bow him out. Then, we all sat down.

4

Surety? How the hell would I get one? Although most of my friends knew about my predicament, I had not told any particular one to come and stand surety for me. I had decided to keep my problems to myself. After all, I had been so sure I would be released on my own free bond that the question of surety did not occur at all. I knew the catch in the surety clause; but I had to hear it from somebody else.

"What qualifies anyone to become a surety for another?" I found myself asking the prosecutor. He grinned at us and told us that the qualifications needed were either a car and having the log-book in one's name or a piece of land and having the land registration certificate in one's name. The same person must not be a Police Officer or an Officer of the court.

He also hinted to us that we, as Police Officers, should know what a surety was. He was wearing an embarrassed smile and I felt like clouting it off his face.

Then, I started feeling the pinch. I realised that I was no longer free. I was a prisoner. I had done what the Kikuyus term 'eating with a double edged dagger'. I got so shocked after the realisation that, I was not even aware of where the policeman on my left, who was tugging at my elbow was taking me. I only half-heard him talking about putting us in safe custody, pending the arrival of our sureties. Safe custody!

We were marshalled through flights of stairs while some pressmen were pushing one another to get a proper position to take photographs of us. Stupidly, I felt kind of important. For the press to cover my short walk from the court room to the cells!! It was something that had not occurred to me before.

We were taken to the Police cells and immediately I was there, I fumbled in my pocket and produced a cigarette which I lit. I puffed on it slowly, letting the shock and the impact thereof settle. I was on my fifth puff when the cop sentry walked to where we were standing.

He was a cop I had known for a long time during my service and I smiled nervously at him, hoping that he would register surprise at seeing me behind bars, possibly utter a none-too-sympathetic '*pole bwana*', but he did not smile. He looked at me straight in the face and **told me without mincing words that I was a prisoner and I was not** supposed to smoke, repeat, not supposed to smoke, in cells. I continued wearing my smile and attempted my humour on him by telling him that I had not been searched and so, I had slipped the cigarettes through into the cells.

That did it! He ordered us to remove all the things we had in our pockets and place them on the floor. I thought he was going to take **all the things for 'safe?' custody but he picked only our cigarettes and matches and ordered us to pocket the rest of the things. Then, he** pointed a finger, straight at my nose and warned or rather reminded me that I was a prisoner and that his job was to see to it that I did not escape from custody.

He added insult to his lengthy submission by saying that he knew, that ex-police officers were worse than ordinary *wananchi* and that he would make sure that we did not escape. "*Apana mwagia mimi unga yangu, bwana*". He sealed his trap. I felt like landing a ten-stone punch on his dirty mouth but then, I did not. I just looked at him, looked at my cigarette stub smouldering on the floor and made a mental calculation that, if I survived to finish the case, either being convicted or acquitted, I would quit being a cop immediately. I **would not, repeat not, be in the same Police Force with a mug like** that sentry!

5

His behaviour reminded me of what a good friend of mine had told me once. We were drinking. It was my first meeting with him since I **had joined the Police Force, at the lowest rung. Ready to climb? And I** had just finished telling him some of my interesting adventures in the Force. He had looked at me steadily for a long time and then deliberately cleared his throat before saying:

"Wamatu, what I am going to tell you is strictly between me and you but, please, listen to me very carefully. You have chosen the wrong career. You can never make a good policeman. I know you only too well and that is why I am telling you this. You see, your kind of life is not what a cop would be expected to lead. You are too care-free. You are too social . . . I mean . . . you are so easily sociable that you might as well make friends with prisoners in custody and you might as well go ahead and release them and land yourself in hot soup—I mean they will charge you of aiding prisoners to escape.

"You would do quite well as a teacher although I doubt whether **you would resist the temptation to take your class, I mean the girls, to** bed. You see, in the Police Force, there is something like a curse. You'll find that you will lose all your friends, me included . . . don't interrupt me!" he said as I tried to put up my hand to defend myself and my fellow cops. I wanted to tell him that not all cops were bow-legged but he would not listen and he continued with this tirade:

"You will find that there is a contagious disease in the Force that somehow, despite all efforts by anyone, affects all of you. Corruption! You will follow the shilling in my palm all the way to jail. Like a dog will follow a man with a bone. Once a dog of corruption, always a dog of corruption. There is always a bone in the bargain. That bone is money. You will take it the first time—want more—take—want—take—want until you are jailed because when you start depending on a bribe for daily subsistence, then there is no way that you will be able to budget your pay without the extras!

"Look at me; I am only a P.2 teacher.—'*Kamwalimu*'—as you policemen call us; but I am doing my job quite well. I am married with two kids and well . . . I don't know whether you have any **proper girlfriend, except maybe the numerous professional pros-**titutes you cops claim to own . . . don't interrupt me! You see . . . now, what was I saying? . . . I see . . . about marriage—why don't you quit before they have corrupted your brain and join us? You might as well share your brains at least with your brothers and sisters in this world. This country needs more teachers than policemen. Of course, I know your standard of education but that will not be a very big hindrance. You will start low but with your intelligence and aptitude, you can rise!"

He had paused and had taken a long swig from his bottle. He had swallowed, blinked and pulled again on his bottle. I was pondering what he had just said. I was just about to open my mouth to defend the whole force when I realised that, what Michael Gathambo had told me, was true. But, it could not be accepted.

"No. Mike, we can not all take one job. Who would be arresting the criminals if all people in the Republic hated being cops like you do?" I asked.

"Who was arresting them before you joined them? I am not telling every bow-legged, boot-licking copper-mug to resign. I am only telling you—as a friend. Pull out when the going is still smooth and please, let us not argue about that!!"

We had continued with this banter for another twenty minutes before Michael decided to go. He had made some sincere remarks to me and some had touched where he had intended them to scythe— my conscience. One of the most memorable remarks was: "I wish they'd sack you before you waste all your brains on them!!" Coming from a friend, I found that remark very threatening.

But, like all good friends did on me, Michael's advice bounced off like a golf-ball hit against a concrete wall. Once a dog, always a dog. I was going to remain a cop and Michael could go on teaching his brothers and sisters.

At that time, I could not even dream of being in a cell. Me? A cop?

I gave the sentry a long, hard look and visioned him as a dog, licking its own vomit. That picture of the cop as a dog somehow consoled me. The cop in turn, must have realised the murderous thoughts that were going on in my head because he quickly turned and went to sit on a chair at the corner. Next to the chair was a riot baton.

His intermezzo served as a good interval. I looked at my two friends and noticed that they too had understood our plight. We had been condemned as ex-police criminals even before the magistrate had convicted us.

We sat on a wooden bench and for no apparent reason, we avoided talking. **What would talking have helped? We silently waited for the** sureties to come. We all know they were not coming; but we did not want to put it in words. We did not want to believe it.

6

At 15.30 hours, things started happening. First, all prisoners were **moved from police cells to prison cells. This killed even the small** flicker of hope that was glimmering in my soul. We were actually handcuffed and ushered into the cells. I was handcuffed to a man who was charged with murder! We started loose talk.

Every prisoner wanted to know what the other prisoner had done. I found some sort of friendly and sincere sympathy among them. Peter told them of our cases and by the time he finished, the other prisoners were sadly shaking their heads and muttering incomprehensible words, all aimed at consoling us.

Some ten minutes later, a Prison Warder came and opened the door to our cell. He hustled us out and told us to squat on our haunches. He told us, in a pitiable tone that, it was his unfortunate task to see that we did not escape from custody and, woe unto whoever tried to make him fail in that task. He started calling out our names.

"James Fredrick Wamatu!" he bawled.

"Yes," I stammered. I was still squatting.

"James Wamatu!'" he repeated, looking directly at me and curling his thin lips back in a snarl; just like a dog.

"That's me!" I shouted. I thought he must have been deaf not to have heard my first answer.

"Stand up!" He shouted. He was menacingly waving his metal key-chain. I stood up awkwardly feeling like crying.

"When you are called here, you have to answer respectfully!" he shouted at me. I was feeling very embarrassed. My six feet and one inch height could not allow me to stand straight as I was still attached to my fellow prisoner—the murderer—with the fetters.

"How?" I asked innocently. Honest; I did not know how to answer a Prison warder. According to the dress he was in, he had no rank symbols and I thought that he was a private or something. Although I was a constable, I did not think that I should call a Warder, Sir. Infact I thought he should call me Sir!

"Have you ever visited a motor garage here in Nairobi?" he asked. He was looking at me like something the cat brought in.

"Yes, I have."

"Do you know what they do to bent metals at the garage?"

"Of course, they straighten them."

"Well, for your information, I will repeat what I have just told you. **I do not know why you are here but it is my unfortunate duty to see** that you do not escape from custody. This is a job I have been given by the Government of the Republic of Kenya. At the same time, it is my duty to see that the bent metals in your criminal mind are straightened," he said this and then he stood on his right heel and swung a fist at my poor unprotected face.

The bang could be heard all over the room as I catapulted over the **heads of the other prisoners, head over heels. I did not fly far though; the chain held to the murderer's wrist and served as a brake. I felt the metal bite into my wrist. I also tasted salt in my mouth where the** son-of-a-bitch warder had hit me. I sat down properly and he pointed an accusing finger at me.

"The Government has found that you are not fit to stay in a free society and that is why you have been brought here. When I call your name, you have to say, '*Affande*' or if you think you know English, 'Sir'. Failure to do that will be earning you a fist just like the one you got now, every time your name is called." He gloated. I moved my tongue around my mouth and felt the place where the skin had ruptured after the impact. I swallowed the blood, as there was nowhere to spit, hating it and hating the warder so much that, except I knew that he would call his fellow warders who would clobber me to death, I would have challenged him to remove the handcuffs and give me five minutes for a man-to-man fight with him. He was flogging a dead horse. God! I felt like dying. Why must some things happen? I felt tears well in my eyes and my nose started running. My hanky was on my left-hand side trousers pocket and I had a very difficult time removing it with my right hand. I was fettered on the left. I awkwardly blew my nose with one hand, wiped the tears from my eyes and sobbed once.

"James Fredrick Wamatu!" the Warder called again. I felt that I would be failing even my prisoner self if I called him Sir or *Affande*, I felt that even if it had been at gun-point, I would not have called the stupid bully 'sir'.

"Yes," I said huskily. I was looking at him with cobra eyes. I thought he was going to hammer the subject of Sirs and *Affandes* again, but he did not even seem to have noticed the ommission. He proceeded to call the other names while each answered *Affande* or Sir.' I guess the warder felt so much of a hero after being called *Affande* twenty times and Sir twelve times!

Our handcuffs were removed and then we were all stripped to the skin. I had repeatedly come across the word 'Thorough Search' in my cop career, but I had always believed that, to conduct the search whereby someone is supposed to be completely naked, one is taken to a private place, stripped and then searched. This was a different case all together. It was like a parade or show of manhood! Long black uncircumcised ones; brown bent pricks, short thick ones, hammer-headed ones; unproportionally large balls and other variable specimens were all displayed here!! I looked down at my incher and noticed that it had a tendency of inclining on the left ball. Hell!! My own nakedness on parade in front of all kinds and sorts of criminals!! I felt desperate. I felt lost. I felt all pains and aches that I had never felt before.

The warders came then. They carefully went through our clothes and then came the most humiliating part of the whole operation.

We were each told to stand with our legs wide apart. Then we were told to bend forwards so that the warders could check whether we had hidden any cigarettes in our arses!!! Goddamned them! What did they think we were? How would I slip a cigarette in my posterior orifice??

I felt tears burning inside my eyes but I fought them back. I felt a choking sensation in my throat but I fought off the persistent urge to scream. I would have given anything I owned in the world to get out of that torture chamber. I would have given all, even my life to get out of the place. I wished I had not joined the copper mugs! I wished, oh how I wished, but, like the old saying goes, there were no horses.

The few prisoners who had a few cigarette stubs in their clothes received several slaps from the warders. I wondered whether it was legal to beat up a handcuffed prisoner, but I reserved the question for a later date. The punch I had received from one of the warders had reminded me of a framed message in my room: 'Never argue with a fool' and I wondered who was more of a fool than the other one—the warder or me. I decided that I was more foolish than the warder because I had managed to get myself to a position where I would be at the mercy of the semi-literate bastards! What a fool I felt!

We were then ordered to redress and our names were called again. There were about ten warders now, all ranging from the rank of Private to Superintendent. I managed to answer when I was called although a lump in my throat was obstructing me. I was also careful to say Sir this time. You never know. If one fool does a stupid thing, the same thing would still be stupid even if done by a million fools. I did not for once think that a Prison Officer could have a higher brain—because of his rank—than the lowest rank—the warder—I had met. Also, their number could not stop them doing anything stupid!

We were again handcuffed and marched, two-two, to the waiting lift on the Prison Safe-Custody Transporters. We were locked in from outside and our custodians went and sat at the reserved partition between the driver's cab and the rest of the truck. The vehicle croaked into life after the fifth ignition kick and lurched slightly as it started on the road to hell!! Again, I was surprised to see that we were still handcuffed even when the vehicle was moving. I wondered what would happen if by a devilish catastrophe, the truck overturned. We would be still linked to one another in chains with only one free hand! I said a short silent prayer.

As we were driven along Uhuru Highway, I felt a change in my mood. I suddenly did not care what would happen to me. I was even almost anxious to see what went on inside the prison barbed wires. I felt that, if I couldmanage to live through the torments, I would have a story to tell my friends. Already, there was enough to keep me busy talking for a whole week. Yes, why not see what the warders did right inside their kingdom!!

The so-called thorough search by the warders had not lived up to its expectations. A few prisoners lit some stubs of cigarettes which must have been hidden in thier noses or mouths. A half-inch stub would go through four mouths before the filter started fizzling. A newly acquired friend of mine offered me a butt and I puffed only twice before the filter divorced the ember!

On arrival at the remand prison, we were again searched. This time in an open yard with about three hundred and one eyes on my naked body. Prisoners and warders and anyone else who is allowed access into the barbed wires was inspecting my nakedness. There was even a warder with only one eye.

Anyway, after the first humiliation, I had developed some very strong immunity. I hardly noticed the gazes from all sides. Even when my clothes were handed back to me, I walked for a few paces from the rest of the prisoners, just to give the spectators a better view of myself before dressing. The belt and tie, shame on me; for having donned a tie! were however taken away. Even my hanky. Also my wallet plus the little change I had. My Kienzle too. I felt almost naked without the watch. It had become so much a part of me.

These items were carefully booked down against our names in a big register and then we were taken to a stinking store where we were told to pick blankets.

Every order on instruction was being passed to us in an excessively authoritative tone. Even the 'one-eye' shouted at us to be quick about picking our blankets. I looked keenly at the hole where his right eye once was and when he noticed my steady gaze he shyly turned to one side and unnecessarily pushed a prisoner who had already picked his blankets and was waiting for the next in the chain of command.

There was a scramble for the less tattered blankets but I waited until the others had picked their choices before taking the two last ones. I could see through them. They were as thick as mosquito nets!! We were then paraded to an open area where our supper was supposed to be served. We were given beans in aluminium half-bowls-half-sufurias and a white-clad convicted prisoner would add a ladle-full of what appeared to be a half-fermented malt, by look and smell, into the beans. I felt the very first signs of getting sick after merely smelling the concoction. Anyway, hunger won. I had tasted nothing the whole day except the morning mugs of coffee and my bitter saliva.

I sat on my blankets and dipped my fingers into the mud coloured mixture. We were not offered any spoons and I did not ask for one. I felt solidness just below the floating beans and when I removed the fingers, I noticed that there was some greying substance at the tips. I dipped my fingers again and produced a lump of watery '*ugali*'. This time, the sickening sensation I had felt before escaped my throat and I felt a rush of bile and saliva fill my mouth. I looked right and left and noticed that none of my surly masters was looking at me. I spat into the bowl and wiped my mouth with the back of my hand. Some of the prisoners were looking at me with surprise intermingled with awe. I was still brooding when one of them, white-clad prisoners, asked me whether I had had enough of the food. I told him yes and before I could say 'Industrial Area', he had the bowl in his hands and was dipping his fingers into it and stuffing his mouth with what appeared to be brown *ugali* which he got from the bowl. I got so surprised that I found myself staring at him unbelievingly. Two minutes and the food was gone. He even had the courtesy to mutter a faint thank you before his eyes started darting among the other prisoners foraging for more left-overs. I decided that he was a mad crank and I left him to his foray.

We were then taken to separate cells. I watched my friends go with a sinking heart. The cell into which I was taken was occupied by about eighteen other prisoners most of whom I recognised as cheap pick-pockets and petty thieves from around the City. They also recognised me and, within seconds of my arrival, they were all shouting at me:

"What is a copper doing here?"

"Have you been bribed?"

"Tell us, copper, what makes you come to visit our holiday resort?

"Maybe he has come to record my statement."

"Or you stole?"

"Let him do some parade for us!"

"Yes, copper, by the left, quick march!"

"Hey, cop . . ." they were then pushing me between themselves. Everyone of them wanted to touch me. One pinched my nose while another was fumbling with my zip. I guess he wanted to feel the size of my balls, but the zip is as far as he got.

8

I punched him so hard on the nose that I felt my whole arm jar against the impact. He, in turn, landed flat on his back, with a well of blood where his nose stuck from his face. The rest of them scampered away from me and I opened my mouth for the first in a long time:

"If any of you would like to see the sun tomorrow morning, just keep off me. If on the other hand, anyone of you has written his last will and testament, let him try his hand on me!" I said sharply. I meant it. I was ready for murder then!

They were looking at me only when I was not looking at them directly. Then, one stepped forward and came to help his colleague who was still lying on the floor at my feet. I mistook his kind act as an intention to assault me and kicked him so hard on his balls immediately he was within reach. He screamed and doubled, holding his balls and that is when the door to our cells was flung open by a warder. He opened his eyes a trifle wider, when he perceived the scene.

"What is happening here?" he asked. He was still. He was looking at my still clenched fists.

209

Ask them," I answered him waving my hand to cover the whole bunch of prisoners. He turned his gaze on them, and one stepped forward;

"They were beaten by this . . . policeman," he accused me.

"Are you a policeman?" the warder asked me in a voice that was almost a whisper.

"Yes," I whispered back, although I felt that the absolute true answer I should have given should have been; 'I don't know.

"And who brought you to this cell?" he asked and even before I had a rude-enough answer to give him, he hastily added, "take your blankets and come with me."

I folded my two blankets under my left arm, jumped over the legs of the fellow I had punched, who was then sitting on the floor, holding his head between his bloody hands.

Outside the cell, the warder turned to lock the other prisoners in. They had started an insulting competition—all words aimed at hurting me, but I was already out of the cell and thus out of reach. When the warder had locked and tested the door, he turned to me.

"What is your name?"

"Wamatu,—James Fredrick Wamatu."

"And why didn't you tell us that you are a policeman?"

"Well, I thought you knew—I mean is it all that important? After all none of you has asked me what I was or am since I was handed over to you at the law courts."

"Were you just alone, I mean the only Police Officer?" The word officer sounded like 'Lucifer', to me.

"No, we were three—the other two must have been taken to other cells.

"Okay, you sit here," he indicated the ground, "while I go and look for your friends." He hurriedly left me and I started biting my finger nails. I felt that I had released some of my pent-up feelings by delivering that punch and kick. I stretched my right hand fingers and they made a satisfying cracking sound. I rolled my tongue inside my mouth and felt where the other warder had punched me. I smiled at myself.

My mind attempted to make out what my punishment would be, punishment for punching and kicking other prisoners. The chances of taking me to court would be remote indeed but the mugs might decided to mete out justice their own way. What would they do to me? I was so absorbed in my thoughts that I did not hear the warder approaching. His voice sounded excessively loud when he called my name.

"Okay, now, let's go," he said and I turned and saw my other two friends. I felt more at ease with them than in the company of the other prisoners: rapists and sodomites!!

9

Being a cop aint' so bad after all. They changed our tattered blankets and gave us newer ones. We were taken to a different cell—the three of us. Inside that cell, we found four other prisoners. We were told that we would stay there overnight while arrangements for proper 'accommodation' were being made. The warder promised us that he would see to it that we were given our own separate cell.

He then asked if any of us wanted anything like food or . . . and I was the first one to answer. The contrast between the bully warders and this almost polite warder was so great and it had so mesmerised me that I almost shouted:

"Yes, some food please."

"Okay, then, I will be coming back," he said and we all heard his boots clatter–clatter away. I smiled at my two friends and they smiled back. I wanted to brag to them about the episode in the previous cell but I held my tongue because of the other prisoners.

I looked at the new specimens of prisoners that I had as companions and found that, one was extremely dirty. From head to his shoe-less feet. The other three were cleaner although one appeared to have been half-shaven on one half of his face while the other side had a bushy growth of both beards and side-burns. They were all half-naked, with only trousers on—no shirts.

At that time, I had no idea that I was in the company of ex-Mathare patients. They looked quite normal—on the face of it. Even the way they conversed with us was quite normal.

The warder came back with three platefuls of beans. He must have miraculously known about my dislike for the *ugali* because he gave me a bowl full of beans only. The only problem was salt. It was irregularly applied and I could have a bite with and another without even a trace of salt. All the same, I did not complain. The action of the new warder were so friendly and polite that I felt that he was kind of apologising on behalf of the other warders.

He chatted with us for about twenty minutes while we munched our mealies, assuring us that we would be okay in his hands but warning against provoking the wrath of some of the warders who, as he put it, thought that prisons were their eternal living places. He told us his name—Fetus Muriithi—and said we were welcome to call on him any time we had a problem like of sending mail if we wanted anything that was within the regulations of the prisoners. We murmured our thanks.

Hey! That was good. The meal was only beans but it tasted good to me. Also, I felt good to have noticed that, amid the scum and filth of the prison warders, there was at least one with a reasoning capacity. I did not require anyone's sacrifices or extreme favours. All I needed was understanding, only.

By the time he left, my morale had been raised at least three degrees.

We asked the other prisoners who they were and what they had done and for the first time, I noticed some semblance of insanity in them. The half-shaven started by telling us how he had been arrested for stealing a gear-box but when the story was half-told, the stolen item turned into a complete wheel and by the end of the story, he was referring to it as a motor-vehicle.

The other two told us incoherent stories which were plain lies and did not make any sense.

The last one told us in a boastful tone of how he had raped a White woman and how he had been admitted to Mathare Mental Hospital and how he had raped a female mental patient there, gloating over the details so much that I felt disgusted. His analysis kind of triggered off the reserves of the others and they started talking. They all gave us their stories of insanity and at the end of it all, I was sure that they were insane. I was locked in a cell with nutters!!

Beause I had only two blankets, I folded one on the floor and felt it with my hand. I could feel the stone hardness through the light sheen of comfort that was created by the blanket. The nutters advised us to remove all our clothes; if we did not want the clothes to become breeding nurseries for bed-bugs and allied blood suckers.

I stripped off all my clothes and remained with only pants. We hung our clothes over the air-aperture but they obstructed the scanty air that was filtering through it and so we had to remove them from there. I folded mine into a pillow and my two colleagues followed suit.

The air was already getting stale. We did not need to cover ourselves anyway. There was enough warmth as it was. There was also another stench emanating from the other prisoners that was enough to make one sweat.

We huddled ourselves at one corner and I pretended to be fast asleep. I could not sleep, however. Not with a mad man within three feet of me. Suppose he ran amok at night and strangled me! Jesus!! I felt a chill run down my spine, and end at the small of my back. I said another short prayer. If matters went on like they had started, I would very easily become a Saint!!

10

I must have fallen heavily asleep somehow. Maybe because of the previous night's sleeplessness or the beans I had eaten. The only thing I know is that I slept so heavily and did not stir until the following morning at 05:00 hours. Of course I did not have a wrist-watch but we were quickly made to know, by our cell-mates, that the first census of prisoners is done daily at 05:00 hours and what we had heard was the sign of the census: the rapping on the doors and the bawling of the warders:

"*Simama kwa hesabu!!!*" they were shouting after rapping on each door.

"Hey! *Wewe! Simama kwa hesabu,*" he would repeat when a particular bunch in a cell appeared drowsy. He came to our cell and although we were all standing with our blankets draped over our shoulders, he shouted the same order of, '*simama kwa hesabu*', and then he peeped through the slot at the door and asked: "*Ngapi hapa?*"

"*Nne,*" one mad man answered readily. I think he must have been repeating the 'nne' for so long that it had stuck firmly in his mad head.

The warder opened the door, raged at the fellow for about three minutes before he made the physical count of us and then locked the door. That is what he should have done right from the beginning. I did not see the reason why he should rely on the answer from a prisoner while he had the key to the cell.

After the first census, there was a break of about thirty minutes before the next group of 'counters' arrived. This was led by a warder who must have been higher in rank than the others. He had a decorated larn-yard. I really had never been over-keen in knowing what the other departments in the Government wore as distinguished marks of ranks and as I looked at the officer, I made a mental calculation that I would at least be more interested in them, when the case was over.

Then, the doors were opened and we were allowed to go and empty our over-full bladders and bowels, and also pour the urine, in a pail which was available in the cell and which was completely full. My limbs were numb and stiff and there was a dull ache around my hips.

After washing our faces with a very hard piece of soap and very cold water, we were served with breakfast. This consisted of *uji* which was contained in a dirty half-drum. It was served by another convict who splashed it so roughly that it was filling the bowl and overflowed onto the hands of the prisoners, before it settled to fill only one third of the bowl. I picked a bowl from the metre-long stack of them and to my utter surprise, I found it filthy. It had bits and pieces of what we had for supper the previous night and greasy film all over. I took it to the tap and try as I would, I could not make it any cleaner and so I removed the bits and pieces one by one, and joined the queue waiting to be served the *uji*. When I was served, I noticed a black unidentified floating object in the *uji*. I asked what it was and I was told that it was some new kind of *uji*. Festus, the kind warder, was not around and so I had no one to turn to, for help. I sauntered back to our cell. I tasted the *uji* and noticed that it was neither sugary nor salty. It was not even tasting like *uji*. The taste was something between wheat dough and stale *ugali*. I gave up the attempt to drink it, barely after the third sip and was eagerly helped to pour it by one of our cell-mates: down his mad gullet!!

Another convict came and picked our empty bowls and then the door was again locked. We sat in silence for about five minutes, scratching our backs where lice and bed-bugs had passed through in the night and biting our dirty finger-nails. Then, the warders came again and announced that all the prisoners who had arrived the previous day were required at the main gate. My heart skipped a beat! I thought that by some kind of miracle, we were going to be released! The three of us stood hurriedly and I was just about to start grinning, when a word from one of the cell-mates stopped my grin in the tracks.

"You are going for T.A.B. and Photographs. That's the only way you can stay with us. You've got to be immunized so that you may not pick any diseases from us."

I did not know what T.A.B. was and I thought that it must be a very powerful drug: to be able to immunize against madness!! The door was opened and we were paraded, two-two to the main office at the gate. The only nagging problem was that at every stop, we were supposed to squat on our haunches. A very uncomfortable position for me and my height!

T.A.B. turned out to be an injection on the upper arm. Very brief and not painful at all. Then, we were taken to the Photographer who took three snaps of each of us.

Another headache rose from that trip because, every bugger warder wanted to know why we, Police Officers, had been remanded in custody instead of being released on bond. I could not go into all the details. After all, I myself did not know why we were not released on bond. I also did not want tell them what had led me to the cells.

That is, how we had left our houses—how we had gone to a bar for a drink—how a fight had broken from one end of the bar—how the fight had drifted to our table—how we had defended ourselves and arrested the participants in the affray—how we had taken them to a Police Station—and how, since that was not our Station, the cops there would not accept the prisoners—and how, at last the culprits had bribed their way up the ranks to whoever it was—and how that person had turned the culprits into complainants and we—poor we, into the accused persons thus being taken to court and subsequently being remanded. I had repeated the story so often to my superiors that I felt like going to the john and leak, every time someone asked me what I had done!

Unfortunately for me, somehow, my innocence had not been appreciated. That is why I was in custody. That is how I had lost my powers, immunities and privileges relating to a police officer.

I was telling them only the rind of the matter. The core and the kernel were reserved for the magistrate. I hoped that he would see the real truth in the case and that justice would prevail.

We were led back to our lonely cell. We found the other occupants outside the cell with their blankets and other belongings. On asking where they were going, they told us that the warders had told them that they must be moved from that cell because it needed spraying. There were far too many lice. That also made us feel more at home. It was bad enough on the cement, without a biting louse here and there.

Our room was sprayed under the close supervision of Festus. Seeing all what he was doing made me resolve that, when I came out of the cells, I would arrange to meet him and buy him a bottle of beer.

11

Inside the cell, the three of us started arguing about our case. We argued heatedly until we came to the final verdict: acquittal. We did not see any other way of ending the case. Not in the prevailing circumstances. Then we all kept silent—not wishing to mention the other verdict of the case that is conviction—and then frown or click our tongues at the sight of a louse or bed-bug, crawling aimlessly to death, after being poisoned by the spray. The other prisoners had been moved to another cell and we had been left to face ourselves and possibly think clearly—without interruption. An unkind warder commented that since he had been in that prison, he had not smelt insecticide, let alone witnessing the extravagant spraying that had been done in our cell. He commented contemptously that we must have been V.I.P.s—Very Important Prisoners!!

For the nine weeks that I stayed there, not one of my friends came to see me. Not one dared sacrifice even an hour to come and see me in cells. They kept aloof. They kept away from me like I had leprosy. They had all deserted me.

After every fortnight, we appeared in court, but on being asked about sureties, we all answered, "I do not see any in this court, Your Honour." I wondered where all my 'friends' had gone.

We appeared in court on the hearing day. We were smelling like something between a he-goat and a rotten pumpkin. I could even smell myself. Not that we were not taking baths. We simply did not wash our clothes. We did not brush our teeth—and mine had accumulated enough *ugali* for a complete meal! We did not comb our hair and we looked like original Rasterfaarians! We did not cut our nails or shave and—and—Oh God!—there were so many basic human necessities that we did not have!

As we were ushered through the corridors, from the cells, I could see so many of my so-called friends. Where had they sprang from on this day? Some of them were wearing stupid embarrassed grins while others had the guts to say hello. I guessed they had all come to gather more news about my downfall to go and preach to others. I was in no mood to answer any hellos or grins. I even noticed that there was a mammoth turn-out of cops from all departments. Most of them my friends but I was so bitter about life that I did not even give them a second glance.

I had in the nine weeks grown into my independent self. I had revealed myself to myself, learnt to act alone. Nine weeks and I felt that even if I would be left in this wide world alone, I would still survive and smile at it. They were nine weeks that taught me the real meaning of the word F.R.I.E.N.D.

Nine weeks without light! Nine weeks without even rolled tobacco for a smoke! Nine weeks without a drop of beer—which I had sworn then to completely abstain from and not take even a drop in my life! Nine weeks without a woman—only to see her but not to touch or feel her! Not unless you make friends with Succuba but I guess she died several years ago.

I had heard rumours about men making love to other men in cells but apparently this practice was unknown to my friends. Again, I can not, for all the gold in Fort Knox, stand a man stuffing my arse with his thing! The very thought makes me want to climb a tree!! And of course vice versa: I would not erect at another man's arse! What with all the shit! How they do it, and maybe enjoy it, is past all my understanding.

Yes. I learnt quite a lot in those nine weeks. But to top it all, I learnt about the hypocrisy of mankind. I even made a mental note that if I struck gold worth about thirty million shillings, I would build myself a castle on a mountain and keep a few animals for company rather than grinning friends in the form of men!!

The agonising memory of the nine weeks was making me bite my finger-nails, trying to reduce their length, and hating all mankind and beast and fowl and other living things. Even trees and flowers and weeds and algae. I was so bitter with the whole of the universe that, the magistrate had to call my name twice before I heard him. Then I shot to attention, stood up and answered him:

"Yes, affande," even the word affande had been indoctrined into my brain!

218

"Your case will be heard today. I will remind you of the charges. You may plead guilty after which I will either convict you or find you not guilty. You may as well choose to keep silent which I will automatically take as a plea of not guilty and we shall proceed with the case as provided for by the law.

"John Kimtai, Peter Mwasya and James Fredrick Wamatu were all brought to this court on the 18th. of March this year, each charged with two counts of wrongful confinement and a third count of assault causing actual bodily harm contrary to sections 263 and 251 of the Penal Code respectively. What is your plea, accused number one?"

"Not guilty, Your Honour."

"Accused number two?"

"Not guilty, Sir."

"Accused three?"

"Not guilty, my Lord." Although I knew that only Judges of the High Court are referred to as My Lord, and although the trial magistrate was only a Senior Resident Magistrate, I wanted to praise him. I wanted to do anything that would convince him that we were innocent. He scribbled on the paper at his desk and then cleared his throat.

"The prosecution will call ten witnesses in this case indicated by the Police Prosecutor on the first day of plea. Needless to say there has been enough time for the Police to prepare their evidence and I hope that they are ready to proceed with the case. First, I'd like every other witness in this case, and who is in this court to leave the court-room, save the first witness, Chris Matabula." The magistrate raised his eyes at us, told us to sit and addressed the court clerk;

"Swear in the first witness—Chris Matabula."

The court clerk proceeded to the witness box, fingered the Bible and Koran listlessly and turned his eyes on to the Police Prosecutor. My heart was hammering like that of a rabbit in front of a cheetah! I had arranged my defense so neatly in my brain but now, I found that I could not even remember the first question that I had planned to ask the witness. The question and subsequent questions that would help me wriggle out of the jaws of darkness.

I looked at the Prosecutor who was nervously getting to his feet. The court was so hushed that I could hear the starched uniform of the Prosecutor creak as the creases stretched and straightened.

"Your Honour," he stammered.

"Yes, Prosecutor . . .?" the Magistrate querried.

"Your Honour, the witness was bonded to appear before this court but I have not seen him since morning," he said. He was blinking his eyes like a person from a dark cave who suddenly gets into bright sunshine.

"Where is he?" the magistrate asked, still scribbling on his pad.

"Your Honour, I have not seen him since morning."

"You have already told me that—what I am asking you now is where he is. Where is Chris Matabula?" The magistrate was no longer writing.

"Your Honour, Sir, if you could wait for a while, I could check whether he is outside the court."

"Okay, check," the magistrate finished. The Prosecutor hurriedly left the court-room and we could clearly hear him calling Matabula's name outside the court. He called the name five times, each time louder than before. Then, he came back into the court-room panting from shouting and told the Magistrate that Matabula, the first complainant and witness, was not available outside the court-room.

"Has he been bonded?" the magistrate asked.

"Yes, Sir, in fact I have got a copy of his bond right here," he indicated the Police file and was about to go to the magistrate to show him the bond when the magistrate waved him back.

"Okay, the second witness is Maluki Mutie—can we proceed with his evidence?" the magistrate suggested.

The prosecution again left the court-room and we could hear him calling the other witness. I was enjoying the shouts. I was also enjoying the way the magistrate was creasing his face in a frown, every time Maluki's name was shouted outside the court-room. The prosecutor came back into the court and solemnly declared that, Maluki Mutie, the second complainant and witness in the case, was not available.

12

"What do you want me to do?" the magistrate asked in a sneering tone.

"Your Honour, we could wait for a little while and see whether the two will turn up. I am sure they will be coming but they could be a little late," the prosecutor concluded.

"What is the time now?" he magistrate asked, not bothering to hide the annoyance in his voice. The prosecutor did not have a wrist watch. I had my Kienzle back but it had long ceased to function. He was helped by the court-clerk who, without turning, announced that it was ten-thirty.

"Ten-thirty. You have until 2 p.m. this afternoon. Failure to produce your witnesses at that time will mean that I will proceed with the case as demanded by justice," the magistrate concluded. He rapped the table and we all bowed him out.

As we were taken out of the court, I could hear a heated argument between the prosecutor and the investigating officer—the fellow who was so intent on seeing that we were condemned by the world!

Some of my friends, who had come to hear about my mischievous deeds were showing relief and disappointment on their faces as we were rushed to the basement cells.

On arrival there, we were pushed into one cell and our handcuffs were removed. We rubbed our wrists where the cuffs had been biting into and the police sentry with us lit a cigarette. The smell of it was so tantalizing that I could not help myself but beg for a puff from it. I asked the police sentry if he would allow me to have two puffs from his cigarette.

"Capital NO!" he answered readily. I just looked at him and swallowed my bitter shame. I asked him if I could have a glance at the newspaper he was holding and he repeated his capital NO. He went on and told me that he had just bought the paper and that he himself had not read it. He left us in the cell and walked away in a swagger.

Some few minutes later, the same sentry came and called my name through the iron bars.

"What is it?" I snapped.

"There is someone here who wants to see you:

"Who is it?" I did not want any of my 'friends' to come and laugh at me. They could laugh their silly heads off anywhere else but not in my face.

"Well, I was just trying to help. I did not ask her name." At the mention of 'her', I forgot all my bitterness. I wanted to know who that dare-devil 'she' would be.

"Okay, okay, that's very kind of you, but, do I see her while I am still in here?" I asked the cop.

"Oh, sorry, I thought the door was not locked," he opened the door and led me to the main door of the cells. Even before I reached the door, I discerned the person of Esther. Esther Wanja. My one-time chick! Esther whom I had left some months earlier, in disgrace. She had cheated me and I had given her the boot. I don't share women if I can help it.

Now, there she was. Although it was only through the bars, I could see that she must have shed a cupful of tears. I boomed a hello at her and sneaked only two fingers through the wires for a hand shake. She did not answer my hello but she held the two fingers warmly. Just that touch and it sent my blood coursing faster through my body. It raced from the hand, to the head, to the chest, to the belly and ended somewhere below my waistline. I felt hardness start swelling up somewhere but I did not try to check it. After nine weeks inside the wires, I realised that I still had not forgotten some things. Damn it! I wanted to grab her and hug her and fondle her and do all the things that we used to do.

"Sorry, Jim," she had never called my full name in our almost two years' love, "I know you will say I was unkind to you but, honestly, I did not know where they had taken you," her voice was shaky. I withdrew my fingers.

"Of course you could not know. How could you? Besides, did you care?" I said. She released a strangled moan and sobbed once.

"Please, please, Jim, I didn't know. For God's sake, please believe me," I could almost hear pain tearing her heart. I believed her. It's funny how a woman's emotions show so openly.

"Well, they took us to Industrial Area Prison and that is where my new quarters is now. We . . ." she did not let me finish.

"If there is anything I can do, just tell me—I mean anything." she begged. But what? Just what could she do then?

"There is nothing you can do now, Esther, except maybe, pray for me," I pleaded.

"But I have heard that they want to release you on bond, with a surety. I had arranged with my brother to stand surety for you. He has come with me here and he is ready to stand surety," she was saying urgently. That sort of touched me. To have persuaded her brother to come and stand surety for a long forgotten love was something worthy of note. The very thought almost moved me to tears. Maybe she cared, after all.

"Is that it?" I asked.

"Yes, he is infact outside the court house. They would not allow both of us to come and see you together." She was pleading with her eyes. "Please, I want to help." She added.

"I really don't know what to say but, even if he would stand surety for me, what about my two other friends?" I asked. Suddenly, I did not want to be bailed out. I had stayed inside for so long that I could not imagine what freedom would feel like. Again, I had been so attached to my two colleagues that I could not for one moment think of how I would enjoy the so-called freedom, knowing that they were still languishing in cells. Bail me out—and bail my friends out as well. Or leave us all in cells. That's what I was thinking.

"But—but . . . I came because of you . . . surely your friends must be having their own friends too," she insisted. I could hear the impatient shuffling of the sentry's feet behind me. We were clearly taking too long.

"Okay, thanks—but we can not know what will happen until this afternoon's court session. Just do this—come to the court in the afternoon and hear what the magistrate says. Meanwhile, please get us something we can eat—we will have no lunch here and the *uji* I had in the monring has evaporated." I was confused.

"Thanks, darling—I'll be back." Darling? And she quickly turned on her heels and fled. I just had a passing glimpse of her rump. It had added in size since the last time I had held it. I watched her feet fade from sight. I was working out her size when the sentry called me.

"Hey, it's time you got back. Infact I have allowed you extra time." he said.

I reluctantly went back to my friends and when we were all locked in, I told them, "We are going to have a decent meal for lunch today. That was one of my old babes."

"Which one was that" Peter asked.

"Esther, she was . . ."

"You mean Wanja, don't you?" John knew her. "But, I thought you two were ceremoniously divorced ages ago?" He was laughing.

"Well, it seems that she retained one ring. She has come to bail me out." I announced.

"Bail you out?" Peter and John exclaimed in unison.

"Yes, you wait and see."

We argued about the failure of the witnesses to turn up and Peter suggested that they must have died of heart failure. I almost believed him. We had cursed the two so much that anything could have happened to them. We had held prayers against them and even invoked the Almighty to destroy them!

At last we agreed that they would turn up in the afternoon and give evidence. I also told them the intention of Esther to use her brother to stand surety for me and we all agreed that I should refuse the offer. To that, I agreed only half-heartedly. I had other plans. I wanted to get out of the place and have that girl all to myself. I imagined how it would be after such a long abstinence.

There would be the usual lies and apologies. There would be the process of the ritual of Venus. The bolting of the door—the slow deliberate walk to the bed—the avoidance to look at one another's face—the getting into the sheets—the first nervous caresses—the building up of the tension—the union—the mewing sounds by the girl—the heavy breathing by the man—the union—the union where two persons become one—the works—oh the wonderful works—the climax—with the groans from the 'she' and the pants from the 'he' and then the filling of the balloon until it bursts itself into shreds and then the hollow nothingness. Only peace and strange quietness which follow the act of love. I was so engrossed in my amorous imaginations that I started visibly when the sentry called my name again.

"Yes," I stood up but had to put my hand into my left-hand pocket to hold the cobra that was rearing and making even walking difficult.

"You have been brought some food and I think you had better come and have it outside here—all of you." He was smilling slyly. He unlocked the door and I went to the main door again.

12

Esther was there, with three paper-bags that were so full that she had difficulty in wrapping her arms around them. Trying to remove one would have surely dropped the others. I begged the sentry to allow her to bring them into the corridor and he consented. Maybe he thought he was going to have a bite out of the contents.

Esther came in and she placed the parcels on the floor. She had to squat to reach the floor and I could not restrain my wicked eyes from looking between her legs. Wow!

She was ordered to taste from each of the bags; so as not to poison us. That was the very first sign of welfare and care that I had noticed from the goddamned keepers.

She removed a piece of grilled meat from one bag and a potato chip from another but the third bag contained items that could harldy be poisoned: boiled eggs and bottles of soda. Then she wished me a good time until the afternoon and left us. My mouth was full of saliva.

We could not eat comfortably from the paper-bags and so we asked the sentry if we could have an old newspaper on which we could spread the eats. He so eagerly consented to our using his own newspaper that I could not hide a grin. I guess he must have gone through the paper then.

We spread the paper on the table and poured the contents of the first paper-bag. There was what one could call mixed grill. Beef, liver, kidneys all so carefully grilled. The liver was still bleeding a little and I could not hold my appetite any longer. I picked a chunk of liver and was stuffing it into my mouth when the sentry displayed yet another of his acts of kindness and care.

"You can wash your hands from the tap at the corner," he said indicating the direction.

"You go and wash," I told my friends, "me I will not, don't forget that I have still got T.A.B. running through my veins." I almost choked. I was swallowing and talking at the same time. I blinked repeatedly, as the chunk of liver found its way down my aesophagus.

That was a meal that reminded me that there was a friend somewhere outside. There was still one friend amid the deserters. Like an answer to a shout in the wilderness: something that you really do not expect but that comes all the same.

My friends came back after washing their hands and we fell to. The fist paper-bag's contents were gone before you could say 'Industrial Area'. We poured the contents of the second paper-bag and my mouth sagged in wonder—chicken! A whole chicken surrounded by chips. I started regretting why I had rushed into the beef session first. We had no carving knives but we ripped the chicken with our hands.

Behind me, I heard a deliberate cough and turned slowly, with a chicken leg in my hands and my mouth over-full. The sentry had been joined by another and together they were looking at us with such hungry eyes.

"Hey, fellas, fall on it—we can't finish all this," I invited them, indicating the remains of the chicken. Peter scowled at me but I grinned at him.

The cops marched to us in quick time and fell on the chicken like ravens. They were smiling awkwardly and swallowing so fast that I could see a lump drop down the throat of one and disappear into his chest before springing back into position. They must have been pot hungry! You would think they were from remand homes where they had not smelt food for a week. They did not even wash their hands.

The eggs followed and I took only one. I was already feeling the effects of overfeeding. But, when it came to the sodas, we declined to share with the cops although they were still standing around with grimy hands and embarrassed grins. One was looking at me with his eyes following the bottle as I tilted it to my mouth and all the way down when I removed it. And each time I swallowed, he also swallowed!

The other offered to take the empty bottles to Esther and when he was leaving, he said: "That girl sure loves you."

"Sure she does!" I applauded.

We washed our hands but, unfortunately, there was no soap to remove the grime from them. We used the paper-bags to wipe up. I belched contentendly and without asking I proceeded to the table where there was a packet of cigarettes and procured one. I used a match box which was still on the table to light it and inhaled deeply. My two friends followed suit and we all lit up. When the cop came to pick a cigarette from the packet, it was empty and he folded it and threw it out of the window in open disgust. I had to hide a grin. The bastard was so mean that he thought three cigarettes were more valuable than the chicken and eggs they had eaten—from our own hands! They did not object to our smoking however. They also did not mention about locking us in cells again. We just lolled there and I had to sit down on a chair to steady myself against the giddiness that was enveloping me because of smoking after a long time of abstinence. The cops picked the paper-bags and took them outside the corridor. When they came back, I thought they were going to tell us to go back to the cells but they did not.

When there is something palatable, a cop is always pallable. I must have been very contented with the world because I fell asleep against the table and slept through some two hours before I was roused when the court resumed in the afternoon.

As we were entering the court, we saw Esther and her brother seated just next to the dock. I winked and smiled at them. The brother smiled back but Esther did not. She was looking at me with such motherly eyes that I felt like shouting to her that all was well. Then, the magistrate came and we all stood up, bowed and then sat again. The police prosecutor was glancing at us accusingly and shuffling his feet.

"John Kimtai."

"Sir."

"Peter Mwasya."

"Sir."

"James Wamatu."

"My Lord."

"I read the charges to you in the morning and so I will not repeat them. You pleaded not guilty. Do you want to change your plea, John?"

"No, Sir."

"Peter?"

"No, Your Lord."

"Wamatu?"

"No, My Lord."

"Sit down," he told us and then focussed his eyes on the police prosecutor. "Prosecutor, we could not go on with the case in the morning because your witnesses were not in court. I gave you until this afternoon to bring them, and I hope they are here now." He turned his eyes to the general public. "Will every other witness in this case please leave the court-room except the first witness—Chris Matabula."

Before the court clerk stood to go to the witness box, the prosecutor stood up. He turned his face towards the listeners and then back to the magistrate. I was watching his every movement. I had in the short time that we were in the court noticed that Chris

Matabula was not anywhere in the court. My other two friends had also noticed it and we had nudged one another. I was feeling a thrill all over me.

"Your Honour." the prosecutor stammered, "Your Honour, I am sorry to inform the court that I have not been able to trace the two first witnesses but I am applying for court summons in respect of the two. Meanwhile, I would beg the court to proceed hearing the evidence from the other witnesses in this case." He finished and swallowed hard. I could see his Adam's apple rise and fall. The magistrate did not even bother to write his pronouncement down. He placed his pen on the table, cast a casual glance at the whole court-room and then looked hard at the prosecutor.

"Have these two witnesses been bonded?" he asked.

"Yes, Your Honour."

"And who are the complainants in this case, if I may know?"

"Unfortunately Sir, they are the two missing witnesses."

"Yes. Unfortunately. For how long have the accused persons been in remand?"

I almost answered that myself but I kept quiet and instead looked at where Esther was seated. She was wringing her hands and having that vacant look in her eyes, the look that women always have when in distress.

"About two months, Sir." the prosecutor answered after referring to his file.

"About two months. I see. And for how long have the witnesses been aware that they were supposed to come to this court today?"

"About the same time, Sir. I'd say they were bonded on the same day of the plea."

"Where do the witnesses live?" the magistrate probed on.

"Here in Nairobi." the prosecutor answered promptly.

"Particularly where?"

"One is living in," the prosecutor consulted his file, "one is living in Jericho Estate while the other is in South 'C'—Nairobi South 'C'." I could see despair starting to curl its horrible tentacles around the prosecutor's face.

"And you said that they are fully aware that they are supposed to be here today to give evidence?" he took his pen and started scribbling hastily on his pad.

"Yes, Your Honour."

The magistrate reached for his big leather-bound black book of Law. He ruffled through the pages and meticulously picked his horn-rimmed spectacles from his breast pocket, placed them on his nose and bent slightly over the book. He cleared his throat.

According to Section two hundred and two of the Criminal Procedure Code, contained in Chapter seventy-five of the Laws of Kenya, when a witness, who, having been bonded or summoned to appear in court, fails to appear in court, the court shall thereby dismiss the charge and acquit the accused unless," he paused, gave the whole court a sweeping glance and then his eyes fell on the book again. My heart was beating so violently that I thought it wanted freedom from my chest! ". . . Unless there are reasonable grounds for non-appearance of the witness after which, the court shall adjourn the hearing of the case and remand the accused person at a place blah-blah blah. Now Prosecutor, Mister Prosecutor, in your own opinion, is there any reasonable ground or excuse for the non-appearance of your witnesses?" The magistrate removed his glasses and closed his book.

"Well, Your Honour," he croaked.

"Yes . . . ."

"Well, Your Honour," he paused and cleared his throat.

"You are repeating yourself." The magistrate reminded him.

"I really don't know what to say but, I think that if we could issue court summons in respect . . ." he did not finish.

"And what do we do about these three?" he waved a hand at us. "They have been in remand for about two months," the magistrate continued without waiting for the answer from the prosecutor. "and for that same length of time or thereabouts, your witnesses have been aware that they should be here in this court today. Due to reasons best known to them, if not to you, they have decided not to come here. After all, they are not in remand like the accused persons.

230

Do you know what I think they are saying? 'Let those three rot in prison—they should not joke with people like us! Mister Prosecutor, do you have that same opinion like your witnesses?" the magistrate was then furious.

"No, Your Honour. Of course not, Sir," this time it was a whisper.

"Then, I hereby dismiss the charges against the three accused person and acquit them forthwith," he looked at us. "You are free, you can go home." He rapped the table and left the court-room even before I had had time to stand up.

14

My heart stood still. Although I had eaten to my satisfaction and beyond, just some time past, I felt hollow in the stomach. My vision started blurring and I had to blink repeatedly to focus the scene. The prosecutor was still standing.

"The hell with it!" He cursed.

Esther came and, unshamedly, in front of all the people in the court, her brother included, kissed me right on the mouth. Her tongue moved over my closed lips and when I opened my mouth to reprimand her, she slipped right inside darting it left and right and I could not say a thing. She was weeping and holding me so lovingly. Then, she staggered back and said: "Let's get the hell out of here."

Our handcuffs were removed and we looked at one another in disbelief . . . . Fellows I had not ever seen before were shaking hands with us and the cops who had come to witness my downfall were shaking their heads in disbelief but above all, there was Esther, who was holding my hand and leading me out of the court-room.

We packed ourselves in her brother's car and we were cheered by the by-standers as the vehicle left the parking bay and headed out side of the precincts of the court.

"Thank you—thank you all," I said. I was not very sure who I was thanking but I think it was Esther. She did not seem to mind my he-goat smell as she huddled her head on my chest. Her brother was shaking his head slowly in amusement.

"Where to, brother?" He asked as we joined the major road leading from the court.

"To my place—I have got to get rid of these rags. I can feel lice crawling all over me."

"Nonsense," That was Esther. "I have not seen any lice on you since . . ." she had opened my shirt buttons and was fingering my sparse chest hairs. Few as they were, I was proud to have them.

"But, I am literally stinking," I protested. Esther put her nose on my chest and inhaled; "Not very bad, anyway," she said and again kissed me.

I was feeling like a million dollars! My two friends were not talking. They were just grinning. Somehow, they had found a sure way of emitting unspeakable gratitude: silence.

We arrived at my house and were met by the signs of evacuation. Tall grass around the house and tree leaves crammed against the door-way. Even a spider had erected a mansion right inside the key-hole. A morning-glory I had planted before I was whisked from freedom had grown over the wall and its tendrils hung over the door, like the eye-lashes of a spent whore. I kicked the door open, with Esther standing beside me and together we stopped, horror-stricken.

Just inside the door, Betsa, my gift pussy was sprawled on the floor. The way ants swam into and out of her mouth and every other opening in her body told me that she was long dead. Must have been killed by hunger. So, when I was starving in prison, Betsa was starving at home. I bit my lips ruefully and it was only Esther who stopped me from taking the putrefying puff of fur into my hands saying how sorry I was.

I went into the bed-room and shed off my prison garb. I stood unashamedly naked and Esther came shyly and wrapped a towel around my middle.

"Go and take a shower, dear. Meanwhile, I will see whether I can fan out some of this dust." She gestured with a hand covering the whole of the house. It had rained outside but the dust had sought refuge inside the house. It had coated my bed-cover thickly and was seething brown in every crevice, crack and hole within my house. I could even smell it with every gulp of breath I took.

When I got outside my house, I saw my two friends and Esther's brother still standing around the car. In my haste, I had completely forgotten about them.

"Hey, Peter and John, why don't you go and remove that jail-bird look you have and then we meet in an hour and know what to do?" They muttered their thanks to Geoffrey, Esther's brother and marched off. I faced Geoffrey and told him, "I want to go and peel off one layer of my dirty skin before I can say hello to anyone. Meanwhile, please get into the house and wait for me."

"No, Jim, now that you are free, I will be on the run. I am sure . . ." he hesitated and looked at the clouds. "I am sure Esther will . . ." he fumbled for more words but could find none. He swallowed hard and slid behind the steering wheel of his car. I also was at a loss for words. All I could manage was:

"Thank you very much, I am sure that we shall meet and have a small chat very soon." He reversed and drove off with me waving him away frantically—the way a child waves off a kind aunt.

I went to the first bathroom and started on what was one of my longest showers. As I was soaping myself, I heard my name being called and when I peeped through the cracks on the door, I noticed that not less than twenty cops had gathered around my house to 'welcome' me home. I told them to go away—I would be calling them for a conference as soon as I was settled. I wanted to tell them to make sure that they came with some Pressmen but I thought it was too insulting.

For thirty minutes, I soaped, scrubbed, rinsed, soaped, scrubbed and rinsed until I felt my skin tingle.

Then, I came out smiling at the still gathered cops and shook all their hands and told them: "Anyone who calls himself my friend should be at the canteen in twenty minutes. I will not demand much from you but I would like to have a beer from each of you." They all roared with laughter and left. I went into the house and found Esther having opened all windows and doors and literally trying to fan the dust out using an old towel. I looked at her as she waved the towel over her head and wondered what had really got into her when she decided to come and rescue me from the remand prison.

Women can be funny sometimes and Esther's actions were not any exception. She looked at me and showed me her tongue. I felt a surge of compassion run through me and before I knew what I was doing, I had got hold of her and was administering several kisses all over her face. Quite like old times, Esther, at my touch, melted against my chest and I lifted her off the ground and carried her to the bed where she started making mewing sounds even before I unwrapped the towel which was around my waist.

234

CHAPTER THIRTEEN

1

It took the bosses in the office three full weeks before they got convinced that I was fully innocent. I was reinstated in my job but, from the first day that I stepped into the office, to be met with howls of congratulations and triumphant smiles from friends, I knew that I could not go on much longer.

I had been let down by the job I had whole-heartedly devoted myself to. I had been utterly humiliated by the same powers that had taught me who an offender was and what to do with him. Yes: they had taught me how to arrest offenders. I had arrested offenders and got the bitter reward of it all: Shame!! I felt that I simply could not go on.

I could not imagine what I could say to an offender—who might have shared the nine weeks with me in remand. He might even spit on my face. I was feeling so vulnerable that I would not have known what to do if I caught a pick pocket with his hand in my pocket!

That is why I did not even know what to say when I found a man in Esther's room.

On that fateful day, I had woken up early to clean my shirts and generally tidy up my house. I had even woken up earlier so that I could finish those domestic chores and have time to rush to Esther's place and check on what was happening to her.

The previous day, Saturday, I had tried to contact her on telephone, to make the usual weekend outing program but, the receptionist at her place of work had told me that Esther had not reported on duty. On further enquiries, I was told: "No, she did not report sick. Yesterday, I was with her and she was still the same bubbling joy she had ever been." Bubbling joy. That is what Esther had become since the day I had left prison.

Except for the normal working hours, most of the other hours were spent in each other's arms. When we were not strolling in youthful abandon around the streets of Nairobi, gaping at the incredible prices of goods on display, we would be in bed, making unlimited love, or, in the kitchen, cooking foods we had never cooked before.

It was known between us, although it had really not been put into words, that our love would go beyond the 'pick and drop' affair that is so common these days. I knew in my heart that I wanted her for marriage. I had not told her in words, because she too displayed the same serious earnestness and determination in every lover's act that happened between us. She had filled my heart to the brim and sealed any crevice which another woman would have penetrated. She had also accomplished what I thought was the most difficult task of all. She had made me almost forget Charity, and no other girl had freed me from Charity before.

I boarded the bus that would take me to my lover's nest and even before I alighted, I felt that there was somthing wrong. I could not put a finger on the cause of my uneasiness, but it was there. I alighted about half a mile from Esther's place so as to give her enough time, as it was still early, to get out of bed. I wanted to walk slowly, savouring the moment when I would see her and what I would do to her first; kiss or embrace. Then, a thought came over me; she could be sick and needing my very presence to give her comfort beyond the doctor's sedatives. This thought made me quicken my pace involuntarily.

I came to her house and noticed that even her window-curtains were drawn. Her neighbour, a pretty little girl with even, white teeth was putting linen on a line outside her house. I gawked a good morning. She smiled and I noticed that she was extremely beautiful although she appeared small. With her lesso around her waist, her posterior appeared very prominently and I thought she would be good for anyone and at the same time, I started wondering who does what to her!

I was just about to rap on Esther's door when the door came slowly open and Esther, my beautiful Esther, stood squarely at the door. She was still in her night-dress, that transparent thing that made her nipples stand out so bossy and firm. She blinked sleepily and

236

focussed her eyes on me. She was starting a yawn but, on seeing me, she froze, spun around and banged and bolted the door from inside.

I was so taken aback, that I did not even know what to think. I fumbled in my pocket for a cigarette and lit it. When it was burning evenly, I nervously approached the door and rapped hesitantly. There was shuffling of feet from inside before a voice came through:

"Please, go away, Jim," It was a voice that was both begging and commanding and it had a finality about it.

"Esther, are you alright?" I inquired, fear knotting my bowels. I was so sure that she must have been sick. For her to have seen me and to flee back into the house and later beg me to go away; I thought the worst malady had accidentally attacked her. My mind had started racing in circles: where was the nearest telephone? I wanted to call an ambulance or the police or . . . but my thoughts were again stopped by the unlatchig of the door.

Standing squarely was a man. A man who had only a towel around his waist and even that could not hide the push of his cock from showing. It led him. He had heavy muscled legs and arms and a dark patch of hair on his chest. This patch was decorated by a horizontal scar from one dark nipple to the other. He opened his mouth, showing an ugly toothless gap in his front teeth.

"Yes-zs?" He inquired. At that, I felt such revulsion and hatred that I had to hold back a wretch and at the same time, restrain my temper because if I had allowed it to flare and wander, I would have left that brute with more than one tooth missing!!

At least Esther should have done a bit better in choosing! I pictured the brute exhaling rotten airs into her mouth as they kissed and I felt my chest muscles tighten. I wanted to know whether she had given in or some sort of fraud—she could not have willed!! I wanted to know how it came about but I did not need to bother my brain so much. The answer came in the form of Esther herself. She came and placed herself on the left hand of the brute—the ugly beast—and took his hand in hers so possessively before she opened her mouth—that mouth, which had been a cradle for my tongue, to say:

"'Am sorry, Jim," she sounded apologetic, "but, Isaac is my

boyfriend. I could not tell you . . ." but she did not finish. She was roughly pushed back into the house and the guy followed her, bolting the door again. I heard the thud of something falling heavily before Esther screamed. I could not bear that noise and so I turned and almost ran from the place. As I left, the neighbour was slowly shaking her head. I told myself that I would avail myself the first opportunity to get her all to myself and maybe taste those teats.

I also told myself that I would avail myself the first opportunity to call Esther on telephone, through which I was sure she would tell me the truth about her relationship with Isaac—or was that the name? I was not sure.

2

I boarded a bus almost blindly. I could not specify what I was feeling. Self-pity? No! I had gone through that before and found that it did not help a thing. Pain? Admittedly, a little. Rejection? Maybe. Esther had rejected me and worse still, she had left me for an ugly toothless beast. What had I done to deserve such a blow? I could not guess but most likely, I thought she must have been lured by money. Maybe I was not giving her enough monetary gifts. Or, maybe she felt that I was dragging her life too slowly. Of course cops are not millionaires and to afford a sophisticated woman like Esther was also a handicap to me! Maybe she thought that with the pace of progress we were making, she would take too long before she filled her wardrobe with the latest fashions. She wanted to run, and running she had done. With a son-of-a-bitch whorerider! All her beauty given to such an unsightly thing!.

I cursed myself for having ridden on that bus in the morning. I wished I had not gone to Esther's place. I wished I had waited for her at my place to come and give me the left-overs. I did not want to think that even earlier, she had been bringing me the left-overs which I had delighted in consuming. When I remembered that I could kiss her everywhere including her private parts, I shuddered to think that maybe one day I had kissed her after a night session with that fellow. Bah!!

But one winning light was still flickering afar. I had won. Once again, I had proved, practically, that Esther would be a neer-do-well throughout her short, whorish life. I felt that I had won because I had nipped the bud that was sprouting, right at the stem. The bud that would have grown into a disaster: marriage between me and Esther. It is one thing to be cheated while you are still lovers instead of finding a man without pants in your wife's bed, while your first born is crying his eyes dry in the cot next to the bed!

Esther could go where she wanted with whatever lecher she chose and do whatever whorish act she liked. Amen.

I alighted at Eastleigh and suddenly, I did not know where to go. To my house? No. I did not want to go and see Esther's photograph framed and wreathed in the bedroom—with her parted lips and loving eyes. I wanted to be remembering her just like I had seen her last—with her man at her side.

My legs found purchase and in no time I was inside Mathare Valley. One of the best niches of crime and sin in our beautiful city. I had been to Mathare Valley on several previous occasions but then, on strickly official duty. I was going there on a totally different mission this time. I noticed that people were looking at me suspiciously. In Mathare, the presence of a cop means only one thing: trouble.

I met with an elderly lady and asked her where one thirsty man could have a beer and she told me that in the last twenty years which she had lived in Mathare, she had not seen beer or any other alcoholic drink in Mathare. Period.

I knew how to handle her kind and after several assurances and a ten-shilling note firmly stuck into her brassiere, she led me to a card-board shack and I was left outside for five minutes before she convinced the owner that I was a harmless, thirsty customer-to-be. I was then called in and met the proprietor—an ageless lady with about half an inch of make-up over her skin, smoking a cigarette which produced what must have been poisonous gas. I had to

steadily smoke to keep the stench of that cigarette from choking me!
She eyed me suspiciously and then parted her lips in a half-smile and
I noticed that she had a tooth missing in her front dental row. Shit! It
was my day of meeting toothless people. I called for my beer, plus
that of my 'guide' and on top of all, I also told the proprietor to have
one on me. She actually laughed out loud after hearing that she was
also to have one on me.

Before I finished my third beer, the room was full to capacity and I
was receiving so many offers of drinks which I declined but I could
not really refuse the very last one: chang'aa. I had not tasted the
bloody stuff before and the first sip left me shuddering. It tasted like
dry naked gin. I could also feel as it evaporated right in the mouth
and I had to sip some more. This time, I swallowed a bit of it and I
could feel it as it found its way all the way into the stomach where
instantly, it put a glow that I almost enjoyed. I took more and more
and at last, I really do not know what happened but I got myself so
drunk and incapable that I could not follow the sequence of events.

I only roused myself from a drunken stupor in the night. My
sodden brain could not recall or locate where I was. The room was
completely dark and before I could start feeling with hands, I felt
movement next to me. I moved my hand stealthily and noticed that I
was completely naked before I touched the warm naked belly of a
woman. No mistake about that.

At my touch, she cooed in her sleep and nudged closer, parting her
legs slightly. Although I had no idea who she was, I felt my prick rear
like a striking cobra. I had to pat her flank three times before she was
fully awake. I did not dare open my stinking mouth but a movement
with my hips suggested to her just what I wanted. She spread herself
and I reached for the goods which I found to be warm and tender.

In the morning, I woke up again and in the half-light, I watched
my queen. Not bad, I mused. Although her hair was streaked with grey
and the folds on her breasts made them look like the scrotum of an
old man, I convinced myself that she was okay. Failing that would
have sent me screaming from her house. I touched her cheek and she
fluttered her eyes open, and I noticed that the eyes looked very

240

beautiful amid the age and delapidation of her other features and I could not help a smile.

"Morning, dear," I said hoarsely.

"Morning, darling," she opened her mouth which reeked of cheap whisky and cigarettes. She closed her eyes again.

"I want to go," I told her. She knew what that meant and she got up from bed, still stark naked and walked to a low table at the corner. She came back with my clothes, my wallet and my wrist-watch. Looking at her as she handed the clothes to me, I compared her with Esther but I only managed to click my tongue in disgust. Disgust for Esther—the cheating hussy!

The clicking of the tongue was mistaken by the woman and she nervously slipped between her coarse blankets, covered even her head and pretended to be fast asleep.

I dressed, peeled a pound from my wallet and left it on the table for 'mama' before I smiled good-bye at her covered form. I walked out of her house and as I went through the ghetto, I felt light headed and relaxed.

3

A few weeks after I was reinstated, the mood in the office changed. I noticed that even the bosses were eyeing me suspiciously. My own rank was avoiding and warding me off with little or no pretext of friendliness.

I had grown from a smiling companionable constable to an aggressive easy-to-annoy public reject. I was eating less and drinking more. My eyes were turning dull brown with streaks of red all over.

Mathare Valley had become my frequent haunt each time I wanted to get drunk and stupid or drunk and a mother-fucker. I noticed that it was very easy to make friends in Mathare: with mugs and ageless whores.

I had twice been forced to produce my Police Certificate of Appointment to Police Officers who had come to arrest chang'aa drinkers and I had been found with them.

Chang'aa was an easy drink. I only needed ten shillings for a beer and several tots of the stuff which would quickly turn me from a cop to an amiable boozer. And the hang-overs! Gosh! I could live in semi-delirium for a whole week!

Even the bosses commented on the slackening of my work. I was working—yes; but I was not devoted to the job. I was only doing it because it was paying me. I did not care really. My eyes were the subject of comment one day. A boss told me that it would be better if I went to an ophthalmic optician for an eye-check because the colour was not healthy!

This made me angry and I wanted to be so far away from the bonds of supervision that, one day, or rather one night, after a bout of all alcohols, chang'aa included, I took a pen and paper and addressed a letter to my boss. One month's notice—I gave him and he accepted only too eagerly.

I proceeded on my terminal leave and started to regret my very literacy. I had wasted ten good years with the cops and had got nothing besides the reward promised to fools in Proverbs 3:35.

So, I resigned. Would you have allowed the embarrassment of arrest and subsequent shame to sink anyway?

But all the same, there are times when I wish I had not resigned and again, when I feel that it was the only way out.

But, wishes or no wishes, the fact was that I was no longer a cop. I returned all the items that they had issued to me on enlistment. What annoyed me most was that they had to deduct some money from my final pay, to cover the loss of some of the silly items that I had lost. They were also very strict that I did not remain with anything with which I could fraudulently identify myself as a cop.

CHAPTER FOURTEEN

1

Immediately after resignation, I joined à friend of mine for lodgings, John. John Karanja worked for Chibuku. Those guys who brew and sell 'civilised' *busaa*. We were so close with Karanja that he did not mind me moving my scanty belongings from the police lines and putting them in his house. After all, there was very little: a bed, a mattress, two blankets and two pairs of sheets, a small table and four stools plus of course my two suit-cases, containing all my clothes. I had pawned the rest of the goods to willing buyers at the police lines, at throw-away prices.

I still had my meagre savings and we got along fine with Karanja for two months. He was already negotiating with his boss about my employment in their firm as a Security Assistant at their plant in Industrial Area. There was an earlier Assistant but the lucky fellow was being promoted to Chief Security Officer, to fill in a vacancy which had cropped up following the expiry of an expatriate's contract. Good. I was going to get a job as easily as that. I had not yet formally gone to see the Personnel Manager but Karanja was working on the issue, or so I thought.

Then, things abruptly went awry. The first catastrophe was Karanja, who was supposed to be a wholesaler of the brew—the fellows who scurry around town with Chibuku trailers, selling to retailers and his driver, selling a full tanker of the stuff and pocketing the money. I think they must have been fooled by the drunken look of the Chief Accoutant at their place. Karanja had repeatedly told me that the Chief Accountant hardly opened his eyes when he was receiving money from wholesalers, and maybe they thought he would put a tick against their delivery without actually receiving the money.

They got a shock when, at the end of the week, two thousand and fourty shillings was demanded from them, Karanja and his driver tried to put on an innocent front, but the red light was already up.

I came home from my job-seeking strolls and found that Karanja was not at 'our' place in Eastleigh. I had my own key to the house and I opened the door and entered. I warmed the previous night's leftovers and had a light supper. I left some for Karanja. Then, I went to Liliput Bar where we used to spend Karanja's stolen money and ordered an Export, thinking that Karanja would turn up any moment. I finished the first one and ordered another. I still had twenty shillings and so I drank the second beer slowly, waiting for Karanja to come and drink from the remainder of the pound—before he started buying me beer. I had learnt that Karanja could be extra magnanimous after stimulating him with a beer or two.

Time was running fast and at 2230 hours, I decided that Karanja must have been hooked somewhere by a whore. He loved them so much. I paid for my drinks, which were already generating a remote head-ache in me and walked back to our place. I thought that he had arrived with a new whore and decided to work on her instead of going out to the bar but I was disappointed and relieved to find that he had not arrived.

Then, I started feeling sort of uneasy for no reason. Karanja was usually at home or in Liliput Bar long before 2200 hours. Even when he picked any woman from anywhere where his Chibuku errands took him, he would always bring her home or around Eastleigh. All the same I went to bed after swallowing two tablets of Algon. I did not lock the door from the inside because I thought Karanja would come in any time. I also did not put off the light. That night, I had a really terrifying dream in which I was fighting with Karanja over a bottle of beer!

The following morning, I peered at Karanja's bed from my bed across the room and noticed that the bed was unruffled. I dismissed the numerous ideas and imaginings that whirled and danced and swirled in my brain. Imagining disaster. I summarily dismissed them as effects of only a dream. I lit the pressure stove, put water on and went out to look for milk. There was a newspaper vendor just next to the milk kiosk and when he saw me, he started shaking his head and saying *'pole'*.

"What is it?" I demanded. He looked at me with wide eyes and then asked.

"Are you not sorry that your house-mate is in?"

"In? Where?" I asked, startled. Instead of answering me, he pulled a *Taifa Leo* from among the papers, and turned to page three and pointed out a story to me. I looked at the page and shuddered.

Karanja's and his driver's photographs, flanked by grinning cops! The story followed: 'A Chibuku salesman and his driver were yesterday remanded in custody by the Chief Magistrate after they denied a charge of stealing by servant contrary to section 281 of the Penal Code. John Karanja and Wilfred Muteti aged 32 and 23 respectively, appeared before the Chief Magistrate yesterday . . ."

I closed my eyes briefly and when I opened them, it was still there: the newspaper carrying the story and Karanja's photograph.

Milk forgotten, I handed back the newspaper and slowly walked back to our house. I put off the stove. I did not even take a shower but just hurriedly dressed up and headed for Industrial Area. I had to know the truth and the truth would only come from one source— Karanja's employers.

"It was not the first time," the drunken-looking Chief Accountant told me, "but, as the saying goes, the days of a thief are numbered." He had been telling me of how Karanja and his driver had been repeatedly stealing small amounts of Chibuku and selling it to what the Chief Accountant referred to as ' unregistered retailers'.

"This was the last straw—I had to expose them, or pay the amount from my own pocket, which would also have cost me my job."

I swallowed hard.

"But, you should have given him time to pay the money. I am sure you would have recovered each and every cent if you had given him time. Alternatively, you could have deducted it from his salary. I am sure he earns more than that per month and . . ." I suggested but the Chief Accountant waved a dismissing hand at me: "I tried that," he told me, "I told the General Manager just that but you can not imagine what a stubborn son-of-a-bitch he is," he checked himself and looked through the window to see whether anyone had heard him making that obscene remark about his boss. Satisfied, he went on in a near-whisper; "You know what, between you and me, I think the General Manager has been looking for just such a chance to get Karanja off. You can not imagine the hurry he was in to call the police—Karanja and the driver were taken to court in the afternoon and the discovery was made in the morning! I think he must have even bribed the police to rush the case. I have not even recorded my statement.

"He does not want to see anyone who does not belong to his tribe working here. In fact he wants this company to be a family enterprise and is trying as much as possible to bring in his cousins, nephews and such into the company. I am just lucky because I have got my CPA Part II. That is why I am here. Even my qualifications do not stop him from gazing at me like I was a piece of well done meat" he paused and I looked at him and noticed that he looked exactly like something the cat brought in.

"While we are on the subject, Karanja had told me that he had talked to the Personnel Manager about this vacancy of Assistant Security Officer. You see . . ." He did not let me finish. He raised his hands in a desperate gesture.

"Futile. Futile, I tell you. the Personnel Manager has no power to employ anyone here. The advertisement you saw in the papers was just to bluff the Labour Ministry bosses. If Karanja had told you that he would talk to the Personnel Manager about your employment here, then, besides cheating you, he had cheated himself. It is my heart-felt belief that a nephew or even a niece will take the post. It is unfortunate that his mother is so old otherwise she might have taken the job. The Personnel Manager is here perfunctorily and is just a stooge!" He sighed.

Well, there goes my job, I thought. If the General Manager was also the Personnel Manager, then I had no job to hope for. If he also had been hell-bent to see Karanja off, sure he would be hell-bent to see that no acquintance of Karanja got the job.

I did not waste the Chief Accountant's time any more. I left the office with only one idea: to get to Eastleigh and look for someone who could put me up for a few days.

I walked along Enterprise Road. I was in no hurry. I walked slowly and unseeingly, thinking of what to do with my poor self. Who would agree to live with me?—a poor job-less ex-cop? I tried to weigh my drinking friends but quickly dismissed them all. A drinking friend is a drinking friend and you are friends only when there is a drink. So what? They would have no room for me except in a bar!

My legs carried me and I found myself next to the Kenya Co-Operative Creameries. Then, my face brightened. Industrial Area Prison was just ahead of me. I knew it. I also knew what went on inside there. I knew that a visit by a friend to someone who is in remand would bring a lot of relief.

I walked to the main gate of the prison and the warder who was manning it immediately recognised me.

"So, what can I do for you this time?" he asked me, grinning and stretching his hand for a shake. The blighter did not know that I was no longer a cop and he accorded me all the respect that a warder should accord a cop. I grinned back at him, shook his hand lightly and told him that I had a friend who I believed was remanded there.

"Name?"

"John Karanja. John Ngumbu Karanja," I answered him.

He rifled through his thick register. I was feeling ill at ease but I did not show him.

"Date of admission?" he asked.

"Yesterday."

I was looking around. I would have liked to see Festus, if he was still stationed there but I felt that that could wait.

"Yes, he is in block D-2. Could you sit here and wait? He gave me a chair. I sat on it and looked beyond the warder pretending to be busy thinking about this and that but inside, I was blank. He then called one of his colleagues and gave him a small piece of paper on which was written Karanja's name in block number. Then, he turned to me.

"So, how is the job?" he asked. My smart clothes could easily camouflage my joblessness. I was not going to let the mug know that I was then a street-walker.

"So-so—we are still trying to minimise the number of hooligans but you bet we are making little progress."

"Yeah, I have noticed that these days, we always have the cells full. I should think the more a country is developing, the more criminals we have." That was the most intelligent remark I had heard coming from a Prison Warder. Within another ten years, there would be philosophers among them.

"Yeah!" I said. I did not want to go on discussing things that did not concern me any more. Then, I heard foot-steps from behind and on turning, I saw Karanja and the warder who had been sent to fetch him. I grinned in a nervous way and pulled Karanja to one side, away from the warders' earshot. However, we still kept within sight of the warders.

"What happened, man?" I asked urgently. He was twitching his mouth and looked like he was at the point of breaking.

"It's terrible, I swear I did not mean to steal the money—it's just one of those mishaps that befall man—and now this—God! What do you think I should do?" He sobbed.

"As matters are, you will definitely be found guilty. I'd advise you to plead guilty and beg for leniency instead of rotting here in remand," I said. I could not think of anything more worthwhile to say.

"For how long do you think they will imprison me, if I plead guilty?" he asked with that dry vacant air of hopelessness. I wanted to assure him and maybe make him feel that stealing is not murder, but I could not.

"Well, I just can't exactly say. The maximum sentence for theft by servant is seven years but that again depends on the magistrate and the circumstances of the case. But considering the nature of your case, the magistrate might give you anything from six months to two years, and that's a bargain." I finished. At that, Karanja hid his face in his hands and sobbed again.

I tried to calm him by telling him that anything could happen and that he might not even be imprisoned. He could as well be given an option of a fine. A long shot but it brightened him a bit. I also told him that these things happen to men and, of course, above all, there was God who has plans for everybody. Imprisonment was not the end of life.

"But, jail . . ." he shook his head slowly. Then, he looked up and I thought there was a flicker of hope in his eyes. He looked like one who had just roused himself from a day-dream.

"Anyway, I'd like you to go to Ofafa Maringo. There's a cousin of mine by name Muthukia—Christopher Muthukia. Tell him to come here and see me. You could come together . . . no tell him to come alone. Meanwhile, please take care of the house and the few belongings we have there," he paused, "anyway, Muthukia will tell you what to do."

"Is there anything else that maybe you would like me do for you in the meantime?" I asked. I was puzzled. I did not know what Karanja would tell Muthukia to come and tell me but, I had a premonition of disaster. For no apparent reasons, I started feeling afraid.

3

Suddenly, Karanja could not look at me in the face and he had started shuffling his feet like a woman being seduced and not knowing what answer would be appropriate between yes and no. He gave me the Block and Door number of Muthukia's house in Maringo and then he was taken back to his cell.

I wasted another ten minutes with the warder, discussing things which could never build our nation development-wise, before I walked slowly towards the Nairobi City Stadium.

Police teams were rehearsing for Inter-Provincial Championships and I walked fast past the stadium. I did not want any cops who knew me to spot me and start their boring conversations. I had started to detest the cops like one detests a pain in the neck.

It was still too early to go to Maringo. I had no wrist-watch, having pawned my Keinzle earlier, for three pounds, but the sun was far from the horizon.

I entered Burma Market, and I bought a piece of readily roasted meat and ugali and noticed, to my dismay, that there was only fifty-five shillings between me and starvation. I also remembered that in my Post Office Savings Bank, I had not more than two hundred shillings and after using that up, I would be left with no alternative but to pawn my belongings. Then, after that, I would be forced either to steal or go foraging in the dustbins for meals!

My meal through, I walked all the way to Bahati Estate. I knew of a girl who used to sell Kenya Charity Sweepstake tickets there but, on approaching the kiosk, I noticed that it was occupied by a man!

I passed on, hardly able to hide the disappointment on my face. Where the hell had they taken Gathoni? I did not even ask the reliever. I walked on wondering what *'bahati'* the Estate had but I remembered that an old resident of the place had told me that the name had come from the way the houses were allocated to the residents when the Estate was new. It was through balloting, (*kubahatisha*) hence *Bahati*.

I passed through Kimathi Estate envying the owners of the posh cars parked in their bays and wondering how the lucky few owners came to own, let alone live in such mansions and drive such cars. I remembered our bed-sitter at Eastleigh, the bed-sitter from which I was going to be evicted and felt the wreaths of despair slowly enfolding my heart.

Of course, I had several friends around Nairobi but I did not know how to go about telling them the problem I had, the problem of looking for a buyer for my scanty belongings.

The last look I had had of Karanja had clearly told me that he was going to send his cousin to evict me from the house. I had no doubts about that. Where the hell would I go? Home in Nyeri? I could not say yes to that because I had not even seen my parents for . . . how long? I could not even remember! The truth was, I did not even know whether Mum and Dad were still alive. What a useless product of both! I felt that it was time I got off my high horse and went home to Mama. What would she do when she saw me? Maybe she'd rush from inside the house and 'break a pot'—a curse. Or, maybe she'd shed tears of love and welcome me back home—prodigal as I had been.

But what would I show them as my '*itaha*'? How would I account for all those years? What if I don't pawn my belongings, but, pack them up instead and take them home . . . would that convince the old couple that I had really endevoured to become what I had always promised them while I was young. The house was there; it had always been there: the '*kahii*' was also there—that was me; but, where was the '*mutwe*'? I was savouring the idea of going home deliciously but I had to have answers to those questions before I put it into practice.

I decided to set those ideas aside first and headed for Maringo in search of Muthukia's house.

It did not take me long to spot it and I went and sat on a dust-bin opposite the door to watch whoever went in or came out. I did not want to go and knock on the door. People in Nairobi are very suspicious of those who go knocking on doors before 16:30 hours. You can never know who a thief or a genuine visitor is.

A small girl approached me and asked my name.

"Maina," I lied to her.

"And what about your teacher's name?" she went on.

"I don't go to school," I laughed out loud.

"Then, you will be beaten by Daddy, he always beats those who don't go to school." She sang and then started calling her other play-mates to come and see a person who did not go to school. I felt that I had had enough of the children and I walked away, escorted by their taunting song" . . . daddy will beat you if you don't go to school . . . daddy will beat you if you don't go to school . . . ."

I walked aimlessly for about an hour within the estate and, next, when I asked a passer-by the time, he told me it was 17:30 hours.

When I knocked on Muthukia's door, I was welcomed by a young woman who reeked of rural life all over. She even had gum-boots on although the last rains we had had in Nairobi had long dried.

"I hope I am in Muthúkia's house," I told her.

"Yes, yes—this is Muthukia's house but, he is not in. He will be here between eleven tonight and midnight. Won't you sit down?" she offered me a dirty, rickety folding chair.

"No, thanks, I will leave the message I had with you," I told her all about Karanja's theft and subsequent arrest and, by the time I finished, she was on the verge of tears. I expressed my sorrow at the whole episode, told her that I hoped all would be well and bade her bye.

I had enough walking for the day and so I walked to the bus-stage and boarded route 7B. I alighted at the Bus Depot at Eastleigh, feeling lost. So much so that I felt that death would have been a welcome relief. I started imagining what it felt to be dead, as I walked towards St. Teresa's Church. I was so engrossed in my thoughts that I almost jumped out of my skin when a motorist applied breaks and his tyres screeched. I had wandered to the middle of the road without realizing it. I was shocked. That was too close to death. I shook the head and shrugged my shoulders at the laughing driver who was now tapping his temple with the fore-finger. Passers-by had come to witness the kill, but were drifting away, disappointed. For them, it was an anti-climax. Nairobi is not a rural village; squealing tyres that don't get a man to hit the tarmac don't bring in what people expect. Anyway, I walked on, more careful this time.

<h1 style="text-align:center">4</h1>

Five days later, I was drinking in town, with five hundred and twenty shillings on me, the money that my scanty belongings had fetched. Having been evicted from Karanja's house by Muthukia who said that he had been instructed to do so by Karanja, I had to sell my bed, mattress, and clothes. I had left only three shirts, four pairs of trousers, a coat, two jackets and a few other items. The conspiracy to evict me was a mystery to me. There were no explanations from either Karanja through Muthukia or Muthukia himself. I just found myself a victim of their blood relation. And God had seen it, and compensated my misfortune somehow. Karanja had earned himself three years in jail.

I was on the road proper. I was sleeping in nightclubs and finding it quite cheap. All you needed was a bottle of beer to hold onto while you slept on the sofa sets in the club. A very comfortable place, if you asked me.

But I was dying inside. Yes, I used to smile, but I could feel the death reaching out its fingers to caress my very heart. Somehow, I felt I did not care at all. I had had enough of the world. I would not have had much to regret if a cop suspecting me for whatever reason had shot me through the head. I did not know where I was headed, nor what was good for me—to die or not to die. But I was slowly decomposing. I could feel it in the awkwardness of my gait as I walked the streets, in the very thum-thump of my poor heart.

I knew Githaiga. That man who kept greasing himself from head to toe every day on Grogan Road. I had watched him doing it several times, occasionally feeling like joining him. But part of my mind would be negative about it, saying I should not let myself grease my clothes while with rolled up sleeves I looked for loose, misplaced or worn out pieces of metal under other people's cars or trucks. In any case, I still had some coins in my pocket, even though they were running out, fast.

I was still making frequent visits to Mathare Valley, where I had a very motherly whore; motherly in both age and kindness. She had warned me against drinking, but how could I do without it? I had often to hide from her and have a sip of the hot stuff—chang'aa. I had given her a hundred shillings when I sold my belongings and she went and bought herself a pair of trousers. She looked so ugly in the pair that I swore never to see her again. She also must have got tired of me because she did not even try to trace my whereabouts.

After three months, I heard that my dear sugar-mummy was involved in an assault case. I did not bother to go and look for her in any police station or remand home. I was having enough problems of my own as it was! Yes. So much so that I did not want to be involved in other people's problems at all. Can't a man have enough of his own? Can't this world know when a man has had enough!

After three weeks of her being remanded in custody, I heard that she had been acquitted and was back in Mathare. Although I had said goodbye to her, I felt triumphant that she had been able to elude the long arm of the law. Any incident in which a person defeated the forces of either the law or nature made me happy. I was happy at other people's successes because I had none to claim. I did not know what was good or bad for me. I really did not even know the very purpose of my existence. I was existing in form only but inside, I was dying. Each passing day carried away a part of my happiness: a part of my gaity; of my laughter, my youth and sadly, my life.

I do not know how it came to be, but I found that I really did not care about anything. I did not care how I dressed. I did not care where I spent my days or nights. I did not care what whore I screwed, as long as she was a woman—age, shape and size were things that mattered little, if any, to me.

I exhausted the few coins I had in a very short time and then started going two or three days without a meal. It might sound funny but the first day that I spent without lunch or supper, I wept. Real salty tears!

I had gone looking for my Mathare Valley sugar-mummy. I was banking on the saying that 'absence makes the heart grow fonder' and, because about five months had elapsed without us seeing one another, I thought she would give me a king-size welcome. I had gone with only half suppers the previous two days and the truth is, my going to see her was aimed at foraging for food! I waited until it was about 2100 hours by which time I knew she would be drunk and possibly amiable. So good!

I went cautiously towards her shanty and noticed that, although the oil-can lamp was still on, the room was extremely quiet. I nervously rapped on the door and a bed creaked from inside. I rapped again and she sleepily asked:

"Who's-zere?"

"I don't know!" I answered. I just wanted her to hear my voice. She knew it like the inside of her pants.

"What d'you want?" There was an unmistakable note of alarm in her voice. Maybe she also had grown to fear me.

"You." I answered, and added, "Surely even small children have not yet gone to bed. Are you growing younger or older as the days go by?" I was laughing; but only with my mouth. My heart was as black as tar. I was so hungry that I was feeling cold. The thought that food was only a few feet from me made me even more hungry and my tummy rumbled involuntarily.

"I think we said good-byes some weeks ago, Fred," she suggested.

"Did we?" I asked. Then, I started sweating. There was a finality about the way she talked that told me that she would not open the door. I was also feeling doubly embarrassed to be standing outside her house for more than five minutes while she was inside. A passing neighbour hailed me and I grunted back his *salaams*. Gosh! How much lower can one sink? For me to be rejected by a fifty-year old bag of flesh and bones! What was I waiting for in the world?

<h1 style="text-align:center">5</h1>

I did not want to say any other word. I suddenly noticed that the room had grown dark. She had put off the lamp!! I retraced my steps just the way I had gone there—without invitation.

I walked to St. Theresa's Church and felt an urgent need to go and kneel in front of the statue of the Blessed Virgin Mary and ask for mercy from God. Surely, I had had enough of problems.

I walked towards the statue and before I got there, there fluttered above my head, an over-size bat. It passed left and right and a morbid liquid fear gripped me, so suddenly that I could hardly stand. I did not know what was happening to me, but that kind of fear had never caught me before, I have never gone near that statue again.

I walked past Pangani Police Station and I had to fight tooth and nail against a force that was urging me to go and set the whole place on fire. I even knew where they kept their petrol and . . . .

I trudged on and found myself inside the one-mile Globe Cinema round-about. I sat down and felt tears streaming down my face. I let them run, but they were so cold that I had to wipe them off. Then, like a switch that had been activated, I went to sleep so suddenly and did not stir until the following day when I was roused by the watch-man who guarded the trailers there. I would have liked him to have taken me to any Police Station on suspicion that I wanted to steal from the motor-vehicles but the blighter only wanted to know whether I had a matchbox on me so that he could smoke. I did not have any and so he went away after clicking his tongue and looking suspiciously at me. I surmised that the kind of sleep I had had was just the way death comes. One minute your are breathing and the next moment you have gone, clean bonkers!

Necessity is the mother of invention, or so someone said. I found a very easy way of getting meals. I should have known before that there existed some vacancies for casual labourers at the City Council retail market every day! All I needed was walking to the market named "Marigiti" each morning, load and unload the delivery vans there, earn myself between twenty and forty shillings a day, not counting the numerous different types of fruits that I ate at the place.

Sleeping was no longer a real problem. My 'Marigiti' co-wokers had all kinds of places to sleep in. Sometimes under lorries and sometimes in the open air. I only made sure of one thing: none of them knew that at one time, I, James Fredrick Wamatu, was a police officer! I was actually ashamed of ever having been one!!

CHAPTER FIFTEEN

1

I was getting to know a bit of mechanics. I joined Githaiga as he had urged me to. He had managed to convince me that as an ex-police officer, I would not get decent jobs. Besides, a job is a job as long as it feeds you, clothes you and affords you a beer and a woman.

He had gone further in his discouragement by telling me that the most 'decent' job I would get would be that of a watch-man. I would have to join one of the security companies that were sprouting all over town like mushrooms. In the job, I would be guarding other people's property, risking my very life in the event of a robbery! Again, I had whole-heartedly sworn not to join those companies. I could not have resigned from a job in which I carried a gun, to go and be employed in a job where my most advanced weapon would be a wooden mallet. Capital NO!

Again, watch-men, like any other security guards you see around town are always partially under the direct supervision of the police and the last thing I wanted to associate myself with was the police.

Marigiti had become a bore. The City Council askaris had started demanding bribes from us so that they could allow us to operate and I felt cheated so much that I called it quits after only one month.

So, mechanics had become the only thing I would do. After all, I was tired of starvation, hopelessness and the fear—always the fear, of what would happen to me tomorrow; the fear I had to live with each tormenting moment of my life.

To join Githaiga, there were no interviews but I had first to learn how to steal. I had to steal some wind-screens so that I could become a member of the mechanics. As I learnt later, the boys force you to steal so that when you joined them, and they stole from a car, you would not have the guts to go and report to the police because they could also accuse you to the same policemen of your theft!

When I asked Githatiga how to go about stealing a wind-screen, he told me to go and ask an Indian. I did not do that since I knew just where to obtain one.

I made the first steal from an Asian's Datsun. This was parked near the Race-Course Road Bridge and I suppose the Asian was in one of the houses near-by: African women brothels. The Asian must have gone there to have a good time. It was about 22:30 hours. I was shown the car by Githaiga himself. I did not know what particular grudge he had against the Asian but he pointed out the car to me and left me to carry on. He even showed me where to fix the screw-driver so that the screen would 'just peel off!

By the time I had the screen in my hands, I was sweating so badly and my stomach was making strange noises that warned me that I would soon diarrhoea. Stealing is not a very easy job. It needs a person with cast-iron guts!

I took the windscreen to Githaiga who was hidden somewhere but who had been watching my progress at the same time and by the way he smiled, I knew that he was happy. He would obtain quite an amount of money after stealing the wind-screen, most likely from the same Asian from whose car I had stolen it!

The second time, I went to an African's Toyota and I was almost caught! I had just fixed the screw-driver at the edge of the screen when some two men approached from nowhere. It was at midnight. The lining of the screen was half-way out when these two intruders came. I started moving away from the car, in deliberately slow steps, and pocketing the screw-driver. The two men stopped at the car. One moved around it and I felt a heat-wave spread over me. Was it the owner? Or who was . . .? Then, they came towards me as I was trying to quicken my pace. I had a mind to bolt right away but then I did not. I pretended that I was looking for a particular vehicle by peering at the number-plates and the guys just closed in on me.

"Have you been here long?" One of them asked me. I had almost lost my voice and I was trembling so badly that, except for the darkness, maybe even the two guys would have noticed that I was shaking.

"No. Why?" I stammered.

"We just wanted to know whether you saw the direction towards which the owner of that car (pointing to the car that I had been tampering with) has gone?" the guy said.

"No, I haven't seen him. In fact I have just come. I am trying to trace my friend's car here." I said. The guys seemed convinced. They moved off and I let off a sigh that you could have heard from Australia!

I was back at the car in a flash and had the wind-screen in my hands within minutes. Walking with it in my hands again was bothersome. What with the ever-suspicious police all over!

When I took the wind-screen to Githaiga, who had all the time been watching me from a safe distance, he commented that I was walking like Jackie Paper on the Dragon's tail! I told him that I would not steal again and also warned him that if he did not share the proceeds from the sale with me at fifty-fifty, I would definitely expose him and his under-world activities!

Honest, I was not going to steal again. Those two experiences had taught me that even a thief should be respected! His job is really difficult. Githaiga told me that I need not threaten him and I need not steal any more on his instructions. He even referred to me as a 'brother' . . . "I know you will be forced to steal on your own!" he maintained.

2

I started learning by cleaning spanners and other tools and keeping my eyes and ears very wide open. There were no theory lessons and if I missed what was being done, I had to wait until another car with the same problem was brought to the workshop for the process to be repeated so that I could see it. Everything was practical.

Githaiga showed me some place to sleep; in the old warehouse which some Asians had abandoned when they hurriedly left the country. I did not know why they did not sell it or why the new owners—if there were any had abandoned it when they hurriedly left the

the way it was. They had provided lodgings for five of us.

We did not go there in day-light. There was a fire-exit at the rear of the building and we were careful to enter the house only in the early hours of darkness. We were also careful and put some rubbish and used oil-cans at the door as a sign of disuse. One passing there would not have easily known that the house was occupied.

Those Asians had been real kind—leaving the house. In most cases when the dukawallahs are leaving the country, they sell all they can and what they cannot, they burn. Those particular ones were kind. Very kind indeed. Blast and screw them and may their plane crash in some ocean—Indian Ocean—if they were going back to Delhi!!

Within three months of joining Githaiga, I was a real mechanic. I had no grade but I was a mechanic all the same. All you needed was to bring your car and by merely looking at the engine and listening to its sound, I could tell you what was wrong with it. I was as good as that. The problem was only a house to live in.

I had moved from the warehouse and was living at Kariakor with another mechanic. The house was only a bed-sitter and we were sharing it. The lease was in my colleague's name but we were sharing the payment of the rent.

Days as a mechanic are very exciting, especially for open-air mechanics. There is a lot of competition. When a car is driven towards our yard, we compete in winning the owner into 'employing' us. You find some of us smearing a lot of grease on our clothes to show how 'skilled' we are. But, the motorist might be one of those who like clean mechanics; so, the mechanics in greasy clothes would lose!

Some of us have keen skill in one part of the vehicle while others have not. So, when one gets a car with a problem that he is not skilled in, he calls for 'paid help'. Sometimes the one who was originally hired to repair ends up with only 10 per cent of the proceeds!

In the evenings, I would go home and take a bath, trying to remove all the grease and oil from my body but no matter how hard I scrubbed myself, I could not rid myself of the faint smell of grease that hovered around me. I guess no real mechanic can eliminate that smell. Not unless he has a Sauna bath.

260

After cleaning up, I used to dress smart and then go to town proper. I was getting my share of 'life' once again, including an occasional woman, prostitute of course.

It was when I was an open-air mechanic that I met Gladys for the second time. Gladys is that school girl from Tumu Tumu who I had left without having consummated love with.

On this day, I went to Kaka Hotel. At Kaka, they sell good food and the prices are not exorbitant. There was also a waiter who had caught my eye and I was going there with a hope that I could make a pass at her.

So, I had dressed in almost my Sunday-best and when I got into the hotel, I took the seat nearest the kitchen-door so that I could observe her as she entered and left the kitchen, delivering foods to ravens.

I made my own order of chicken and rice and started to eat. I also winked at the waiter as she delivered my meal and told her that I would like to have a word with her in private, after the meal. She smiled at that and I knew I would not have a lot of problems in coaxing her.

As I was eating, Gladys came in. She had grown into an older woman but, man—was she a woman.

Her hair was piled on top of her head in a complicated series of twists and turns. Her skin was the colour of coffee and cream and her bosom did some rhythmic bounces as she walked. I was almost hypnotised. She was all round, big teats, big curves and a fanny I admired. She also saw me as she was looking for a vacant table and must have recognised me because she came where I was seated, smiling.

3

"Hello, Fred, where did they unearth you from? You have certainly tried to hide yourself!" she exclaimed as she pulled a chair and sat herself opposite me. I could not shake her hand because I had chicken stew all over my hands. She was laughing. She looked excited. I was also happy. By a fluke of a chance, I might lay her instead of having to wait for a hotel-waiter until possibly past midnight. I also don't like falling in love with women and leaving them without a lay. Makes me feel cheated. After all, what I call love between a woman and a man cannot be called real until there is that body union.

"Hello, Gladys dear, nice to see you—but it's you who got lost. Your husband must be very strict and does not allow you out of the house," I said turning the question around. That is the only method I know. People will always try to convince you that they have been around and in fact, it is you who has been 'lost; and if you don't give up, you can argue for an hour. One wonders where it all started. I found it going and just copied it.

Gladys ordered chicken and rice too, and then started talking about the bad old times. She told me that I must have been very cruel to have beaten that epileptic mono. So, the story had gone around! She told me that after we were expelled, there was no more monolisation and such things.

"Those are days that I do not like to remember. If you remind me of them, I will also remind you that you refused to give me a lay," I told her knowing too well that it would offend her if she were married. It was meant as a stale joke, to stop her from reminding me of the bad old school days. She laughed it off however, and told me that I was too young then for a screw.

"What about now? I asked. I wanted to know her opinion.

"That remains to be seen. I have known some bigger men than you who can not accomplish it satisfactorily . . ." she said and laughed. That made me feel jealous.

"But, they did not fail with you, I presume." I challenged.

"Oh, no. I am not telling you that I went to bed and they failed. But have been told by several of my friends that success in that game does not depend on the size of the body but size of . . . ." she did not finish. I felt reassured at heart. I don't like a woman bragging to me about how she handles men.

262

"I bet I can make it now," I suggested.

"What do you bet?" Surprise.

"A Canon camera" Don't know where that one came from.

"Anyway, these are things to be seen. Tell me, where have you been since those days you call 'bad'? she probed on.

I would have liked to tell it all. It would have taken time and that is exactly what I needed. Time, so that I would know whether she was 'for' or 'against' me. But, I thought I was being hasty—too hasty—to even imagine that I would have her for the you-know-what.

"It's a long story, but right now, I am here in Nairobi." I told her.
"Where particularly?"

"I am down at Grogan Road. I repair cars there. I am in partnership with some other two men. We have a garage there but not a very big one." I lied. I lied because I did not want this woman to know that I was not formally employed and that I depended on sheer luck for my daily bread. Open-air mechanics are most of the time not very well-up. One can miss a customer for a whole morning or afternoon and then, the only solution would be to use one's savings.

Girls in Nairobi, and other urban centres I guess, want to know exactly where you are working—whether you are a managing director or a messenger or what. They need all the details. Whether you drive a car or depend on the Kenya Bus Services for all your travelling.

I wanted to lie to her that I had a car, a Datsun 120 Y but thought it would be futile to tell her such lies. She might have suggested that we go to her place or my place and you bet I would not know how to make the car issue disappear from her head as I led her to the bus-stage.

"Oh, you mean it? And I have been taking my car to rogues who charge me so much!" She exclaimed. But I heard right? Gladys had a car?

"You—have a car?" I could not hide the surprise in my voice.

"Not a very big one, though, but it takes me around," she tried to console me. Maybe she had read my mind. It was a day of surprises.

"What make?".

"It's a Honda Civic." More surprise. A Honda Civic is not a very small car!

We finished our meal and I was about to call for the bills when Gladys suggested that she would pay for the meals and that I would go and buy her a drink in compensation.

"By the way, I hope I did not stop you from meeting anybody, Fred?" she inquired.

"Of course not—I just came here for a meal," I replied and threw a fleeting glance around the room.

The waiter I had 'booked' was moving from table to table, taking and delivering orders. I would not have known what to tell her if she had come just then and asked me what I wanted to tell her in private.

Anyway, I waved her to come over and Gladys paid the bill with a hundred shilling note. She made sure that I saw that there was more where that one had come from.

The waiter eyed her with hostility before leaving our table, dragging her feet on the floor. Gladys was too busy looking inside her purse and did not notice the reproaching look that the waiter threw at me and the subsequent embarrassment that I displayed. I was grinning stupidly though.

When the change was delivered, Gladys ordered me to take it. I was going to protest but she stood up and headed for the door and so I had no choice but to pick the money from the table where the waiter had thrown it. I pocketed it and started feeling a sucker. However, because we were going for a drink, I would use the money there and even spend some of my own to show her that I was not really a beggar!

4

We walked downstairs and came to her car. It was a swell piece of metal, glittering red under the electric light and had a fancy aerial, about five feet long. It was only after looking at the paint-work on both the front and rear fenders that I noticed that, at one time or the other Gladys threw all care and caution to the wind and allowed the car to stop itself, either against another car or an electric pole.

"Yes. This is the junk. My junk. The dents you see all over it occur when I am in the 'mood' she laughed, as she opened the car door. I got into the passenger's seat and Gladys drove the car off.

"Where to?" she asked. Now, that was a difficult question. I had been so much used to bars in Grogan Road and the like but you can bet your last farthing that I would not suggest them.

"Sarova; do you know it?" I asked.

"Yes—in Ambassadeur Hotel?"

"Yes—I like the atmosphere there." I lied once again. I had been to Sarova only once. I had been taken there by a rich client, who was going to buy me a beer there, in appreciation for the service I had rendered his car. In real truth, I had not liked the atmosphere of the place. I mean the sadly quiet kind of boozing that goes on there. Me, I like a place where I can get drunk, yell and curse if I want.

We quickly arrived at Sarova and parked our car. I was feeling like a boy in a successful orange-stealing mission. We started climbing the stairs. I had no tie on but the door-man did not seem bothered about that this time. The previous occasion had embarrassed me and my client had had to hire a tie for me at 10 shillings. We passed into the bar-room and seated ourselves at the table next to the fellow who spends all his time strumming an organ.

Before I could make up my mind what to drink, Gladys called for Vodkas. I protested, telling her that I was not used to Vodka, but, she told me that she could not drink any other stuff without first downing Vodka. So I accepted.

I swallowed the Vodka, feeling its bite all over my aeshophagus and a pinch somewhere else—my pocket. I did not have enough money for such exotic drinks. True, I had about a hundred and thirty shillings of my own, plus about fifty-five or something shillings which was Gladys' change, but I was not ready to part with everything that I had. The cops had taught me how to be mean in buying drinks and despite the fact that I hated them, I was still very reserved where buying drinks was concerned.

Gladys must have noticed my uneasiness because she called for Exports immediately after we finished the Vodkas.

She was drinking and getting drunk and excited and I was making some mental calculations. She was telling me a lot of funny stories. Like that one day, a guy had wanted to rape her and she had slapped him so hard that he had fallen down. She had then ran away. The stories all sounded childish to me. She was getting more and more drunk but it did not come to me as a surprise. She was drinking an Export in only about five minutes and then calling for another and the waiter was always at the ready to come and serve us. I even noticed that the occupants of most of the other tables had somehow turned their chairs so that they had a constant view of our table.

Me, I was not getting drunk. I was having a thousand and one thoughts that could not allow my system to get drunk. I was thinking, besides other things, of how I would come to own a car—no matter how small. Then, I would not have to depend on Kenya Bus Services or beg rides every time I wanted to go some place. I was wondering how people like Gladys came to own cars and such. How did it happen? I had already swallowed about eight Exports, not forgetting the double tot of whisky but, unfortunately, instead of the alcohol relaxing me, it was only sharpening my self-consciousness and making me feel inadequate for a woman like Gladys. I was so pre-occupied with these thoughts that she had to recall me to the present.

"I think we had better get out of this place now," she suggested, "maybe your wife is tired of waiting for you," she told me, looking at her wrist-watch. I looked at mine and noticed that it was already past 2200 hours.

"I have no wife," I snapped, grinning.

"And I have no husband—gosh! aren't we getting a bit too old for bachelor life?" she looked at me pretending to be worried.

"How old are you now?" I asked.

"One hundred years—let's get the hell out of here, Fred. I am feeling drunk." She looked drunk alright.

I was going to pay for the drinks but again, she beat me to it. She produced a roll of fivers and extracted two from it. Before the waiter could bring the change, she got up, picked her hand-bag, held me by

the hand and we started walking towards the door. I could not help
but calculate that, given an average of about four shillings per Export
and the price of the Vodka, the waiter had got away with over eighty
shillings tip! What a waste! We reached downstairs and she leaned on
me, looked up at me and parted her lips. She half-closed her eyes and
I kissed her. Just there in front of the usher who was looking at us like
we were Martians.

4

We then went to her car and she told me that she could not drive
any more. She asked me whether I could drive and I answered her
positively. That was not a lie anyway. One cannot afford to be a
mechanic without knowing how to drive. Otherwise how could one
conduct road-tests?

"Okay, drive me home?" she told me. My heart automatically
changed its tempo.

"Which home?" I asked. A very stupid question, I presume; but I
had to ask it. Having not even suggested about being together for the
night, I did not know where she wanted me to go.

"To my place—you can go to your place with the car if you find
mine unsuitable for you." She handed me the car keys and I
wondered how many other men had had the opportunity of getting
her drunk and driving her home. I opened the doors and she slumped
on the passenger seat and closed her eyes, pretending to be asleep and
then she fluttered them open again and smiled at me. I wished she
could go on smiling, but for only as long as she had no husband. I had
an idea of making love to her just there and then but, I did not put it
across to her.

I started the car, and she pointed the corners where to turn here
and there and presently, we were in Uhuru Estate. She walked
unsteadily to the door and handed me a bunch of keys.

"I am not used to so much drink, Fred. You must forgive me if I
appear drunk but, it was you who made me drink—for old time's
sake eh . . ." she laughed out loud.

"But, you are not very drunk," I assured her. I was fumbling with the lock of the door, trying almost every key and she was holding on to me to stop herself from staggering. At last, I opened the door and she staggered in, snapped on the light and embraced me.

"Welcome to my den," she told me and then she flopped on a sofa set.

"Thank you." I said and made for the same sofa set but she held up her hand.

"No. It's time for a shower," she told me.

She showed me the bathroom. The house was real big. Two bed-roomed! There was no way of comparing it to the small bed-sitter which we shared with my fellow mechanic at Kariakor.

In the bath-room, she told me to remove my clothes. I opened my mouth.

"What is it, Gladys?" I asked, but I did not need anybody's answer. She was already undressing. Just like that and suddenly she was naked! Waters hit her, she gasped. I was looking at her. Boy! Those thighs! The arse! The apple! I was having one hell of a time. I had to remove my clothes fast or jack-off in them.

I hurriedly stripped and walked into the shower with my prick leading me.

5

"Gosh! I have got myself a job there!" she exclaimed, pointing at my incher which was at full cock!

The cold water enveloped me and my prick went a step down. Not fully down, however. It could not fully go down when Gladys was fully naked in front of me. It remained at half-mast.

We showered and towelled up. She held me and kissed me. She was hot again. She then led me to the master bed-room. We left all our clothes in the bath-room.

"Say you love me." she told me.

"You love me." I repeated.

Not that—I mean. Say, I love you!" she corrected me.

"I love you!" I repeated. This reminded me of a word game I used to play with Charity. I tried to make a mental comparison of Charity with Gladys and Charity won. Damned it! I did not know what that woman had given me. I should not even have thought of her when I was in another woman's house.

"Okay, babe," she muttered sitting on the bed. I moved and held her. I placed her in the middle of the bed. I kissed her. A long kiss that left her legs apart.

At 0600 hours the following morning, I woke up. I made the usual adjustments and remembered where I was. I kissed Gladys on the nipples, watching them rise and harden at my touch, and she woke up. She looked at me sleepily and then parted her legs. I mounted her.

This morning act had been introduced to me by Charity. We used to call it 'Morning call-up! If I missed a morning call-up with Charity, I was sure of having a cold eye at break-fast table.

At 0700 hours, I was up and bathing. Gladys was also up. She was in the kitchen quarrelling with the pots and pans. As I showered, I was whistling the song called 'Love the second time around'! I was, for the first time in a long time: happy. Gladys was surely a hot bird. I hardly had slept throughout the night. I also had given her a hell of a night because she too had hardly slept. I was amazed to notice that the drunkenness she had so openly displayed in the evening had vanished immediately we started the game. She did not leave me to the works alone like Mary had done.

I finished my shower and joined Gladys in the kitchen. I told her that there was really no need for us to go to the table-room for breakfast and so we had our breakfast right there in the kitchen. After eggs, bacon, bread and two mugs of tea, I held her and kissed her and I started erecting all over, but she held me short;

"No, Fred, there is this evening and of course any other evening that you want—okay?"

"Yes," I answered. I felt that I would have liked it to be every evening.

She took the wheel on our journey to town and we could hardly talk on the way. She was holding the wheel like her very life depended on it and so I did not want to disrupt her concentration.

She dropped me at the East African Road Services Bus Terminus on Race Course Road. I could easily walk from there to Grogan Road. After arranging how we would meet that evening, I waved her off and started walking down the road. I was still whistling 'Love the second time around'.

On arrival at the open-air garage, I found my house-mate already there. He asked me where I had spent the night and I told him. I told him everything. I praised Gladys so much that I noticed he was getting envious. That's what I like. I like men to envy me.

Even as we started our work, I noticed that there was something that was disturbing his peace of mind, but I did not ask him what it was. I had learnt to keep quiet on matters that did not directly affect me. Proverbs had told me that 'a man who finds others quarrelling and joins in is like a man who holds a lion by the tail'. You can guess what happenes to such a man.

He was clicking his tongue from time to time and once, when I told him to pass a spanner to me, he pretended not to have heard and I had to go and get the spanner myself. He was wearing a frown all through the morning.

We used to have our lunches in one of the shanty 'Hiltons' along the river. The food was cheap and the atmosphere was very friendly. You found that everybody talked only about cars and women and because we were all mechanics—of cars and women?—one could not feel out of place.

On that particular day, my house-mate told me that he was going to have his lunch in town. When I asked him why, he told me that he was tired of eating in cheap stinking hotels which were not licensed. We laughed at the deprecation of our 'Hilton', but I noticed that my friend was forcing himself to laugh. He would have very easily wept instead. I suggested that I accompany him to town and that did it. The bomb that had been ticking the seconds away slowly inside him, then exploded:

"I will not go with you! You can go and look for your prostitutes anywhere; but don't drag me to them!" he shouted.

Just imagine that. What was the guy saying? I was shocked. I was really hit back. What was the cause of the uproar? Why was he so angry?

The man had been living with me for the past six months and we had had no quarrel of any kind. I realised that there was something amiss and that I had the right to know.

"What is wrong, David?" David Gitau was from Murang'a. I had been introduced to him by Githaiga before Githaiga got a regular job with the Cooper Motor Corporation and also a Company house. I occupied the place that Githaiga had been occupying and we got along quite fine with Gitau.

"Nothing! Nothing is wrong, but I want you to move from my house tonight. I can pay the rent alone. This evening, before you go looking for your prostitutes, I want you to remove all your belongings. Everything! When I arrive there, I do not want to see anything that is called yours inside that house!" He spat out the words.

Why? Why was he telling me to move from the house? I had not refused to pay the rent any time. In fact, the previous month, I had paid the whole amount hoping that he would do likewise the following month. He had told me that he had had to send his aging mum some money for a brother's school fees and so he did not have any money to spare for rent.

The house was registered in his name but then ... he was my friend. Where would I go? I suddenly realised that I had been very stupid all along. I had had enough time to look for my own house. I had just sat and lived my life with blinkers on. Trouble was, I had never thought that Gitau would ever chase me from his house. I was living like the house was actually mine. Gripes! What a situation! Gitau was surely not my brother or kin and so he had every right to tell me whatever he wanted any time.

The first person that came to my mind was Gladys. She had a big house of course but, would she accept me? And if so, for how long? I was not sure whether the love she had shown towards me the previous night was genuine or was the effect of drunkenness. Maybe she was even feeling ashamed of having thrown herself to me the way she had done. Again it was just by chance that we had met. The question of love was out.

Lodging houses? Of course the most readily available solution. But where was I going to keep my few belongings? Maybe I would fold them and Gitau would not refuse me to keep them in his house for about a week. I would need that long to get myself a house.

I decided that in the evening, when I met Gladys, I would joke with her about moving to her house and then see her reaction. I would be looking at her to see whether she would curl her upper lip in disgust or smile lopsidedly. Those thoughts raced in my brain within about ten seconds.

"Okay, David, if that is the way you want it to be, then, it shall be. Only don't forget the rent deal we did last month and so, I will need a refund." I said conclusively. If he did not want me, then surely he should not want my money?

Anyway, I did not want Gitau to go on shouting at me. I was not deaf. I would not have been employed as a cop with defective ears!

David walked away and left me still standing there. Kanyi, a mechanic neighbour told me that maybe he had something disturbing him. I just nodded my head in assent but had no words to say. I was trying to think where the sudden urge to chase me from his house had originated and I did not need to eat my heart out thinking about it. What I would do was just leave his house. If that would please him, well and good. I wished him luck.

I walked towards Kiriti Bar. I decided that I would not have any food for lunch. I would rather have a beer and then, in the evening, I would look for the best 'cheap' lodging where I would put up for a few days. For the first time in a long time, again I felt the tentacles of hopelessness start to caress me. I mean, ever since I had joined Githaiga at Grogan and had started my mechanics lessons, the air of utter hopelessness that had enveloped me immediately after resigning from police had completely vanished—to be replaced by a hope—however forlorn—of progress. David had started that sense of being 'lost' in me again.

I entered Kirit and ordered an Export. It was delivered and I swallowed it slowly. The time was still early—11.35 according to my wrist-watch and I still had twenty-five minutes. We took our lunches earlier than the other people—11.30 to 12.00 so that we might be at our places of work during the real lunch break.

I asked for another drink and finished it in no time. I felt that I needed more alcohol in my system but I put a stop to it. That is another silly problem with me. Whenever I have cause for anger or worry, the only solution I find is in taking alcohol. That way, my mind is numbed and I do not concentrate on the problem any more. I did not want to go on drinking because of two things. First, I had to spare the money I had otherwise I might find that lodging houses are more costly than I anticipated. Again, I did not want to get drunk when going to repair other people's cars. They might end up being worse off than they were when they were brought to the garage. Then again I might end up with an injured hand and there is no worse handicap for a mechanic than a wound on the hands.

I walked back to my place of work and found that David was already there again. He was still sulking. His explusion of me from his house had not eased the tension that was in him. I did not want to show him any enemity at all. In fact, I would have liked to buy him a beer just to show him that he had not really offended me at all. There was nothing unusual in what he had done.

"Where did you go? I came looking for you but could not trace you" I told him. I just wanted to show him that I harboured no ill feelings towards him.

"What was it that you wanted from me?" He asked. He sounded very furious.

"Nothing in particular. I just wanted to buy you a beer. I also did
not feel over-inclined towards those river-side hotels and had a beer
for lunch." I found myself saying.

"Do you think I am one of your prostitutes?" he asked very
harshly. I then decided that David had no right to insult me at all
even if I lived in his skin! I don't like to be insulted by anybody
whatever their relationship with me. I decided that David had gone
far enough and had to stop. He was a man like me and if he was
doubting my manhood, I would not tell him to go and ask Gladys
but I would beat him up and urinate on him. That way, he would see
my manhood.

"Why are you insolent to me, David?" I asked, very furiously as
well. I was looking at him. He was looking for a tyre-lever which I
reckon he wanted to use on me in case of a physical confrontation but
then, a tyre-lever is to me no weapon at all. I had been trained in
unarmed combat and I could even disarm armed combatants.
David was forgetting my past and so thinking that he could wipe me
clean. He was wrong though. Very mistaken.

"What will you do about it? I have insulted you alright but what
do you think you can do? If there is anything, just go ahead and do it
now!" He challenged, sneering. Before I advanced towards him. I
already knew the hold I would use to get the tyre-lever from his
hands.

I jumped on him and before he could raise his hands to strike me, I
was already holding it. I was holding it with my left hand and I gave
him a punch on his death-pressure point with my full right. Gas
hissed through his clenched teeth. He let go off the tyre-lever and I
picked it and threw it far from us.

People were coming from all over and cheering like mad. I don't
know whom they were cheering but I guessed it was me. I was giving
David real punches and he was accepting them. He was giving me
next to nothing. He was swaying some wild lefts and rights and none
was connecting with any steam on me.

7

I gave him a full lift with my right and he went flat on his back. I was going for the throat—to finish off the rest of his resistance—but before I could strangle the day-lights out of him! Wao! The cops! They had arrived. Two of them walking quickly to where we lay in a heap, and a patrol-car following behind them slowly. It had its siren on. I stood up and one of the cops held my hand in a none-too strong grip. I would easily have wrestled my hand free by just twisting it but I let him have the heroism of holding me. They allowed David some two minutes before he could recover his senses fully. He then stood up.

He did not seem to know where he was. Looking at him, I noticed with disappointment that I had done no real damage to his handsome face. Then, a feeling of relief as I knew that the cops would have a very difficult time proving any case against us. We could have been merely practising wrestling.

He then saw the cops and suddenly 'woke' up. He focussed his eyes on them as he tried to wipe dust from his head.

"He has refused to move from my house." David said. I didn't know who he thought the cops were. One of the cops, the one wearing the Chevrons of a sergeant, laughed and told him that he would be given all the time in the world to say all he wanted, in a court of law. He even cautioned us against saying anything until we reached the police station. I did not know whether that was the proper way to caution offenders but then, I was no longer a cop. Maybe they changed the form of caution when I left. We were both handcuffed and led to the police car.

"Excuse me sirs, but, I have left all my spanners and other tools there." I said pointing at my tools, and then added, "Could I be allowed to collect them and . . ." But the cop had already started dragging me forcefully towards the car.

"There is no workshop in the police cells. We take our cars to D.T. Dobie and so you don't need your tools." The sergeant retorted.

Although I had reserved some respect for them, especially the way they came to know where trouble was brewing any time, I felt that that was not the most intelligent way of answering me. He did not need to tell me even where they take their cars for repair.

"But, they will be stolen. I just . . ." I did not finish. The sergeant slapped me on the mouth and called me shit. Me? Shit? I shut up and moved my tongue all over inside my mouth but there was no dent. I maybe would have worsened the situation by reacting to any taste of blood in my mouth.

The driver started the car and we were driven to Kamukunji Police Station. The sergeant instructed the constable on duty to lock us up and book us for affray. He then left. The constable told us to sit on the floor. I promptly sat down but David hesitated and was slapped by him. So hard that blood lined his lips. I thanked the cop in my heart. That slap evened the score.

The cop took our particulars and searched us. He gave us receipts for our money and wrist-watches and told us to wrap the rest; belts and handkerchiefs together. He then pushed us to the cells. Luckily, he put us in one cell. That way, we would have a chance to reconcile and 'finish' the case. I waited until the cop had locked us up and the click-click of his boots and died out before I turned to David.

"Do you see where your folly has landed us? I will tell you what we shall do. We shall say that we were merely playing. Do you hear that? Since you don't have any visible injuries—and neither do I, they can not prove that we were fighting. If you don't say as I suggest, then, we shall be in trouble." I advised him. It was the only solution to a case of affray.

"Go to hell! I don't want your philosophy. All I want you to do is move from my house. I don't care whether we are jailed or not!" David snarled.

I advanced towards him blindly and gave him a slap that you could have heard from Embakasi. He returned the slap and before you could say 'Industrial Area', we were having the wildest fight I have ever fought. We were exchanging punches like we were in a boxing ring. I was a head taller than David and so he could not bang me very hard on the face. He was rather pumping my tummy.

I was banging his nose repeatedly. He was already bleeding from it and the blood was making my fists dirty. I gave him a kick on his crotch and he doubled forward. I lifted him with a 'short' knee and he thudded on the floor. Flat out! That's what he was. I walked to the opposite wall and sat down. I wiped David's blood on the wall. David too sat up and faced me from the other wall. We were then silent and I started flexing my fingers, one by one.

At 1600 hours, the cell door was opened. Do you know who I saw? Wafula! Inspector Matthew Wafula. My old squad-mate. It was him alright. He had come to check on the prisoners in custody. There and then, I realised that I would not be in custody for long.

8

"Hey, Fred, what are you doing here? You know I was still doubtful when I read your name in the Occurrence Book and I was just coming to the cells to confirm. What the hell are you doing in cells?" He asked, bewildered. He was looking at me and then looking at David. He seemed not to believe his eyes.

"Trobules, brother, tell me first, are you here now?" I asked him.

"Yes, I am here, I am the Deputy O.C.S. here. Come along, cells are not the best places for conversations. I arrived just last week and I am happy to see you although you must admit that these are not the best circumstances." He was laughing as he pulled me out of the cell. David made as if to move and Wafula snapped at him to sit down. I was smiling shyly as Wafula locked the door again and we walked towards the offices. I heard David click his tongue loudly. We walked to Wafula's office and he offered me a seat. I sat opposite him, bare-foot.

"Before we carry on, tell me; why are you here?" he asked. He was a cop all over.

"You see that fellow we have left in the cells; we have been sharing a house, but, today, he came and told me to move out of it. It is in his name. We exchanged a few bitter words when I was trying to know the reason for the eviction without notice but apparently, we could not understand one another. You know the way with men. If you cannot understand one another with words, you use swords and that is exactly what we were doing when your patrol-men came and arrested us." I had to tell him the truth because I knew he would do his best. He was still shaking his head:

"Why did you not tell them that you are a Police Officer?" he asked doubtfully.

"Because I am no longer one." I answered firmly.

"You mean . . . what you are saying is that you have left the Police Force; isn't it?" He asked me.

"That is precisely what I am trying to say."

'Why?" What a question. And what was I supposed to tell him?

"Anyway," he said on second thought, "I know you are going to tell me all the details. As it is, this case of affray is dead. Is any of you injured?" He was examining me the way a doctor would examine a baby.

"Not really. David could be having a bleeding nose but that one can come even without a fight," I answered.

He lifted the telephone handset and told the recipient at the other end to deliver the O.B. When the cop brought it he saluted Wafula respectifully. Wafula was at last worth saluting!

He conducted a short lecture to the duty constable; about the points to prove a case of affray—like medical examination—independent witnesses—visible injuries—et cetera all aimed at trying to show the duty constable that he and the officers who had arrested us had fallen short of the term 'efficient in duty.' He almost termed our arrest 'wrongful confinement!'

My heart was doing the cantata right inside my chest. He then ordered the constable to release us and he noted in the remarks column of the O.B. No further Police Action (N.F.P.A.)

We walked to the counter where our items were handed back to us. I put on my shoes and buckled my belt and we walked out of the Police Station and into freedom.

Wafula was telling me how he had left the Rift Valley Province. He said that there was a Provincial Police Officer there who thought the Rift Valley Province was a Republic with its own sovereignty and that he, the P.P.O., was the Head of State there. Wafula had been transferred from the Province because he had refused to salute the P.O.O.'s wife!

We were walking towards the canteen. David was following us and so I signalled to Wafula about his presence. Wafula told him to go away and not to repeat such childish behaviour. He walked away without even saying thanks!

We entered the canteen and Wafula called for a beer for me. I accepted it. He ordered a soda for himself and when I asked him why he was not drinking, he told me that every time he went to a new station, he gave himself some few weeks of abstinence, so that he could 'know' the safe areas to drink.

We related to one another the things that we had done since we had parted at Kakamega. At the end of it all he assured me that as long as he was the Deputy O.C.S. at Kamukunji, I would not be harrassed by the cops at the stations.

Then, I remembered my spanners.

9

"Hey, *bwana*, since you and I are here all the time, let me go and see whether any kind of mechanic collected my spanners for me when we were arrested. You know the damned things cost a fortune these days." I told him.

"Oh, yes, let us see whether the driver is around. I can drop you there as I proceed on patrol." he told me and then snapped his fingers at the seller. He paid for my three beers and then we went back to the police station.

We got the patrol car but no driver and so Wafula drove me to the open-air garage. We found the place deserted but I assured Wafula that somehow, I would recover my spanners.

He told me that he was going on patrol and asked me to be seeing him often . . . at least once a day. I promised him that I would be doing just that. He left, laughing.

I walked home and found David there. When he saw me, he scowled at me.

"Get your things out and make it snappy!" He snarled at me again. I could see that he had changed his clothes and had applied a coat of vaseline on his broken lips. What a cursed son-of-a-bitch.

"I will get them out but not before I know where I am going to put them. I am going to talk to Gladys now and, I will be coming to collect them in may be an hour's time. Meanwhile, keep your serpent tongue to yourself and learn how to behave. I am surprised that you do not realise or appreciate that it was me who triggered your release from the police station. You should be thankful, at least for once." I told him very calmly although my heart was beating, fit to burst. He did not argue.

I went to the bath-room and washed off the smell of the police cells and the grease. Then, I dressed smart and walked off to Terrace Hotel: our rendezvous with Gladys.

I had not even finished my first beer before Gladys came in, apologising for keeping me waiting and blaming the traffic lights for the delay. I assured her that I was quite alright and then told her of my episode with Gitau. She listened, nodding her head silently. Then I said as I was joking, "So I would like to sleep at your place for a few days before I get my own hovel!"

"So you want to marry me?" she asked me, equally jokingly.

"Yes. But only for a week! Within one week, I am sure I will have got a house for myself." I told her. I was smiling like I had hit the jackpot. I thanked the Almighty. Gladys did not even protest. It's good to have a friend like her! She was a real friend in need.

She further told me that I need not carry all those 'beds and mattresses'. I could pawn them.

When I asked her on what I would be sleeping, if I pawned my beddings, she smiled and pointed at her bosom.

I was not going to pawn my belongings. You never know with a woman. She could very easily grow tired of me and kick me into the wilderness again. After all, what was I going to offer her in return. I mentally calculated what I was worth. My height—six feet, two inches, my weight, about eight kilos, personal assets—don't mention it! I, as I sat there smiling at Gladys, was not worth more than five hundred shillings in assets—not counting my body with its numerous scars, and a nose that was too long for a Bantu!

I was going only to pick my suit-case, full of the clothes I had bought to replace the ones I had pawned and join Gladys for a few days while I looked for my house.

I thanked Gladys with a Vodka and then I borrowed her car. It would be only a few minutes drive to Kariakor and I could pack my suit-case alone.

As I stepped out of Terrace Hotel, I noticed that it was raining heavily. That's the trouble with Nairobi hotels. They are constructed in such a way that, at night, you would not know what the weather was like outside till you got out.

I doubled up and ran to Gladys' car, wincing as the cold rain fell on me. I quickly got in the car and started the engine. One of the wipers, the left hand one, was not working but that was to be expected.

I arrived at our place after only a ten-minute drive. The rain had made me drive slowly; so I was a bit too late. David had already spoiled my evening.

10

Scattered outside, were all my earthly belongings. David must have mistaken them for rain-gauges. They were all there; soaking wet and still absorbing more from the rain which was now abating its intensity.

There was light in the house and the radio was on. Full volume. David was having a good time inside. I touched my mattress. It was wet. I tried to lift it but it was too heavy. Foam mattresses really know how to 'drink' water. My blankets were spread on the mud. Even my

Sunday-best suit! The coat was here and the trousers there. David had clearly prepared a noose for himself. I would not forgive him. I could not forgive him. I could not bring myself to look at all I owned, soaking wet there and then think of forgiving the cause of all the wetness!! I was saying to myself that maybe that would be the last day in freedom but, even when I am in jail, David would not be able to pronounce 'S'.

I banged on the door loudly and the radio was switched off.

"Who's there?" David asked from inside. I did not want him to know that it was me. If he did, he would not open. I knocked again. Again, he asked who it was and I still knocked again. Above the whisper of the drizzling rain, I could hear foot-steps approaching the door. He was coming towards the door.

When he reached the door, again he asked who it was. I kept mum. I was just about to knock again when I heard that he was removing the latch. The door was hardly released from the latch when I gave it a horse-kick sending it open and David sprawling five feet inside the house. I walked in, dripping water.

When he saw me, he started screaming 'Thief! Thief!' I had to stop him. I went to him and gave him a silencing punch, right on his dirty screaming mouth.

"If you scream again, I will kill you!" I said with all the menace I could manage in my voice. I meant it. David must have caught the live threat in my voice and he shut up. He was trembling from head to toe. I listened but above the roar of the rain, which had incidentally added its intensity again, there were no people coming to answer the hue and cry that David had raised.

David was standing in front of me with his hands on his mouth. I was also trembling. Trembling with rage and wrath and anger. I wanted to grab his neck and squeeze and watch him die. I felt that that would be my only satisfaction. I wanted to kill him with my bare hands.

"Why did you throw my things in the rain?" I asked him. I had to restrain my voice from getting too high. David just looked at me. He was looking at me like I was a dragon. He had his mouth open but no words were coming out of it. I took another step towards him and repeated the question:

"Why did you throw my property in the rain?"

He opened his mouth wider. I guessed he wanted to scream again. I slapped him across the face. He got hold of my shirt-front and we started fighting for the third time during the day.

I was determined to show him that I was a man. I was so determined that I was not feeling the weight of the punches that he was landing on me. He gave me an over-powerful punch on my mouth and I felt my tooth crack. I felt the broken piece and spat it out. Blood was coming from a lacerated cut he had made on my face with his nails—like a woman! He was on me proper. I was feeling my face with my hand so I was not aware of his coming.

He got hold of both my legs and hauled me to the floor. I banged my head so hard on the cement floor that I thought I would go nuts! David had borrowed some power from the devil and he was using it all on me! If I did not act then, he would surely have killed me. He got hold of my neck with both hands and started squeezing. He was slowly and carefully strangling the life out of me.

I could not use my hands on his body as I was trying to release the grip on my throat. I was feeling like my head was swelling and some unnatural heat was enveloping me. I was going to die like a rat. At the very last moment, before I lost consciousness, I brought my right leg from behind David and manouvered it so that I hooked it under David's chin. That done, despie the rapidly fading consciousness, I felt a bit assured. I stretched the leg and David released hold of my neck and doubled. He was doubling backwards and despite his resistance, I thought I heard something snap in his spinal cord and he gasped once. Just once and then his whole body went limp.

I was trying to regain my breath and massaging my neck which I thought had already started swelling. I held him in the backward double position for about three minutes and then I released him.

I stood up, feeling my neck with my hand but David remained in the same position I had left him. I bent and straightened him up. The way his head banged against the floor and bounced told me that he was dead and panic gripped me. I quickly bent over him and felt his pulse; it was fast but very faint. I suddenly got the shock of my life! I could have killed the guy. The real truth is that I just wanted to show him that I was a man. Not to kill him for God's sake!!

I stirred him with my foot. He moaned softly but did not open his eyes. Blood was slowly oozing from his nose and mouth. He had smeared me with it all over my shirt and body. I wanted him to stand and fight. Not just lying down there giving me the scare of my life. But he just lay there groaning. I tried to lift him up but his hands were as limp as the tentacles of a dead octopus.

A tap on the door made me turn sharply. I told myself that it could be the police. Not again! At least not so fast! I did not want anybody to find me inside the house when David was thus sprawled on the floor. Someone might start screaming 'Murder! Murder!' and I might land in for good. I went to the door and opened it a crack. There was a woman outside. She was dressed in her Sunday-best. I guessed she was the woman who had made David decide to throw me out of his house.

"Come in." I said. I did not care what she would say or do. She was smiling, showing me some very white teeth and folding her umbrella. She came all the way in. I was still standing between her and David's prostrate form on the floor. I waited until she was fully inside the house and then moved aside so that she could see her man. She looked past me at David's prone body. She looked at me as I stood between her and the door and she started screaming: "Ooooohhhh!" and I noticed that she had an unproportionably bigger voice than her body-size. I allowed her to let off three screams before I left the house, banged the door and walked quickly to Glady's car. I started it and drove off but on driving for only about ten minutes, I remembered my suit.

Throwing all care to the wind, I reversed and went back. I alighted, picked the wet suit and dumped it on the rear seat. Then, I drove off again.

12

I did not go far though. I drove to about five blocks from our house and switched off the engine. It had stopped raining then and I got out of the car and stood there, watching the direction of David's house to see what would happen.

My belongings were still scattered there. Already, some nosy people were going to the house to check on what was happening. The woman was still screaming her silly head off.

Then, she came out of the house running. She was still screaming. She ran towards the social hall and I gave her one notch in her score card. She must have been going to call the police or ambulance.

The people who had gathered outside the house were touching my things. Some were even peeping into the house and then withdrawing. The situation was such and that one could not understand at first glance.

Five minutes later, the woman came running back to the house. She had stopped screaming but as soon as she entered the house, she was at it again. This time hoarsely. People were then entering the house and coming out but I was too far to hear what the hell they were saying.

A police car's siren could be heard from a distance. Yes. She had called the police. Maybe it was the same siren I had heard in the after noon when I was arrested for affray. The car was at the Market and the siren was cutting into the dark night. It came on and passed me just where I had parked Gladys' car. Surely, it was the the same Ford Transit Van, that had picked us during the day. I did not want to think that Wafula could be the car commander. The blue warning dome-light made a beautiful contrast on the red of Gladys' car. They passed me and headed straight for David's house. I counted the cops as they jumped out of the van and saw Wafula, in a great-coat issuing orders to his men. I smiled mischievously. There was a total of eight policemen including the driver. Too many for any Goliath and so, I slid into the car and waited for them there.

They came out of the house about two minues later, carrying David. They put him in the rear of the van and the woman also went with them.

They passed where I was, for the second time and now I was a bit scared. Although I knew that none of the cops would connect Gladys' car with the incident, Wafula knew David and even knew of our previous quarrel and so it was not very hard for him to put two and two together. I did not want him to see me.

I waited until they had driven a few metres in front of me and then started the car and followed them. I wanted to know where they were taking David. The mortuary or hospital.

As soon as we joined the main-road, the siren started its wailing again and that kind of reassured me that David was far from dead. Cops don't apply the siren for corpses. I kept my distance, though.

We drove all the way to Kenyatta National Hospital. They entered through the casualty entrance and I parked Gladys' car very far away from the entrance—but where I could see what was going on.

When the police van stopped, the cops literally jumped out and ran to the rear of the van. The caution that they were taking while moving David from the car to the stretcher told me that he was not dead. I did not need any more information. I just wanted to know whether he was dead or alive and so I drove off and headed for Terrace Hotel.

I had to button up my coat to stop everyone staring at the blood on my shirt. I entered the hotel and noticed that Gladys was nowhere in sight. I only saw the waiter I had an eye on but I did not as much as say hello to her. Gladys must have gone. I must have taken too long.

I hurriedly drove to her house in Uhuru but the darkness around the place, and the silence that answered my knock showed that she was not in the house. So, I drove again to town and went again to Terrace. I went in and again Gladys was not there! Where the hell was she?

I wanted to give her car back and flee. I was no going to wait for David to die so that Wafula could come and arrest me. Oh, no! I had to get the hell out of Nairobi.

I decided to try Uhuru again, thinking that if she was not in, I was going to park her car just where we had parked it the previous night and leave it there. I would write her a small note, giving an odd reason why it was necessary for me to go away. Luckily when I drove there, I found that the lights were on. She was in.

I knocked nervously on the door and she opened it. She saw the state of my clothes and at once, she must have sensed that something was wrong. She stepped away from me and was opening her mouth to say something but, before she could frame her first question, I held my hand up and silenced her. It was my time to speak and not hers.

"Whatever has happened was destined to happen. I just took part because I was forced to. If you try to give me time, I will tell you all." I told her as I sat myself on a chair, unbuttoned my jacket and allowed her to see the blood that was all over my shirt and other clothes. She had her mouth very wide open. I was afraid that she too would start screaming.

"Wha-t ha-happened?" She asked, hesitantly.

I told her everything, truthfully. I was not very sure of how she could react but I guessed that I could trust her not to run to the nearest telephone booth and call the police. I was sure she would not do that.

"Are you sure he is not dead?" She asked as I concluded the story.

"That I am sure of. The way the police were handling him at the casualty entrance of the hospital told me that he was not dead. However, I am not really certain of it but I think there is no cause for alarm," I assured her.

"Okay, let's get rid of these clothes. You look awful. May I tell you what you look like—and don't hate me for it please . . . you look like Al Capone!" We both burst out laughing inspite of the state of things.

Then followed the removal of my clothes. I stripped to the pants. Gladys put all the clothes in a basin and filled it with water. She then sprinkled a detergent all over them and told me that they would have to soak overnight so that the blood would be absorbed in the water.

I was uneasy. If David kicked the bucket, I would be in the wanted list—for murder. The police at Kamukunji Police Station already had a record of our quarrel and fight and Wafula would not need to conduct an Identification Parade to know who had done what. I tried to count the number of people who knew that I was living with David for the previous six months and they were too many for comfort. I said a silent prayer to the Almighty God that David should not die.

"Go to bed, Fred. I will bring you supper there," Gladys told me. She was taking care of me. She was taking a risk for me. If David died, she would be arrested as an accesory after the fact. She too would face the music of the law-breaker. Sweet music!

I went to her bed and covered myself half-way. I took a Daily Nation that was lying on the bed-side table and started reading it. As I reached the police reports column, I realised that the following day, David's case would appear there with the police appealing to anyone who might have witnessed the incident to volunteer information to the nearest police station. They might even give a description of me! It made me feel uncomfortable.

I could not make anything out of the National news columns and so I went all the way to the small ads, where the first thing I saw was an advertisment for jobs by the Ministry of Power and Communications. They wanted five Grade II Mechanics to fill in some vacancies that they had. I knew I had the necessary skill but I had no certificate. I also could not attend the interview unless and until David recovered. I was wondering why I had not earlier tried any of the Government Trade Tests that were being conducted everyday. When I could not attend any interviews, vacancies were appearing all over. I went on reading.

Gladys brought me food and I started eating. Then, she asked me a very queer question:

"Do you know why I am keeping you in my house after you have told me that you have almost killed a man?" She just asked from out of the blue. I slowly put my spoon on the plate and faced her. I could not even have the vaguest guess.

"No. Any particular reason?" I asked.

<h1 align="center">12</h1>

Then she told me briefly all that she had done since she had left
school. There was quite a lot. From a marriage to a divorce. She left
the husband when they had one child. Then the child died mysterious-
ly and the post mortem revealed that she had died of food poisoning
and Gladys was arrested and kept in custody, pending trial on a
charge of infanticide. She was kept in remand for over three months
after which she was acquitted.

She told me, apologetically, that one day, she had drunk herself so
volunteer to give them any information that would lead to conviction
in a case, even if she was the sole eye-witness. The case of her child
whom she swore to have loved more than she loved herself, affected
her so much and so adversely too, that, when she was released from
remand, she started hitting the bottle; not half measures but she
could drink until she forgot where she was or who she was!

She told me, apologeticaly, that one day, she had drunk herself so
silly the following day she had found herself in bed, naked, with a
very old man. She said that there was nothing in this world that
retained any taste for her. She swore that she would never marry
again.

It was my turn to gape at her.

She told me that her friends had even got to the extent of
nicknaming her 'Ma Barker', after the confessed criminal woman of
the United States. She explained even how she had come to acquire a
car. Not from the meagre salary she got as Personal Secretary to the
Managing Director of Mali Moto Holdings, but that she had hooked
a White millionaire who had come on tour to Kenya and who
besides wishing to see the wild life, had also wanted the company of
tame life—women—and had found it in the form of Gladys. She had
shown him so much affection, confessing that she would have gone
with him to the States if only he had suggested it, but that the White
man had not, and so, when his time to leave came, he had left Gladys
right here in Nairobi, but a hundred thousand shillings the richer. He

had left her all the money that he had had in cash form and promised he would come back and pick her.

That's how she had come by the car and the 'small' house that she lived in at Uhuru Estate. She told me not to feel cheated anyway because she had no feelings towards the White man any more. In fact she wished he was dead so that she would not meet him again.

After she had told me all that, I had nothing to say except: "You are great," and added, "Ma Barker!" and we burst laughing again, but only for a short while. I had more serious things to think about just then than reminiscence over past history.

I suggested to Gladys that the only solution for me was to leave Nairobi. I simply could not sit and wait for news of David's progress be it towards hell or anywhere else.

Gladys at once protested saying that she could keep me under cover for as long as I wished. There was no hurry. She even suggested that she was going to reverse her decision not to get married again, if I could consent to stay with her. We laughed again.

We slept at midnight. Gladys had taken all the time telling me how easy it would be to 'hide' myself at her place. She had even gone to the car and removed my wet suit. We had also soaked it in the water and hoped that it would not lose its texture.

She told me that she would go to town and buy me some clothes the following day. She did not ask for money that would be required but she told me that she had enough for two jeans, two shirts and a jacket. She was being excessively kind. By the time she joined me in bed and we started making love, I had told her several thank yous.

The whole of the following day found me in Gladys' house. I stayed indoors and did not see the sun except through shutters. I almost went through all the books in Gladys' librabry—most of them on crime. I was bored stiff by the exercise.

I lunched on some bread that Gladys had bought in the morning and got so tired of sitting down that I started to do some silent drill.

I could march from one bedroom to the other, with all the left and right turns, to the kitchen, bathroom, tableroom. I even practised marking time in slow march. That was one advantage of having been

290

a cop. There are so many different things that one can do alone.

Gladys came earlier than usual from her place of work. She told me that she had not even told the boss that she was leaving the office but she knew that he would not do anything about it. Part of her interview for her job had been a night out with the boss, and a promise that she would be available should the boss need her later and thus, she had a real strong hold on him.

The clothes she brought me fitted me so well—just like they were made to measure. I tried them all on. The answer to what I would be wearing while hiding was thus found. It was also a step towards the success of the plan I had, a plan that was concealed even from Gladys.

After supper, she went and brought me four beers. She must have noticed the thirst that was lurking in my eyes. Good woman. As I drunk them, she was telling me that she had tried to inquire from her friend, who worked at Kenyatta National Hospital, about the state and condition of a casualty who was taken to the hospital the previous night, and the friend had confirmed that David, was not yet dead and was not even in the critical list. I let out a sigh that you could have heard from Ol Joro Orok.

In my pocket, I had only eighty shillings. I had some two hundred in the bank but I was afraid of walking to the bank, lest the police spot and pick me. Yet, I had to move out of Nairobi, and I had to have money. If I suddenly asked Gladys for money, she would know that I wanted to go away and I was not sure whether she would accept that. My plan was to steal from her.

The following day, after Gladys had left for her place of work, I rummaged through all her lockers, drawers and suitcases and obtained a total of four hundred shillings. I felt that three hundred shillings would be enough for me then, and so, I placed the remaining one hundred shillings in an envelope and wrote a small note to Gladys; it was brief and to the point: "Sorry for leaving like this. I promise you that I will post the dues to you soonest. I.O.U. three hundred shillings. Thanks very much for everything. Love, J.F.W."

I walked to the shops across the street and bought myself a pair of goggles. I went back to the house and viewed myself on the mirror. I looked just a bit different from yesterday. Then, I went out of the house and boarded a bus to town, carrying the small bundle of clothes I had in a plastic bag. I walked nervously to the East African Road Services bus terminus and booked a seat for Nakuru.

The previous night, I had put all the towns in Kenya on a drawing board, and weighed them. Some were automatically out of line for me. Mombasa was one of these. Although I had heard that one could disappear into thin air in Mombasa, I could not imagine myself living in the humid heat that I had heard was the order of the day there. Another failing factor was the women—prostitutes. I had heard that they were twice the number of decent women we have at the place and that the total number of women was about three times the number of men. There was also the threat of me being raped by my own fellow men. Ugh!

Kisumu was also out of the question. I had gone there on a number of visits while I was at Kakamega and had not liked the place at all. There was a perpetual stench of fish and I hate fish especially the smoked stinking type that is sold in the open market.

I had been to Kakamega and Nyeri long enough and would not have liked to start re-living in these towns any more. That left only Nakuru out of all the towns I knew. I had heard of the peace and quiet in Nakuru and so I decided to give it a try. Being one of the towns on the Trans-Africa Highway, Nakuru was bound to have enough motor traffic for a mechanic to be on great demand.

After booking a seat, I did one very daring thing. I walked down Grogan Road and surprisingly, I was not feeling as nervous as the previous day. I just walked there and found my fellow mechanics. I was expecting them to start shouting 'Huyo!' when they saw me or do something hostile but they did not do such a thing. They had not even known of my later fight with David and after talking to some for some time, I learnt that they thought we had been taken to court on the charge of affray for which we had been arrested. They thought that we had either been convicted and jailed or were in remand.

Kanyi, who was our neighbour mechanic had collected all our

spanners when we had been whisked away by the police. He had wrapped them together—that is mine and David's.

I lied to him that I was going to repair a car in town, and, despite his eyeing me suspiciously on account of the clothes I was in, he handed the spanners to me. He asked me where David was and I told him that he had gone to see his ailing mother. He bought that as well although I could see that he was doubtful.

I picked the spanners and walked away, looking at the place where I had learnt all my technical skills and feeling sorry that I was leaving it for good. I walked to one of the dukas on Race Course Road and bought myself a cheap suitcase into which I crammed all the spanners plus the bundle of clothes that I had. Then, I bought a newspaper and quickly scanned through it, looking for any hint of David's case but found none. I guessed that the police were keeping it quiet with a hope that I would think that the matter was over and reveal myself and get caught!

By the time I went back to the O.T.C. Bus terminus, the bus for Nakuru was already parked at its bay and I entered the bus and sat down. I pretended that I was reading the newspaper but I was furtively looking at the door of the bus to see whether any cop or suspicious character was coming towards me or paying any particular attention to me.

13

When the bus finally started, I sighed in relief. Nakuru, open your arms! I am coming! I wondered what Gladys would say after reading my note. She would definitely feel cheated but then, that is something I could not help. I was sorry for her.

At Kijabe, we encountered a road block, manned by armed policemen and my mouth automatically went dry.

They came into the bus, looking at each of us in the eyes and I had to hold my breath and stare back at them to stop myself from crying out that it was me they were looking for. However, they passed me without comment and went out of the bus without saying a single word to anyone on the bus. I wondered what they were looking for but did not ask.

I arrived at Nakuru at about 2130 hours—only three hours after we had left Nairobi. I remembered the first journey that I had made to the place in a train and felt that buses these days were really 'flying'. I alighted and walked towards a street where noise from juke-boxes proclaimed the place to be a bar or some other entertainment place.

I removed my goggles as I neared the place and cleared my throat. I wanted a cheap place, a place which could accommodate me comfortably but cheaply. I entered this bar, from where music could be heard and gave the place a once-over.

As it was still early, 2000 hours according to the wall-clock above the counter, the place was not crammed full but the few patrons who were inside were scattered all over the tables. I spotted a table which was only occupied by an elderly couple and headed for it, disregarding the probing scrutiny that I was receiving from the other patrons. Just when I was about to reach the table, I thought that the best thing would have been first to know the charges for rooms and so I turned again towards the counter. That sharp turn made my suitcase bang against the leg of a table, shaking it and spilling most of the drinks that were on the table. Before I could open my mouth to apologise, a guy who was sitting at the table was already on his feet, pointing an accusing finger at me and shouting at me; "Hey, you! This is not the railway station waiting room!" and although I had made up my mind to apologise, I felt that his reaction was over-done. I looked at him, sweat starting to break over my nose and retorted; "Sorry, I know where I am but thanks all the same for your kind counsel." I am also a man where men want to show themselves.

All eyes were trained on me. I felt very embarrassed. Some guys can embarrass you very deeply when they want to.

The fellow spat. He spat on the floor and then wiped his mouth with the back of his hand. The girl he was drinking with, and who had been watching the exchange of words silently, took her drink, stood up and made as if to go away from his table.

The fellow, in one swift movement pulled her back so violently that she lost her balance and landed on the table. The table slid and the girl fell heavily on the floor, breaking the bottle and glass that she was holding. The fellow slapped her—a loud bang across her face and she screamed.

The guys who had been gazing at me then turned all their attention to the woman and the fellow. One of the men stood up, walked slowly to where the fellow was and gave him a punch that connected under the jaw and the fellow was sent catapulting to the floor. Another guy moved to where he had fallen and gave him a kick on the ribs. The fellow stood up but there were four converging on him. It was evident that he would be licked if he was going to fight with all those men. It was a totally unfair war.

Despite his effort to throw punches left and right, the four men were quickly gaining an upper hand. I could not understand why they were all against him. I thought quickly and made a wild guess that maybe they all wanted the woman, who was not very ugly anyway, and so they wanted to show her that they could protect her. A man wanting a woman can do some very silly acts sometimes.

I looked at the poor fellow and noticed that his shirt-collar was torn and he was bleeding from a cut lip. Although I did not know him, and although he had riled me by attacking me with words, I felt that he was still a human being just like me, and like me, he had a right to be in this universe.

A picture of David's prone body flashed across my mind but that did not fully discourage me. I threw all care to the wind and moved into action.

I placed my suitcase on the floor and joined the battle. I gave the guy who was holding the fellow's collar a flying kick right on his mouth. A very deadly kick if you know what I mean. He flattened on his back, screaming like a woman and holding his mouth which had turned into a well of blood. I cought the legs of the one who had kicked the fellow's ribs and pulled them from under him in a swirling tackle. That one fell, some ten feet away in a heap that was fun to see. The fellow was hammering the third one with all his might while I went to the fourth one. He was already making for the door but I could not allow him to go away without tasting some of his own stew. When he saw me, he raised his hands above his head and begged me not to hit him but my fury was so intense that I did not heed his plea. I gave a double-handed karate chop on his thick neck and I thought I heard him fart before he hit the floor.

The woman who had been the cause of the fracas took an empty bottle, and, with all her strength, broke it over the fellow. The bottle flew in all directions in a thousand pieces. I caught hold of her hand, and despite her screams of 'don't! don't!'", I threw her right through the door and oustide the bar. She might have landed on her head or arse for all I cared.

The fellows who had gone through our hands were hurriedly leaving the bar. The others, who had not been involved were prematurely calling for their bills and showing us their backs as they also left.

The whole operation had taken about three minutes but, if you had entered the bar then, you would have thought that a bull-dozer had passed there. Everything was then as silent as a tomb.

As if by an unseen signal, the fellow and I smiled at the same time. We moved towards one another. He was wearing a bare tooth grin while I was wearing an embarrassed smile.

14

"Have one on me, brother. That was a good show! Hey! Those guys wanted my heart. You just came in time . . . ha . . . ha . . . ha . . ." The fellow said. He was laughing and shaking his head and feeling with his hand where the bottle had banged him. He was also caressing his beard.

We shook hands vigorously and the fellow patted me on the shoulder. The pat was in reality a heavy bang and I had to stand firmly to steady myself. I felt a strong liking for him immediately.

I picked my box and we re-arranged one table that had not been fully affected by the 'hurricane' and sat down. He called for a beer for me and himself and continued thanking me for 'rescuing' him.

'My name is Jackson Kabuthu. Jack for my friends, and I would feel honoured to know yours." He told me grinning. I did not even stop to think whether it was safe to give him my real name, knowing that the police would be looking for me, but I felt that I could trust this man. He did not look like the 'Judas' kind.

"James. James Fredrick Wamatu, but Fred or Jim would do. In fact I like it as Fred," I was also grinning.

"I don't need to tell you that it has been a pleasure to meet you!" Jack was saying as he yelled for the waiter to bring the beer quickly. The woman who brought the beers brought me an Export just like she knew what I was going to drink and I was quick to tell her that. She smiled at me, winked and told me that she could tell what a man drinks merely by looking at the size of his nose. We laughed out loud but I did not agree with her, seeing how short an Export is compared to my long nose.

The beers were opened and we started to drink. I also started to know Jack.

He had been employed by Premji for some eight months, after he had resigned from his job, as a mechanic, in the police workshop at Nakuru. He told me that he had had his own frustrations and had decided to quit the police employment. At the mention of the job of mechanics I emptied all my heart to Jack.

I told him of my busy practice in Nairobi and asked him whether there was any chance for me to be employed by that Premji. He told me that he would make arrangements for me to do a grade test with the Ministry of Power and Communications the following day, and that he would 'force' Premji to employ me. He sounded very confident.

He further told me that the Grade Certificate would just be a formality as Premji did not regard them so highly, but that one had to have one before employment.

When I told him of the motor vehicle components that I was specialised in, he told me that instead of sitting for the Grade Three examination, which was the first examination for all mechanics, he would arrange with the Inspector at the Ministry, to have me sit for Grade Two without having first to go through grade three. I felt so thankful to him that I bought him a beer.

Then, I asked him about lodgings in Nakuru and he told me that, right at the bar we were, there were lodgings which were not very costly but which were clean and decent. He called the waiter who was serving us and told her to reserve one room for me.

"You mean you want to spend the night here?" She asked, opening her eyes and having an anticipatory smile all over her face.

"Yes. What's wrong with the place?" I also pretended to be puzzled.

"Wrong? There is nothing wrong with the place. In fact it's one of the best—no—the best place in Nakuru!" She was laughing.

"Then, that's why I want to spend the night here—and—besides, you are here . . ." I also winked at her. She looked so happy. This world is always admiring a hero and just then, I knew that I would not need to go very far to get a woman for the night.

After a few more drinks each, Jack told me that he would be leaving and that I should be ready as early as eight the following day. He would take me to the Grades Inspector.

There were only two more customers and the waiter told me that she was going to show me my room. She carried my suitcase to the room and when we got in, she sat and bounced on the bed, to show me that it was soft and springy. I latched the door from inside and smiled at her. She asked me why I was latching the door while she was still inside and I told her that, from that moment, she was not leaving the room.

I walked to the bed, held her face and kissed her. She started mewing and I had to hurry up in undressing myself and her.

By the look of things, Nakuru was not going to be a very bad place for me. Jack, I felt, was the mascot that I had been looking for all my life. And I had found him.

On the following day, Jack took me to the Grades Inspector. They held some brief, closed door consultations and when I was called into the office, the fellow beamed at me and conducted only an oral interview. He told me that I could rest assured that I was a Grade Two mechanic and that I could go to pick my certificate, and take the fees in my own free time. I felt that that was irregular but I did not mention it. As long as the irregularity was to my benefit. We left his office and arranged to meet in the evening at a certain bar which Jack chose.

Then, Jack took me to Premji's Garage, where the foreman, an Asian told me to re-assemble a dismantled carburetor as my interview.

That was as easy as A.B.C. and I did it within minutes. Even Premji marvelled at the skill I displayed. I was afraid that he would ask for my certificate but he did not. In fact, he told me not to show it to him, even if I had it.

"Mimi pana andika karatasi. Mimi andika mutu fanjia mimi kanji manjuri. Karatasi pana fanjia mimi kanji!" He told me in his lousy Asian accent. Thus, I was employed, and I was to start working right there and then.

15

That evening, Jack and I went and picked the Grades Inspector from his home. We went to the same bar where I had met Jack. I had two reasons for wanting to go there. One was that I had left my suitcase there and the other that I wanted to see Nduta, the girl I had spent the night with. I wanted to see her and buy her a drink in appreciation of the service she had rendered me. I had offered her money but she had refused it and told me that she had loved me at first sight, because she thought that I was extremely humanitarian in the way I had gone to Jack's rescue. She was not after my money but 'love'. That's why I wanted to go and buy her a beer to at least off-set a bit of the debt that I felt I owed her. I was also going to apologise to her for having grabbed her out of her employment before time and I also wanted to know whether she had been made noise at for accepting to go with me.

When we got into the bar, Nduta smiled at me and at once came to the table we occupied. She shook hands with each of us and asked us what we would drink. We made our orders and I told her that she too could have a beer and charge it to my account. I was buying the beers and Jack even subsidised my financial stand by adding me some two pounds.

By 2130 hours, I could hardly direct the glass of beer to my mouth. The effects of the hectic time I had had the previous four days, were telling on me. I begged Jack and the Inspector leave to go and rest my weary bones. They did not protest and even Jack, who must have noticed that my pocket was almost exhausted paid for my lodging that night. I left them right there drinking and again Nduta took me to the room. This time, she told me that I should not lock up because she was coming to join me when the bar closed. I smiled sleepily at her and told her to latch the door from outside.

I undressed and lay on the bed. Sleep was easy to come by and I had to be shaken awake by Nduta when the bar closed. I explained to her that I could not satisfactorily participate in the game, in the state that I was in and she understood. After all, she told me, there was the endless tomorrow.

CHAPTER SIXTEEN

1

Jack and I became real buddy buddies. We were two and yet we were one. We drunk together, fought together, hunted together and even laid women together.

He had shown me a house for hire. A cheap house but ideal for me. It was a bedsitter with the toilets and bathrooms outside. If there is anything I hate, it is common toilets. Some guys can be real messy and somehow, they can not direct their shit to the toilet basin when helping themselves. Blast them!

Jack and I repaired cars together too. Although I was single and he was married with one kid, you could hardly tell the marital status difference between us. His wife had accepted me as part of the family immediately I was introduced to her and the kid. Anne, a small girl of only about two years had immediately 'fallen in love' with me and she actually used to cry when I was leaving their home.

Jack showed me where to go and where not to go in town. He showed me where decent prostitutes haunted and where a screw might mean contracting V.D. He showed everything that I would have liked to see in Nakuru.

The fear of arrest that had been so rampant in me in the first few days at Nakuru went off just like that. I guessed David did not die and was afraid of telling the cops the truth about the whole issue, particularly with the knowledge that Wafula was my friend, and that he himself had provoked me into fighting with him by throwing my property into the rain. Again, he had enough compensation. All my property had remained at his place and maybe he knew that I was not going back for it.

When I received my first pay from Premji, I posted five hundred shillings to Gladys and wrote her a small note, telling her that I still remembered her kindness and that I would go to see her soonest. I however did not give her the address to which to send a reply and the truth is, I had closed the chapter of me and her in my heart.

I had already met another girl who had almost touched my heart at the soft spot. Nduta—Rose Nduta. Two weeks after I had met her at the bar, she had been employed as a cook in the Army Training School at Lanet. She was far from me but she used to come to Nakuru—rather to me, every alternating week-end. The other week-end was spent with her parents. I was afraid of telling her that I wanted to marry her, knowing the few disasters that I had had in love with other girls and so we just let our relationship 'live'.

"There is always a car that needs repair, Fred," Jack would tell me. I would agree with him. That was our consolation every time we got broke.

At first, we blamed the women and reduced the number of 'paid' screws that we had. Still we got broke. Next, we blamed beer, and so we reduced the amount per day. Still we got broke. Then, in desperation, we continued what we had been doing before.

Jack would tell me: "When you are broke, think of the day when you had so much money. Think of the meat you ate, the beer you drank and the woman you screwed. Then think of the source of that money. Go back to that source and get some more out of it."

I would do just that. The only source of money that I had was in repairing cars. So, I would go and look for a car that needed repair and that way, I would get money and would repeat the 'wasteful' process of meat-beer-women and I would get broke again!

2

"I don't like Asians. Fred." That's Jack telling me. He hates them anyway. I also hate them.

The other day, Jack told an Asian foreman at the garage that he would shave him with a screw-driver, if the foreman did not take his pink-pigment from Jack's sight.

The foreman reported the incident to Premji who summoned Jack to his office. When Jack was asked whether it was true that he had threatened the foreman, Jack answered in the affirmative and even warned Premji that he too would get the same treatment if he continued treating him like a coolie. Jack has not been on good terms with the boss since then. I am also not on good terms with the whole of the management because Jack is my friend.

"Do you know what we are going to do?" That's Jack again. I do not know. Since I was employed by Premji, I have lost all thought of the future. I only think of repairing cars, and then queuing in front of Premji for my meagre monthly emoluments.

I look at Jack and shake my head.

"I don't know, but, please do tell me" I say. I am feeling a bit drunk. We have been in the bar for over two hours and we have not been sitting idle. We have been swallowing beers like we are either employed to swallow them or we are being given them free.

I wonder why the Breweries do not award medals to the heaviest boozer in a particular area. I could easily win the medal for Nakuru.

Jack is toying with his glass. I reckon he is drunk too. His woman for tonight is leaning on his left shoulder. When I look at her, I wonder what Jack sees in other women that his wife does not have. But, I don't comment a thing.

"We are going to open our own garage." I pop my mouth open. "A garage where we shall be repairing cars. We shall employ our own mechanics, some who will be poached from Premji's garage. I can not stand an Asian telling me when to eat or when to shit and such-like things. I am a grown-up and this is not Delhi or Bombay. This is Nakuru—Kenya!" he finishes.

I agree with him.

There was evident colour and cast discrimination in almost every act that the Asian group at the workshop did. Led by the foreman, the other Asian mechanics were openly prejudiced in each act.

They showed contemptuous doubts in every repair that we, the African mechanics did and although we could not understand their dialect, it was apparent, from the shaking of their heads that they were talking about the poor workmanship that we Africans portrayed.

Any facility, brought to the workshop for repairs, and the repairs being done by a black, would not, and it was almost a written law, be handed back to the owner without an Asian first checking it and if possible, double-checking it.

I myself had on several occasions tried to kind of socialise with them, but the most intimate socialising that I achieved was being told to check whether I had tightened the nuts on a wheel even when I had double-checked them!

Premji had made it so that even the toilets were separate. Asians and Blacks. As there were two toilets, one was always securely locked and the key was hung in Premji's office where we would not go of course. The other key was hung right there at the workshop.

Every time an Asian got the key to the other toilet from Premji's office, and finished his job in the toilet, he would make sure that he locked the toilet securely and took the key back to Premji's office.

There was about twenty-five of us Blacks compared to only six Asians at the workshop and sometimes, we, Blacks, had to queue just to empty our bilges!!

Jack was overly bitter about the treatment we received but as he said it, there was nothing that we could do, at least then. As time went on, however, God who created the Blacks and the Whites and the Reds and Yellows and all other colours, would shed light on the Blacks' path and we would be independent of the Yellows and Reds.

As I reflected on Jack's words, I wished that that time would come sooner.

As I lay on this bed, drunk, and unable to sleep comfortably I remembered Jack's words. He had said that we would open our own garage. When Jack said a word, most of the times he meant it, whether he was drunk or not. If he told you that he would fix you, run away my friend because it might turn out that he would do just that.

If we opened our own garage, I would definitely earn more money and have enough to spend and spare for my poor parents. You never know, I could call them to come and live with me at Nakuru. There are these land-buying companies that are sprouting all over the country and I could buy shares for them in one of the companies. That way, they would bless me at the time of their death. I need their blessing surely. I also need God to forgive me the numerous sins I have committed.

I also would like to earn enough to keep Rose eating and dressing up. Honestly, I feel that I have drifted for too long and would now like to settle, get married, breed a few kids and then wait for age to come and disable me. I have wasted enough time as it is. In fact I have been all along behaving like a man with a worm in his head. A real, big, hairy, green worm.

Yes. We shall try the idea of a garage. We shall of course start in the open air but, given the determination that Jack seems to have, we shall overcome somehow. That's what we shall do. So help me God.